5/D

BLOWING SMOKE

Books by Barbara Block

CHUTES AND ADDERS

TWISTER

IN PLAIN SIGHT

THE SCENT OF MURDER

VANISHING ACT

ENDANGERED SPECIES

BLOWING SMOKE

Published by Kensington Publishing Corporation

BLOWING SMOKE

Barbara Block

KENSINGTON BOOKS
http://www.kensingtonbooks.com

Although the city of Syracuse is real, as are some of the place names I've mentioned, this is a work of fiction. Its geography is imaginary. Indeed, all the characters portrayed in this book are fictional, and any resemblance to real people or incidents is purely coincidental and completely unintentional.

KENSINGTON BOOKS are published by

Kensington Publishing Corp.
850 Third Avenue
New York, NY 10022

All Kensington titles, imprints and distributed lines are available at special quantity discounts for bulk purchases for sales promotion, premiums, fund-raising, educational or institutional use.

Special book excerpts or customized printings can also be created to fit specific needs. For details, write or phone the office of the Kensington Special Sales Manager: Kensington Publishing Corp., 850 Third Avenue, New York, NY 10022. Attn. Special Sales Department. Phone: 1-800-221-2647.

Kensington and the K logo Reg. U.S. Pat. & TM Off.

Library of Congress Card Catalogue Number: 00-110393
ISBN 1-57566-670-7

First Printing: July 2001
10 9 8 7 6 5 4 3 2 1

Printed in the United States of America

To my mother

ACKNOWLEDGMENTS

I would like to thank Michael Morris for taking the time to chat with me about how investigators work.

I am extremely grateful to Robert Strickland for the psychological insights he has given me.

Thanks to Carolyn Hanlon, Janet Fulgenzi, O.P., and Kenneth Untener, bishop of Saginaw, for helping me with my Latin problem.

Larry, thanks again for your opinion.

And lastly, my undying gratitude to Sherry Chayat for taking time from her busy schedule to read my manuscript.

Chapter One

Sometimes I wish my eyesight wasn't so good, because then I would have kept going.

I was on my way out to Cazenovia to see a family about a case involving their runaway daughter. I'd just rounded a turn and was daydreaming about renting a place on a beach for a week when I spotted a discarded pile of clothes lying by the side of the road.

As I whizzed by I thought I saw a hand. I told myself I was seeing things, that it was a piece of an old doll someone had thrown away. Or a store mannequin. I told myself it was none of my business. But I couldn't let it go. Five minutes later, I made an illegal U-turn and went back for a second look. Just to make sure.

Half-hidden in the dried-out grass, the man was lying on his side with his head resting on his arm and his hand out. At first, I thought he was dead, a hit-and-run left on the side of the road along with the discarded soda cans and fast-food wrappers. But there was no blood. Then his hand moved, the fingers faintly motioning me to come near. As I got closer, I could see he wasn't injured; he was sick. His cheeks were sunken. His eyes were glassy. His brown skin had taken on an ashy undertone. The spot he was lying in must have been as far as he could get before he collapsed.

"*Por favor,*" he gasped.

The edges of the tall grass scratched my arms as I squatted down beside him. He began coughing. His face went red with the effort as the cough rattled around in his chest. Blood and sputum flecked his lips. I felt his forehead. His skin was dry and hot to the touch. I was about to ask him what was wrong with him when he reached up and grasped my wrist.

"*Da este a Dorita,*" he whispered, opening his left hand. I noticed he had a small comet tattooed on it as a crumpled piece of paper fell onto the ground. A turkey buzzard sitting on a tree branch a short distance away flew down and hopped toward it.

"Get away," I cried. Offended, the buzzard pulled in its neck, hissed, and took off.

I picked the paper up and looked at it. It was a Polaroid of a family—a smiling man, woman, and a young child—all in their Sunday best, standing on the steps outside a church in a town square.

"*Por favor,*" the man repeated. He coughed again, spit blood onto the ground, and closed his eyes.

"Hey, don't die on me."

He gave a slight nod.

"I'm going to get you to a hospital."

A choking noise exploded in his throat. For a moment, until I saw the rise and fall of his chest, I thought he'd died. I looked around for someplace I could go for help. But there wasn't any. No houses. No stores. No nothing. Just trees and brush. I realized that the nearest house that I knew about belonged to the people I was going to see, about fifteen miles away.

"Hang on," I told him as I went through his pockets, looking for some identification that would tell me who he was and where he was living. But there wasn't any. "It's going to be okay."

His eyelids fluttered. I stuffed the picture into the pocket of my jeans and half-dragged, half-carried, him over to my car. He was so thin, I could almost circle his wrist with my hand. But even though he was as light as straw, maneuvering him into the backseat of my car took more strength than I'd anticipated, and I was covered with sweat by the time I was done. I rolled up the jacket I'd been carrying around for the last couple of months, slid it under his head, then wiped my hands off on my jeans, got into the front seat of my car, started it up, and took off.

The rattle of the man's breathing filled the car. I kept glancing in the rearview mirror as I drove. His eyes were closed. His right arm dangled over the seat, moving each time I took a turn.

"*Como se llama? De donde viene?*" I asked in my faltering Spanish.

But he just shook his head and began coughing again.

I hit the gas. A couple of minutes later, I zoomed into the driveway of the Petersons' house. I slammed on the brakes, ran out, and rang the bell. A blonde that had had too much plastic surgery came to the door.

"You must be Robin Light," she said. "We've been waiting for you."

I explained about the man in my backseat and asked her to call 911.

The smile turned to a frown, and she half-turned back toward her house. "Arthur," she called. "My husband will be here in a minute," she said, turning back to me.

He must have been just inside the door, because he was with us before I could say anything.

"What is this about, then?"

I explained again.

"Millie, go ring up 911."

"I'll take a glass of water for him, too, if you don't mind."

She nodded and vanished into the house.

"I still don't understand why you brought him here," Arthur Peterson complained as he hurried toward my car. A heavyset man in his early forties, he had pouchlike bags under his eyes and a salt-and-pepper beard.

"I couldn't leave him on the side of the road, could I?"

"Don't you have a cell phone?"

"Not on me." I'd forgotten it.

Arthur Peterson snorted and peered through my car window. "I can tell you where he lives, though. In the trailer park. All the Mexicans around here do."

"I didn't know there were any trailer parks in Caz." Cazenovia was a town where rich people lived.

"Just this one." He ran a hand through the remaining wisps of hair on the top of his head. "I wish they'd tear the damned thing down."

"Now, now, dear," Millie remonstrated as she handed me a glass of water and a wad of paper towels. "Those people have to live somewhere. How's he doing?"

I glanced into the car. "Not well, I'd say. Not well at all."

The ambulance and a sheriff's car rolled in ten minutes later.

"Where are you taking him?" I asked one of the EMTs as they loaded the man I picked up onto the gurney.

"Upstate." The EMT, a guy who looked as if he should be riding a Harley, paused for a second, then added, "If I were you, I'd check with the county health department in a few days to see if his TB test comes back positive."

"TB?"

"I ain't a doc, but that's my best guess. We're seeing more and more like him." He jerked his head in the direction of the ambulance. "They should stay where they belong."

"Jeez." I brushed the lock of hair that had fallen into my eyes out of the way and, when that didn't work, refastened my ponytail. Who was it who had said that no good deed goes unpunished?

"That poor boy," Millie said, watching the sheriff walk back to his squad car after he'd taken my statement.

Arthur, the corners of his mouth pulled down, waved his hand in the direction of the sheriff's car as he maneuvered it down their driveway. "They can come out for an undocumented worker, but I have to pay someone to look for my daughter." He shook his head disgustedly. "No wonder we're in the shape we're in."

"Now, Arthur, you know you don't mean that," his wife tittered as he led the way into their house. "Arthur's just upset," she explained to me. "We both are. Bethany." She stopped and took a deep breath. "This has been hard to deal with."

The husband took me into a pleasant living room that was furnished with expensive wood and leather modern furniture. There was original art on the walls and pieces of pottery sitting on the end tables and the fireplace mantel. A modern brown and orange patterned rug completed the design. I started reaching into my backpack for a cigarette when I noticed there weren't any ashtrays. I sighed and settled for taking out my notebook and pen.

The moment I sat down on the sofa, Arthur Peterson put a photo of his daughter in my hands. "This is our Bethany," he said. "She's fifteen. We took it outside our house this spring."

I couldn't tell from the sullen expression on her face whether she wasn't happy about having the photo taken or she just wasn't happy, period. She looked about five feet five and was on the plump side, though she might have looked heavier because of the oversized T-shirt and windbreaker she was wearing.

She'd bleached her hair platinum blond and pulled it back off her face and tweezed her eyebrows till there was nothing left but a thin line she'd augmented with black pencil. Even though she was trying to make herself look older, all she'd done was emphasize the baby fat in her cheeks and the softness of her chin. But the thing that caught my attention was her jewelry. She had large gold hoops in her ears and a gold necklace with her name written on it around her neck.

"That's real gold," her mother said, following my glance. "We don't know where she got the money to buy it. When I asked her, she told me it was none of my business." Millie put her hand to her mouth and blinked back tears. "I'm sorry," she said. "I'm just so worried."

Arthur patted his wife's shoulder. "It's been obvious from Bethany's choice of friends that something has been wrong for a while. We've tried being patient. We've tried talking to her in a nonthreatening, nonconfrontational way. We've tried counseling. It hasn't made any difference. We did one of those drug tests, the kind where you get a lock of hair and send it off for analysis. It's come back clean, but her grades keep dropping, and now we're getting these calls from the principal of her school saying she isn't there." He took a deep breath.

"And then, last night, Millie and she had a big fight. Naturally, I stepped in to back up my wife."

"What was the fight about?"

"A kid I'd never seen before—he was older, maybe eighteen—rang the bell and asked for Bethany. She started out the door, and I told her she couldn't go; then I told this kid he had to leave. Well, he took off, and Bethany started screaming at me. I told her she had to go up to her room."

The wife sighed. "I can't believe some of the things she said to us."

"Neither can I." The husband's voice was grim. "Anyway, I gave her an hour to cool off, and then I went up to speak with her. Only she wasn't there. She'd climbed out the window. We called her friends. No one has seen her. Or at least that's what they're telling us. But I don't believe them. One of my friends, Matt Rydell, said you were good at finding runaways."

I'd managed to locate his son for him last spring. I looked up from the "B" I'd doodled in the margin of my notebook. "Finding them is the easy part. The problem is what happens when they come back."

"I think we've got that covered." Arthur Peterson squeezed his wife's shoulder. "So you think—"

"Can I keep this?" I lifted the picture up. "I'm going to have to get copies made."

"Of course."

I left the Petersons' house armed with the photo of Bethany, a list of her friends, and a retainer. Now that it had cooled off a bit, the evening was pleasant. I decided that as long as I was out here, I might as well be efficient and call on some of Bethany's friends and see what I could find out. But as I drove over to Somerset Road, the first address on my list, I wasn't thinking about Bethany. I was thinking about the man I'd picked up on the road, wondering who he was, who Dorita was, and hoping like hell the EMT guy was wrong about his having TB.

I remembered a story my grandmother had told me about her husband's family not wanting him to marry her because she was too thin and they were afraid she'd come down with TB. They called it Jewish pneumonia back then. I'd told her we didn't have that stuff around anymore, and she'd looked at me and said something like things like that would always be around.

Of course, now they had pills to take care of it. Pills you had to take every day for a year. The problem was you couldn't drink when you were on them because it would stress your liver. That would be a lot of fun. Still, I suppose it beat the sanatorium. Especially since I didn't have health insurance. One of the perks of being self-employed.

I wondered if the pills were expensive. With my luck they'd probably be five dollars each. That was a little over eighteen hundred dollars a year. I never thought I'd be in a position where eighteen hundred dollars mattered one way or another, but unless things turned around at the pet store I owned, I was going to have to declare bankruptcy. At least that's what my accountant had told me during our last meeting.

Which brought me back to thinking about Bethany. Here we had these upper-middle-class parents. A father who was a psychologist, a mother who dabbled in interior design, nice house, carefully cut hedges, tended flower beds, the whole schmear—but according to the photo I had, their kid was decking herself out like someone from the projects.

All the CDs in her room were rap. The posters plastered on her bedroom walls were hard-core gangsta rappers. The clothes in her closet seemed to consist of oversized sweats and microminis in equal proportion. I could imagine how pleased Mr. and Mrs. Peterson were at the music she was listening to and the clothes and jewelry she was sporting. Like her parents, I wondered where she'd gotten it from and how she'd paid for it.

The first two of Bethany's friends on the list her parents had given me weren't home, but the third one, a Karim Nettanhu, was. He lived in a big, expensive new colonial on a road filled with houses just like it. He was a tall, thin brown-skinned kid with a bad case of acne and the kind of black-rimmed glasses I vaguely remembered people wearing back in the fifties. I wanted to talk to him alone, but his mother hovered right by his side.

"Bethany," she said carefully, picking a piece of lint off her yellow silk shell. "I already told her parents we haven't seen her. Isn't that right, dear?"

Karim bobbed his head obediently, but his eyes told me a different story.

"Perhaps if I could talk to your son alone," I ventured.

"He doesn't know anything," the mother asserted, putting her hands on her son's shoulders. "Now, it's late, and he still has homework to do. If you'll excuse me." And she closed the door in my face.

I stood there for a few seconds, breathing in the laurel-scented air. Then I got back into my car and drove away. That was that. If the woman didn't want to let her son talk to me, there was nothing I could do to make her. This wasn't the slummier part of town. People here not only knew their rights; they were quick to exercise them. Some of them probably had lawyers on retainers.

The fourth kid on my list was a girl by the name of Michelle Morgan. She lived a ten-minute drive away, in a gimcrack development a little bit outside of town. Judging from the look of the houses, I'd be willing to bet that they were a good deal cheaper than the other places I'd been to so far.

"Yes," she said, opening the door without bothering to see who was there.

A heavy girl, she was dressed in fat-girl clothes. Her face was plain, with too big a nose and a receding chin, and even if she lost the hundred pounds she needed to, she still wouldn't be attractive. As I introduced myself and explained what I wanted, I couldn't help noticing that she was wearing the same type of earrings Bethany had on in the photo.

"Nice," I said, indicating them.

She felt one and smiled. "Thanks. We got them in the city."

"Syracuse?"

She nodded.

"Where are your parents?"

"They're out seeing a movie. Do you want me to tell them you came by?"

"Not really. I want to talk to you."

"Me?" The girl pointed a finger at herself.

"That's right, Michelle, you. Bethany's parents have hired me to find her. You know she's run away, don't you?"

Michelle nodded, her eyes wary.

"Well, I was hoping you could help me out."

The girl shook her head and fingered her earrings again. "There's nothing to tell. The last time I saw her was a week ago."

"Are you a good friend of hers?"

The girl nodded again, unsure of what was coming next.

"So why do you think she ran away?"

The girl looked down at the ground. "She wasn't happy."

"And why was that?"

"You've met her mom and dad?"

I nodded, even though the question was rhetorical.

"That's why."

"They seem like nice enough people to me."

Michelle made a face. "You wouldn't say that if you were their daughter. They're always watching her. Asking her these dumb questions. Wanting to know how she feels." She gave the words a sarcastic spin. "They won't even let her go out at night during the week. That's so lame."

Seemed sensible to me, but then what did I know? Once

again I gave thanks that I didn't have children. "How does she like school?"

"She hates it! We all do. That's another thing. Bethany wants to go to school down in the city, but her parents want to transfer her to private school."

"Why the city? Usually people pay to keep their kids out of the schools down there."

"Because that's where the real people are."

"As opposed to robots?"

Michelle gave me a sour look. "Everyone in our high school thinks we're freaks. At least it's not total white bread down there."

"You're probably right." Syracuse City high schools were like a mini-UN these days. Bosnian, Russian, Vietnamese, white, black. You name it, the schools had it. "So where did she go?"

Michelle shrugged. "I don't know."

"I think you do."

"Well, you're wrong."

I took a cigarette out of my backpack and lit it.

"My mother doesn't allow smoking in the house," Michelle said self-righteously.

"I'm not in your house. Listen," I said taking a puff, "your friend could be in a great deal of trouble."

"She's fine."

"Why are you so sure?"

Michelle folded her hands across her chest. "Because Bethany always is. She knows how to take care of herself."

I flicked the ash toward the grass. "There are lots of men out there that prey on fifteen-year-old girls who know how to take care of themselves."

"Don't be ridiculous," Michelle scoffed.

I leaned an arm on the doorframe. "You know why I think you're not worried?"

Michelle didn't say anything.

"I think you're not worried because you've spoken to her and you know that she's fine."

"That's not true," Michelle cried.

"I think it is. Maybe I should just wait till your parents come home."

Michelle tossed her head defiantly. "Go ahead. Wait as long as you want."

I reached out and lightly touched one of Michelle's earrings. "Where did you get the money to buy these?"

Michelle jerked back. "Baby sitting. What do you think?"

"How about Bethany? Does Bethany do much sitting?"

"I have no idea," Michelle said stiffly. "You'll have to ask her."

"Why was it so important for her to go out last night?"

"I told you I haven't spoken to her."

"You know," I continued, swatting at a mosquito that had landed on my hand, "in the last month or so the cops have been picking up a whole group of nice, suburban teenage girls who have been hooking on the streets. . . ."

"Bethany would never—"

I interrupted. "Are you so sure?"

"Yes," Michelle blurted out. "She's been taking money . . ." Michelle put her hand over her mouth.

"From who?"

Michelle developed an intense interest in a copper beech tree off in the distance.

"Tell me. Her mother? Her father? The local convenience store? You started the sentence. You might as well finish it. I'm not going to leave until you do."

Michelle looked down at the ground, back at the tree, then at me. "She's been stealing money from the lockers at school."

"You know this for a fact? You've seen her."

"She told me. The other thing that you said . . ."

"Yes?"

"That's a lie."

"I hope so." But I wasn't convinced. "Michelle, if Bethany's your friend, if you care about her, tell me where I can find her. She needs to be home—even if she doesn't like it. Her other options are even worse."

Michelle bit her lip while she thought.

"This is something you need to do for her."

"But her parents . . ."

"Want her home. Of course they're upset, but they'll get over it. I wouldn't say that if I didn't believe it. Honest."

It was getting darker now. The streetlights were beginning to come on. I watched Michelle as she struggled to make a decision. "She could die," I told her. "No kidding around."

"All right. All right. She's gonna kill me for telling." Michelle took a deep breath and let it out. "Bethany's at Karim's house."

"But I was just there," I protested. "Karim's mother said she hadn't seen her."

"His mother doesn't know. She's staying in their attic."

"The attic?"

"That's right. She snuck in when Karim's parents went to work. You won't tell her I told you, will you?"

I promised her I wouldn't. Then I turned around and headed for my car. The attic. It figured. All the time Bethany's parents were going nuts, imagining the worst, Bethany had been at Karim's house, probably playing video games and talking on the phone. That house was so big, I could see how you could have someone living in it and not know. Actually, a house didn't even have to be that big for something like that to happen. When I was in high school, one of the kids in my class had run away. They found him two weeks later. He'd been living under his girlfriend's bed the whole time. And this was in an apartment in the Bronx, unbelievable as it sounds.

I wanted to corroborate Michelle's story before I called Bethany's parents. To do that though I had to convince Karim's mother to let me in the house. At least that's what I thought as I drove over there. But Michelle must have had a change of heart and gone in and called Bethany the moment I'd left her, because just as I was pulling into the circular drive-way of Karim's house, I saw Bethany dash out from behind a clump of bushes.

"Stop! I just want to talk to you," I shouted at her.

She looked in my direction, then jumped into the waiting SUV at the other end of the driveway. The car took off.

I cursed and took my foot off the brake of my car, but as I did, Karim's mother ran out of the house and planted herself in the middle of the driveway. "I demand to know what's going on," she said.

I slammed on the brake again and leaned my head out the window. "Why don't you ask your son?"

"What's he got to do with anything?"

"Bethany was hiding in your attic."

She put her hands on her hips. "He'd never do anything like that."

"Well, he did."

"You're lying."

"Go on. Ask him."

"Do you know who my husband is? He's the head of—"

"Lady, I don't care." I started maneuvering the car around her.

"My flower beds," she screeched. "Watch out. You're driving over my flower beds."

"Sorry about the daylilies," I said as I flattened them. The damned things were like weeds. They'd come up next year, anyway.

"I'm going to sue you for this."

"Go right ahead." The nice thing about being practically broke is that you have nothing to lose.

By the time I got to the end of the driveway, it was too late. The SUV and Bethany had vanished. I spent the next hour cruising around, looking for them, before I wrapped it up and went home. Zsa Zsa, my cocker spaniel, was waiting to greet me at the door. As I bent down to pet her, I thought once again how much nicer than children dogs are.

Chapter Two

To clarify in case you're wondering, I'm not a licensed New York State private detective. I don't work for an agency. I don't advertise in the Yellow Pages. My business comes to me strictly by word of mouth. I also don't carry a gun, although I can shoot one if I have to. And have. I also run a pet store called Noah's Ark, which specializes in exotics—read reptiles—though these days I seem to be doing more detecting and less pet storing, if I can coin a word.

I started doing investigative work to save my own ass and turned out to be good at it, good enough so that people keep asking me to help them and I keep saying yes. I usually work a handful of cases a year. Mostly, I find lost children and animals and leave the high-end sexy stuff to the big boys.

It was almost eleven-thirty at night by the time I walked through the door of my house, and I was not in a good mood, possibly because I hadn't had anything to eat since ten o'clock that morning. When I saw the blinking light on my answering machine, I was hoping it was Bethany's parents calling to tell me their daughter had come home by herself. But it wasn't. It was someone called Hillary Cisco, wanting to hire me to do a job for her.

Normally, I would have turned her down. I prefer giving people their money's worth by concentrating on one thing at a time. But with the proverbial wolf at my door in the form of quarterly tax payments to good old New York State, I figured it was time to make an exception to my rule. The next morning, before I went to work, I phoned her back.

"How'd you get my name?" I asked her while I let James in and got a can of cat food out of the cabinet.

"Calli gave it to me."

Calli was an old friend of mine who'd gone out to California and was now back. At the moment, she was covering the Metro section in the local paper.

"She said you'd be perfect for this."

"Really?" As I set James's food in front of him, I told her about my fees and how I worked.

It sounded fine to Hillary, so I said I'd swing by her place later that afternoon. As I hung up, I noticed that James's ear was torn.

"Fighting again, I see."

He answered me with a growl. I wondered why I kept him around as I went to get the peroxide. Of course, he'd disappeared by the time I'd come back, and after searching the house for five minutes or so, I gave it up as a bad job and called Calli.

I wanted her to tell me about Hillary Cisco, but either Calli wasn't home or she wasn't picking up. I left a message on her machine, got Zsa Zsa, and finally left the house. I was only twenty minutes late.

Tim, the guy who works for me, and I spent the rest of the day restocking shelves, cleaning cages, and feeding the snakes. Bad day for the mice, good day for the snakes. In between, I popped into the back, arranged to go in and have a TB test, and made calls about Bethany while I tried not to listen to the asthmatic wheeze of the store's air conditioner.

The temperature was in the nineties, and the machine was not happy. It probably wanted a vacation, but then didn't we all, a fact I was reminded of when I stepped outside. I was drenched in sweat by the time I walked to my car. Which didn't improve my mood any. If I wanted heat, I'd be living in the Southwest instead of central New York.

On my way to Hillary Cisco's, I swung by Warren Street, but Bethany wasn't there, and after about twenty minutes or so, I gave up and drove over to Starcrest, the development in which Hillary Cisco lived. When I saw her leaning against the porch railing, I was reminded of a kid who'd been locked out of her house and was waiting for her mommy to come home. Even though she wasn't a kid. Not even close. And 113 Wisteria Lane was her house.

Listening to her voice on the machine, I'd pictured her as blond and big-boned, but this woman was as small and brown as a wren. Her gauze dress, incongruously long-sleeved and high-hemmed, fluttered around her thighs as she came down the steps to greet me. She moved with a slow, languid pace, but then, I reflected, it was too hot to move any other way.

Her hair, straight, black, and chin-length, hung like a curtain on either side of her face. But it was her eyes I noticed. They looked as if they belonged to someone else. A pale grayish blue, they were too light for her complexion, casting a vacant expression over her features. Her eyeliner and mascara had run in the heat, smudging into dark circles underneath her eyes. Beads of moisture ringed her hairline. She looked tired, as if she'd been wrestling with something for a long time and lost.

"Robin Light?" she asked. In person, she sounded breathier, less self-assured than she had on the phone.

I nodded. "Hillary Cisco?"

She bobbed her head and nervously plucked at the hem of her dress, trying to make it longer. "You're late. I thought you might have decided not to come."

"I got lost." I'd been circling around streets that all looked the same for the last twenty minutes, kicking up plumes of dust and growing more and more irritated by the second.

"Everyone does." She swiped at her forehead with the back of her hand. Her arms, I realized, were exceptionally long. "They designed these roads like a maze, you know. That's so the blacks from the inner city can't come up here and rob us." For a moment I couldn't tell if she was serious or not.

Then the corners of her mouth formed a slight smile. She shook her head as she contemplated the houses on either side of her. "As if they . . . or anyone would."

I followed her gaze. The place didn't seem so bad to me, just raw in the way that new housing developments are. They were popping up all around Syracuse, siphoning off its population. In twenty years, when the trees and the hedges grew in, it would be a pleasant enough place. At six o'clock, the day was just beginning to cool off. Somewhere a cardinal was singing his song over and over again, the notes rising and falling away like a benediction.

His notes mingled with the happy shouts of children chasing each other with water guns while their parents, still in their suits from their day in the office, were busy adjusting and readjusting the hoses and sprinklers on their lawns before they went inside and changed into shorts and T-shirts.

Hillary snorted her opinion of them and beckoned for me to follow her. "My brother and sister are anxious to meet you," she told me, as if she'd invited me to tea instead of to discuss a job. "Nothing big," I remember she'd said on the phone. "We just need to clarify a few issues."

Issues. Right. The new buzzword. As in, he has issues with alcohol or she has issues with men. Meaning he drinks and she sleeps around. I wondered what particular issues Hillary Cisco had in mind. They had to be substantial. People don't hire a private detective otherwise. Then I thought about how much I wanted it to rain as I mounted the three steps that led to Hillary's house.

A small white colonial, 113 Wisteria Lane was indistinguishable from the ones sitting to its left and right, even though Hillary had made a stab at decorating. Two wind chimes constructed from spoons hung from the eaves of the porch. A blue banner with several white music notes stitched to it jutted out from the porch beam. Half-dead red geraniums lay wilting in the ceramic pots lining the path to the house.

"The banner is my sister's handiwork," Hillary explained. "She does crafts," she continued, making the word crafts sound like some arcane sexual practice. "I sing, you know. Professionally. Teaching is my day job."

I nodded politely. I guess I should have acted more impressed, because a spasm of irritation rippled across her face. She compressed her lips, pulled the door to her house open, and stalked inside. But I didn't feel bad. I got the feeling she got irritated a lot.

The air in the hallway smelled faintly of cooking grease, room deodorizer, and kitchen trash. It had a dank, underwater quality to it, the kind you get in cheap motels in which the windows don't open and the air vents need to be cleaned. The living room was done up in a Chinese motif.

The rug, furniture, and walls were all white. Badly painted Chinese scrolls hung on three walls. A lacquered screen, dotted with someone's idea of a bamboo tree, stood off in the corner of the room, while a matching black lacquered coffee table sat in front of the sofa. Even the cabinet housing the television was in had an Asian motif. It looked like the kind of room they advertised on TV at two o'clock in the morning. Five pieces for seven hundred dollars. No money down. Two years to pay. By which time it would have come apart.

"My brother, Louis," Hillary said, pointing to the man in Bermuda shorts and polo shirt sprawled on the sofa, watching television.

"At last." He clicked off the program he'd been watching, hoisted himself up, came forward, and shook my hand, engulfing it in his. "And yes," he said, laughing. "We have the same mother and father. Everyone always wonders."

It was easy to see why they did. If Hillary was the mini version, Louis was the jumbo king-sized. A bear of a man, everything about him was big, from his ears, beaked nose, and lantern jaw to his hands and feet. Looking closely, though, I could see a similarity in the shape of the mouth between him and Hillary.

"I'm glad you could come." He was about to say something else to me when a woman burst out of the kitchen and planted herself next to Louis.

"I still think this is wrong," she told him, ostentatiously ignoring me.

Hillary took a deep breath and let it out. "My sister," she explained as her eyes lightened to an even paler shade of gray. "Evidently, Amy still has a few doubts about the wisdom of what we're doing. Although I thought we'd straightened that out."

Amy flushed. "No, we haven't." She drank from the can of soda she was holding and brushed a strand of frizzy hair off her face. She seemed as if she were one of those women who always looked permanently disheveled. The jewelry she had on, a squash-blossom necklace and matching wristful of silver bangles belonged on someone five inches taller. The peasant-style white blouse and pleated gauze skirt she was wearing accentuated her pendulous breasts and stomach. She was as short as Hillary, but she outweighed her by a good seventy pounds or so. "Listen," Amy went on, "all I'm saying is that Mom is going to be furious if she finds out."

"She's not going to," Louis snapped.

"She always does," Amy countered.

Louis glowered at her. "Don't you think it's time you grew up," he said. "She's not God."

Amy's face turned sullen. "That's not what I'm saying, and you know it."

"Amy," Hillary said, tugging at her sleeves. "Please. We've already had this discussion. We've decided—"

"You decided," Amy snapped.

"No. You agreed. We all agreed."

"I never said—"

"Yes, you did," Louis replied. "If you can't remember, maybe you'd better change those antidepressants you're on."

"That's a lousy thing to say," Amy flung back at him.

"You're right," Louis apologized. "It is." Even though he didn't look particularly sorry.

Amy put her can of soda down on the coffee table and began fiddling with her bracelets. "All I'm saying is that I'm not sure that this is the right thing to do."

"Well, I am." Exasperation underlined Louis's words. "Why do you always do this?"

"Do what?"

"Say yes and then change your mind?"

"But what if she finds out?" Amy wailed.

"So what?" Hillary's eyes flashed. "Big deal. So what if she does. We're certainly not going to be any worse off than we are already."

When Amy started to reply, it was all I could do not to say, Hey, people. Why don't you all shut up. Instead, I picked my backpack up off the floor and said, "Call me when you've decided what you want. I have other things I have to attend to." Like finding Bethany. Like finishing restocking the shelves. Like repairing one of the filters in the big fish tank. Like ordering five more geckos.

"Please." Hillary took my hand and began leading me to the sofa. "Don't go."

"Only if we can get down to business."

It was the money that made me stay. Though if you asked me, I'd say that what these folks really needed was a therapist instead of a private detective.

Hillary glanced at Amy. Amy shrugged.

"All right," she said. "But I'm not taking the blame for this."

"How novel," Louis sniped. "It's not as if you ever take the blame for anything."

"Both of you stop it," Hillary ordered. "It's the heat," she said to me. "The heat is making everyone crazy. Let me get you a drink," she continued. "An iced tea." And, without waiting for my answer, she went into the kitchen.

As I listened to the air conditioner's rattle and hum, I watched Amy wind a lock of her hair around her finger. Her face was round. She looked younger than her siblings and paler, as if she never got out in the sun. The outline of a faint mustache was apparent above her upper lip.

"It must be nice to still be able to do that," she said wistfully, referring to the high-pitched screams of the children playing outside that were seeping into the room. Then she sighed and sat next to me. A faintly sour smell came off of her. "Do you believe in life after death?" she asked suddenly.

Louis rolled his eyes and flopped down on the armchair to the left of the sofa. "Ah . . . we're back to the great unknown."

Amy sucked in her cheeks and straightened her back. "What's wrong with that question?"

"Well—" I began when Louis interrupted. Doing that seemed to be a bad habit of his.

"Anyway, what she thinks is besides the point," he said.

"It most certainly is the point."

"No, it isn't. The point is that we don't want Mother taken advantage of."

"That's right," Hillary agreed, entering the room. As she handed me an iced tea, I could see that her nails were bitten down.

"I was just curious," Amy said, but her tone had changed from defiant to defeated.

"You'll have to forgive my sister," Hillary told me. "She's just concerned about our mother."

"As are we all," Louis chimed in.

I took a sip of my tea and put it down. It had that chemical aftertaste of the powdered instants. "Does your mother have a name?"

"Oh." Hillary paused. "I thought you knew."

"Should I?"

"Of course not. Why should you?" She gave a dismissive little laugh at her own foolishness. "It's Rose. Rose Taylor," she continued, idly caressing her arm with her hand.

The name sounded familiar, but I couldn't place it, and I didn't ask, figuring I could always do that later.

"I suppose," Hillary continued, "I could go to one of the larger detective agencies, but that seems like overkill."

"Not to mention expensive," I couldn't help volunteering. As an unlicensed part-timer I charged bargain-basement prices.

"That, too," Hillary conceded, her gray eyes widening a fraction. "I won't lie about that."

"One hundred dollars an hour is a lot on a postal worker's salary," Louis griped.

Evidently they'd already made inquiries at other places. Hillary fingered the hem of her skirt. "Actually, I thought we needed a more personal touch."

"So what is this job about?" I asked.

Louis and Hillary exchanged glances as Hillary sat down on the other side of me. She crossed and uncrossed her legs. She seemed to like the way they looked. I noticed she had a small half-moon tattooed on her left calf.

"Tell me," Hillary asked, turning her head in my direction. "Do you believe in psychics?"

"Psychics? You mean people who communicate with the dead?"

"Yes."

"No." I'd tried one after my husband Murphy had died. It had cost me a hundred bucks and left me feeling like a fool.

Hillary and Louis exchanged another look. "Do you believe people have the ability to talk to animals?" Hillary asked me.

"I think we can communicate." My dog, Zsa Zsa, was pretty good at letting me know what she wanted.

"I mean talking."

I looked to see if she was joking. She wasn't.

"As in my cat telling me, watch out, the lady down the street is in a bitchy mood today?" I asked.

"Something like that."

"Not outside of the movies."

"Well, my mother does."

"She believes she can talk to animals? I don't think . . ."

"No, she believes a woman named Pat Humphrey can." Hillary spread her hands and studied what was left of her fingernails.

"Go on," I finally prompted.

"This is so embarrassing."

I waited.

Hillary sighed and brushed a strand of hair off her fore-head. "All right. Three months ago—more or less—my mother's cat disappeared from the house. At first, we thought someone let it out by accident. Now, of course—" Hillary stopped. "Well, you decide. My mother was hysterical. She's very attached to . . . this animal. Anyway, the next morning at nine o'clock, this woman—"

"Pat Humphrey?" I asked.

Hillary nodded. "She appeared at my mother's door with the cat in her arms. She said she was a pet psychic. She said she'd found the cat wandering in the park and the cat told her where my mother lived."

"So you're saying you think this woman might have stolen your mother's cat and then brought it back?"

Hillary gave me the kind of smile a teacher bestows on a promising pupil.

"She said she didn't want any money," Louis continued, "but my mother insisted on giving her a reward."

I leaned forward. "How big?"

"Five thousand dollars."

I whistled. "Five thousand dollars is a fair chunk of change—even these days."

"Not for our mother," Amy blurted out. "She's rich."

Hillary glared at Amy, who turned her eyes downward. "Comfortable," Hillary corrected. "She's comfortable."

While Amy bit her lip, Louis took up the narrative.

"In any case," he said, "our mother talks to her every day now. Sometimes twice a day. We're worried. We think our mother is giving this woman money."

"I assume you think this woman is running a scam."

Hillary nodded.

"So, then, why don't you go to the police?"

"We will if we have to," Hillary said. "But we're hoping to avoid that. We don't want to upset Mother unnecessarily.

She's a very private person. She would be furious if she thought we involved the authorities in her private business."

"It would be like saying we thought she's losing her grip," Louis said.

Hillary nodded her head in agreement.

"But going to me isn't?"

"She's not going to know. At least until we have something definitive to tell her."

"I'm confused here. Now, what is it exactly that you want me to do?"

Louis looked at Hillary, and Hillary gave a nod.

"We've been thinking about that," Louis said. "And this is what we've come up with. We want you to get an appointment with this Humphrey woman. And then we want you to tape your session with her. I don't care if it takes one, two, or five times. We want tangible proof that this woman is a fraud."

It seemed as if that wouldn't be too hard a task to accomplish.

Chapter Three

The first thing I did when I left Hillary Cisco's house was drive over to Upstate. I'd been thinking about the man I'd picked up on the road yesterday. The picture he'd pressed into my hand felt like a hot potato, something I wanted to get rid of as quickly as possible. I had enough to do without finding Dorita. Especially now. All I wanted to do was give the damned thing back to him.

On my way down I called Calli on my cell phone, hoping she could tell me a little more about Hillary. But she wasn't in. That's probably because she was busy screwing her brains out with her latest fiasco of a boyfriend. She specialized in unredeemables.

"Call me, you black-hearted bitch," I said when I heard the beep from her answering machine. "I need to speak with you."

Then I rang up Pat Humphrey, told her I was Nancy Richardson, and asked for a consultation on my German shepherd, Duke. All business, she informed me that a phone consultation was thirty-five dollars for fifteen minutes, or we could do a half an hour face-to-face for seventy-five dollars, which is what she recommended for her first-time clients. Either was payable by major credit card. Naturally. These days everything is.

I could hear the pages turning as she consulted her book. "I can squeeze you in this Thursday at four o'clock. Two days away."

"That's fine. Should I bring Duke along?"

"No. That's not necessary. I can read your companion's vibes through you."

I guess vibes must be like dog hair; they stick to your clothing.

I was wondering how well Humphrey was doing with this gig as I pulled into Upstate's parking lot and went into the hospital. Probably better than I was. I'd seen ads for pet psychics in several of the pet magazines the store sells and discounted them. But maybe I shouldn't have. After all, a pet psychic combines three current trends: spirituality, treating animals as humans, and lots of free spending cash. In these days of doggie day care and homemade doggie biscuits, not to mention doggie treadmills, doggie portraits, doggie albums, doggie downers, and doggie hip replacements and MRIs, it stands to reason that someone who claims to be able to tell you why your precious pooch keeps peeing on your Oriental rug would be making money.

I was mulling over the possibility of taking our back room and offering it to a visiting pet psychic—a kind of itinerant spiritual vet—when I ran into my first roadblock of the evening.

"You can't go in there without permission," a nurse the size of Big Bertha barked as I started to enter the room my John Doe was in. "Can't you read the sign?"

The sign said Respiratory Isolation, which was new speak for quarantine. I took my hand off the door handle and held both of them up in the air.

"Okay. You got me."

"That warning is there for a reason, you know," she huffed.

"Gee and I thought you just hung it on random rooms. Sorry," I said as her frown deepened. "I was told the unidentified guy the EMTs picked up in Caz last night is in there."

"That's correct." She folded her arms across her chest. "Are you family?"

"I could be."

No response.

"I have something to return to him."

She held out her hand. "I'll put it with his belongings." But I didn't want to give the photograph to her. I wanted to give it to him. Suddenly, it was very important that I put the picture in his hand.

"Thanks, but I'd like to wait till he's up and about."

"Suit yourself." Her tone made it clear that she didn't think that was going to happen any time soon.

"Do you have a name on him yet?"

"Even if I did, which I don't, I can't tell you without proper authorization."

"You're just a regular ray of sunshine, aren't you?"

"If you don't mind." Her uniform crinkled as she folded her arms across her chest again. When I didn't leave, she added, "Do I have to call Security?"

"Only if they'll take me out to eat."

She didn't smile. But then, if I looked like her, I probably wouldn't be smiling, either.

I went home and had a drink and my dinner, which consisted of two chocolate doughnuts left over from the morning, looked at the picture of the family, then tucked it back in my backpack and went to sleep.

I spent some of the next day and most of the evening looking for Bethany. I called up her school principal and found out she'd gone from a straight-A student to someone that was barely passing. The school psychologist said she was "at risk" but wouldn't provide me with any useful information.

I showed Bethany's picture at the malls and pizza parlors and handed out my business card, and when I was done with that, I cruised downtown and talked to the women working the street who would talk to me. One of them, a skinny spandexed ghetto-talking blond, identified Bethany.

"You ain't gonna be finding her around here parading her fat white ass up and down the street, I can tell you that," she said while keeping her eyes open for squad cars and customers.

"How can you be so sure?"

" 'Cause I told her, she tried any of that shit down here, I'd put a strap to her so fast it would make her head spin. Her and those other burb bitches, thinkin' they can just waltz in here. Now we got the cops swarmin' all over us."

"So I take it you haven't seen her today?"

"What I be telling you?"

I handed her my card and told her there was a fifty in it for her if she called me if Bethany showed up. Jeez what a world. I couldn't believe that she was just doing this because she wanted money to buy a gold necklace. Although that's what a social worker who'd interviewed a couple of these girls before turning them over to their parents had told me one night over a beer at the bar.

"Oral sex," he said, wiping the beer from off his mustache. "It's not a big deal to some of them. It's like kissing."

God. I hadn't even known what that was at fifteen.

I tried calling Karim, but his mother hung up on me. Michelle wasn't home, and neither were the first two names on my list of Bethany's friends. What I was really hoping, even though I wasn't going to say this to her parents, was that she hadn't decided to take off for someplace like New York City or Buffalo with the guy who'd picked her up from Karim's house, the guy no one knew, because then my chances of finding her were going to go from good to slim to none.

Around nine that evening, I stopped at Dunkin' Donuts for a coffee and my chocolate-peanut doughnut fix, then drove over to Satan's End, a place off of East Genesee Street that showcased punk and hard-core. It looked like Bethany's type of scene, and I was hoping she'd be there.

Tonight, according to the handwritten sign at the door, Bad Breath and Scum were playing. Who was going to be there next? Puke and the Amputees? A wall of noise hit me when I walked through the door. I wondered if I could collect workmen's comp for hearing loss. I looked around. The place was jam-packed full of black-clad and pierced boys and girls, most of whom I placed between the ages of fourteen and twenty, though it was hard to tell. I was scanning the dance floor when I felt a tap on my shoulder.

"What do you want?"

I spun around and glanced up. A granite block of a man with the blond curly hair of a Botticelli angel was staring down at me.

"I'm looking for someone." And I showed him Bethany's picture.

"You her mother?"

"No. I've been hired to find her."

"What's she done?"

"She's a runaway." I was yelling to make myself heard. "Have you seen her?"

"These kids all look the same to me."

"Mind if I look around?"

"As long as you don't cause any problems—no."

I nodded and started walking through the place. The kids ignored me, pretending I wasn't there. When I tried to show them Bethany's picture, they all shook their heads and averted their eyes. There were lots of kids that looked like Bethany—maybe she was even there—but between the lighting and the constant motion, it was difficult to tell. I found a relatively quiet corner and stood there and watched. After about ten minutes my eyes and ears adjusted, and I spotted Bethany leaning against the wall, sipping something out of a paper cup and watching the band. She looked lonely standing there by herself.

"Bethany?" I said once I'd worked my way over to her.

She shot me a glance and started moving away. I grabbed her arm, which in retrospect was a mistake.

"Let me go!" she cried.

"I just want to talk to you."

She tried to wiggle out of my grasp. "You're hurting me."

I tightened my grip. "Your parents want you to come home."

"Tell them to screw themselves."

"Bethany . . . please . . . all I want to do—"

"Get away from me!" she screamed.

By now we'd begun to attract a considerable amount of attention.

"She's trying to kidnap me!" Bethany yelled. "Help, help!"

Suddenly, we were surrounded. Everyone was yelling things like "Let her go" and "Leave her alone."

The next thing I knew, my feet had left the floor. "I warned you about creating a disturbance," Granite Guy said as he deposited me outside.

I called Bethany's parents from the parking lot and told them to come down. Hopefully, they could talk some sense into their child. I waited around till they showed half an hour later, and then I went home. The phone rang about two minutes after I walked through the door.

It was Bethany's dad. He just wanted to let me know they'd lost her. She'd jumped out of the family car and run off again. He sounded furious, and I didn't blame him.

The next day, I kept my appointment with Pat Humphrey. She lived in Strathmore, one of the last upscale areas left in the city of Syracuse. The area has a Fort Apache feel, since it sits like a citadel looking down over Onondaga Park, grandly ignoring the slums that are creeping up on all sides of it. It has streets with pretty French names, lilac bushes in the front yards, and houses made of quarried stone and stucco, parquet floors, oak doors, cove molding, and mullioned windows, houses made by craftsmen who expected them to last for a hundred years instead of twenty.

The cottage Pat Humphrey lived in looked as if it had been built during the Arts and Crafts Movement era. Small and tidy, the outside was painted a teal blue, and the windowsills, a deep matte red. The pillars supporting the wide front-porch roof were made of quarried stone. A rocking chair and three weathered Adirondack chairs faced out to the street. It was easy to imagine myself sitting there, drinking a tall iced coffee, smoking a cigarette, and listening to the cicadas. Alongside the house a stunted perennial border of coneflowers, shasta daisies, and black-eyed Susans, decorative grasses, and deep purple petunias struggled in the afternoon heat.

I checked one last time to make sure the voice-activated tape recorder in my backpack was working, then got out of my car and rang the bell. A moment later, Pat Humphrey came to the door. She didn't look the way I'd expected her to, but then I hadn't expected her to live in a place like this, either. I thought I'd be meeting someone who favored ethnic dresses and wore sandals and large, dangling earrings, someone like Amy. Instead, Pat Humphrey was cool, unwrinkled, and in control. Just looking at her made me feel hot, sweaty, and dirty.

Tall and thin, she wore her carefully tailored short sleeve beige linen blouse and slacks well. She had a long, narrow nose, eyes set a shade too far apart, and a mouth that looked as if it didn't get to smile too much. Her hair was an indeterminate shade of blond. Straight, it came to right below her ears and was cut in the sort of style that looks as if it's easy to do and actually takes hours in front of the mirror with a brush and blow-dryer to accomplish.

The diamond studs she had on were large enough to be noticed but small enough to be tasteful. But for all the care Pat Humphrey had taken with her appearance, she couldn't completely conceal the rough red patches across her cheeks and on her chin. Then I noticed she had similar patches on her wrists and arms. Little pinpricks of dried blood marked where'd she'd been scratching. Eczema, I'd be willing to bet. One of my cousins had had it. The doctor had told him it was caused by stress.

"Come in," she told me, casting a somewhat jaundiced eye on my wrinkled black linen short skirt and bubblegum pink

T-shirt. "I should have told you to wear neutral colors. Vivid ones can interfere with reception."

"Now I know why my TV isn't working too well," I quipped as I stepped inside.

Pat Humphrey smiled politely.

The house was pleasantly cool. I caught a faint aroma of sandalwood. Everything in it, from the hardwood oak floor to the diamond-leaded windowpanes, sparkled. The walls of the small vestibule I was standing in were covered in an expensive, textured, wheat-colored paper, which contrasted nicely with the ocher-colored living-room walls. The pictures on them, mostly landscapes, looked like original oils and watercolors. The worn nut-brown leather Chesterfield sofa and club chair sat on a fair-sized Oriental rug. A bouquet of baby's-breath, sunflowers, and daisies sat in a polished copper vase in front of the fireplace. The mantel, painted white, was covered with photos and ceramic candlesticks.

"Very nice," I said. The place dripped with good taste, the kind it takes a fair amount of money and knowledge to accomplish.

Pat Humphrey nodded her head graciously. "Most of the furniture is my grandmother's. This"—she indicated the lamp to the right of the sofa—"is a real Tiffany. The table under it is a signed Stickley." Pat tucked a strand of blonde hair behind her ear.

"We're talking what? Maybe fifty to sixty thousand dollars?" I posited, realizing I'd spoken out loud. "My mother was in the trade for a while," I explained.

"People say I should sell this stuff and invest the money, but having it here makes me feel closer to Gran."

I made a noncommittal sound. I had no reason to believe Humphrey was lying about where she'd gotten the stuff, but she didn't strike me as the sentimental type, either.

"I guess I've been fortunate," Pat Humphrey added as she led me into the dining room and sat me down at the table in the center.

Maybe. Or maybe she'd made her own luck. I positioned my backpack on the table, close to where she was sitting. "No pets?"

Pat Humphrey spread her fingers out and studied her carefully manicured nails. "I find them a distraction. I need quiet."

She certainly had that. Aside from the whir of the overhead fan, the only other sound I could hear was the swish of the dishwasher running. Out of the corner of my eye, I watched a metallic green beetle march its way over the fringe of an old Herez and onto the floor. When it got to the leg of the sideboard, it stopped and waved its feelers around for a few minutes, wondering what to do.

"How did you get into this line of work?" I asked her as the beetle began its climb.

"I've always had the ability. From the time I was a little girl. I'd get these flashes. My grandmother had them, too, so I guess you could say I inherited it. This is a way to use my ability for good." Pat Humphrey clasped her hands together and cocked her head slightly to one side. "Tell me, how can I help you?"

"I thought you'd know."

Pat Humphrey frowned a little. The gesture brought out the furrows between her eyes. "I have lots of other clients who need to see me. If you think this is a joke . . ."

"Not at all," I hastened to reassure her, after which I proceeded to give her the story I'd decided upon when I'd phoned. "I'm worried about my German shepherd, Duke. He's not eating well. He looks different. Not right. I was hoping you could tell me what's the matter."

"Have you taken him to a vet?"

My respect for her went up a notch. "Of course." I allowed my voice to grow indignant. "He's had all sorts of blood work done. Nothing's shown up."

"I see. When was he born?"

"August of last year."

"So that would make him a Leo," Pat Humphrey mused aloud as I watched the beetle clamber over a carved wooden rose.

"Does it matter?"

"Of course it does. Let's get started, shall we?" And with that she closed her eyes.

Her face grew slack; her breathing became shallow. The only discernible movement was the occasional flicker of an eyelid. It was a good act. I wondered how long she'd be able to keep it up. Probably for a while. It seemed as if she'd had plenty of practice. I checked my watch. Two minutes later, I checked my watch again. Five more minutes and I began to get antsy.

I got up. Pat Humphrey didn't move. Probably because she was on another plane, a spiritual one, chatting away with her spirit guide. Right. I restrained myself from snapping my fingers in front of her face or sticking my tongue out or any of the other ten-year-old maneuvers I wanted to perform. After all, I was just here to see the show and make a report, and it seemed to me the report I was going to make was pretty conclusive.

Instead, I went into the kitchen, got myself a drink of water, and came back into the dining room. Pat Humphrey was still in her trance, and the beetle was on top of the sideboard. He looked as if he didn't know where to go. It was probably tough living in a psychic's house, with all that spiritual energy flowing around you. Of course, in ancient Egypt beetles were holy, so maybe he was used to this kind of thing. I was about to pick him up and take him outside, anyway, when Pat Humphrey's eyelids fluttered and she opened her eyes.

She gave a slight cough. I sat back down and waited to hear what she had to say. Her face looked drawn. A delicate trace of sweat was visible over her upper lip. As she wiped it away, I noticed there was a slight tremor in her hand. The woman really did put on an excellent performance. I'd give her that. Suddenly, she began to talk. Her voice sounded weary. But, hey, I get tired when I fly to New York City and back.

"Your dog, Duke, is surrounded by a field of negative energy. It is impinging on his ability to heal himself. If you want him to get better, you must work on your own negative emotions and those in your immediate environment. You must become more positive. The universe is a vast sea. Whatever you throw out comes back to you."

"What should I do for him?" I asked, trying to get her to say more about my nonexistent pet.

"Duke wants you to know that he needs your support," Pat Humphrey continued. "He is in pain."

"What kind?"

"In his hind legs. He needs to sleep off the floor."

Considering he was a German shepherd and most shepherds have hip problems, that wasn't too hard a guess.

"Also," Humphrey continued, "I sense he has a problem in the area of his liver. The food you are giving him is rife with negative karma. You must change it. If you do these things, he will begin to heal."

Since most commercial dog food is made with ground-up animal by-products, that wasn't too surprising, either. That's why I don't feed it to my dog Zsa Zsa. But then Zsa Zsa doesn't eat dog food. Of any kind. Out of the corner of my eye, I watched the beetle pause on the edge of the sideboard. He wavered for a few seconds, then plunged over the edge. He landed on his back and stayed there, legs frantically waving. Finally, he managed to right himself and scurry under the sideboard.

I was trying to spot him when Pat Humphrey pushed herself away from the table and stood up. I redirected my attention to her.

"And now, if you'll excuse me, I must lie down for a few minutes. I hope I was helpful."

"Oh, you were," I assured her. After all, any animal could benefit from the advice she'd given me. Feed your dog healthful food, be nice to it, and cut down on the fighting around the house. I hoped she was giving Hillary's mother more detailed readings for the money she was getting.

"Good." Pat Humphrey clasped my hands in hers. Her palms were dry and cool. "Tell me if Duke begins to feel better."

"I will," I promised.

I started for the door. I was thinking that all I had to do was run a background check on Pat Humphrey and give Hillary Cisco the tape of this meeting along with my report and I'd be done with the job when Pat Humphrey called out to me.

"Wait," she said.

I turned.

"Do you have a cat called James?"

"Yes, I do. Why?"

Pat Humphrey licked her lower lip. "Because he's locked in somewhere and can't get out. Somewhere dark. Somewhere without windows."

I felt the hairs on the back of my neck go up. "A van?"

"I can't tell. It's too dark."

I was having my bedroom painted. The guy doing it owned a covered truck. I glanced at my watch. It was four-thirty. John said he'd be done and out of my house around now. Could James have jumped into the truck and gotten himself locked in? It was possible. He'd done something like that a couple of years ago.

She held up a finger as I began to speak. "There's something else. Something about a person . . . a man. His name starts with an M . . ."

"Murphy," I blurted out.

Pat Humphrey shook her head. "I don't know. I'm sorry. I've lost it now." She looked genuinely upset.

She wasn't half as upset as I was.

Chapter Four

I watched George—who was what? My boyfriend? My some-time live-in?—take a long pull from his bottle of beer and listened to the dull click of glass on glass as he put the bottle back on the table. It was a little after ten in the evening, and we were having a nightcap in my backyard—it was too hot in the house—and discussing the day's events.

"If it had been me, I would have handcuffed that little shit to the door of the car," he observed.

I swatted at a fly and inhaled the sweet scent of nicotiana wafting from my garden. A sliver of a new moon hung un-certainly in the night sky. "Now, that's a constructive sugges-tion."

"Hey, at least what's her name . . ."

"Bethany . . ."

"Whatever. Wouldn't be out on the streets roaming around now."

"She's probably sleeping in the basement of one of her friends' houses."

George yawned and put his arms over his head and stretched. "God, I'm glad I don't work juvie anymore. You can't imagine how nice it is not to have to deal with that kind of stuff."

"I bet the kids on the street are glad, too."

"Har. Har." He made a dismissive gesture with his hand. "So what now?"

"Her parents want me to keep looking."

"She's just lucky she's not my kid, that's all I can say."

"What would you do?"

"I'd put her in a friggin' all-girls Catholic boarding school like my aunt did with her daughters."

We both lapsed into silence. I was thinking about how George still sounded like a cop even though he was off the force when my phone rang.

"Aren't you going to get it?" George asked.

"No. Let the machine pick it up." It had been a long day, and I didn't want to talk to anyone now.

A shaft of light from my kitchen illuminated the planes on George's face as he leaned over, took the tape of my session with Pat Humphrey out of the recorder, and tossed it to me. I missed, and it landed in my lap.

"You want my opinion on this?"

"I wouldn't have asked if I didn't."

He ran a finger around the mouth of his bottle. "You don't believe this Humphrey woman is for real, do you?" he asked.

"Of course not," I lied as Zsa Zsa chased a moth around the deck. She snapped at it, missed, and snapped again. She hadn't caught one yet. "I'm just asking for your explanation of the last part of the session."

"For openers, she obviously recognized you."

"I hope not. If she did, why didn't she say so? Why did she go along with it?"

George shrugged. "I don't know. Go ask her. But that's the only reasonable answer." He spoke quickly, compressing the words together, the way he did when he was talking about something he didn't want to. The fact that discussing Murphy still upset him endeared him to me. "That's how she knew."

I studied the glowing white petals of the nicotiana languidly drooping in the darkness instead. A giant moth, attracted by the lamp in my kitchen window, was fluttering its wings against the glass.

"The paper covered his death," George added. "Remember?"

How could I forget? Although, God knows, I would like to. I took a sip of my scotch and tried not to think about that time. "All right, maybe she did know who I was," I conceded, tracking a pair of yellow-green eyes that had materialized out of the bushes and would, I knew, shortly metamorphose into my cat. All black, he was practically invisible at night. In the Middle Ages they would have called him a familiar and consigned him to the flames. With my red hair and my big mouth, I probably wouldn't have been far behind.

"Maybe she was playing me, but what about James? How do you explain that?" I demanded as he brushed by my leg. I scooped him up and buried my hand in his thick fur. He moved his neck, letting me know he wanted me to scratch behind his ears. I'd reached my house just as the painter was pulling out of my driveway and gotten him to unlock the back of his truck. If I hadn't, my kitty would have been God knows where instead of sitting in my lap. "Pat Humphrey was right about him being in the van."

George snorted and took another swallow of beer. "Get real. It was a lucky guess. That's all it was. That's all it usually is."

"I wish I was as sure."

"Humphrey is running a classic textbook con." George put his beer down on the table. "Think about it. She made a general statement about James."

I took a sip of my scotch before replying. "No, she didn't."

"Yes, she did. Robin, saying James is in an enclosed space is like saying he was up a tree. Crawling into nooks and crannies and climbing up trees are two things that cats do."

"What about the van part, then? How did she know that?"

"Easy. You gave it to her."

I flushed and fished a Camel out of the pack lying on the table.

"See," George said, taking my silence for assent.

I went to light the cigarette, and James, disgusted with my actions, jumped onto the ground and disappeared back into the hedges. "You still haven't explained how she knew I had a cat?"

George cocked his head and studied me for a second before replying. "Like I said before, she probably knew who you were."

I drew in a breath of smoke, then exhaled. "How do you explain the fact that she knew James's name? That's a fairly specific piece of information."

George drummed his fingers on his chair's armrest. "Come on, Robin. This is a small town. Maybe Humphrey knows one of your neighbors. Maybe you guys have a mutual friend. You've been written up in local papers. Maybe they mentioned James there. Or maybe you mentioned James to her in your conversation and you've forgotten that you did."

I thought back. I was fairly positive I hadn't, but I could be wrong.

"That's the way people like her operate," George continued. "She's good at remembering what other people say. She's also good at reading people cold, reading their body language. It's a knack." He stifled a yawn. "Good salesmen have it. So do con artists. I read that some professor even teaches a college course on how to do it. He calls it debunking psychics."

"Still . . ." I began when George pushed his chair back and stood up.

"You want a beer?" he asked.

"I'll stick with scotch, thanks." I enjoyed watching him walk into my kitchen, the way he strolled along. When he came out a moment later, he had a beer in one hand and the picture of the Mexican family in the other. I'd left it on the counter by the sink.

"Who is this?" he asked.

I reached up and took it. "Just a photo I picked up some-where," I lied, the words flowing out while prickles of guilt blossomed in my gut.

I hadn't told George about the man lying in the hospital. I hadn't told him about having to get tested for TB, either. Maybe I should have. But we weren't married, I rationalized. Therefore, I didn't have to tell him everything. Of course, I hadn't done that even when I was married, but that was be-side the point. Anyway, it had been a long day, and I wasn't in the mood for the argument I was sure would ensue.

George sat back down. "You want me to ask Paul to run Humphrey's name for you?"

"Think he can leave the golf course long enough to do it?"

George frowned. "What's that supposed to mean?"

"Nothing. I'll ask him."

Paul was a friend of George's. At the moment, George was going for his Ph.D. in medieval history, but when I'd met him, he'd been a cop, and he still had lots of friends on and off the force. Paul was one of them. He'd recently opened a security agency, and so, even though I didn't like the guy too much, any kind of checking that had to be done, I threw his way. It wasn't worth it not to. That's the thing with relation-ships—they always involve compromises.

Half an hour later, after George had finished his second beer, he grabbed my hand and pulled me up. "Come on," he said, kissing me, his hand lingering on my hip. "Let's get a lit-tle action going here."

I kissed him back.

"Let's go upstairs."

My hand went to his waistband. "It's too hot upstairs, let's stay down here."

He kissed the side of my neck. "I don't think so."

"How come you're so conservative?"

"How come you're so reckless?"

We compromised on the living-room sofa.

* * *

After George left, I went back into the garden. I smoked another cigarette and sipped my scotch and pondered the last two days. Watching Zsa Zsa and James playing hide-and-seek, I thought about ghosts and spirits and whether I believed in them or not. By the time I was ready to go to bed, I'd convinced myself that George was right, that what I'd seen that afternoon was a fluke. Pat Humphrey was an exceptionally talented con artist. Nothing more. I could understand why Hillary and her sister and brother were so upset, why they'd wanted to hire me. I'd want to hire me, too, if I were them.

That night, I dreamed about Murphy, something I hadn't done in years. I woke up before my alarm went off to Zsa Zsa licking the tears off my cheeks. The dream had had something to do with a green skeleton that turned into a straw mat that became a cluster of blue and yellow butterflies. I tried to remember more and failed as I dragged myself out of bed, stood under the shower, got dressed, and drove off to Noah's Ark. But the dream had become lodged in my mind like a cinder in your eye. I couldn't get rid of it.

I was still trying at ten-thirty in the morning when a man walked through the shop door. Zsa Zsa immediately ran out from behind the counter and started barking. Looking at him, I figured two things. One: He wasn't a customer. And two: He wasn't from around here. His clothes, expensive, casual, pressed khakis and a dark green polo shirt with an Izod logo, marked him suburban. And then I caught sight of his car and amended the suburban to rich.

"Nice ride," I said, indicating the Mercedes parked by the curb after telling Zsa Zsa to stuff a sock in it.

Actually, now that I'd taken a closer look at him, he wasn't so bad, either. Attractive rather than handsome. Tall, loose-knit body. Clean-shaven. A chin a shade too narrow, a nose a little too big for his face, eyes that never seemed to come to rest, but somehow together the features worked.

He grinned, revealing a set of prominent canines. "Personally, I like the Jag better."

"Personally, I like the old MGBs."

"Me, too." He winked. "I'm trying to get the boss to buy one. I spotted a beauty down in Tully the other day."

"So what are you? A chauffeur?"

He cracked his knuckles. "Something like that."

"It must be nice to have that kind of money."

His grin grew wide enough to split his face. "I think so." He planted an elbow on the counter and leaned toward me. I caught a whiff of his aftershave. "Here." He pressed a small envelope into my palm. "This is for you."

"Who's it from?"

"The boss lady."

"And that would be?"

"Rose Taylor."

"Rose Taylor?" Hillary's mom. I lifted an eyebrow. "Why? Is there a problem?"

"Not at all." Well, that hadn't taken long. Maybe George had been right about Humphrey knowing who I was. I flushed, thinking about what a fool I must have looked like.

"Nice place you have here," he said, looking around the shop as I absentmindedly tapped the edge of the envelope on the counter. "Although your air conditioning could use a little help."

"I know. I've been trying to get the repair guy on the phone for the past two days."

He pointed to one of the saltwater fish tanks alongside the left wall. "Are those hard to keep going?"

"They're not recommended for beginners."

"Pity. That's the story of my life."

"What is?"

"Always wanting things above my ability." He clasped his hands together, straightened them, and popped his knuckles. "So aren't you going to open it?" He indicated the envelope with his chin.

"Sorry." I loosened the flap and slid the card out. It was the expensive kind, the kind made out of vellum, the kind with the embossed black letters. I flipped it open. Rose Taylor was inviting me to cocktails at five-thirty that evening. Her handwriting was precise and even. She'd written the invitation out with a fountain pen in bright blue ink.

"I didn't think people drank cocktails anymore."

"Most people don't use fountain pens either," the chauffeur observed.

"Why does she want to see me?"

He shrugged. "She didn't say. Can I tell her you're coming?"

Watching him, I got the feeling that no one refused Rose Taylor. "And if I say no?"

The chauffeur smoothed out the logo on his shirt. "You'll miss a good martini."

"I prefer manhattans."

"We have those, too." His smile was positively wolfish. "I'll even have the maid put a cherry in your glass." He leaned forward. "You like cherries, don't you?"

"Doesn't everyone?"

"Good. I'll have her put in two. It's a great house. You'll like it. Oh," he said, turning when he reached the door. "One more thing. Try to be on time. She hates it when anyone is late."

"Don't we all."

After he left, I picked up the card Rose Taylor had sent me and studied it. Amy had said her mother was rich. The card and the car confirmed that. They also told me something else. They told me that not only did Rose Taylor have money; she wanted people to know that she had it. Given the way her children had acted, I had a feeling she wasn't above using it to get what she wanted.

I put the card down next to the photograph of the Mexican family. Well, one thing was for sure: It was going to be an interesting visit. I went into the back and poured myself a cup of coffee and checked in with Bethany's parents. She hadn't shown—big surprise. Then I called up another one of Bethany's friends and got a possible line on one of the boys she was staying with. I was just looking up his name in the phone book when Calli called me.

"B&N. Tomorrow night around nine. Okay?"

"Okay."

"Great. Gotta go. I'm on deadline."

"Just give me a two-minute précis on Hillary and her mother."

"You got it." I took notes while she talked.

After she hung up, I went back to looking up Bethany's boyfriend's address. Matt Andrews lived on Seymour Street, which wasn't that far away from the store. I called the number listed and was informed by a man with a thick Russian accent that he was out painting houses and would be back around four that afternoon. I thanked him and hung up. Maybe if I was lucky, Bethany would be there too.

Chapter Five

I intercepted Matt Andrews just as he was going up the steps of his house. He was a good-looking, compactly built guy in his twenties with closely cropped blond hair and a killer tan. I could see where Bethany would want him, but why would he want Bethany?

"Yes?" he asked as I approached him. His face closed up as if he were expecting trouble, and he hugged the six-pack of beer he was carrying a little closer to his chest.

I gave him my card. "Bethany's parents would like her to come home."

"I don't know what you're talking about."

I pointed at the SUV parked in the driveway. It was the same one I'd seen drive away from Karim's house. "You picked her up the other night."

"I don't have to talk to you." He started back up the steps.

"Do the words statutory rape mean anything to you?" I called after him.

He kept going.

"Her parents don't want to prosecute, but they will. She's just fifteen."

He stiffened and whirled around. "Fifteen? You're kidding me, right?"

"What do you think?"

"She told me she was eighteen," he protested.

She looked eighteen the way I looked twenty-five. "Well, she's fifteen. Now where is she?"

"I don't know. Honest," he added after a few beats had gone by.

"Think about it. No. Don't shake your head. At this moment, you're liable to prosecution. You know, being labeled as a sex offender—that wouldn't be good at all."

"Hey." He shook a finger at me. "I didn't force myself on her. She gave it up of her own free will. She wanted it."

"Legally, a fifteen-year-old girl doesn't have free will. Is she in your apartment?"

"No."

"You mind if I take a look?"

"Be my guest." I followed him inside. Salsa music and the smell of frying potatoes wafted down from upstairs. "I keep telling them to lower the volume," he groused as he unlocked the door.

The inside of the apartment was surprisingly neat. It was furnished with odd pieces of mismatched, tattered, nicked furniture, but the windows, floors, and walls were spotless.

"See," Andrews said as he followed me from room to room. "I told you she wasn't here."

"So who else does she hang out with?" I inquired when we were back in the living room. When he didn't answer, I nudged him a little. "Remember, a sex-offender status will follow you wherever you go."

He tugged at his painter's hat. "Sometimes," he said reluctantly, "she hangs at this tattoo parlor on the North Side." And he gave me the address. I wrote it down. "She has a friend that works there."

I consulted my watch. I'd have to drop in there later. The drive out to Rose Taylor's would take me at least a half hour—if there wasn't any traffic on the road. Plus, I was stopping on the way and seeing Bethany's parents before I hit Rose Taylor's. It was a meeting I wasn't looking forward to. After all, how do you tell someone that their fifteen-year-old daughter is stealing money from people? And that was the good news?

I took my card out of Matt Andrews's hand, scribbled my cell phone number on the bottom of it, and handed it back to him. "If she comes by, be smart and call me immediately."

"Don't worry. Believe me, I will."

"Good. Because you don't need the kind of trouble she's going to cause you." And I got in my car and took off. Hopefully, I'd scared him enough so he would.

As I drove along Route 92, I pondered what Calli had told me about Rose Taylor. She was definitely a high-powered lady. The widow of Sanford Taylor, a down-home guy who had been known as one of the powers behind the throne in the New York State Republican Party. A power broker and financier, he'd inherited the family fortune from his dad, Hubbell Taylor, who'd made *his* money manufacturing office equipment. Sanford had dramatically increased his fortune by strategically aligning himself with certain prominent families that had widespread interests in construction, trucking, waste disposal, and real estate. Rose Taylor was his second wife, his first one having died in an automobile accident.

Twenty-five years younger than her husband, she'd been a nurse, training that had served her well when her husband had come down with rheumatoid arthritis. He'd remained bedridden for five years before he died at the relatively young age of sixty-five. It was rumored she'd become the brains behind his particular operation, the person in charge. Nothing went through without her say-so.

Maybe that's why Sanford had left everything to her. She, in turn, according to Calli, was supposed to look after her children's needs out of the money in the estate. Then, when she died, they'd inherit what was left over. The kids had outstanding debts all over town that the mother was refusing to honor. Not a good recipe for family harmony, I decided as I lit a cigarette. Not a good recipe at all.

* * *

Eagerness made palpable, Arthur and Millie Peterson were waiting for me when I pulled into the driveway of their house. Once we were seated in the living room, I told them everything I'd found out about their daughter. I kept my hands folded and my eyes focused somewhere in the middle of the room, because I didn't want to see their reactions.

"You're wrong," the mother cried when I was done. "Bethany would never do those things. She's still a baby."

I felt as if I'd just shot Bambi.

"I just want her to come home." She covered her face with her hands. Sobs flew out between her fingers.

I couldn't think of anything to say. I studied a piece of pottery and tried not to see her. Her husband put his arms around her and held her close.

"It'll be all right," he murmured. "You'll see. We'll get through this."

I couldn't get out of the Petersons' house soon enough. I hate giving people this kind of news, I wished I was back in Noah's Ark, taking care of my fish, cleaning out the bird cages, and feeding Zsa Zsa her dog biscuits. Everything is so much simpler there.

Like Bethany's parents, Rose Taylor lived in Cazenovia, but in a ritzier part. Normally, I liked driving through the town. Bordering on Cazenovia Lake, it is one of those quaint summer resorts that turn up in tour guides under the heading of undiscovered American gems. It has its share of bed-and-breakfasts, hotels with colorful faux British names, and shops selling amusing postcards, expensive, imported scented soaps, and candles.

Until recently a WASP stronghold, although not as conservative or rich as Skaneateles, another small lakeside resort town in our area, it still harbors a sizable contingent of the wealthy, though their numbers are dwindling as the middle class moved in. What's even worse, from some people's point of view, is that the college there, once an all-girls school, in an attempt to shore up their enrollment, not only turned coed but was now recruiting minority students from New York City. The barbarians were no longer at the gates. They were inside. But they hadn't reached Rose Taylor's house yet.

A white plantation-style manor, it looked like some of the ones I'd once seen on a trip to Newport, Rhode Island, except smaller. Located about forty feet back from the lake, the house was surrounded by a vast, manicured emerald green lawn, which gently unfurled itself as it ran down to the dock. It was a Henry James kind of lawn. I expected to see men and women dressed in white playing croquet. Several sprinklers were set up on the grass, the fine mists of water dancing in the sun, catching the colors of the light. Maybe there was a drought in the rest of Onondaga County, but there wasn't one here.

The bucolic nature of the place was further emphasized by the series of gently rolling hills off in the distance. They were so evenly spaced, they looked as if they had been airbrushed in. The only thing missing was sheep dotting the hillside. Naturally, there was a tennis court and a swimming pool off to one side. I parked the car in the circular driveway a little over to the left. As I walked up the black brick road—no tarmac for Rose Taylor—two gardeners stopped and watched me go by. The sun had turned their skin the color of walnuts.

A maid answered the door a few seconds after I rang. She was dressed in the traditional maid's uniform, a black dress with a white apron, something you don't see too often anymore. Or let me correct that. Something I don't see too often anymore—something that I actually had never seen at all, if we're being accurate.

"The service entrance is around the back," she told me in heavily accented English.

I guess I should have changed out of my jeans and T-shirt. I handed her my card and told her who I was.

"Really," I said, giving her my best middle-class smile. "Mrs. Taylor is expecting me. Check if you want."

"That is not necessary." The maid's disdainful glance lingered on the place on my T-shirt where I'd wiped my hands after I'd scooped some algae out of one of the fish tanks. Up until now I'd forgotten about the yellow-green stain. Then she gave a slight, resigned shrug, as if to say she only worked here, it wasn't any business of hers who came in.

"Mrs. Taylor is waiting for you in the sunroom."

I stepped inside, and she closed the door. Constructed from wood, with palm-sized metal rivets, it reminded me of the doors you see on old buildings in Florence or Rome. The maid's short-legged body and the slightly flat shape of the back of her head made me think she was Mayan, probably from Chiapas or the Yucatán. At one time, I would have thought that was unusual, but in the past few years I've been seeing more and more Mexicans in this area.

She turned and started down the hall. I trotted behind her, my slides click-clacking on the black-and-white marble floor. My stomach started to clench. At first, I thought I was nervous about the upcoming meeting, but then I realized it was the house itself. It reminded me of my mother's apartment. The house was perfect. Like a museum. Filled with beautiful objects, it was devoid of the clutter that would have made it a home. From what I could see, it was also devoid of things like computers, television sets, and stereos. The furniture in the rooms we passed was mostly French, the rugs Persian. There were landscapes on the walls and a collection of blue-and-white Chinese pottery displayed in the hall, along with two large antique Japanese scrolls. An old Coromandel screen, similar to one I'd seen in an exhibition at the Metropolitan Museum of Art, stood over in one corner.

As I slowed down to contemplate a fifteenth-century Buddha sitting, palms upraised, staring out at a blank wall, consoling no one, I wondered why Hillary had chosen to decorate her house the way she had. Most people in her situation would have picked another motif instead of coming up with a cheap copy of her mother's. I know I had. Maybe Hillary was making an ironic commentary on the nature of wealth and possessions, except she didn't strike me as either distanced or sophisticated enough to do that. I was still wondering about that when I walked into the sunroom.

"Come in, come in," Mrs. Taylor said, indicating she wanted me to come closer with a crisp wave of her right hand. The gesture was as precise as her penmanship.

She was seated on a cushioned wicker chaise longue, stroking the lilac-point Siamese cat resting on her lap, the cat, I presumed, Pat Humphrey was talking to on a regular basis. A cluster of weeping ficus trees that almost reached the ceiling stood behind her. To her right was a priestly-looking man in a lightweight navy suit, while to her left was the man who'd delivered her note to me this morning.

"Did you have a nice drive over?" she inquired.

I nodded as I advanced across the floor. The place smelled of dead flowers and cloves.

"Good."

The room was all windows and oak. Off to one side was a small greenhouse that could be closed off from the main room by a sliding-glass door. Baskets of large staghorn and maidenhair ferns hung from the ceiling, while pots of improbably colored orchids sat on the center table.

"Orchids are a hobby of mine," she explained, following my glance. "I like them because they're a challenge. They're difficult to propagate and difficult to raise. Unlike some other flowers, such as my namesake—roses. Which, despite what some people say, are essentially boring."

If I were going to guess, I'd say Rose Taylor was about seventy. It was easy to see how pretty she must have been forty years ago. She still had the cheekbones, the large eyes, and a wide, generous mouth. Her gray hair was pulled back in a chignon. Her makeup was light. She hadn't made the mistake of trying to disguise the wrinkles on her face. Her dress was simple, a pair of black linen pants and a thin white linen shirt with decorative embroidery around the collar. Her only jewelry was a pair of large emerald earrings.

"This," she said, pointing to her cat, "is Sheba, and this," she said pointing to the tall, painfully thin man in the blue suit, "is my old friend and lawyer, Mr. Moss Ryan. And this person, whom you met in the store this morning, is my husband, Geoffrey Lang."

I don't know if my jaw dropped or not. But her expression told me how much she enjoyed the look of amazement that had to be appearing on my face.

We were talking about what here? An age difference of twenty-five or thirty years?

For some reason I found myself thinking of the Cheshire cat. Maybe it was Rose Taylor's smile.

Her smile showed off her teeth. They were very small and very white, and they looked as if they could still take a nasty bite out of someone.

"You see," she purred. "People are wrong when they say money can't buy happiness."

Chapter Six

I wondered how long ago the happy couple had gotten married and what Rose Taylor's children thought about the nuptials and whether or not they'd been invited to the wedding, let alone gone, while I watched the flesh around Geoffrey's nostrils turn dead white. His entire face reddened. He looked as if he'd been slapped.

"Is there anything wrong, dear?" Rose Taylor asked, touching her husband's sleeve.

He flinched and drew away. Rose Taylor's face crumpled. Her lower lip began trembling.

"Oh, my." She lifted her hand away from the pink cotton material and shook her head. "I don't . . . what did I say?" Then her eyes widened, and her hand flew to her mouth as she understood what Geoffrey thought she'd meant. "Oh, no, darling . . ." she stammered. "You can't think I meant . . . my comment about being rich . . . I just meant I've been lucky . . . having this house. . . . You know I'd never . . . ever." Her voice cracked. She ducked her head to one side.

I studied the terra-cotta tiles on the floor. They were Italian, like the marble in the hallway, I decided as I watched two small black ants scurrying along a thin line of beige grout.

"Of course we know," Moss Ryan said, hurrying into the breach of Rose's silence. He had one of those professionally calming voices, the kind religious leaders and doctors cultivate, the kind that makes you want to believe that everything will be all right even when you know it won't be. He glared at Geoffrey, the irises of his eyes dark with anger. "I'm sure Geoff does, too. Don't you? Don't you," he repeated after a few seconds had gone by.

Geoffrey forced the corners of his mouth upward into a rictus of a smile. "Yes. Absolutely," he told Rose Taylor, pointedly ignoring the other man. "I know you'd never say anything to hurt me."

"Because . . ." Her voice quavered. She looked small all of a sudden, as if her body were shrinking in on itself.

"No. I was just being silly." His voice had a hard, shiny quality to it, like a beetle's shell.

Rose Taylor reached up and clutched his arm, pulling him toward her. "So, you'll forgive an old lady her mistake?" she asked him anxiously as her kitty meowed to be petted.

"Don't be ridiculous; you're not old," Geoffrey countered with a gaily practiced, painfully false gallantry as he leaned over and hugged her.

She clung to him, relaxing in his embrace. A moment later, he excused himself, claiming he had business to take care of. I watched Rose watch Geoffrey as he hurried across the floor, his chin tucked in, his eyes hooded over, looking neither to the right or the left.

"My," she fretted after he'd gone. "I think I really have upset him. He's so sensitive, and I always seem to be saying the wrong thing." She gave Sheba an absentminded pat.

Moss Ryan bent over Rose and made soothing sounds in her ear. "Do you want me to speak to him?" he asked, patting her shoulder, reassuring her the way a parent would a child.

"Please. I'd be ever so grateful." Rose flashed him a smile, and he scurried off like a courtier on a mission from his queen.

"I know I must appear ridiculous to you," she said to me as soon as we were alone. "No." She wiped a tear from the corner of her eye and held up her hand. "Don't say anything.

I know what you're thinking. I would have thought the same thing at your age. I don't expect you to understand. How could you? Why should you? No one thinks I should be doing this. Not Moss. Not my staff. Certainly not my children. And they're probably right. My life would be much simpler without Geoff. I'm not denying that." She fingered one of her emerald earrings as Sheba, bored, twitched her tail.

I waited for Rose Taylor to continue. After a few seconds, she did.

"Rheumatoid arthritis is a terrible thing. My first husband suffered horribly with it. In the end, his limbs were so twisted and swollen, even morphine wasn't enough to keep the pain away." She shuddered and quickly studied her own hands as if she were afraid she'd see the signs of the disease there. "I nursed Sanford for years. I never asked for anything. I was never unfaithful. I was at Sanford's beck and call night and day. I did everything for him. Everything. He wanted it that way. He never wanted anyone else to touch him. Do you know what that's like, watching someone you love slowly dying?"

Her speech, which was designed to elicit sympathy, left me cold. Maybe it was the practiced quality it had to it, or maybe it was because it made me start thinking about Murphy. I wanted to say to Rose, but at least you had time to get ready, time to prepare. Your whole world wasn't taken away from you in the snap of a finger. I'd gone out to get some food and come back to find Murphy dead in the car in the garage from a heart attack brought on by a cocaine overdose. Which way was better? Did it really matter?

"That's when I began raising orchids," Rose went on, interrupting my thoughts. I tried to focus on what she was saying. "They're like my children. You see that one? The one on the end of the table." She pointed at a small white bloom.

I nodded.

"It cost me fifty thousand dollars. I bought my first orchid for thirty dollars. I read everything I could get my hands on.

And Sanford encouraged me. He insisted I add on the green-house. For a long time they were my only consolation."

"But now you have something else."

"Yes, I do," she parried without missing a beat. "And what's so wrong with that? With wanting to enjoy myself while I still can?"

"Nothing," I replied hastily, even though the question had been rhetorical.

"Exactly. Not that my children share that attitude." She shook her head and watched as Sheba jumped off her lap and began stalking the ants on the floor. "Maybe I shouldn't expect them to." She sighed and began twisting her wedding ring around her finger. "They were furious when they found out what I was going to do. Louis was the worst. The way he carried on . . ." Rose Taylor's voice fell again. She raised her chin. "I don't know. Sometimes I think children are more trouble than they're worth, but then I'm glad I had them. I feel sorry for any woman who misses the experience of motherhood."

I didn't say anything.

She brightened. "Now, let's have that drink I invited you for, shall we?" And with that she pressed a buzzer by her seat. Two minutes later, the Mexican maid appeared with a tray containing a martini glass, a silver cocktail shaker that came straight out of the twenties, and a glass filled with a manhattan for me.

"I'm glad people have revived the cocktail hour," Rose Taylor said as I moved the chair I'd sat down in closer to the table. "Not that I've ever given it up. Sanford and I indulged every evening at five-thirty. Toward the end, he was sipping his martini through a straw while I held the glass. Would you mind pouring, dear?" she asked, nodding toward the shaker. "Since my stroke my hands tend to shake a bit. So tedious growing old, but I do what I can to amuse myself."

I managed to restrain myself from pointing out the obvious. "Was it a bad one?" I asked instead, remembering my grandmother's.

"Bad enough." Rose Taylor grimaced at the memory. "I

lost partial use of my right side. It took months of physical therapy to get back to where I am. Now I have to take a blood thinner and have these stupid blood tests. So boring, but Geoffrey has been marvelous through it all. I don't know what I'd have done without his encouragement."

I had a feeling his encouragement didn't come cheap. I made a noncommittal noise as I remembered his comment in my store about wanting an MGB. He'd sounded pretty certain that he'd get it. And he probably would, too, if the loafers he was wearing were any indication of the way things were.

Made of Italian leather, they cost five hundred dollars a pair if they cost a penny. No wonder Louis was pissed. Here he was working his ass off at the post office while his mother showered what he probably considered to be his money on her second husband. Not to mention all the money that was going to the pet psychic. I wondered if Louis had ever gotten a sports car from his mom. Somehow I thought not.

"How about that drink?" Rose asked. I realized I was still holding the pitcher in my hand. "Now, then," she said when I'd filled her glass and handed it to her. "You look like an intelligent woman." She took a sip of her martini, savoring it before she put the glass down on the table. "I'm sure you can see that you've been put in an untenable position."

"Not really." I picked up my Manhattan. A cherry was floating along the bottom, just the way Geoff had promised. I fished it out and ate it, wondering, as I did, why I liked these things so much. It had to be the color. It certainly didn't taste like a cherry. It just tasted sweet.

"Quite frankly, my children are involving you in something that is none of their business."

"Ah." I put the stem back in my glass and took another sip of my manhattan while waiting to hear the rest.

"Pat Humphrey is a close friend of mine. I don't wish her disturbed."

"I wasn't planning on disturbing her." A lie, but then I've always felt telling the truth is an overrated virtue.

"You already have by coming to her house, and don't bother denying it," Rose Taylor snapped before I could.

"I wasn't going to. I just asked for a reading. As far as I know, I have a right to do that."

"You gave a fake last name. Richardson, wasn't it?"

"True. Maybe I was embarrassed. Maybe I didn't want anyone to know what I was doing."

Rose Taylor began tapping her fingers on her martini glass. "Don't demean my intelligence."

"Excuse me. I didn't think I was." I took another sip of my manhattan and put the glass back down on the tray. "So who told you? Pat Humphrey?"

"It's irrelevant."

"Not to me." I had another thought. "It was Amy, wasn't it?" She'd been so scared of her mother finding out, it made sense that she'd be the one to tell. I've noticed that people who are extremely anxious about something often precipitate the event just to get it over with.

"What a ridiculous notion," Rose scoffed. But I could tell from the way her eyes blinked that I'd hit home.

"Hasn't it occurred to you that Pat Humphrey could have stolen Sheba and . . ."

"Let me worry about that," Rose Taylor said. She leaned forward. I could see that the effort cost her. "I'm not a sentimental person, and I'm not a fool. I don't believe in lying to myself. About anything. And that includes Pat Humphrey as well as my children. They don't like the fact that I control the money. I can understand that. You probably think I'm terrible, but there's a reason why my husband wrote his will the way he did.

"It pains me to say this about my children, but all of them have problems. All of them have been in therapy on and off for as long as I could remember. I don't know . . ." She looked away for a second. "Maybe we asked too much of them when they were little. It's true Sanford wanted them to be strong . . . but we only wanted what was best for them . . ."

The plaint of parents everywhere. Especially when their children turn on them, demanding explanations.

"Perhaps we should have been more . . . understanding . . . but that wasn't the fashion then, you know. When I was raising children, you expected them to listen to you. You weren't supposed to be their pal. You were supposed to teach them values. Now, I don't know what they told you about me. . . ."

"Nothing bad," I quickly said.

"That would be a novelty," Rose said dryly. "I know they feel as if I'm not giving them their fair share, but I've given them lots of money in the past—hundreds of thousands of dollars—and believe me, they've spent it all and had nothing to show for it . . . nothing." She took another sip of her drink. "I don't know what I can do besides protect them from themselves." She pointed to my glass. "Aren't you going to finish yours?"

"In a minute. They're worried about you."

"That's what they told you?" Rose Taylor's laugh was short and unpleasant.

"It's true," I protested.

Rose Taylor looked down at Sheba, who was batting a piece of lint around the floor. "Did they also tell you they tried to have me declared incompetent and the case was thrown out of court? I didn't think so," she said when I didn't answer. "No. They hired you to protect what they perceive as their money." She emphasized the word perceive. "Pure and simple. They're worried there won't be enough left over for them. Well, the money is mine to spend as I like. And you can tell them that for me. In fact, I insist on it.

"I've learned valuable things about Sheba from Pat . . . Very valuable . . . as well as other things . . . things that there is no way she could have known."

"Pat is very impressive," I said cautiously. "I'll grant you that. She's very good at what she does . . ."

"Which is why I won't have her bothered. Not by you. Not by anyone. I appreciate my children's concern, but it is not necessary. Believe me, I know how to take care of my-self."

"I'm sure you do." I heard a cough and turned. Moss Ryan was standing by the door. I wondered how long he'd been there following the conversation.

He cleared his throat. "Before you arrived, Mrs. Taylor and I were discussing how we could best utilize the talents of someone such as yourself."

I raised an eyebrow. "Really?"

"You sound surprised." He took a couple of steps into the room. "But my firm frequently has the need for a private in-vestigator. I'd be happy to put in a word for you."

"And what firm is that?" I asked as I rose to my feet.

Ryan named one of the big ones, the kind that routinely did work for corporations. "Naturally, your compensation would be in line with what we pay our other operatives."

"Do you buy everyone off this easily?"

Ryan glared at me. "I find your remark extremely offen-sive."

"And I find your attitude offensive, so I guess that makes us even."

Ryan opened his mouth to say something else, but Rose put her hand up, and he closed his mouth, clasped his hands behind his back, and moved off to the left. The cat began rubbing the side of its head against Rose Taylor's arms. "I won't have you going around questioning people about her."

"Is there something you're afraid I'll find out?"

Rose Taylor's eyes assessed me as if I were a piece of meat she was getting ready to eat. "At the very least my children could have chosen a professional."

I could feel my cheeks redden. I told her I'd show myself out.

She nodded distractedly, her attention having shifted from me to Sheba. When I left, she and her lawyer had their heads bent together, quietly conferring, confident, I was sure, that they'd taken care of the problem—me. And why shouldn't they? After all, that's what they were used to. They summoned, they demanded, they offered a little crumb from their table, and people scurried to do what was asked of them.

As I walked through the hallway, my footsteps echoing on the marble tile, all I could think of was what it would be like growing up with Rose as my mother, someone who always wanted her own way and was prepared to do anything to get it. It wouldn't be Brady Bunch time, that was for sure. Rose could have yelled at me. She hadn't. Instead, she tried to enlist my sympathies, to sweet talk me around to her point of view. That kind of thing is harder to fight. Much more insidious.

I was wondering how much of what Rose Taylor had told me about her children was true as I stepped outside into the heat. Most of it, I was willing to wager. I took a deep breath and put my sunglasses back on. The air was soupy with humidity. Two seconds and my T-shirt was sticking to my back. God, did I wish it would rain. It kept threatening to but didn't.

The weather made me want to head to the mall and stay there, along with the rest of the population of Syracuse. This global-warming thing definitely sucked. Why hadn't I bought an air conditioner for my bedroom when I could have? Now there were none left in the entire city. Or at least none that I'd been able to find. I was on three waiting lists, at three different stores, and nary a one of them had called.

As I walked to my car, I found my eyes drifting toward the pool. It was a classic, kidney-shaped, with white chaise longues around it. The water was so blue. I was imagining myself in it, thinking how nice it would be to just jump in clothes and all when I noticed two figures standing very close together.

One was a small redhead in a bikini. The other one was Rose Taylor's husband.

They both looked as if they were having a very good time. Very good indeed.

Chapter Seven

I was more than halfway to the pool before Geoff and the redhead realized anyone was there. They were so engrossed in each other, they probably wouldn't have seen me until I tapped them on the shoulders if a little white bichon frise with a red bow stuck between its ears hadn't come tearing out at me, yapping its head off.

I grinned and waved at Geoff as he turned toward the noise. His face froze for an instant. Then he recovered and put on the smile I'd seen in the store that morning.

"Nice place you've got," I commented as I walked toward them.

The bichon frise continued growling, retreating as I advanced. Since the dog weighed ten pounds, if that, I didn't pay it much mind.

"Maurice," the woman called as Geoff took a hasty step away from her. "Behave yourself."

Maurice wagged his tail, barked at me again to show he had matters in hand, then, duty done, scurried to the safety of his mistress's feet.

"He's shy," she explained, scooping the dog up in her arms and rearranging his bow.

I nodded to Geoff. "I see your business wasn't that pressing."

"The people I had to call weren't in," he mumbled, digging a hole in the grass with his toe.

"Aren't you going to introduce me to your friend?"

He reached for his shirt, which was hanging on the back of one of the chaise longues. With it off, I could see that he had a good start on a potbelly.

"This is Shana Driscoll, Rose's nurse."

I extended my hand, and she put the dog down and shook it.

"Irish?" I guessed.

"From outside of Dublin." She had a slight brogue. "Could it be me name that gives me away?"

Geoffrey stepped between us. "Shana has been with us since Rose's stroke."

I stepped around him. "Your wife doesn't seem as if she'd need a nurse."

Shana smiled. She was pretty in a girl-next-door kind of way, with her blue eyes, white skin, and freckles. "She likes to pretend she doesn't, but actually she still needs help getting dressed and putting on her makeup. She's a very gallant lady, Mrs. Taylor is. She's working very hard to get all her faculties back."

"I bet she is."

Geoff shot me a glance.

"I mean, who wouldn't," I replied as I watched the bichon frise start trotting down a heavily landscaped path that led away from the pool.

"Maurice," Shana called. "Come back. Mommy will be with you in a moment."

But the dog kept going. As if it were going home.

"You live here?"

She looked at Geoff, seeking guidance, but he was avoiding her eyes. She looked back at me and squared her shoulders. "Why, yes. In the cottage around back. It was a grand gesture, Mrs. Taylor offering the use of that little house to me. It used to be the groundskeeper's, but now she hires out. It's hard finding a place close by that will let me keep Maurice. I'm so lucky. Mrs. Taylor lets me use the pool and the tennis courts."

"How convenient."

"She's a generous lady."

Possibly more generous than she knows, I thought.

"Really," Shana protested in the face of my silence. "She is. I know some people don't think so, but she's a dear."

"Shana and I were planning Rose's birthday party," Geoffrey explained before I could say anything else.

"We want it to be a surprise," Shana added.

I took my hair out of its rubber band, pulled it back, and redid my ponytail before replying. It's weather like this that makes me want to cut it all off. "Rose doesn't strike me as someone who likes surprises."

Shana frowned. "It's true she's been going on about not wanting a party, but I think she's just blathering. Everyone likes a cake and candles."

Not when you're in your seventies and your husband is twenty-five or thirty years younger. I was about to say something to that effect when Geoffrey took me by my elbow and steered me around. I glanced down at his hand. He removed it and started buttoning his shirt instead.

"Here," he said. "Let me walk you to your car."

"By all means. I wouldn't want you to be remiss in your duties as a host."

Geoff didn't reply, but by the way he was clenching his jaw muscles, I figured it wasn't because he didn't want to. He was remarkably thin-skinned, given his living circumstances.

We skirted a large bed of roses. There must have been twenty different varieties, each one neatly pruned and labeled. For someone who'd just told me she didn't like them, Rose Taylor certainly had a fair number of specimens in evidence. I reached over, plucked a small yellow blossom, and held it to my nose.

"Hybrids aren't perfumed," Geoff informed me.

I lifted my head up. "You know about roses?"

"Enough to get by."

"It's funny, but when I first saw you, I wouldn't have pegged you as that kind of guy."

Geoff gave me a sidelong glance. "What kind of guy is that?"

"The kind that likes roses."

"And why is that?"

"Because roses are old-fashioned. You seem like a—"

"Let's just drop the subject, shall we?"

"What subject? Your horticultural expertise?" I took another couple of steps. The grass smelled so sweet, I wanted to lie down and bury my face in it. "Fine. Here's a different question. How did you get this gig, anyway? It seems to me you have a pretty cushy deal going on even if you do have to run a few errands now and then."

Geoff stopped and grabbed hold of my arm. Hard.

"If you don't mind." I shook his hand off. "I can do without the black-and-blue marks."

"I don't expect someone like you to understand this, but I love my wife." This from between gritted teeth.

"Someone like me?"

"A prying, low-life sleaze."

"Prying, low-life sleaze?" I repeated. "That's a little harsh, don't you think?"

He scowled and shoved his face closer to mine. "What I think is, I'm tired of your insinuations. Understand?"

"Oh, I understand. What I'm wondering is whether your wife would understand if she saw you and Shana together." And with that I turned and walked toward my car.

Even though I'd parked it in the shade, I could feel the heat inside lapping at my arms and chest when I opened my car's door. The steering wheel was hot to the touch. I was thinking that the next car I bought would definitely have air conditioning while I started it up and drove around the driveway. As I headed for the main road, I caught a glimpse of Geoff in the rearview mirror. He was standing where I'd left him, watching me. I waved good-bye. For some reason, he didn't wave back.

*   *   *

I inhaled the hospital odors of fear and antiseptic as I walked down the corridor toward Raul Montenegro's room. Raul Montenegro was the name I'd given to the guy I'd picked up on the road. It had popped into my head on the way over. Somehow it seemed to fit him. I wanted to ask him if he liked it, but I couldn't. His room was empty. The beds were made up, blankets taut with expectation, waiting for the next person to inhabit them. A whey-faced man wearing a loosely tied bathrobe and slippers, eyes trained on the floor, shuffled by me down the corridor.

"Excuse me," I said to him. "Do you know what happened to the man in this room?"

He shook his head and shuffled on, his world shrunk to the few inches of linoleum in front of him.

Right.

I knocked on the door across the hall. A woman told me to come in. She was sitting in a chair, crocheting an afghan square. In the bed beside her lay a stick of a man hooked up to a welter of machinery. I asked her about Raul.

"Are you a relative?"

"A friend," I lied as I watched her fingers work, feeding the wool into the pattern.

"I'm sorry, dear, but he went to his reward this afternoon. Around three-thirty." But she didn't seem sorry at all. Just weary. She glanced at the motionless man lying in the bed, assessing him, while her fingers flew. "It happens to us all sooner or later. Sometimes sooner is better."

I'm not sure why Raul's death upset me. After all, I didn't even know the man. Maybe because it seemed a shame that he had to die alone, surrounded by strangers. The elevator doors opened with a whooshing noise, and I stepped inside. It was crowded with departing visitors. No one talked. Everyone faced straight ahead and looked at the numbers on the floors. In the back someone was crying quietly. Everyone pretended they didn't hear it. It was a relief when the doors opened and we disgorged into the lobby. I took Raul's picture out of my backpack and looked at it. So much for giving it back.

I stopped at a trash can near the door, but I couldn't bring myself to throw it away. I examined it again. The man in the photo looked as if he were a younger, healthier version of Raul. I wondered if the woman in the snapshot was his wife, the child his child?

"All right, Dorita, whoever you are," I murmured. "I'm not promising anything, but I'll see what I can do."

I was slipping the photo in my backpack when my cell phone rang. I thought it was going to be Hillary screaming about my meeting with her mother. I knew I should have alerted her first before going over there. But it wasn't. It was Calli telling me she wouldn't be able to meet me at B&N tonight. Something had come up. And I knew who that something was. Richard. Calli's taste in men was awful, but this one was the worst yet. He was a boozer and womanizer who grew grass on the side. But of course Calli was going to save him—just as she was going to save the man who had taken her to California and dumped her or the one who had a thing about having sex with women over twenty-five.

"You are such a moron," I told her.

"I know. I know."

"Call me and tell me what happens."

"Of course. Talk to you soon." And Calli hung up.

God, I thought as I walked out of the hospital, what is wrong with us? Why can't we ever hook up with nice men? I knew there were some out there. Somewhere. And then my thoughts drifted back to Raul. Had he been a nice man? I thought I'd call Paul in the morning and see if anyone had reported someone missing. Not that I thought that would be the case. Especially if he was an undocumented worker. It would probably be a good idea to make time to visit the trailer park Arthur Peterson had bitched about. Maybe there was someone there who knew who Raul really was.

*   *   *

By the time I got back to Noah's Ark, Tim had already closed it up and left. I said hello to Zsa Zsa and fed her a couple of doggie cookies; then I called Hillary and Pat Humphrey. Neither one was in. I left messages on both their machines while I looked over the messages Tim had left for me. There were five all together—two from distributors wanting money and three from people wanting me to get them snakes. I was thinking about who I knew that was breeding emerald tree boas when Manuel walked through the door.

It had been about a month since I'd last seen him, and he didn't look good. More like a stray cat that's been hanging out in the woods for too long. Always on the thin side, he was now verging on emaciated. Plus he had rings under his eyes, and his skin, normally light brown, was grayish. He'd cut his dark hair Caesar style and was sporting a pair of long sideburns, both of which only served to underline the gauntness of his face.

"Hey, Robin. How's it goin'?" he asked as he yanked his baggies up.

I don't know why all the kids insist on wearing clothes that are four sizes too big for them, but then I guess that's what our parents said about what we wore.

"Not bad." I reached for a cigarette as Zsa Zsa came dashing out from behind the counter and started rubbing up against Manuel's ankles.

"You been a good girl?" he crooned to her as he squatted down and began to rub her rump. "You miss me?"

She groaned with pleasure. The months Manuel had stayed in my house, she'd slept in his bed at night, curled up beside him. They'd made a cute couple, though Manuel hadn't appreciated the observation. After about five minutes, Manuel straightened up and turned his head. Now that he was closer, I could see that the lower side of his mouth looked like a rotten melon.

I pointed at the bruise. "Nice. What happened?"

He shrugged, reflexively touching the damaged side of his

face. "Just a fight." Then he reached over, grabbed six of the small toy mice I keep in a box by the register, and began juggling them. "Think I can keep all of them up in the air?"

"Sure. How's your dad these days?"

"Haven't seen him," Manuel said, concentrating too hard on the toy mice. "Why are you asking?"

I wanted to say: I'm asking because I think your father gave you that bruise; I'm asking because I want to know how much longer this is going to go on; I'm asking because I care. But I didn't. The last time I'd tried, Manuel had turned around and headed out the door. If one of Manuel's friends hadn't let it slip that Manuel's father slammed him around, I never would have known. He'd never said anything. Even when I flat out asked him.

I'd seen Manuel's father once. He was a big man. Way bigger than Manuel. If it were up to me, he'd be in jail. But Manuel protected him. He took the beatings when they came, then vacated the premises, waiting a week or sometimes more until his father left the house before he returned. Fortunately, his dad wasn't around much anymore.

I was wondering whether I should call social services, anyway, when Manuel lost his rhythm and two of the mice dropped on the counter. "Guess I need more practice," he said, putting all of them back in the box. "Tim here?"

"He's gone for the day. Anything I can do?"

"He said he had a job for me."

I tightened the drawstring on my backpack and picked up my keys. It was late, and I was tired, and I still had to go to the North Side and check to see if Bethany was at the tattoo parlor Matt Andrews had mentioned. "Do you mean moving stock?"

"Yeah." Manuel shifted his weight from one leg to another. "Something like that."

"We needed you here three days ago." On Tuesday, we'd had a big shipment come in, and we'd had to make room for it in the storeroom. Tim and I had spent the better part of the day moving and unpacking cartons.

Manuel shrugged his shoulders again.

"Jesus." But I stopped myself from making the speech about having to take responsibility for your own actions. His mother had made that speech. So had his teachers, his social worker, and his probation officer. The more everyone talked the less Manuel seemed to listen.

"I don't suppose you got anything else for me?" he asked

I thought about Bethany. "Actually, I think I might." Over the years I've used Manuel for investigative work. He smart, he's fast, and most of all, he's plugged in. "Feel like going for a ride with me and Zsa Zsa?"

On the way to the tattoo parlor I explained about Bethany and showed him her picture.

"She's friggin' whacked," he said, handing the photo back to me.

"That seems to be the general consensus."

"How much her parents paying you to find her sorry ass

"Enough. I'll give you two hundred bucks to help m

He scratched one of his sideburns. "Four hundred."

"Two-fifty."

"Two-seventy."

"Done deal." We shook.

Manuel reached over, turned on the radio, and began dling with the dial. A moment later, the sounds of Beet ven's Ninth came pouring out. He grinned. "This is d man." And he began conducting the music. "What?" he s reading my face.

"Got a new girlfriend?"

He shrugged. "There's nothing wrong with movin' u the world."

The Piercing Palace was located on North State, near L and if there was anything palatial about it, it wasn't appa from the outside. I wouldn't get Zsa Zsa's toenails cli there, let alone anything else. I dropped Manuel off watched as he went inside. Five minutes later he came and tapped on my door.

"I need you to front me eighty bucks."

"Why? What's going on?"

"The guy's gonna give me a deal on getting my tongue pierced."

"Get in the car," I growled. "Now."

"But you're giving me the money."

"After we find Bethany. Has he seen her or not?"

Manuel got in the car and slouched down in his seat. "She was here a couple of days ago. But the guy said she'll be back because she's gonna have a dragon tattooed on her arm. I gave him your number and told him there was a hundred bucks in it for him if he called when she turned up."

"Did he say anything else?"

Manuel started peeling one of his nails. "He said sometimes she hangs at Wooden Oaks."

"Oakwood?" Oakwood is a cemetery. Founded in 1859 as a park for both the dead and the living, it's over 125 acres of winding paths, hills, gullies, and large monuments. Recently, it's become a gang hangout as well.

"There's this crypt. It's pretty hard-core. I can show you if you want."

"I want."

We stopped at McDonald's on the way. As we approached the cemetery's main entrance, I killed the lights so I wouldn't attract the attention of the police. They'd stepped up their patrols there recently and tended to frown on cars driving through there at night.

"Go to the left," Manuel instructed.

The car vibrated as I swung off the main road onto a deeply rutted dirt path. "Do you believe in ghosts?" he asked.

I was too busy trying not to hit the tombstones on either side of me to answer.

"I do. My momma goes to this lady down on the West Side at least once a month to ask her for advice. She throws the coconut shells for her. She talks to the spirits. My momma says this lady tells her things, important things."

As I crested a hill, an obelisk, spectral in the dark, sprung up in front of us. "Do I keep going?" I squinted, looking for the path. Everything was a blur of blacks and grays.

Manuel clicked his tongue between his teeth. "I'm not sure," he admitted.

I slammed on the brake. A picture of us circling endlessly around the cemetery until the morning took root in my mind. "You don't know?"

"Well, everything looks different at night," Manuel replied. He got out of the car and walked up a hill. "Okay," he said when he came back. "Take a right."

"You're sure?"

"I can see the crypt from here." A moment later, he asked, "You think the dead can talk to us and tell us things?"

"I think you should shut up and let me drive."

"This place doesn't scare you?"

"Oh, it scares me, all right," I hissed as the tires crunched over the gravel. "It scares me because I don't want to pop a tire and get stuck here and come face-to-face with a couple of pit bulls." That would be very unpleasant indeed.

Manuel gave Zsa Zsa an absentminded pat. "So what do you think happens to people when they die?"

"Can we get off this topic?"

"I think they stick around."

"Good for you." I killed the engine and pointed to a marble crypt about thirty yards in front of us. "Is this it?"

"Yeah."

Even in the dark I could tell it was the Crenshaw Crypt, final resting place of one of Syracuse's important people—though I didn't know what he'd done to rate that appellation. I'd passed by the square white marble building numerous times in the daylight and admired its columns and arches. But I wasn't admiring it now. The word Gothic sprang to mind, followed by the words vampires and the undead.

"I hope you're right." I took a couple of flashlights out of the glove compartment and handed one to Manuel. "Because breaking into a crypt is not the way I'd planned to spend the evening."

"The last time I was here, there were a whole bunch of Bethany clones rolling."

That was the new slang world for taking ecstasy. You know you're old when the kids are doing drugs you've never tried, I decided as I told Zsa Zsa to stay in the car. Manuel and I got out. He took the lead. We were almost at the crypt's front steps when the door swung open. For a second my heart stopped.

Literally.

I wanted to scream, but no sound came out. Then I heard someone saying, "Richie, come on. Richie, we gotta go," and I wanted to kick myself as four people ran down the steps.

"Hey," I said as one of them came directly at me. I could smell the beer on him as he veered away. I tried to grab him, but he pushed me off. I stumbled backward and landed on my ass. When I looked up again, they were gone.

"Friggin' assholes," Manuel said.

We mounted the steps slowly. The door was open. The odor of cheap beer was overwhelming as we stepped inside. I switched on my flashlight. A pentagram was spray-painted on the floor. I saw candleholders and lots of beer and liquor bottles around it, and then I heard a groan.

Chapter Eight

The girl was lying on the marble floor with her skirt up around her waist and her underpants down around her knees. She closed her eyes and put up her hand to shield them from my flashlight's beam.

"Are you the police?" Her words were slurred.

"No." I clicked the flashlight off. "Are you all right?"

"I'm fine." Then she moaned, turned her head, and vomited. I jumped back just in time to avoid getting my feet splattered.

"You don't seem fine." In back of me I heard Manuel saying, "I'm out of here." I didn't blame him, because I was getting a little nauseated from the smell myself.

"Don't look at me," the girl ordered while she fumbled to pull her underpants up.

"Listen . . ."

"No." She stumbled out the door and threw up again.

"Should I call the police? Take you to the hospital?"

"Leave me alone," she cried, collapsing on one of the steps. She brought her knees up, bowed her head, and buried it in her arms. "Just leave me alone. I'll be fine."

Yeah and I was the new pope. "Sure you will. We'll talk in a few minutes." I told Manuel to keep an eye on her and went back inside.

There had to be a better way to make money than this, I

decided as I tried not to breathe in the stench. Maybe I should take a couple of computer courses. Sit in a nice clean office. I played my light over the walls. There was graffiti everywhere. On the walls, the ceiling, even on the marble coffin. Fat and thin letters. Squiggles that looked like worms. Over in the right-hand corner I saw a scrawl that could have read Bethany. I was moving closer to it when I heard Manuel cry out. By the time I got outside, Manuel was cradling his arm, and the girl was gone.

"The bitch scratched me." He pointed to his forearm. A little blood was oozing up from a small abrasion. "She probably gave me rabies."

"What happened?"

"I asked her if she knew a Bethany Peterson, and she said she knew lots of Bethanys, so I showed her the picture, and she said she hadn't seen her."

"And then?"

"And then she scratched me."

"Just like that?"

"Just like that."

"You didn't say anything to her?"

Manuel paused for a fraction of a second. "I did tell her I thought she was lyin'."

"And?"

Manuel hesitated again.

"Let's have it."

"Well," Manuel allowed. "I also said we were gonna call the cops and they were gonna throw her ass in jail if she didn't answer me."

"Jesus, Manuel." I could have killed him for making the girl run. "She was a possible lead."

"I was just trying to scare her."

"Well, you scared yourself out of ten bucks."

"That's not right," he yelped.

"Make it fifteen." Nothing makes a point to Manuel like losing money. I headed for the car, Manuel muttering and trailing along behind me. "Let's see if we can pick her up."

Aside from everything else, this was not a good place for anyone to be alone on foot. We circled the cemetery for an hour without finding her. Finally, I gave up and dropped Manuel off at a friend of his. Then Zsa Zsa and I hit the Onion for a drink. I wanted to talk about nothing with people I didn't know well and get the evening out of my head. It was a little after twelve by the time I walked through the door of my house. James was waiting on the doorstep. I fed him and listened to my messages. Hillary had returned my call. So had Paul. He'd turned up some stuff on Pat Humphrey. George wanted to know if I was coming over.

But it was too late to call anyone back now, and even if it wasn't, I didn't want to. I didn't have the energy. Thinking of that girl lying on that floor had left a bad taste in my mouth that the scotch hadn't been able to get rid of. Had she gone there of her own free will? Had she been tricked into going? If she kept going the way she was, she'd be dead by the time she was forty. And so would Bethany, for that matter. I don't know why it was, but seeing the girls going bad always bothered me more than watching the boys. Maybe because they hit bottom so much faster.

I stripped down and got into the shower. Then I got into bed, but sleep wouldn't come. The *kechunking* noise of the window fan set my teeth on edge. I briefly thought about getting up and turning it off, since it was just sending hot air into the room, but I couldn't summon up the energy. After another twenty minutes spent studying the cracks in the ceiling, I pulled myself out of bed, put on a T-shirt and a pair of underpants, padded downstairs, and poured myself a shot of scotch; never mind that I'd already had three and I'd promised myself I'd keep it down to one a night. Two at the most. Then I lit a cigarette, breaking another vow about cutting back. Screw it, I'd start tomorrow.

I listened to Zsa Zsa snoring as I drank my Black Label and peered out through the blinds of my living-room window into the dark. Outlined by the streetlight, a raccoon ambled across the sidewalk and disappeared into my neighbor's privet hedge. It was a large male. Thirty pounds at least. There'd been lots of coons around lately, enough so that I didn't let Zsa Zsa out in the backyard by herself at night. She was stupid enough to start a fight but not vicious enough to finish it.

The drought was drying up the berries and bringing the raccoons down from the woods and into the backs of the houses to forage for food. Some of my neighbors wanted to trap them, but I liked watching them. I stubbed my cigarette out in a saucer sitting on one of the end tables and took another sip of my drink. I swirled the amber liquid around in my glass, admiring the little whirlpool I'd created, when the kid who lived across the way roared into the driveway. He slammed the door of his Jeep Cherokee shut and half-ran, half-stumbled, inside his darkened house. A few seconds later, the downstairs exploded in a blaze of lights, and I caught a glimpse of his bathrobe-clad mother advancing toward him. Then they moved out of my line of sight. I wondered what it would be like to have someone waiting up for me? Nice, I thought. Real nice.

But then I remembered Manuel used to do that when he was living here, and I hadn't liked it one bit. I put my glass down on the coffee table and walked into the dining room. All this crap about talking to the dead must have been getting to me, because I bent down and dug out my picture of Murphy from the bottom of the sideboard drawer. I stared at the photo for a moment, wondering what my life would have been like if he were alive.

I'd probably still be working at the newspaper and writing on the side, still trying to write that Pulitzer Prize book, instead of getting involved in other people's messes. Or maybe we would have gotten divorced and I would have left Syracuse and gone back to New York City. Or moved to an ashram in Colorado. Or become a social worker. Impossible to know. But one thing was for sure. Murphy had been a good-looking guy. Too bad he'd been so screwed up. But maybe that had been one of the attractions.

"What do you think?" I asked Zsa Zsa when I walked back into the living room.

She lifted her head off the sofa armrest, yawned, and went back to sleep. I lay down next to her and curled my fingers around the fur along her legs. The last thing I remember thinking as I drifted off to sleep was that I really had to cut the mats off Zsa Zsa's belly.

My day started at eight o'clock in the morning with Paul calling.

"Don't you return phone calls?" he demanded.

I made an unintelligible noise.

"I thought you wanted this stuff ASAP."

"Just a minute." I stumbled into the kitchen, grabbed a cup half filled with yesterday's coffee from the counter, and dug my pad and a pencil out of my backpack, then settled myself back on the sofa and told Paul to get started.

"Okay. This is what I have. Pat Humphrey's parents live in a little Pennsylvania town. The father owns a garage. The mother is a housewife. There are no brothers or sisters. Our person got good grades through high school. Went to Clark Community College. She didn't finish. She dropped out after twenty credits. I don't have a work history for her. You want me to get it?"

"Not at the moment. Go on."

"She owns her car free and clear. Has a mortgage on her house, which she's current on. But three years ago she left her job as office manager in Prevention Plus, one of those fuckin' HMO things. She declared bankruptcy about three months after that. She's still working on paying off her creditors."

"Interesting." I thought about the furnishings in the house. She'd either acquired them recently or hidden them. "You have a reason."

"On the surface it looks like credit-card debt. She just got in too deep. She started advertising her services as a pet psychic about a month after her bankruptcy. I've got the name of two vets who've used her, and they say good things."

I wrote their names down.

"Any priors?"

"Some low-level shit. Two for kiting checks. One for disturbing the peace. A couple for shoplifting." And he gave me the dates. "Nothing major. You want me to invoice you?"

"Please."

"Anything else?"

"Maybe later." I drummed my fingernails on the table while I thought about what Paul had told me. Humphrey's offenses were minor, but they indicated a pattern at odds with her dress and demeanor. Underneath I was willing to bet something else was going on. A man? Drugs? Gambling? Alcohol? If I had to choose one, I'd pick the booze. I called Hillary to fill her in on my progress.

"You know, my mother called me," she said as soon as she heard my voice. "She wasn't pleased."

"I figured she would." I could imagine the conversation.

"You could have let me know."

"You're right. I'm sorry about that." Trying to come up with a plausible explanation as to why I hadn't, I lit a cigarette and let out the cat and Zsa Zsa into the backyard. It felt as if it were eighty outside. The paper had said it was going to be in the nineties this afternoon. "I think your sister told her."

"Amy always was a loser." Hillary drew the word out.

"Do you still want to continue with this?"

"More than ever."

"Fine." I told her I'd drop by to talk with her later.

"I can hardly wait."

I sat down on one of the deck chairs, smoked the rest of my cigarette, and watched a woodpecker working on the stump of an old elm. A little ways away, five sparrows were clustered on the branch of a honey locust, pecking at the berries. I had a feeling this was the only quiet moment I was going to have the whole day. Zsa Zsa came running up with a piece of paper in her mouth. I traded her a dog biscuit that was lying on the table for it and called Pat Humphrey. There were a few things I wanted to clarify before I went to see Hillary.

"I knew who you were the minute you walked in the door," she said to me before I'd even begun, a faint note of amusement in her voice.

Her tone made me want to smack her. Instead, I stubbed out my cigarette and flicked the butt in the ashtray. "Because Amy told you."

"No one told me."

"If you knew who I was, why did you put on a show?"

"I wanted to see if you'd buy it. How'd your tape turn out, by the way?"

"Good. You're running a low-level con."

Humphrey snorted. "What do you want me to say? That I am? Are you recording this by chance? Because you know that's illegal in this state."

"Thanks for the lesson."

"Murphy said . . ."

I cut her off before she could start in. "Don't go there. I'm not buying it, so don't even bother."

"What are you so afraid of?"

"I'm not afraid of anything." But as I said it, I wondered if she could hear my blood pounding in my veins. I focused my attention on the blue jay on the telephone wire.

Humphrey laughed. "Yes, you are. You're terrified. I can hear it in your voice."

"Don't worry about me. Maybe you'd better start thinking about giving Rose Taylor's money back." I slammed the phone down harder than I'd intended. If Humphrey thought I was going to fall for her particular load of crap, she was very mistaken.

The fact that the two vets I went to see were complimentary of Pat Humphrey did not improve my mood any.

"No, she really was helpful with a cat we had," the vet at the Wee Creature Clinic in Dewitt told me. "Of course, I was skeptical at first, but the owner insisted, and damned if the cat didn't have a small growth in her kidneys we'd over-looked."

The second vet out in Fayetteville told pretty much the same story. "We had a German shepherd I'd operated on to repair a tear in a tendon in his knee. But he wasn't healing right, and I couldn't figure out what the hell was wrong. We even had him MRI'ed in Rochester, but nothing showed up. Then this woman the owner called, Humphrey, comes in and lays her hand on the dog. A few minutes later, she tells me the dog's in pain because a small piece of cartilage is adhering to the socket joint so the ball of the bone can't come all the way down.

"I thought it was a load of crap, but the client insisted we go back in—we were going to take off the leg—and damned if it wasn't what Humphrey said. I don't know how she did it, but she did."

"So you believe she's psychic?"

"I don't know if she's psychic. But she's a damned good di-agnostician. That I will tell you."

Maybe she was, I thought as I walked out of the office, but she still hadn't talked to Rose Taylor's cat.

Even though I tried, I couldn't get my telephone conversa-tion with Pat Humphrey out of my mind. I knew she was scamming me . . . and yet. But that's what people like her do—take advantage of everyone's desire to believe. Which was why I decided to pay her a visit. Off the clock. I wanted to make her admit she was lying about Murphy.

I arrived at her cottage a little after two-thirty the follow-ing afternoon. By that time, my T-shirt was sticking to my back, and the khaki skirt I'd put on that morning was a crumpled mess. I took my sunglasses off, wiped the sweat off the bridge of my nose, and redid my ponytail before heading for the house.

It was just as well, I decided, as I rang the doorbell, that I'd left Zsa Zsa with Tim. Cocker spaniels—in fact, dogs in gen-eral—don't do well when the temperature is in the nineties, and we were into triple digits. Of course, I don't do well, either. Unfortunately, I didn't have a nice owner who was willing to take care of me, not that Zsa Zsa was showing any signs of gratitude. But then, when you're a princess, you don't have to.

She hadn't even protested when I'd walked out the door. Usually she hates it when I go anywhere without her. But not now. She'd just opened one eye, then closed it again and gone back to her doggie dreams. Right now I wished I could join her. The one good thing about working these days was that the store was air-conditioned. I rang the bell again. No one answered.

I was turning to go when I noticed Humphrey's car was still in the garage. Which meant she was probably down the block, or maybe she was across the street visiting a neighbor. I rang the bell one more time just to make sure. When no one came to the door, I sat myself down on one of the porch chairs and reviewed the questions I had for her while I fanned myself with a pizza flyer that I'd found lying on the armrest.

Everything was quiet. The surrounding houses were closed up against the sun, their curtains drawn. The birds were hiding in their nests. The cats were snoozing under bushes. The air shimmered in the heat. A faint breeze brought with it the smell of hot tar mixed with roses. I listened to the murmur of the traffic down below and dreamed of iced tea. Somewhere, far away, a dog barked. Finally, after about twenty minutes or so, I roused myself from my torpor and walked around the back.

Pat Humphrey's backyard had a Mediterranean feel to it. An ornamental shadberry tree, its branches heavy with fruit, sat in the middle of the yard. Toward the rear, hugging a white wooden fence, was a medium-size vegetable garden, while perennial and herb beds, their curved borders marked with different-colored rocks, ran around the rest of the perimeter.

Three ceramic pigs of various sizes nestled in among the

rosemary and lavender. Sunflowers grew along the back. A white wrought-iron table and two chairs sat on a small stone patio. A squirrel was sitting on the table eating the remains of a breakfast roll from a plate. When he saw me, he grabbed his bounty and ran away.

As I walked to the table, my feet sank into the ground. I felt something wet and looked down. A stream of water was running out of the garden hose. It must have been running for a while, because it had formed a small channel in the ground. Somehow I couldn't image Pat Humphrey leaving the water running like that. For that matter, I thought as I looked for the faucet handle, I couldn't image her leaving her breakfast dishes on the table. From the way she kept her house, she was much too neat a person for that.

After I shut off the water, I went over to the table. A line of ants was snaking its way over a half-eaten piece of toast and circling around the top of the capless jar of strawberry jam. Where the hell was the cap, I wondered as I looked at the almost-full cup of coffee sitting nearby. A drop of sweat working its way down my spine felt chilly as I contemplated the dead fly floating on top of the brown liquid.

I bit one of my nails as I tried to visualize what had occurred. Pat Humphrey had made herself breakfast and taken it outside, at which point she'd probably begun watering her plants.

And then she'd left.

Without turning the water off. Or putting the top back on the jam.

And she hadn't returned.

I pictured her standing here, garden hose in one hand, a piece of toast in the other, listening to the birds.

What had happened?

Had someone come along?

Had there been a sudden emergency?

Then another idea occurred to me. One I liked even less. Maybe Pat Humphrey was still here.

Inside.

And she hadn't answered the door because she couldn't. I was probably overdramatizing, I told myself. She was probably at a neighbor's. Nevertheless, I hesitated for a few seconds before I walked over, grasped the door handle, and pulled. It swung open. Steeling myself for the body that I hoped I wouldn't find sprawled on the floor—I can never get used to the look of surprise and indignation on the faces of homicide victims—I took a deep breath and stepped inside.

"Pat? Pat Humphrey?" I called, walking toward the middle of the room. "It's Robin Light."

Nothing.

I tried again. All I heard was the humming of the refrigerator. I glanced around the kitchen. A coffeepot with a filter on top was sitting on the counter, a few cups and a knife and fork lay in the sink, but the cupboard doors were closed, the countertops were clean. *A place for everything and everything in its place,* my mind sang.

I don't know why, but I tiptoed through the living room and the dining room as if I were walking through rows of mourners at a funeral parlor. Since my last visit, Pat Humphrey had changed the flowers in the crystal vase on the mantel to orchids, just like the ones Rose Taylor grew.

I opened the hall closet. It was filled with the usual stuff: coats, sneakers, golf clubs, a couple of tennis rackets—nice ones—a canoe paddle. There were no signs of violence, no signs of Pat Humphrey having been dragged away. I backtracked and walked down a narrow hallway and took a quick peek into her bedroom. It smelled of sandalwood, just like the rest of the house. The walls were painted lavender. The trim was white. The bed was made. The curtains were partially open. The dresser drawers were closed. The room was neat and clean and tidy.

So was Pat Humphrey's office. A hot breeze from the open window billowed the voile curtains hung over it. I gingerly stepped over to the window and looked outside. All I could see was a bird feeder hanging from a small magnolia tree. I turned back and considered the room. The walls were decorated with Mexican ceremonial masks. A large staghorn fern hung from the curtain rod.

Seeing it reminded me of the one in Rose Taylor's house. I wondered if it was a relative. The bookshelves were lined with volumes on animal behavior, psychology, myths, and anthropology. The computer on top of the desk was brand new. The box it had come in was on the floor below it. There was nothing to see in here, so I returned to the kitchen. I was just about to leave when I noticed the blinking light on Pat Humphrey's answering machine. I hit the PLAY button.

"Call me as soon as you can," a voice I recognized as that of Rose's nurse, Shana, commanded. It sounded, what? Concerned? Frightened?

Bingo, I thought, playing the message again. Gotcha.

Chapter Nine

My meeting with Hillary took a little less than half an hour. I thought she looked even paler than she had the last time I'd seen her.

"So let me get this straight," she said to me when I told her about the message on Humphrey's answering machine. "You think that my mother's nurse is working with Pat Humphrey to defraud my mother."

"I think it's a possibility."

She leaned even farther forward on the edge of the armchair she was sitting in. "But you don't have proof."

"No," I admitted. "I don't."

Hillary clicked her tongue against her teeth and pulled her yellow cardigan closer to her, a gesture that accentuated the narrowness of her rib cage, and looked down at the papers I'd given her. "I wonder if my mother knows about Humphrey's arrest record?"

"I'd be surprised if she did." I pointed to my description of my visit to the two veterinarians. "To be fair, on the other hand, these people gave Humphrey a good report."

Hillary balled my page of notes up and threw it in the trash. "It's a fluke."

"All right." I wasn't about to argue the point. "You want me to find out about the nurse?" I asked, wiping a drop of sweat out of my eye.

"It would be nice if Pat Humphrey didn't come back, wouldn't it?" she mused aloud instead of answering my question.

I didn't say anything.

Hillary smiled unpleasantly. "Maybe we got lucky and she got hit by a truck on the way to her neighbor's house. Maybe she's sitting in the morgue waiting to be claimed. It would save us all a lot of trouble."

"Unfortunately, things don't work out that neatly," I said, thinking of Raul. I got up from the sofa. "Do you want me to see what I can find out about your mother's nurse or not?" I repeated. Hillary's tone was making me uncomfortable.

"Not yet. Just send me a bill for your expenses so far." She gathered up the musical score lying on the coffee table and rapped the pages into place with short, sharp gestures. "If you please. Out of curiosity, when you spoke to my mother, did she tell you I was irresponsible, that we all were?"

I allowed as how she had.

"Did she tell you we were after her money?"

I nodded, regretting I'd answered Hillary's first question truthfully. I needed to get going.

"That we'd tried to have her committed?"

"She mentioned it."

"Bet she didn't tell you why, though?"

I waited.

"She was addicted to Valium. Valium and liquor. That's how she got herself to sleep every night. She got her prescriptions from three different doctors. What's the matter?" Hillary demanded. "Don't you believe me?"

"Sure. I just wondered, if that was the case, why you bothered intervening?"

"What do you mean?"

"Figure it out."

Hillary glared at me. I glared back. She laughed and changed the subject. "I'll give her the house, though. She does have good taste."

"It's impressive."

"Not like this place." The flash of anger in Hillary's eyes as she looked around telegraphed what she'd lost. "Did you see the Japanese scroll in the hallway?" I nodded. "Isn't it beautiful? It's almost seven hundred years old." She swallowed, as if her mouth had gone dry with desire. "It just came back from an exhibition at the Met. My father wanted me to have it, he told me, but she's giving it to Geoff." She hugged her music to her so tightly that the skin around her hands lost color and forced out a laugh. "Oh, well," she said as she escorted me to the door, "if it's meant to be, then it'll happen, and if not, then so be it. By the way, I'm playing downtown this Wednesday. Come and see me if you have the time."

I promised her I would.

As I stepped outside and took a great big burst of fresh air into my lungs, I realized Hillary's house reminded me of a tomb. I was halfway to the store when my cell phone rang. Manuel was on the line.

"Yo, *vieja*. I think I know where Bethany is," he said.

"Think or know?" I asked as I maneuvered around a group of kids playing ball in the middle of the street.

"I've been talkin' to T." T was a friend of Manuel's. "Remember that kid Karim you told me about? The friend of Bethany's. Well, T knows Karim's older brother."

"And?"

"And Karim's been paying him to transport this girl out and back to a shack right alongside the Erieville Country Club."

I slammed on my brakes as a squirrel ran in front of my car and ran back again. "Would that be Arrow View by any chance?"

"Whatever. Anyway, I told my friend you'd pay him fifty bucks if she's out there."

What Manuel was telling me made sense. When teens run away, most of them tend to remain in close proximity to their friends.

"So what do you say?" Manuel asked. "Feel like going for a ride?"

"I'll be over in twenty."

"I'll be waiting."

The Arrow View Country Club was the ritziest golf club in Syracuse. Located outside of Manlius, it was frequented by the well-to-do and the well-connected. I was willing to bet that Bethany's parents played golf out there. I dialed up Mrs. Peterson to confirm my guess.

"We joined last year," she said. "Why? Does this have something to do with Bethany?"

"Possibly. I'll call you if I have something to tell you." And I turned my phone off.

So Bethany had been out there before. She probably knew about this shack. Probably all of her friends did. As I honked for Manuel, I decided that if she were there, I'd send him in while I waited outside. Despite his performance at the cemetery, he was usually pretty good at talking to kids.

Then, perhaps, when he was done, I could take a turn and convince her to talk to her mom and dad. Just talk. Or if that didn't work, perhaps I could convince her to stay at a friend's house until everyone was able to work things out. Turning her over to the courts was, of course, another option. But that wasn't my decision to make, and from what I'd seen, that didn't work too well.

The Arrow View Country Club announced itself with a big white sign. The road leading up to the clubhouse measured a good three-quarters of a mile. The grass on either side of the road was the color of money, while the bushes and flowers looked as if someone had gone over them with a nail clipper and tweezers. The clubhouse itself was a quarried-stone-and-wood affair. A row of golf carts were lined up on the pavement in front of it.

A few groups of people, looking as if they'd just come in from the course, were chatting with each other. As we approached, I saw Geoff walking inside. He had on his tennis whites and was carrying his racket under his arm. Engrossed in conversation with an attractive-looking older woman—

not Rose Taylor—he didn't see me. I was about to honk when Manuel tapped me on the shoulder.

"We take the road that goes to the right."

It turned out to be the service road. We went by the clubhouse and veered around the kitchen. A group of Latinos and Asians in soiled whites, taking a break outside the kitchen door, fell silent when we drove by. They didn't start talking again until we were almost out of sight. Coming around the garbage corral, I could see people playing off in the distance, and then the road turned again, and I was looking at trees. The road got more and more rutted until it gave out completely and we were driving on a dirt path.

"Where the hell are we going?" I asked Manuel as we bounced along. We were closing in on a copse of trees, and as far as I could tell, there was nothing there.

"You'll see," Manuel said. A moment later, we came upon a broken-down wire fence. "Stop here," he instructed.

I parked the car on the dirt, and we got out. Manuel took the lead. We stepped over the wire fence and onto a meadow. Manuel started walking.

"What's here?" I asked.

"This place used to be a farm, but the owner got killed, and now it's nothing. Come on." He gestured, his eyes darting nervously to the left and right. "Let's get going."

It was funny, but you could drop Manuel in the middle of the worst neighborhood in Syracuse and he'd be fine, but put him in the middle of the country and he started to twitch.

About four minutes later, Manuel pointed in front of him. "There it is."

At some point, the shack must have been used for storing farm equipment, but that had been a long time ago. Now it was collapsing in on itself. There were holes in the boards toward the ground where the moisture had seeped in and rotted them out. There was also a hole near the roof so big that you could see through it to the other side. Weeds and vines twined up around the structure, covering it and pulling it back where it had come from.

"Bethany," I cried as we approached. "It's Robin Light. I have a friend I'd like you to meet. Please don't run. I promise I'm not going to take you back to your parents, I'm not going to tell them where you are. We just want to talk to you."

No one answered. When we stepped inside, two mourning doves fluttered their wings and flew out the door. I looked around. Someone was camped out here. They'd made a bed of straw in the corner of the shack that still had its roof intact. A small cache of food sat on a cardboard box. I picked up the box of Cookie-Crisp and put it down. A man's shirt and a pair of jeans were hanging from one of the tines of an upturned pitchfork. I removed the clothes and went through them. A small journal was nestled inside the shirt pocket.

I opened it up. On the front page was written, *"These are the private thoughts of Bethany Peterson."* I started to read.

"You shouldn't do that," Manuel said.

"I know," I said as I thumbed through it.

"Don't know what to do," one passage read. *"Karim says I shouldn't say anything. So does Michelle. Maybe I'll consult my Tarot cards."* In another passage, Bethany had written, *"My mother said I have to lose weight. No more sweets. Snuck five candy bars into the house. She found them and grounded me for a week. My father says I'm going nowhere fast."* Another page contained the phrase *"I love Matt."* She'd written his name on page after page and surrounded it with hearts and curlicues. Looking at it reminded me of myself in the ninth grade. I closed the book and put it back where I found it.

Manuel and I waited around for an hour, but Bethany didn't show up, and eventually we got in the car and went home. I had to get back to the store, and Manuel was meeting some friends downtown.

"I'll come back and check later tonight," he told me.

"With what car?"

"T's."

"Fine." I didn't say anything about the fact that Manuel didn't have a license. He'd been driving since he'd stolen his first car at fourteen. That he couldn't legally get a license till he was twenty-one because of a variety of legal mishaps didn't seem to hinder him.

It was nine at night, closing time at the store—not that I couldn't have closed the place down earlier considering the day's business—when Geoff and Moss Ryan walked through the door of Noah's Ark. Up to that point, we'd taken in a grand total of twenty bucks. Not even enough to cover the day's operating expenses. I was half-lost in thought watching two marbled angelfish languidly swimming between the tall, waving grass fronds, their fins trailing behind them like bridal trains, contemplating everything I had to do and wasn't doing when I saw the black Mercedes pulling up. I waited to see what the two men were going to say to me. Somehow I didn't think they were coming to deliver any compliments.

"Rose wants to see you," Moss Ryan said as he approached the counter. He had to raise his voice to be heard over Zsa Zsa's barking.

"Now," Geoff added for punctuation. He'd changed out of his tennis whites and looked quite spiffy in his pressed linen slacks and polo shirt.

I stubbed out the cigarette I'd been smoking and dropped the butt into the coffee mug I was using as an ashtray. Somehow a strand of tobacco stayed on my tongue. "That's nice," I said after I'd picked it off. "Have a good game of tennis?"

Geoff did a double take.

"I saw you at the club."

"What were you doing there?"

"Looking for Bethany Peterson."

"Oh. So you're the one they hired." He smoothed back his hair with both hands. "I'm sure she'll turn up eventually. They always do."

I shushed Zsa Zsa and moved the tally sheet I was supposed to be working on to one side. "Hopefully."

Geoff's glance strayed to the picture Raul had given me. I'd taped it to the front of the cash register on the off chance that one of our customers would recognize him, since there are a fair number of Hispanics who lived in this part of town.

"Do you know them?" I asked.

"No." He gave a self-conscious laugh. "I usually don't come across people like that."

"You have people like this working for you."

Geoff adjusted his Rolex. "I meant socially. Anyway, Rose deals with the household help."

"If you don't mind," Moss Ryan interjected.

As I turned my attention to him, I saw he was wearing a lightweight navy suit, white shirt, and navy tie. I wondered if he ever wore anything else.

"Rose wants to speak to you about Pat Humphrey." Ryan stopped, waiting for me to say something. After a couple of moments of silence on my part, he reluctantly continued. "She appears to have taken off." He waited again. I continued to keep quiet. He folded his hands behind his back and looked somber. "One of her neighbors said they watched you go into her house."

"So? The door was open."

Moss Ryan put his hands up. "Don't get me wrong. I'm not accusing you of anything."

"Then what are you saying? Exactly."

"Rose is concerned. She still can't reach her. That's most unlike Pat." Moss Ryan dabbed at the beads of sweat on his forehead.

I closed the cash drawer. "If she's that concerned, she should go to the police and file a missing person's report."

Moss Ryan stuffed his handkerchief back in his suit pocket. "It's a little more complicated than that. Mrs. Taylor will explain."

"What if I don't care to speak to her?"

"I'm hoping you will. She's extremely upset," Moss told me while Geoff strolled over and began looking at the fish tanks. "I'm hoping that speaking to you will make her feel better."

"Why?"

Moss Ryan's brittle smile flashed on and off. "Just come."

By now Zsa Zsa had retreated to my legs and was whining the way she did when she wanted to go out.

Moss Ryan shot his cuffs. "I think you'll find Mrs. Taylor is a most generous employer. From what I've found out, you could stand to benefit from her largesse. Shall we say you'll be there in an hour to an hour and a half?"

"And if I'm not?"

He pursed his lips. "She'll hire someone else. But I think you'll find that you've missed a good opportunity." And he gestured to Geoff to follow him out the door.

In the end my curiosity got the better of me, and I loaded Zsa Zsa in the car and drove out to the Taylor estate. As I rounded the curve where I'd found Raul, a picture of him flashed through my mind. I should have gone to the hospital sooner. I tried not to picture him lying in a drawer, covered with a sheet, waiting for someone to claim him and no one coming. Where did they bury people like that? I reached for my cell. I needed to speak to someone. I called Manuel, George, and Calli. But no one was home. I didn't leave any messages.

Rose Taylor's maid was waiting for me. She didn't say anything about the ketchup stain I'd just gotten on my shirt from the two Big Macs and fries I'd eaten in the car on my way over. She didn't comment on the fact that I'd fixed the thong of my left sandal with duct tape or the fact that the make-up I'd started the day with had long since worn away. She didn't even say anything about Zsa Zsa. In fact, she didn't say anything at all. Just opened the door before I'd even rung the bell and motioned for me to follow her.

She looked weary, as if the day had eaten away at her reserves of strength. The wrinkles in her face were deeper. Her uniform was creased. Her gait was slower. She'd developed a slight limp in her leg from when I'd last seen her. As we walked through the hall, the noises our shoes made on the marble floor echoed in the dim light.

The maid led me to a room off the main hall. Looking around it, I had the feeling that this was where Rose Taylor actually lived. Relatively small, maybe twelve by twenty, it was furnished with a comfortable-looking light brown sofa and two club chairs, a desk piled high with correspondence, and a large wall unit containing a television and stereo. The walls were hung with pen-and-ink drawings. An assortment of magazines sat on the coffee table next to a box of tissues, a cup, and a tray filled with pills.

Rose Taylor was reclining on the sofa. One side of her mouth had a definite tremble to it, but other than that, she looked the way she had when I'd last seen her. Geoff and Moss Ryan were clustered next to her. Geoff was sitting in one of the club chairs, stroking her hand, while Moss Ryan was saying something to her that I couldn't hear. Rose made an imperceptible movement with her shoulders when she saw me, and the two men moved back slightly.

"You shouldn't have brought the dog," she told me. "Sheba doesn't like them."

"I can leave if you want," I replied, looking around for the cat. It was nowhere in sight. Maybe it had taken off along with Pat Humphrey. "I shouldn't be here, anyway."

"No. Sit down." Rose Taylor rang for the maid while I sat in the free club chair. When she came in, she told her to keep the cat in the kitchen until further notice and ordered coffee to be brought. "Now, then." She turned to me after the maid left. "Hillary told me everything you told her."

"Is that what you called me here to tell me?"

"Partly. I wanted you to know that Pat had already shared that information with me, so Hillary wasn't telling me anything I didn't already know. But you did a good job, which is why I want you to find Pat Humphrey for me. I know you know she's disappeared."

"I'll repeat what I told your lawyer. Go to the police. They're better equipped than I am to find someone who has gone missing."

"That's your advice?"

"Yes."

"I see." Rose Taylor carefully rearranged a fold of the caftan she was wearing. Bright blue with gold threads, it looked as if it were worth more than everything I had in my closet. "Have you ever made a mistake?" she asked me when she was done.

"Frequently." Out of the corner of my eye I watched Zsa Zsa sniffing around the corner of the desk.

"I think I might have made one."

"Just one? That would make you a fairly unusual person."

She frowned. When I didn't say anything else, she continued. "You've met my children."

I nodded at the rhetorical question.

Rose Taylor stopped talking when the maid came back in with the coffee. "Consuela, put the tray down here." She gestured to the coffee table. Consuela did as told and left. Geoff got up and served both Rose and myself. Rose took a sip of her coffee, then continued. "A couple of days ago I got a call from Pat. She was furious. She said my children had offered to buy her off."

"Like parent, like child," I murmured below Rose Taylor's hearing. "How much were they offering?" I'd been under the impression the three of them didn't have a spare nickel between them.

"Twenty thousand dollars if she left town. Naturally, she told them no." Rose Taylor stirred her coffee. The teaspoon clinked on the edge of the china cup.

"Naturally," I said. Why settle for a little when you could get a lot more.

Rose Taylor went on as if I hadn't spoken. "I was so angry . . .

so mortified that my children . . ." Her voice drifted away. She fluttered her hands in the air. "I . . . I told Hillary I was changing my will . . . that I was going to include Pat Humphrey in it . . . and that I was thinking of allowing her to use one of our country houses."

"She must have loved that."

"She became extremely angry. Abusive, really," Rose Taylor admitted. "I would never have talked to my mother the way she talked to me."

"Did you say anything else?"

"I told her that if she didn't leave Pat alone and stop bothering her, I'd take more drastic steps."

I folded my arms across my chest and watched Zsa Zsa meander over to where I was. "In short," I told Rose after a minute of silence had gone by, "you're afraid that one of your children has something to do with Pat Humphrey's disappearance?"

Rose nodded slightly. If I hadn't been watching, I would have missed it.

"I still don't get what you want from me."

Moss Ryan gently interrupted. "What Rose is saying is that we want you to find Pat Humphrey and make sure that she's all right."

I thought about the running water and the uneaten toast in Pat Humphrey's backyard. I thought about the opened back door. "And if she's not?"

Moss Ryan bit his lip. "If something has happened to her, the police will naturally come to Rose's children first. We would like a chance to prepare for that eventuality."

"I'm glad Sanford isn't alive to see this." Rose's voice quavered. She rubbed one hand on top of the other. They were covered with liver spots. Suddenly, she looked old. "His heart wouldn't be able to take this. I'm not sure mine will, either."

Geoff leaned over again and patted her hand again.

"Of course, we'll be willing to compensate you for your time," Moss Ryan said to me.

"Of course."

"Please," Rose Taylor said. Her lower lip quavered. Tears began trickling down her cheeks.

I told her I'd take the job. For three reasons. One: God knows why, but I felt sorry for her. Two: I could use the money. Three: I wanted to nail Pat Humphrey.

I went to look for Shana Driscoll. We had a few things to discuss.

Chapter Ten

It was still hot outside. The air was thick with the smell of honeysuckle and the promise of rain to come. Little pinpricks of light flickered on and off. Fireflies. The grunks of croaking frogs floated back from the lake. Moored sailboats, looking like toys, bobbed in the water. Over by the hills, a flash of lightning lit up the sky. Fairy lights marked the path that led to the cottage Shana was living in. I followed it while Zsa Zsa ran ahead and to the side of me, chasing moths with translucent wings.

The pool was a still oval of transparent water. The chairs around looked bereft, as if they were waiting for a party. Someone had lit two citronella candles. The smell, a mixture of lemon and wax, wafted over me, reminding me of summers spent at my aunt's camp near Saratoga Springs. A glass, half-filled with a dark liquid, sat on a small round table. As I got closer, I noticed someone treading water in the deep end of the pool. It was Shana Driscoll, out for her evening swim.

I walked over and hunkered down at the edge of the pool while Zsa Zsa pawed at a bug crawling along the edge of the concrete apron.

Shana's face was tipped up, a white oval in the shadows. "What do you want?" she asked.

"To talk to you."

"That's fairly obvious." But she climbed out, water streaming off her body, and toweled herself off in a slow, deliberate fashion just as Zsa Zsa nosed the bug over the edge and into the pool.

"Where's your dog?" I asked Shana as I watched the beetle frantically try to paddle its way back to the side.

She flung the towel on one of the chairs, then plopped on its arm, her left foot swinging like a metronome. "Maurice is back in the cottage."

"You're not on duty, I take it?"

"I go off at seven."

I took my cigarettes out of my backpack and lit one.

"You should quit."

I acknowledged the suggestion with a grunt, then swatted at a moth that had come too close to my face. "So you must have had a pretty rough day today, what with the state Mrs. Taylor was in."

Shana ran a hand through her hair, tugging and patting the strands into place. "Poor, dear lady. Don't you know that all stroke patients tend to become overemotional? It's one of the side effects."

"No, I didn't know that." I exhaled and watched the puff of smoke drift upward. A plane flew overhead, its wing lights winking red and blue.

"It's the truth."

"So you think Mrs. Taylor is overreacting to Pat Humphrey's disappearance."

"Disappearance is a strong word."

"You think she'll show up?"

"That I couldn't say."

"And why not?"

Shana blew out her breath in irritation. "Because I don't know. And now if you'll excuse me . . ." And she picked up her towel and hung it around her neck.

"So you haven't heard from her, either?"

"Mrs. Taylor's friend? No. Why should I have?" Shana took a step to the side and nearly tripped over Zsa Zsa, who had planted herself next to her feet.

"I just thought . . ."

"What?"

"Given your phone call."

"Call?" She'd turned her face into the shadows, making it difficult to see her expression.

"To Pat Humphrey. I was in her house. I played her answering machine back."

"What right did you have to do that?"

"The door was open. I walked in."

"You just go around doing things like that?"

"When it's justified. Yes."

"Does Mrs. Taylor know you did that?"

"She hired me to investigate her disappearance."

Shana's eyes widened. She pointed a finger at herself. "And based on that message, you think that I had something to do with that. Is that why you're here?"

"Did you?"

"Don't be absurd," Shana scoffed.

I dropped my cigarette on the concrete and stubbed it out with the heel of my sandal. I must have had too many today, because this one was making my throat sore. "I thought you didn't know her well."

"Of course I know her. Whatever gave you the idea I didn't?"

"Probably because you referred to her as Mrs. Taylor's friend."

"What's the harm in doin' that?" Shana demanded, her brogue kicking in again. "She is."

"Nothing. It just gives a certain impression." I changed subjects. "So what did you want to talk to her about?"

"Maurice. What else?" Shana idly ran a finger up and down one of her bathing suit straps. A high-cut maillot, it contrived to be even more revealing than the bikini she'd been wearing earlier in the day. "Patricia really does know things, you know. Sometimes even vets ask her to help them out."

"I know. I spoke to two of them."

"Then you're aware of what I'm talking about."

"I still think there's another explanation."

"Like what?"

"I'm not sure," I admitted. "Yet."

"Well, for your information, Patricia told me things about my dog, things none of the vets, not even the ones down at Cornell, picked up. The poor dear was sick—dying—until she came along."

"And he told Patricia"—I emphasized the name—"what he needed, and she told you?"

"Yes," Shana said, squaring her shoulders. "That's exactly what happened."

"It's nice your dog is so smart that he can diagnose himself." I pointed to Zsa Zsa, who was chasing another moth. "I must have gotten the dummy of the litter."

"Have you any other questions for me, then?"

"Not at the moment."

She looked me up and down. "You're doing well for yourself, aren't you? Being hired by Mrs. Taylor."

"I think you may be doing better."

She smiled.

"How did you get this job, anyway?"

"Through an agency. You can check if you want." And she gave me the name.

"Are you really from Ireland?"

"Indeed I am. A little town up in the north."

"Because your brogue comes and goes."

"People here seem to like it, so I put it on a bit. That's not a crime, is it?"

"Not at all."

"Good. And now I really have to leave. My dog is waiting for me."

"Fine." I put out my hand. "But if you're hurrying on Geoff's account, don't bother. It's going to be a while before he shows up at your cottage. He has his hands full right now at the house."

"You leave him out of this."

"You know, I saw him at the country club today with a

rather attractive older lady. He seems to have a thing for them, don't you think?"

"You don't understand."

Now it was my turn to shrug. "What's there not to understand? It's an old story. Not the oldest but old enough. The old lady and the handsome young man she keeps around for entertainment. What do you think Mrs. Taylor would say if she knew you were screwing her husband?"

"Who's to say she doesn't?" Shana spat back.

"Shall I go back up to the house and ask her?"

Shana folded her arms across her chest. "You do whatever it is you like. It's a matter of little difference to me."

"A matter of little difference," I repeated. "Very poetic. Is that how you see your relation with Geoff?"

"Geoff and I are none of your business." Shana took a deep breath. "And I'll tell you something else. It's not me you should be looking at if you want to find Patricia Humphrey," she told me, her brogue having made a miraculous recovery. "It's Mrs. Taylor's darlin' boy you should be talking to."

"Are you referring to Louis?"

"Does she have another one?"

"Boy is hardly the way I'd describe him."

"Ask him what he and Patricia were yellin' about out on the driveway."

"When was this?"

"Ask him yourself. I'm not earning your money for you." Shana turned to go, reconsidered, and turned back. "And another thing. Bother me anymore and I'll call the police and have you arrested for harassment." Then she left.

I whistled to Zsa Zsa and walked back to the house. I was mulling over my conversation with Shana, as I opened the door of my car, when I heard the rattle of tires on churning gravel. I looked around and saw headlights coming toward me. A few seconds later, a car screeched to a halt in back of me, and Hillary got out. She was dressed all in black. Black short skirt. Black rayon boat-neck shirt. Black heels. Silver jewelry. Performance clothes. I wondered what had happened to her gig downtown. Why she wasn't there singing.

"I should have known," she said, putting her hands on her hips and jutting her chin out when she spied me.

"About what?" I asked, even though I knew what she was going to say.

"You're working for my mother."

"Because I'm here?"

"Am I wrong?"

"No," I admitted.

"Exactly. You told me—"

"She asked me to come by after I'd spoken to you."

"You didn't have to, though." Hillary took a step closer to me. She looked like a wraith—it was the black clothes, I decided—and sounded like a disappointed child. "See. I knew you'd end up working for her."

I made a lame joke about coming out for a cocktail, but the hurt expression on Hillary's face embarrassed me. She shook her head from side to side. Now that she had come closer, I could see that she had smears of mascara below her eyes. I wondered if she'd been crying or if it was the heat or she was using cheap makeup.

"Sooner or later everyone does," Hillary said to me. "No one says no to her. Ever. What did she say to you? I have a right to know."

But before I could answer, the front door swung open, revealing a rectangle of white light, and Geoff walked out onto the upper step. "Hillary," he said. "Do us all a favor and go home."

"Fuck you," she flung back at him, her hands now balling up into fists.

"She's in no state to see you."

"I have to see her," Hillary insisted, her voice rising.

"Well, you can't." Geoff rendered the verdict in a lofty voice, the kind a judge might use. "We're waiting for the doctor to come now."

"Why won't you let me speak to her?" There were tears in Hillary's voice. "She's my mother, for God's sake."

"And she's my wife, and her well-being is my responsibility. Now get out of here. And don't try to phone tonight, either. I won't have her disturbed by you or anyone else."

Hillary took another step forward. "Let me in. I need to talk to her."

"How much money do you need this time?"

"It's not about money, you fuckhead."

Geoff moistened his lips with his tongue. "Don't make me call the police."

"You're going to pay for this," Hillary yelled. "You really are."

She flashed me a look that said, What do you think now, traitor? Then she whirled around, jumped back into her car, and gunned the motor.

"Sweet Jesus," Geoff said as he watched her turn right and ride straight over the lawn until she got on the road. "I don't believe her." He ran over and surveyed the damage the tires of Hillary's car had inflicted on the grass. "We're going to have to get the whole thing resodded," he told me when he came back. "I don't even want to think of the money that's going to cost." He pointed at the path Hillary had taken. "She really is crazy, you know. Absolutely nuts. I'm talking clinical here. For a while she was on some drug. Obviously it didn't help."

"How do you know she wanted money?"

Geoff snorted and kicked a piece of gravel out of the way. "Because that's all she ever wants. The only time she ever comes here is when she needs something. Every time she speaks to Rose, Rose gets upset. And that's not good for her. Especially now. After the stroke. In fact . . ." Geoff paused and straightened the collar of his polo shirt.

"In fact what?" I prompted.

"If it wasn't for her, Rose wouldn't have had a stroke."

"Why do you say that?"

"I didn't say it."

"Who did?"

"The doctor. She and Hillary had an enormous fight. Hillary ran out, and I came in. Rose was crying hysterically. I tried to calm her down, but I couldn't. Finally, I went into the other room to call her doctor. I was dialing when I heard a crash and ran back inside. There was Rose on the floor."

"What had they been fighting about?"

"I didn't ask. At that point, I had other things to do. Like save my wife's life." And he turned and slammed the door behind him, leaving me standing alone in the dark, wondering why Hillary had come.

Chapter Eleven

Zsa Zsa and I finished the last of the French fries I'd bought at Burger King earlier that evening as I pulled into Cedar Estates. The place was a trailer park, something Rose had neglected to mention when she'd told me where I could find her son, a telling omission in my view. Located a good twenty- to thirty-minute ride away from her estate, off the main road, it was hidden by a large scrim of trees. Driving by, you'd never know the place existed, which I suppose was the general idea, the poor being present but by general agreement invisible in Cazenovia.

Someone had scrawled *"Cedar Estates welcomes you—yeah, right,"* in red spray paint over the large sign that directed all visitors to report to the manager's office. Another person had scrawled *"Bienviendos a pequena España."* (Welcome to little Spain.) Arthur Peterson's words when he'd seen Raul in the back of my car flashed through my mind.

He'd said, "He lives . . . in the trailer park. All the Mexicans around here do."

He'd been referring to this place. He had to be. How many other trailer parks could there be in the area? Damn. I should have brought that picture with me. Now I'd have to come back later. I brushed a moth off my arm as I read the rest of the sign. Loud music, skateboards, unleashed dogs, and unsupervised children were forbidden. Speed limits would be strictly enforced. Underneath someone had written, *"Chinga tu madre."* Translation: Go fuck your mother. An iconic phrase in any language. A big plastic pot of parched, weed-infested geraniums sat off to one side, someone's idea of decoration.

The trailers, aluminum-sided rectangles, were lined up in a grid pattern, eight to a row. The streets were dirt. Signs marked out the corners. Groups of men in undershirts were sitting outside in folding chairs, drinking beer and playing dominoes and cards. The smell of chorizo wafted through the air. Packs of children were running around as their mothers gossiped with each other. The faint sounds of ranchero music punctuated their conversations. Even with the trees, the scene reminded me of Spanish Harlem on a hot summer night.

I halted at the first group of men and asked if they knew a woman called Dorita. Not that I really expected an answer. They'd gotten that we're-just-poor–humble-peasants-who-don't-know-shit expression on their faces as soon as I'd stopped the car.

"Dorita?" one repeated in broken English. "We're sorry. *Lo sentio. No la conocemos."* They studied their cards.

"I'm not INS."

Their faces remained blank. I described Raul to them and explained the situation. Their expressions didn't change. I didn't blame them. In the places they'd come from you never answered questions by people you weren't acquainted with. I handed out my card and moved on to the next group, and the one after that. But I might as well have saved myself the trouble. I got the same reaction from each one I talked to. The sudden silence as I approached, the wary eyes, the head shaking. Finally, after about half an hour of canvassing the park, I gave it up as a bad job and did what I was being paid to do: find Mrs. Taylor's baby boy and have a chat with him about Pat Humphrey.

I would have loved to have heard what Mrs. Taylor had said when Louis had told her he was living here among the kind of people that she hired to work on her estate. Some-

how she didn't strike me as someone who endorsed the concept of social equality, I thought as I bumped along the road
to Louis's trailer.

It was set on a cul de sac at the end of the street, surrounded by woods; hence, the name Tree Lane, I assumed.
The locale afforded Louis a little more privacy than some of
the other people that lived here. His trailer was one of those
double-wide jobs that are never meant to ride the roads but
go straight from the factory to their allotted plots of ground.
Someone, maybe Louis, had put up a foot-high white picket
fence around it. Inside the fence there were enough garden
ornaments stuck in the earth to stock a nursery. Two deer. An
elk. A family of elves. A couple of rabbits. A woman bending
over. A fountain with a frog on top. And if that wasn't enough,
two rubber tires with flowers growing out of their centers
flanked the doorway.

A spider hopped onto my arm when I opened the door of
my car. I brushed it off. Watching it ride into the night on an
undulating strand of silk, I thought that unless Louis started
living in an ashram in India, he couldn't get much farther
away from the environment in which he'd grown up. I wondered if he'd picked this place for that reason. As a defiant
gesture. Especially since it was so close to his mother's estate.
Had he ever invited her out here? Had she come in her fancy
car? Been shocked? Had he said to her, Look at how I'm living? Or, This is what I like. Accept me for what I am.

Only Rose Taylor wouldn't do that, I thought as Zsa Zsa
jumped onto the grass. She nosed around, then followed me
through the fence. I rang the bell.

A moment later, a voice trilled, "Debbie, thank God you're
here. I'm having the worst trouble zipping up this dress."
Then the screen door banged open, and a big-haired, big-
breasted woman in a beaded dress filled the door. "You're
not Debbie," she exclaimed.

No kidding.

I handed her my card. "I'm Robin Light, and I'm looking
for Louis. I've been told he lives here."

The woman blinked. "Sorry. You've got the wrong information."

I kept looking at her as I apologized. There was something about her. Something about her nose. The way it curved down. I'd seen it before. And that lanternlike jaw. Then it hit me. I did a double take.

"Louis?" I said, my voice going squeaky.

The woman lifted her chin up and turned her head away from me and into the shadows. She'd done it to conceal her face, but the movement was a mistake, because it tightened her neck muscles and displayed the faint outline of an Adam's apple. "My name is Lila."

I took another step forward. Now that I was closer, I could see that her hair was one of those bad wigs that you see gathering dust in cheap hair-salon windows, and even though she was wearing enough pancake makeup on her face to outfit a production of *Macbeth*, it didn't quite cover the faint shadow above her upper lip.

"Not the last time I saw you, it wasn't." I remembered Louis at Hillary's in his polo shirt and shorts. He'd been big and ungainly then. He still was. Only now he was big and ungainly in a long-sleeved, scooped-neck, beaded red gown. He wasn't a good-looking guy, but he made one hell of an ugly woman.

"I don't know what you're talking about," she insisted.

"Yes, you do. You're Louis, Rose Taylor's bouncing baby boy."

"Get out of here." He started to close the door, but I was quicker and pushed my way inside before he could. His nostrils flared. "You can't come in."

"I already have," I told him as I closed the door. The smell, a combination of depilatory, Chanel No. 5, and talcum powder, slapped me in the face.

"I'm going to call the police."

"And have them charge you with a fashion crime?"

"I hope you're not going to make stand-up comedy a career choice. I could have you arrested for invasion of private property."

"Yes, you could." But I didn't believe him. His voice lacked conviction. "Be my guest." I'd be gone before they arrived.

"I'm going for the phone," he snarled, and headed deeper inside the trailer. I followed on his heels.

"Are you sure you want the authorities out here?" I said to his back.

He didn't reply.

"I mean, your mother is pretty well known about these parts. Aren't you afraid someone would tell her about your . . . predilections?"

He whirled around. "You're right. I should take care of you myself."

I put up my hands. "Hey, calm down. I'm not going to say anything."

"You'd better not." Louis moved closer to me. I could smell the Lavoris on his breath. "I used to box profession-ally." He feinted a right to my jaw. "I bet no one told you that."

"You're right. They didn't," I replied, wondering how much a whole new set of teeth would cost me if he punched me in the mouth.

"I was good."

"What name did you fight under? The petticoat kid?" His eyes widened slightly. For a moment, I thought I'd gone too far. "That was a joke," I said.

"A bad one." He moved his head around, stretching his neck one way and then the other, the way professional ath-letes do. "You think I'm a fag?"

"Actually, I don't care if you like to get it on with pink ele-phants. I just want to talk to you about Pat Humphrey."

"That's why you're here?"

"Yup."

He dropped his fists to his side. "What about her? Hillary

said that was settled. She said she gave you your money. Don't tell me she didn't?"

"No. She did. Only now Pat Humphrey has disappeared."

"Okay." He fingered one of the beads on his dress. "But what's that got to do with me?"

"Your mother is worried. She hired me to find out what happened to her." Out of the corner of my eye I watched Zsa Zsa flop down by the door.

"She should be glad she's gone."

"Evidently she doesn't share your opinion."

Louis cracked his knuckles.

"When was the last time you saw her?"

He made a minute adjustment to his wig. "A couple of weeks ago, I think."

"Are you sure?"

"No, I'm not sure. I don't keep my social calendar in my head."

"What were you doing this morning?"

"I was sleeping. I work nights. Not that it's any of your business."

"And you don't have any idea where Pat Humphrey could have gone?"

Louis shrugged. "No. Why should I? It's not as if we keep in touch."

"You don't seem especially upset at the news," I observed. "Could that be because you already know about it?"

The sounds of a baby wailing disconsolately seeped through the trailer walls.

"Even if I did know—which I don't—that doesn't make me responsible. And you're right. I'm not upset. Poor Mom. Not being able to chat with Sheba." Louis shook his head in mock concern. "What happened? Did Humphrey take all of Mom's money and clear out?"

"If she did, your mother didn't tell me about it. Would it bother you if she had?" The smells in the trailer were getting to me. I wished Louis would open up a window.

"Why should it?"

"Considering that it'll all be yours one day, yours and your sisters, I find that answer odd."

He smoothed the front of his dress down. "By the time Geoff is done, there won't be anything left to get." Louis swatted at a fly. Perspiration was beginning to seep through his pancake makeup, leaving creases around his mouth and nose. "My feeling is, let her get what she can. That's less for Geoff. It was Hillary's idea to hire you. Not mine. She was the one who didn't like her."

"But you do?"

"I didn't say that."

I shifted my weight from one foot to another and tried to keep impatience out of my voice. The baby's cry was sharper. Where the hell were its parents? "Shana Driscoll tells a different story."

Louis glared at me. "Yeah? Such as?"

"She says she heard you and Pat Humphrey fighting the other day."

"Well, she's full of shit." And he made a chuffing sound with his mouth. "She was the one that was fighting with her, not me."

"And how do you know that?"

"I saw them."

"Why should Shana lie?"

Louis laughed unpleasantly. "To get me in trouble with my mother."

"And why would she want to do that?"

"Because that's what she's been doing since she arrived. I don't think a word of truth has come out of that woman's mouth since I met her. Shana is without a doubt the worst thing that has happened to Mom."

"The worst?"

Louis flushed. "The second worst," he amended.

"What were they fighting about?"

"I don't know. I was too far away. I just saw them. They were standing on the tennis court."

"What were you doing there?"

"At the house? Visiting. You mean I don't have the right to go see my own mother?" he demanded when I didn't reply.

"I didn't say that." I looked around at the trailer. "So what made you live here?" I asked, changing the subject.

"I like it. It's cheap. It's convenient. The people here are nice."

"They're certainly different . . ."

"From what I grew up with? You'd better believe it, sister. Your car dies and you need to go somewhere, they'll loan you theirs."

"Unlike your mother."

"My mother," Louis said bitterly, "will only give me something if it makes her look good. That's all she cares about. Everything goes for that goddamned house of hers and for Geoff." Behind the fake eyelashes, I could see the hurt in his eyes. "And now, if you'll excuse me, I have to finish getting dressed."

"Going to a party?" I said, trying to keep the conversation going.

"Yes. Not that it's any concern of yours." And he turned and went deeper into the trailer.

He stopped, then turned and faced me when he got to two long, narrow tables, set up on either side of the trailer. They were crammed with cartons filled with blue-and-white-enamel tinware, old cooking implements, irons, paperweights, old coins, framed illustrations, and costume jewelry.

"What are you still doing here?" he said. "I answered your questions. Now get out."

"All in good time." I picked up a paperweight containing the Empire State Building and shook it. Little flurries of snow swirled around. I'd had one like it when I was a little girl. My father had bought it for me. It had stood on my nightstand for years. I shook it again, wondering what had happened to it.

"Put that down," he ordered.

"Sorry." I gestured toward the tables. "What do you do with all of this stuff?"

"I sell it to people that want to buy it."

"You're a dealer?"

"In a small way. Yes. Now, will you leave."

"In a minute. Who do you sell to?" I asked as we moved toward the dining room/kitchen area.

"Other dealers. Collectors."

"Do you ever sell to your mother?"

Louis snorted. "Get real. The most expensive thing I have sells for five hundred. Even the ashtrays in Rose's place cost more than that."

I picked up a rhinestone crescent. "I used to have a pin like this. I threw it out."

Louis took it out of my hand. "Too bad. Because I can sell it to a store in New York City for about four hundred dollars. Now will you go? I've told you everything I know."

"Somehow I don't think that's the case."

"Somehow I don't care."

I pointed to a piece of blue-and-white pottery. "That looks like something your mother has."

"My mother's is antique. That is a copy." He smoothed his dress down. "Unless you have anything more to say. I suggest you leave and let me finish getting dressed."

But I didn't want to. Something on the table was making Louis nervous, and I wanted to find out what it was. I took another look. All I saw was a jumble of costume jewelry. And then I saw it. The thing he didn't want me to see. A gold chain with a pansy charm lying on top of a pink poodle. A similar piece of jewelry had been hanging around Patricia Humphrey's neck when I'd spoken to her. Louis followed my gaze. He went to pick up the chain, but I scooped it up before he could and inspected it. The petals were enameled. A small ruby chip was imbedded in the center. Two tiny emeralds gleamed on each small leaf.

"Nice. Where'd you get this?"

Louis glowered at me. "Forget what you're thinking."

"And what would that be?"

"For your information, Pat gave that to me. She wants me to sell it for her."

"If she gave it to you, why are you so nervous about me finding it?"

"I'm not. I don't give a shit what you think." He extended his hand. "May I have it back now?"

"No, you may not."

"That's not your property."

"Too bad." I slipped the piece of jewelry in my jeans' pocket. "I think I'll let Pat Humphrey tell me what she wants to do with it when I find her."

"Give it back." Louis's voice rose.

"That's if she can talk when I do."

He clenched his jaw. "That's stealing."

"That should be the least of your concerns. But"—I pointed to the phone—"you can always call the police and report me. Go ahead," I urged. "What's the matter? Afraid to dial the number?"

"If I were responsible for Pat Humphrey's disappearance, why would I be stupid enough to leave a piece of her jewelry around? Why wouldn't I have gotten rid of it?"

"I've observed that people are inclined to do remarkably silly things when they're stressed."

Louis moved toward me. "Let me have it."

"I don't think so. Perhaps it's time you called your mother's lawyer and had a chat with him."

Blotches of color blossomed on Louis's cheeks. "Like hell I will. God, you really are some piece of work," he ranted. "You barge in here without calling. You insult me. You steal something that isn't even mine, and to top it all off, you're telling me I had something to do with Pat Humphrey's disappearance. Trust Hillary to hire some brainless piece of shit like you."

"Brainless?" I snorted. "Unlike you, you fashion-impaired cocksucker."

As I watched Louis clench his fist and draw back his arm,

I wondered which words he'd found more objectionable: fashion-impaired or cocksucker? Probably fashion-impaired.

It occurred to me a little too late that this man weighed at least eighty pounds, maybe even one hundred pounds, more than I did. Plus he'd fought professionally. He was not a good person to piss off. And it was too late to take my words back.

I tried to knee him, but he was too fast for me—even with his dress on.

I should have tried ducking instead.

Not that that would have done too much good, either.

There was really no place to go.

Louis caught me on the side of my jaw with an uppercut. I felt my head snap back, I felt a blinding pain behind my eyes, and then I didn't feel anything at all.

Chapter Twelve

I felt something warm on my cheek. The warm became wet. Something tickled my skin. Then I realized Zsa Zsa was licking my face. I opened my eyes. The light on the trailer ceiling seemed to be pulsing on and off in time to the sound of a baby crying. Probably the same baby I'd heard earlier. Why couldn't someone shut that kid up, for God's sake? I wondered how Louis dealt with it. Louis! That cross-dressing putz. I saw his fist smashing into my jaw and closed my eyes again.

Zsa Zsa barked and started licking the corner of my mouth. It tickled. "Okay." I turned my head. "Enough. Go away."

But she kept right on doing what she had been, and I let her, mostly because I couldn't summon up the energy to push her off. Besides, I liked the floor. The linoleum tile was comfortable. Nice and cool. I decided I could stay there for a while. A really long while. I was drifting off again when I heard something ringing. A phone. It went on and on. Someone should get it. Jeez. Couldn't anyone get any rest around here? Then I realized it was my cell phone. Which was where? I searched my mind. Floor? Backpack? In the car? And then I remembered.

"Hello," I groaned into it after I'd managed to extract the damned thing from my pocket.

"Robin? Is that you?"

"No, Manuel. It's Zsa Zsa." I sat up and instantly regretted the action. The room started spinning. I took a deep breath and closed my eyes.

"You sound funny. Are you okay?"

"Not really. But I'll live."

"Where are you?"

I explained.

"I'm coming over."

"Don't. I'll be fine." I massaged my temples with my free hand. "What did you call about?"

"I just wanted to tell you that Bethany didn't go back to that shack tonight. But I've got a couple of other places I think she might be."

"Call me when you get something."

"You sure you're all right? I can come get you."

"I'm fine, honestly. I promise to call you if I need any help." And I hit the OFF button.

Zsa Zsa wagged her tail and began cleaning my fingers while I ran my tongue over my teeth—mercifully, they were all there. I moved my jaw up and down. It hurt—and would probably hurt more tomorrow—but I'd been lucky. Nothing seemed to be broken. It took me another couple of minutes before I was able to push myself up from the floor. Zsa Zsa stayed by my feet, encouraging me with little barks. I dug through my pockets. Pat Humphrey's chain was gone, along with Louis. It looked as if Rose Taylor had been right to be worried about her children's involvement in Humphrey's disappearance, after all. What is it they say about a mother's intuition?

I wondered how far Rose Taylor's extended as I saw the wig and the dress her son had been wearing thrown in a pile by the bed. Guess the party was off. I looked in the bathroom. The wastepaper basket was filled with torn pieces of paper with makeup on them. Louis's false eyelashes were sitting on the bathroom shelf, looking like the spider that had been crawling on my arm earlier that evening.

I wondered where Louis had gone off to as I contemplated them. To where Pat Humphrey was—if she was alive? To move her body if she wasn't? To K mart? To see Debbie? Or maybe he had just panicked and was out riding around, trying to figure out what to do, like the rest of us poor slobs.

I picked up the lipstick sitting on the edge of the sink— Passion Pink. For a few seconds I pictured him buying it. Had the girl at the checkout counter said anything when Louis had bought it? Had he told her it was for his girlfriend? Or was it Debbie's? Then a picture of Pat Humphrey flashed through my mind. Had she been wearing lipstick? I couldn't remember. Not that it mattered.

As I put Louis's lipstick down, I caught a glimpse of myself in the mirror. God, between my swelling jaw, my hair plastered to my head, and the big black circles under my eyes, I looked like a poster child for an abused woman. Or an accident victim. I just hoped George wasn't at my house when I finally made it home. I really didn't want him to see me looking like this. I didn't want to have to listen to what he had to say. It would be nice if he'd hug me and bring me an aspirin and an ice pack. But he wouldn't. He'd get angry and tell me what an idiot I was for getting myself in this situation in the first place. What made it even worse was that he was right.

Oh, well. I opened the medicine-cabinet door and examined the contents. Louis had stocked up on plenty of Q-tips, mouthwash, various pimple creams, and a variety of pills. I took the vials out and examined them. We had sleeping pills and the latest antidepressants, prescription antihistamines, something for heartburn, and over in the corner, buried behind a bottle of aspirin, something a little more interesting. Fifteen tabs of ecstasy in a bottle. The feel-good drug of the nineties. It's not just for kids anymore. Also known as E. Originally used by psychiatrists to help their patients open up, then at raves by club kids, and now by all sorts of people. A couple of tabs are supposed to relax you. Makes any sort of physical contact really nice. Side effects are minimal if you use it once in a while.

Personally, I'd never tried it. It had come on the scene after my druggie days. I swallowed about five of Louis's aspirin. I was thinking that maybe I should take a couple of tabs and go rollin', as the kids like to say, when Zsa Zsa ran out of the bathroom and started barking. Please, don't let this be Louis coming back, I prayed as I went to see what was going on. I sure as hell wasn't up for another dance with him. Maybe I should have let Manuel come get me, after all.

But it wasn't Louis. Zsa Zsa was barking at an attractive skinny girl standing in the middle of the trailer. She was in her mid-twenties. She'd buzzed her hair and bleached it out so it was platinum. She'd colored her lips a deep purple-brown and applied lots of eyeliner and mascara. She had a tattoo of a barbed-wire strand circling her upper left arm. She was wearing a very short black skirt, a tight white T-shirt, and a pair of strappy wedges.

"Where's Louie?" she demanded.

"He's gone."

She threw her hands up in the air. "Friggin' great. Did he say where he was going?"

"No. He just left."

"Is he coming back?"

"I don't know. He didn't tell me."

The girl moved closer. She put her hands on her hips and scrunched her eyes up. "So who are you, anyway?" she demanded. "I don't think I've ever seen you before."

"My name is Robin Light. I'm guessing that you must be Debbie."

She started. "How did you know that?"

"He thought I was you when he answered the door."

"I got held up." She plunked her backpack on a cabinet top. "Was he pissed?"

"A little."

"You saw the dress he was wearing, right?"

I nodded.

She grinned. "I helped sew it. I want to be a fashion de-

signer. We're gonna kick some butt at the party tonight."
And she threw her arms up and did a little victory dance.

I almost felt guilty disillusioning her. "I think he might
have changed his mind."

She came to a dead stop. "Whaddaya mean?"

"I don't think he's going to the party." I pointed to the
bed. "He took the dress off."

"Oh, no." She ran over, picked the dress off the bed, and
cradled it in her arms. "I don't believe this," she cried. "I
worked for hours on this. What happened?" Then another
thought occurred to her. "What the hell did you do to him?"

"What did I do to him?" I indicated my jaw. "Look what
he did to me."

Debbie hugged the dress to her. "Louis would never hit
someone outside the ring."

"Well, he did."

"I don't believe you. I think you're making it up."

"I'm not making my jaw up."

"Then he must have had a reason." She squared her shoulders. "You must have done something to make him."

"Yeah. I asked him about Pat Humphrey."

Debbie tugged the front of her skirt down. "The pet-
psychic lady? The one that's practically shacked up with
Louis's mother?"

I perked up. "You've met her?"

"No. I've just heard about her. Louis talks about her all
the time."

"What does he say?"

Debbie moved her ring finger up and down. "That she's a
fake. That she's ripping his mom off."

"And?" I asked hopefully.

"That ever since she came on the scene, his mom doesn't
want to talk to him anymore. Not that he really cares," she
added. "Now, why are you here? What does he have to do
with her?"

"I'm not sure. She's disappeared, and his mother hired me

to find her. I came by to ask him if he'd seen her, and he punched me." Not exactly the way it happened but close enough.

Debbie carefully folded the dress and put it back on the bed, then took Louis's wig and put it on the stand on top of the dresser drawer. "So, you're some kind of private detective?"

"Something like that." I gave her my card.

She tossed it on the bed. "He didn't have anything to do with Pat Humphrey disappearing."

"How do you know?"

"Because he's a dear, sweet man. That's why."

The room started spinning again. I steadied myself against the table. "I take it you're more than friends?"

She held out her hand. On it was a tiny diamond ring. "He's my fiancé." Her grin was back. "We're going to be married next month."

"His mother didn't say anything about that to me."

"His mother doesn't know. And we're not telling her until afterwards. If she could, she'd control when he takes a leak. We're going to get married at the speedway. Then we're going to travel around the world. To Africa and India and Australia. I'm totally psyched."

"Doesn't the fact that he's a transvestite bother you?"

"No. It's totally cool as far as I'm concerned." Debbie ran her hand through her hair. "So what if he gets off on that kind of thing? People should be able to do what they want. I mean, guy, girl, age, race. They're irrelevant. Pretty soon they'll have a pill so you can change them at will." Debbie hit her chest with her fist. "It's what's in here that counts."

"That's what I'm worried about."

"You are so wrong. What gives you the right to come in here and invade his space and make those kind of accusations?" Debbie was going to say something else when her beeper went off. "I gotta take this." And she went out onto the steps. While she was out there, I took the opportunity to take a quick peek through her backpack.

She had a lipstick, lip gloss, mint-flavored condoms, and a key chain with a can of mace hanging from it—just like I did—jumbled up in the bottom. I lifted out her billfold and opened it up. Her license read "Debbie Wright." I glanced at the address. She lived close to Bethany's friend Michelle.

I wondered if they knew each other as I did a quick count of the money she was carrying. It was all twenties and fifties. She had at least five hundred dollars, maybe more. I put that back and picked up a small plastic Ziploc bag. It had ten ecstasy pills in it. I pulled out another Ziploc bag. It contained twenty. I guess I knew where Louis had gotten his. I was holding one of the bags when she came through the door.

"What the hell are you doing?" she demanded. "Put that back."

I did. "Do you sell this stuff?"

She grabbed her backpack. "No wonder Louis popped you one. I would myself if I did things like that."

"So do you?"

"We were going to a party. These were for my friends, and please don't give me that archaic drugs-fry-your-brain crap. Because they don't."

"I wasn't going to."

"You guys give your kids Ritalin and all those serotonin reuppers, and that's okay, but this isn't."

"I don't have kids."

"Don't confuse the issue." And she stormed out the door. I followed.

"You see Louis, you tell him to come talk to me," I called after her.

She paused long enough getting into her Honda Civic to tell me to go fuck myself.

"Maybe I can keep him out of jail."

She slammed the door and drove away.

So much for that. I motioned for Zsa Zsa and went back inside. I spent the next half hour going through Louis's stuff. I looked in his file cabinet and found the DBA for his antique business as well as his tax returns. A cursory glance told me he was getting by, but that was it. As I closed the drawer, I wondered where he was going to get the money to take his bride on her wedding trip.

I went through his dresser drawers next. Half of them contained the usual socks and underwear, while the other half contained bras and silk panties in sizes I didn't know they made. In a box by his bed I found what appeared to be every birthday card his mother had ever sent him, two pressed roses, plus clippings of his fights. An interesting mix.

Then, off to one side, on top of a stack of local newspapers, I found a bubble envelope addressed to Shana Driscoll. I opened it up. Three Tommy Makem and The Clancy Brothers CDs fell out. A fact that indicated what? I sighed and put them back and checked my watch. It was still early enough to go back and talk to Shana. I had a couple of more questions that I wanted to ask her.

I was the only car on the road. As I drove along, I couldn't get Louis out of my mind. I kept thinking about him. Thinking about the expression on his face when I'd told him about Shana. Thinking of him in his dress. Thinking of Debbie. Thinking of what she'd said about categories. Wondering if she really believed what she said.

What would Rose say if she knew about Louis's clothes? What would she say if she saw Louis's girlfriend? Or maybe she did know about her. And about the cross-dressing. Maybe she knew other things about Louis as well.

And there were other possibilities. According to Debbie, he had reason to be pissed at Humphrey. Had she learned about Louis's other passion? Maybe seen him when he was decked out? Or gone to his trailer and surprised him? Threatened him with blackmail?

What would Rose do if she knew? Write him out of the will altogether? Cut him off without a cent? I rubbed my throbbing jaw and wished I had an ice pack with me to put on it as I watched tree branches weaving themselves into fingers, heads, and bodies, then disentangling to become branches again.

What would it be like to have a child you didn't like? All those dreams, all those expectations, and then you get— what? Something you haven't ordered, something you can't relate to. An orchid that refuses to bloom. And what do you do with flowers that do that? Especially if you're someone like Rose Taylor? You toss them in the trash and buy yourself more.

I wondered if Rose Taylor had done that as I turned between the two stone pillars that marked the beginning of her estate. Everything seemed quiet. The lights along the road I was following cast a gentle illumination. The scent of roses from her garden lingered in the air. I could hear the sound of an owl hooting off in the distance, followed by a dog barking. If this house and land were in Westchester, it would cost several million. Here it was worth just one. But still, that was enough.

The facade of the house was still lit up, but now all the house lights were off. It looked as if everyone were in bed. Glancing up, I thought I saw a slight movement in one of the windows. Then I decided I was mistaken, that it was a trick of the light. I scanned the driveway in front of the house. It was empty.

I parked a little way back from the house and followed the path over to Shana's cottage. The grass was soft under my feet. Zsa Zsa ran ahead of me, chasing after fireflies. It was a perfect summer night. Warm. A night for staying up and watching the stars. A night for building a bonfire on the beach. As George and I had done the summer we'd rented a cottage down in Hatteras. It had been nice, us drinking beer and sitting there and feeding twigs to the fire. What it wasn't a night for was going looking for someone, I decided as I passed by the garage. I'd started down the gravel path and was thinking about how pissed Shana was going to be when Zsa Zsa began to bark.

"Shush," I told her. "You're going to wake everyone up."

"My wife takes sleeping pills."

I spun around. Geoff was standing there in a pair of khaki shorts and nothing else. Unless, of course, you counted the Glock he was holding in his hand.

Chapter Thirteen

"How about pointing that somewhere else," I said to Geoff.

"Sorry." He lowered his weapon. "I thought you were a burglar."

"Really?" I noted the lights around the garage. "I would have thought you could see me well enough."

"Well, I couldn't. You should call first before barging in. Especially at this time of night. In other parts of the world, like Mexico, I could shoot you if I found you on my property without permission."

"But we're not in Mexico, are we? We're in Central New York." I shushed Zsa Zsa again. This time she took the hint, but she stayed close to me in case I needed protecting.

"No," Geoff conceded. "We're not. Any particular reason you're here?"

"I came to speak to Shana."

"Shana?" He frowned. "Why? What possible interest could you have in talking to her?"

"I want to find out more about a fight your girlfriend—"

"She's not my girlfriend."

"Fine. Your 'friend' told me she witnessed between Louis and Pat Humphrey."

"And that couldn't wait until tomorrow morning?"

"Yeah, it could have. But I didn't feel like driving back here again. Tell me, does he ever visit?"

"He might."

"You don't know?"

"He times his visits so I'm not here."

"And why is that?"

Geoff scratched his chin with the muzzle of his gun—not a good thing to do. "About four months ago I caught him stealing from the house. Nothing big, mind you. Some Roman coins. A couple of small Daumier etchings. He told me he had a right to take them. He said they were his. Can you believe that? He steals something every time he comes."

Maybe that was how he was going to finance his honeymoon with Debbie.

"Are you missing a piece of blue-and-white pottery?"

"Yeah. We are. Why?"

"I think it's in Louis's trailer."

"Christ." Geoff chewed the side of his cheek. "If it wasn't for Rose . . ." He let his voice drift off.

"You'd do what?"

"I'd call the cops."

I thought about Pat Humphrey's necklace. "You know that necklace Pat Humphrey wears?"

"The one with the pansy? What about it?"

"Do you know if it's valuable?"

"It's worth maybe a couple of thousand dollars—it's an old piece. A famous jeweler did it. Why? Did you find it?"

"I might have."

"She took it off to try on one of Rose's necklaces, and then she got a phone call and had to run off. When she came back, it was gone. Rose insisted one of the maids took it. She fired her."

"How long ago was this?"

Geoff thought. "Three, four weeks. But it was Louis, right?"

I didn't say anything.

"I swear he'd steal candles from a church. He and Amy.

They're a real pair. I feel bad for Rose having to put up with them. If they were my kids, I would have told them to hit the road a long time ago."

"From what I understand, she practically has."

"My mother took a strap to me when I was bad."

We started to walk. Zsa Zsa kept a little bit to the right of me. "Can I ask you something? What are you doing out this time of night?"

He shrugged. "I couldn't sleep. I thought I heard something and came down to investigate."

"I'm surprised you don't have a security system in here. Other than that." And I pointed to the gun.

"Oh, we did. But Rose canceled it. The cat kept setting it off. Drove her crazy. So now I've taken over."

"How comforting. You know, you don't have to come."

"I want to."

"And if I told you I didn't want you to?"

"I'd tell you I'm coming, anyway."

I was about to reply when Geoff held up his hand.

"What is it?" I asked.

He pointed to the pool with the barrel of his gun. It took me a couple of seconds to see that one of the Adirondack chairs had been knocked over on its side.

"So?"

"It wasn't like that before." I glanced at Geoff's face. In profile it was impossible to read. He picked up his pace, and so did I. We were almost at the pool when Geoff cried, "Oh, my God," and broke into a run.

I was about two seconds behind him.

Shana Driscoll lay floating on her belly, facedown, just under the surface of the water. She had on the bathing suit I'd seen her in earlier in the evening. Her hair swirled around her like an undulating patch of exotic seaweed. Just like the tails of the angelfish in the aquarium I'd been looking at earlier in the evening, I couldn't help thinking as Geoff jumped into the water.

I followed. Zsa Zsa stood on the edge and whined for me to come out. The water was still warm from the day's heat. Shana's body bobbed gently in the wake of the waves Geoff and I had created. Geoff reached out and turned her over. I felt for her carotid artery. There was no pulse. She was dead. But then I had known that the minute I'd seen her. What she was doing wasn't called the dead-man's float for nothing.

"Don't touch her," I said.

Geoff shook his head. "We can't leave her like this." He tenderly ferried her over to the side. "Help me get her up. She may still be alive."

"She isn't."

But Geoff had already clambered out of the pool, grabbed Shana under her arms, and started to pull. Zsa Zsa barked twice at him, then retreated a safe distance away.

"Come on," he cried, his face twisted with exertion.

I helped even though I knew that disturbing the crime scene is a definite no-no.

Shana was heavier than she looked. We hauled her over the edge of the pool and laid her out on the concrete apron. Aside from a black-and-blue mark on her thigh, her skin was clear of bruises. Squatting above Shana, watching Geoff perform CPR, I couldn't help thinking that in the water Shana had looked like a mermaid drifting with the tide. On the concrete, with her blank eyes staring up at the night sky and her wet hair hanging down in clumped strands over her breasts, she looked like a piece of refuse that had been cast upon the shore.

"Let her be," I told Geoff. "This isn't going to help. You're not going to bring her back."

But he kept going, vainly trying to pump life into her lungs.

I'm not sure how much time went by as I listened to Geoff's breathing and watched his back muscles moving. Finally, I roused myself and touched his shoulder. It was warm from exertion. "It's over."

Geoff's arms went slack. He squeezed his eyes shut, then opened them again and rubbed his forehead. "You're right. I know you're right. It's just that . . . it's . . ."

"Hard."

He took a deep breath and stood up. His chest and legs were beaded with water from the swimming pool. He ran a hand through his hair. "Jeez, what am I going to tell Rose?"

I walked over to the chair that had been tipped on its side. A three-quarter-empty bottle of Jameson was balanced on one of the wooden slats. "Did Shana drink Jameson?"

"She was Irish, wasn't she?"

"Did she drink a lot?"

"Sometimes. Why? You think she got drunk, fell in, and drowned?" When I didn't answer, Geoff said, "I don't believe it. Not for a minute. She was a good swimmer."

I made a noncommittal noise. It certainly looked as though Shana could have died that way. I hoped for everyone's sake she had. But I didn't believe it, either. Maybe it was the pool lights, but I couldn't get over the feeling I was in the middle of a stage set. And then there was Louis. He sure hadn't been happy when I'd told him what Shana had said. I was wondering where he'd been when Shana died when my phone started ringing. I took it out of my backpack. Manuel was on the line.

"Not now," I told him.

"But Robin, Bethany . . ."

I cut him off. "Manuel, I'm going to have to let you go. I'll call you back as soon as I can." And I pressed the OFF button. "You want to ring up the police, or should I?"

Geoff ran a hand through his hair. "I'll call from the house. I gotta talk to Moss first," he muttered.

"Use my phone to call him."

"Ryan's at the house."

I raised an eyebrow.

"He stays over sometimes," Geoff said, going defensive on me. "When he's too tired to drive home."

"Fine. Have him call the cops. I'll stay here."

Geoff groaned and brought his hands up to his face. "My mother was right. I should have stayed in Michigan and learned computers." Then he turned and jogged toward the house.

The moment he was out of eye range, I motioned for Zsa Zsa and, with her trailing behind me, started toward the cottage. I wanted to take a look around before the police got here and sealed everything off. We were about twenty feet away from the cottage when Zsa Zsa started barking. I looked where she was looking but couldn't see anything. A moment later, a little white ball darted out from behind a tree and started yipping at Zsa Zsa. Zsa Zsa wagged her tail. Shana's dog did, too. Then she ran over, stood up on her hind legs, and scratched at my legs, begging me to pick her up. Which I did despite Zsa Zsa's protesting growls.

"You look okay to me, Maurice," I said as I checked the dog out. Outside of some leaves and twigs stuck to his coat, he seemed fine. "So what happened to your mistress?" I asked. In answer, Maurice licked my nose, jumped out of my arms, and started playing with Zsa Zsa. Obviously, that famed animal empathy wasn't in force here.

The cottage Shana had lived in was picture-book charming, the kind you always see in travel ads for the English countryside. It came with a rose-covered trellis overshadowing the front of the place, ivy growing up the side of the walls, and a path made of paving stones. I wouldn't have minded living in a place like this myself, I thought as I looked at the flower beds flanking the doorway. Blowsy with cosmos, black-eyed Susans, and lupines, they gave evidence of being well tended.

The old-fashioned wooden screen door was ajar. I used the edge of my T-shirt to pull it open and went inside. The dogs came in with me. Zsa Zsa followed the little white dog over to a bowl filled with water near the door. I glanced around the living room while both of them began to drink. The room seemed tidy enough. If a fight between Shana and her killer had occurred, it hadn't happened in here.

The sofa and the two armchairs were covered with bright yellow-and-orange Indian print cloths and had a variety of contrasting cotton print pillows sitting on them. I walked over to the coffee table. It was piled high with magazines—mostly fashion. A small brown shipping box sat next to it. One of Tiffany's tell-tale blue boxes was nestled inside. I took off the cover, lifted out the dark blue jewel case, and flipped it open with my fingernail. Two good-sized pearl-and-ruby earrings stared at me. A small card had been placed along the top of the case.

Carefully picking it up along the edge, I took it out and read it. Someone had typed the word *love* on it in capital letters. Not written. Typed. Meaning the sender didn't want his handwriting identified. It was probably Geoff, I decided as I put everything back the way I found it and went into the kitchen. He had the money and the taste. Unless Shana had been seeing someone else as well. It was also interesting that the earrings were still in the shipping box. Shana had to have opened the box already. Known what was inside. Had she been going to send them back? It certainly seemed that way.

I glanced around the kitchen. The sink was filled with dirty dishes. At least two days' worth. A frying pan, crusted with egg, sat on the front burner of the small, old-fashioned stove. Obviously, Shana's sense of neatness did not extend to this room. From the look of it, Shana had made herself a salad and a couple of eggs for dinner. I moved on to the counter. A box of opened crackers lay on its side, its contents half-spilled out next to two water glasses. I bent over to sniff them. The smell of Jameson hit my nostrils. Evidently, Shana had started drinking in here and then brought the bottle with her to the pool.

But had she used one glass, then another when she'd dirtied the first, the way Manuel did, or had she had a visitor?

Hopefully, the police would be able to tell. I opened the refrigerator. The contents were depressing, especially since they reminded me of my own. A box of baking soda, a couple of yogurts, a six-pack of beer, an orange that looked past its prime, and a wedge of moldy cheese.

I moved on to the bedroom. The room was small, made smaller by the mess it was in. Looking at it, it was hard to tell if someone had gone through her things or if this was the way Shana lived. The floor was littered with clothes. So was the chair. I picked up a bra that had been flung over the side of the bed. It was made of expensive white lace. I put it back and picked up the teddy lying next to it and peeked at the label. It came from Switzerland. I recognized the name. The thing probably cost three hundred dollars, if not more. I put that down, too, and picked up a black microfiber backpack hanging off the foot of the bed. Prada. That was worth six hundred dollars right there. Shana had definitely been doing well for herself—until tonight.

The mattress yielded as I sat down on the edge of Shana's bed and looked at her nightstand. She had a set of bright pink wooden Buddhist prayer beads sitting around a light green aromatherapy candle with the word *peace* written on it. A little ways away was an envelope addressed to her. I nudged it over with my thumb and read the return address. The Center for Enlightened Self-Awareness. Wolfe Island. Which was located between the United States and Canada, about an hour to an hour-and-a-half ride from Syracuse. I couldn't be sure—it was hard to make out the date because the numbers were so faint as to be nearly illegible—but it looked as if the envelope had been postmarked two days ago. I opened it. The letter gave evidence of having been read and reread.

"Dear Shana," it said. *"I understand your problem. You seem to be caught in a karmic riptide. But things are not always as they seem. There are ways to reverse this tide. Perhaps you would care to meet. I have some suggestions*

*that may surprise you. Until then, remember that a problem
is not a problem but a missed opportunity. Love, Pat."*

So Pat was still alive. Or at least she had been. Shana and
Pat. One woman was dead, and one was gone. I was wondering if the two were related when I heard a cough. I looked
up. Moss Ryan was standing by the door. His hair was tou-
sled. He was wearing a pair of dark navy pants and a partially buttoned white shirt.

"What are you doing?" he demanded.

"Reading a letter."

"You shouldn't do that. You shouldn't even be here. You're
compromising the crime scene. Rose wants to see you," he said
as I folded the letter up, slipped it into its envelope, and put it
back where I found it. "I'll wait here until the police come."

He was still at the door when I walked out, but something
told me that if I doubled back I'd find him doing what I'd
been doing when he arrived.

Rose was waiting for me in the room in which I'd last seen
her. She was sitting on the sofa. Geoff was next to her, patting her hands. She seemed to have gotten smaller.

"Leave us," she told Geoff when Zsa Zsa and I came in.

"But . . ." he protested, clearly surprised.

"I need to talk to Robin alone for a minute," Rose told
him, her voice surprisingly strong.

"Are you sure?"

"Positive."

Geoff got up reluctantly and slowly walked to the door.
"I'll be right outside if you need me."

"Thank you." She watched Geoff leave. Then she told me
to close the door. "Make sure it's shut all the way," she instructed. "What happened to your jaw?" she asked when I
returned.

"Your son punched me."

"I knew Sanford was wrong about letting him take up
boxing," she murmured to herself as she dabbed at the edge
of her eye with a tissue. Then she folded her hands together

and placed them in her lap. "More importantly, Geoff tells me Shana's dead and that you think Louis might have had something to do with it."

I hadn't said that to Geoff. But I didn't correct the statement. Mostly because it could be true. "It's possible."

Rose blinked. I noticed her left iris seemed higher than her right one. I wondered if her stroke had caused it. "Will the police think so, too?"

"They might."

Rose studied her hands for a moment. "In your opinion, should Moss contact a criminal lawyer and arrange for representation for my son?"

"I don't think it would be a bad idea."

"I see." Rose lapsed into silence again. Another minute went by before she spoke. "And Pat? What about her?"

I told her about the letter I'd found in Shana Driscoll's room.

Rose leaned forward slightly. "Do you think she's still there?"

"It's possible."

"I want you to go there and see if you can find her."

"Why?"

Rose stuffed the tissue into the sleeve of her caftan. "Because I have unfinished business that I need to discuss with her."

"Fair enough. Supposing she is there. Then what?"

"Tell her I need to speak to her."

"What if she doesn't want to speak to you?"

"That's not going to happen."

"But if it does," I insisted.

"Then we'll deal with that then. I've lived too long to be worried about ifs and maybes."

I studied Rose's face. "Is there anything else I should know?"

"No."

"Are you positive?"

"Absolutely." She closed her eyes and rested her head against the back of the sofa. "Tell Geoff to come in on your way out," she said. Her eyes were still closed. "I need to put my makeup on before the police arrive."

But Rose wasn't going to get the chance, because when I stepped outside, I could see a squad car making its way up the driveway.

Chapter Fourteen

James came darting out from behind a bush as I put the key
in the lock of my door and gave me a reproachful meow. It
was a little before six o'clock in the morning, and I'd been up
for almost twenty-four hours now. My jaw was throbbing,
my bones ached, and my clothes smelled. All I wanted to do
was strip, jump in the shower, and go to sleep. Feeding cats
was not on my "to do" list.

"Scat. Get your own breakfast. Go kill a mouse."

But James gave me his your-life-is-going-to-be-a-living-
hell-if-you-don't-give-me-something-to-eat look, and I capit-
ulated and went into the kitchen and opened up his can of
food and put it in a dish. As I was rinsing out the can, I noticed that the message light on my answering machine was
flashing. I shouldn't have played it.

I heard Pat Humphrey's voice say, "I see you in the dark. I
see blood."

"And I see you in jail," I said to the machine.

Fuck her. I wondered if this is what she'd done to Rose.
Setting her up. Then moving in for the kill. Probably was.
She was clever. I'd give her that much. I got a glass out of the
sink. Then I went to the refrigerator and put a couple of ice
cubes in it. I liked the sound of their clink as I dropped them
into the glass. It was reassuring. I shouldn't be doing this.
Screw that, too.

For months after Murphy died I'd sat in the dark by my living room window with a razor blade making little cuts on my fingertips to distract myself from the pain I felt. I'd never told that to anyone. It was my nasty little secret. Just thinking about that time again made my stomach twist. The not sleeping. The not eating. The crying I couldn't control. The going to sleep at night hoping it would be better and waking up each morning feeling the same as the night before. I went into the living room and poured myself a hefty shot of scotch. Before I knew it, it was gone. I poured myself another one and sipped it, admiring the color of the liquid in the glass. That warm golden brown. The color of autumn. I'd finally managed to tuck all of that Murphy stuff in a little box and seal the lid, and I was damned if I was going to let someone open it.

I went back into the kitchen and dialed star 69. I was in luck. I got the number. I dialed it. A recording telling me I'd reached the Center for Enlightened Self-Awareness came on. "No one is here right now," a voice chirped above the sound of bells and chanting. "But your message is important to us. Please leave one and we'll get back to you as soon as possible. Peace be with you."

Peace my ass. I hung up and went back into the living room and picked my drink up and lit a cigarette and inhaled. I reveled in the sensation of the smoke filling my lungs. I took another sip of scotch.

The Center for Enlightened Self-Awareness? Okay. I didn't know what game Pat Humphrey was playing with me, but I sure as hell was going to find out.

Now I had two reasons to locate her. Rose Taylor's and mine.

Murphy. Murphy. Murphy. Jeez. I rolled the glass on my forehead. He was dead and buried. Gone. But he kept on coming back and messing up my life, making me feel like shit. Just like when he was alive.

*   *   *

I must have passed out, because the next thing I knew, someone was shaking me. I looked up. Manuel was standing over me on the sofa.

"You okay?"

I rubbed my eyes. "How did you get in here?" Then I remembered he had a key to my house. "What time is it, anyway?"

"Eight-thirty."

I sat up and buried my head in my hands. I had an awful taste in my mouth, a crick in my neck from sleeping the wrong way, and my jaw hurt worse than it had when I went to sleep, if that was possible.

"You look like shit."

"Thank you, Manuel, for your support. What do you want?"

"Bethany is passed out in the kitchen."

I brought my head up. "My kitchen?"

"No. The one down at the Holiday Inn."

"How did you manage that?"

"You don't want to know."

"Oh, yes, I do."

"Fine. T and I caught up with her at a rave going on over on the West Side. She was lookin' for E, and I told her I could get her some."

"And she went with you just like that?"

"She was wasted."

"How wasted?"

"Wasted enough so that I had to stop the car so she could puke." Manuel made a face. "That was pretty gross."

"And she thinks I'm a dealer?"

"Well, she doesn't think you're an English teacher." He laughed. "Boy, is she going to be in for a surprise. I took her in the house through your side door. By the time I got back from takin' a piss, she was out cold."

I levered myself up and walked into the kitchen. As Manuel had said, Bethany was indeed slumped at the kitchen table, her head on her arms, sleeping. Her mouth was slightly open. Her hair looked like a rat's nest. Her eye makeup was smeared over her cheeks. Her complexion was white.

"She looks almost as bad as I do," I observed. When Manuel didn't say anything, I added, "You're supposed to say, 'You look better.' "

"Okay. You look better."

"But she's okay? We don't have to call the hospital or anything?"

"She's fine. She just needs some sleep."

"Watch her," I said to Manuel.

"Where are you going?"

"To phone her parents."

"Thank God," Bethany's mother sobbed when I told her. "Thank God my baby's coming home." Then, before she could say anything else, her husband came on the line.

"It's all right, Millie," Arthur Peterson said. "I'll handle it."

When I walked back into the kitchen, I saw that Manuel had opened the refrigerator and was staring inside it.

"Her dad will be here in a half hour."

He turned. "I did good, hunh?"

"You did real good."

He preened. "That's why I'm the man." Then he went back to staring inside the refrigerator. I had to admit it wasn't an inspiring sight. He frowned. "How come you never have anything to eat in here?"

I reached for Bethany's bag and unzipped it. "Because I'm a single woman and single women don't have food."

"My half sister does," Manuel said, sniffing the milk and recoiling from the smell. "This is disgusting."

"Then throw it out," I told him as I dumped the contents of Bethany's bag onto the kitchen counter and began pawing through it. I wasn't worried about Bethany waking up. She hadn't even twitched during Manuel's and my conversation.

I found a couple of pairs of underpants, bubblegum, three packages of ribbed condoms, a Snickers bar, lots of loose change, and a picture of herself when she was little, with her mom and dad, in front of their house.

"Anything interesting?" Manuel asked, coming up behind me. He picked up the matchbox model of a Porsche and put it down. "Why would she be carrying this around?"

"I don't have a clue." I opened Bethany's address book and scanned the pages.

I found Karim's and Michelle's phone numbers, numbers for the rest of her friends, numbers for clubs, and the number for Debbie Wright. She'd written *"beeper"* under the number in pencil, and after that she'd written the letter e in parenthesis. Could it be E for ecstasy? Let's guess. Well, one thing was for sure, I thought as I scribbled the number down on a spare piece of paper before I put everything back in Bethany's bag. Louis's girlfriend certainly got around.

Bethany was still sleeping when her dad pulled into my driveway twenty minutes later. She was still sleeping when he rang the bell and strode through my house. Arthur Peterson didn't say anything when he saw his daughter. He didn't say anything when I told him about how Bethany had gotten here. The area around his eyes got tighter and tighter while I talked. His anger was like lava, flowing into every corner of the room.

"What are you going to do?" I asked as he approached his daughter.

"Do?" He rubbed the corner of his mouth with his thumb. "Do? The only thing I can do. Send her away."

Manuel moved in front of him and stuck out his chin. "What do you mean, send her away? I thought you were taking her home?"

"Who is this?" Peterson demanded of me, noticing Manuel for the first time.

"This is the person who found your daughter."

"Thank you," Peterson said abruptly, turning away from him and directing his comments to me. "But I have to do what I consider best for everyone. I can't continue to have this type of disruption in my life. Neither can my wife. One of my colleagues suggested a place down in Florida that deals with children like Bethany. My wife doesn't want me to, but obviously staying at home isn't the answer for my daughter anymore. Sometimes we must follow our minds, not our hearts."

"That's whacked," Manuel said.

Peterson ignored him, reached over, put a hand on Bethany's shoulder, and shook her. "Okay, Bethany. Let's go."

When Bethany opened her eyes and saw her father standing over her, defeat settled over her face. I'd been ready for her to fight or run. But she'd come to the end of her road. At fifteen you don't have that many you can go down.

"It's a little late for that, don't you think?" Peterson said as his daughter burst into tears. "Come on. Your mother's waiting."

She walked slump-shouldered out of the house, her father following a couple of inches behind her.

"What an asshole," Manuel commented as we watched father and daughter walk to their car.

"He's upset."

"No wonder she doesn't want to be home."

Peterson was saying something to Bethany that was making her cry even harder. She got in, and he slammed the door after her.

"I should have left her where I found her."

"She's better off at home than on the street."

Manuel bent down and rubbed Zsa Zsa's rump. "She's not going home, remember."

"She's still better off."

"I had a friend who was a PINS person that got sent to one of those places Bethany's father was talking about. They treated him worse there than they did at Hillbrook."

Hillbrook was where they put the hard-core cases. "Maybe this place will be different."

"I sure as fuck hope so."

Suddenly looking at Manuel's face, it struck me. "You like her, don't you?" I said.

Manuel mumbled something and turned away from the window. "You got my money?"

I took it out of my bag and gave it to him. He stuffed the bills in his pocket without counting them.

"I have another job for you to do if you want."

"Like what?"

"A hundred bucks if you can find out a little more about Debbie Wright."

He nodded absentmindedly. I could tell he was still thinking about Bethany.

Chapter Fifteen

Manuel left a little while after Bethany and her dad. Zsa Zsa and I shared a bowl of cereal, after which I tried to go to sleep. Only I couldn't. Pat Humphrey's words kept buzzing around in my head. Finally, I got up and called Paul.

"Listen," I told him, "I want you to get me a rundown on the Center for Enlightened Self-Awareness. Whatever you can. And anyone connected with it," I added as an afterthought.

"You know, Light, you really should stop doing these crappy little jobs and come to work for me," Paul said. "I could hook you up with some decent money."

"Yeah, but then I'd have to take my orders from you."

"Always have to be a wiseass, don't you?"

"That's why you love me."

"Wanna go out sometime?"

"I thought George was your friend."

"He is. Up to a point."

I hung up and went to Noah's Ark, where I fed the animals and cleaned their cages and tried to figure out how five geckos had managed to escape from the aquarium I'd housed them in.

Around one, when Tim came in, I went back to the house to take a nap before I drove out to Wolfe Island. Otherwise, I was afraid I'd fall asleep at the wheel. I'd just drifted off when George walked into my bedroom.

I raised my head off the pillow. The afternoon sun slanting through my bedroom's blinds gave George's black skin an ebony shine and made him seem even bigger than he already was.

"I dropped by the store. Tim said you were here."

"Don't say anything," I told him as he came toward me.

"About what?"

"This." I pointed to my jaw.

"Maybe I wouldn't have noticed."

"You would have." It was impossible not to.

"I can't ask how you got it?"

"No."

"Or ask who—"

"No," I reiterated.

"I'm not going to do anything to him."

"I know."

George scowled. "If you want to be a moron, who am I to stop you?"

"You came here to insult me?"

"No. I came here to do this." And he bent over and kissed my bruise. "And this." He got lower. "And this."

"*This* is good."

"Tell me," I said as I turned toward him. "Do you believe in messages from the other world?"

He laughed. "No. I believe in this," he said as he lowered himself down and slipped inside me.

"So," George said an hour later, when we were sitting out on my deck. "Who's going to cover the store while you go off to Wolfe Island?"

"Tim." I stretched and stifled a yawn.

"That's nice of him."

I poured sugar in my ice coffee. "Nice nothing. I'm giving him two weekends off next month."

George pointed at my cup. "How can you drink it like that? Why don't you just have some coffee with your sugar?"

I picked up a spoon and began to stir. "I like it this way."
He grimaced. "You're going to get diabetes."

"Don't be ridiculous. I'm going to die of lung cancer." I
took a sip, then leaned over, snagged a slice of the pizza
George had bought, and bit into it. The taste of tomato and
oregano exploded in my mouth. God, it was good, almost as
good as the sex George and I had just had, but maybe that
was because this was the first food I'd had all day. "Are you
sure you don't want to come with me? It's a nice drive."

"I would if I didn't have to teach a class."

"Cancel it. I'm sure your students won't mind."

"But the administration would." George drained the can
of soda he was drinking and crushed it. "There's nothing in
here about Shana's death," he said, indicating with a nod of
his head the newspaper he'd brought over.

"I'm not surprised." Rose Taylor was still powerful enough
to keep the incident, as she'd called Shana's death when she'd
spoken to me at the store, out of the papers. Unless, of course,
the coroner ruled Driscoll's death a homicide. Even someone
like Rose Taylor couldn't do anything about something like
that—not that she wouldn't try.

"You think the coroner will find for death by misadventure?"

"Rose Taylor does. She's asked me about representation
for her son."

George grunted. "They'll bargain it down if it comes to
that." He flicked a piece of pizza crust off his khakis. He was
in his teaching clothes, khakis, a light green polo shirt, and
Docksiders. "He'll probably get three years' probation and
community service. Unlike the poor schmuck who gets seven
mandatory for growing grass in his basement."

I could see Rose explaining the incident to the people at
the country club. It would be an accident, of course. My son
the murderer. Somehow it didn't sound as good as my son the
doctor. I took another bite of pizza and shared my observation with George.

"I wouldn't know. I've never joined one. Not Our Kind,

Dear," George affected an English accent. Then he reached down and absentmindedly scratched Zsa Zsa's rump. "She's lawyering up awful quick."

"I was thinking that, too."

"Maybe she knows something you don't."

"I wouldn't be surprised."

George leaned forward. "So what is the Center for Enlightened Self-Awareness, anyway?" He made a face. "One of these New Agey places where people come to find themselves—whatever that means."

"Something like that." And I filled in George on what Paul had dug up for me. I didn't tell him about Paul's hitting on me. I didn't see the point. Why bring up something that was only going to get George pissed? Not that he'd see it like that. He being for truth and honesty. Unlike me.

He made soft clicking noises with his tongue against the roof of his mouth while he listened to me read off my notes.

"Okay. The Center for Enlightened Self-Awareness was founded five years ago by the Reverend Ascending Moon, a.k.a. John Sinclair before he went to court and legally changed his name. The building Sinclair is in was donated to them by a charitable trust called Alternative Strategies."

"Who set it up?"

"Paul's still working on that."

"It shouldn't be too hard to find out." George ate some more pizza while I continued talking.

"The cult has a tax-exempt status and claims a hundred and fifty members. According to its brochure, it's a place of peace and rejuvenation where all are welcomed to come and replenish themselves."

"Anything else?"

"Not that Paul could find. There have been no complaints filed against the center. At least none that he could locate. They're quiet. They pay their bills on time."

"And John Sinclair?"

I consulted my notes again. "Pretty standard stuff. He was born in the Buffalo area. Both parents are dead. No brothers or sisters. Or none that we know about. Our fellow married and divorced twice. Has one child, a boy, who is residing with his mother out in Boise, Idaho. Sinclair graduated from high school and went straight into the army. He made sergeant but was dishonorably discharged for redirecting supplies."

George looked up. "Stealing?"

"Can we say creative management? Anyway, after he left Uncle Sam's embrace, Sinclair worked on the assembly line in a meat processing plant in North Carolina. Got a couple of DWIs down there, then he moved back up here and worked in a restaurant as a short-order cook, where he got tagged for selling pharmaceuticals and put on probation, and then—"

George interrupted. "Let me guess. He found God."

"He not only found God; he founded his own order." I fed a piece of my pizza to Zsa Zsa. "Sometimes I think the penal system is responsible for more conversions than the Catholic Church."

"I don't know. They racked up a pretty good number during the Inquisition. Racked up. Get it?"

"I'm trying to ignore it."

George looked crestfallen. "Anything else?"

"According to Paul, Sinclair supposedly went to India for six months, although Paul hasn't been able to find any record of that, and came back as the Reverend Ascending Moon." I pushed a lock of hair out of my eyes and readjusted my sunglasses. "Paul said he'd see what else he could turn up if I wanted him to. This is just his first pass."

George looked pensive. "It's frightening what you can turn up on someone these days."

"Isn't it, though? And this just took Paul an hour. Imagine what he could do if you gave him a day."

"Maybe you should take a computer course. At least then you wouldn't run around getting punched."

"I thought we weren't going to talk about that."

"We're not talking about it. I'm just telling you that I think it's time you got off the street."

"Really?" I eyed the last pizza slice.

"I'm serious."

"I know you are. Have you considered the fact that I might like it there?"

"Have you considered that's indicative of a problem?"

"Are you saying I need help?"

"I'm saying it's not a good place to be. That's why I left. It messes with your head."

"My head's already messed up, so I guess it doesn't matter."

George scowled. "I just don't like seeing you getting hurt. Is that so wrong?"

"No. It's sweet." And I leaned over and kissed his forehead.

Chapter Sixteen

On my way to Wolfe Island I made a detour and stopped off at the Hispanic Alliance. The organization, founded around ten years ago in response to a growing Spanish presence in Syracuse, was located on the West Side of town, off Seymour Street. The building it was housed in was a ramshackle two-story affair that had been built on the cheap and was only getting worse as time went on.

The steps buckled and groaned as I walked up them. Inside, the director was sitting at his desk, reading the newspaper, while a table fan blew a stream of hot air on him. An elegantly groomed man despite the heat, he would have looked more at home at the Spanish legation. He listened politely to what I had to say about Raul and Dorita and took the picture I'd been given out of my hand and studied it for a few moments before laying it down next to a pile of papers.

"You know," he said in faultless English, "at last count we had over ten thousand Hispanics living in this community. They come from all over—Colombia, Ecuador, San Salvador, Mexico, the Dominican Republic. To most people who live here, they are invisible. Some prosper, but the others . . ." His voice trailed off. He took a handkerchief out of his breast pocket, mopped his brow, folded it up, and replaced it. "If you came here expecting me to help you with this picture . . ." He shrugged, his gesture conveying the futility of the enter-

162   *Barbara Block*

prise. "I'll try, but frankly the outcome is doubtful. As to the other, my grandmother died from tuberculosis." He formed an O with his mouth and blew air out. "I'll talk to the clergy and see if we can raise some money for a funeral. Outside of that . . . well." He waved his hand around. "You can see our funds are limited. I only have a secretary three afternoons a week."

I left him studying the photo I'd given him.

Accessible by a twenty-five-minute ferry ride, Wolfe Island is located between Canada and the United States and bounded by Lake Ontario on one side and the Saint Lawrence on the other. The island is about sixteen miles long and seven miles wide. Once occupied by the Iroquois, it now consists of windswept meadowlands, a sprinkling of farms, cattle, and a few cabins and small resorts, as well as the stores that serve them. Except in the summer and early fall, when vacationers come, the cows mostly have the place to themselves.

The Center for Enlightened Self-Awareness was situated on the Saint Lawrence side of the island. Housed in what had, at one time, obviously been a fishing lodge, the main building was an elongated two-story log cabin set about fifty feet off the shoreline. Several cottages, also done up in log-cabin mode, dotted the perimeter of a large grassy square. We're talking upscale Catskill bungalow colony here. Down by the water, three motorboats were tied up to an old wooden jetty. They were bobbing up and down in the wakes left by the boats zigzagging around the lake. Water-skiers' shrieks vied with the screeches of seagulls.

The place didn't seem very crowded. As I parked on the grass next to a beat-up Honda Civic, I spotted a couple walking down by the shore and a man going into the main building, and that was it. I saw one other person, a woman, as I went into the main lodge. If the Center for Self-Awareness was taking in a lot of donations from its congregation, they sure hadn't spent it on the furnishings.

I was willing to bet the fishermen who'd come here would find things almost the same as when they left. There was a check-in desk at one end of the lobby and a grouping of shabby sofas and chairs at the other. A variety of flyers were spread out on the main desk. Most of them were announcing classes in yoga or tai chi, talks by various people, or the availability of massages. A board on an easel, set up by the main desk, gave the day's menu.

A man materialized on the other side of the desk. He was short and plump, with well-tended pink skin and thinning, mousy brown hair. The white knit skullcap he was wearing matched his white caftan. A large enameled pendant with a circle inscribed in the center hung from his neck.

"Can I help you?" he asked. His voice, high and reedy, didn't go with the rest of him.

"Perhaps. Are you the Reverend Ascending Moon?"

He nodded. "Indeed I am. Would you like to register?" He glanced at the box with the keys in it. "Fortunately, we have a couple of cottages available. Normally this time of year, we're full up."

"Actually, I'm looking for a Pat Humphrey."

"I don't believe I know that name," the reverend informed me.

Right. And I eat cream of wheat and jog five miles every day. "I got a message from her originating from here on my machine yesterday."

"Perhaps she was someone's guest and used one of the phones in the cabin."

"Then what about this?" And I showed him the letter.

He read it carefully and handed it back to me. "Well, it appears from this that she was here, I can't dispute that, but I'm afraid she's not a regular member of our congregation. Her name is unfamiliar to me. She was probably a visitor. You know, we open our facilities to the public. People come and go all the time." The reverend straightened out a crease in one of his sleeves. "I've just come back myself. I've been traveling quite a bit recently. Giving talks. People ask me and I go. May I ask why you're inquiring about her?"

"I'm inquiring because one of her clients needs to speak to her."

"Clients? May I ask what business she's in?"

"She's a pet psychic."

Sinclair cocked his head. "How interesting."

"Yes. Isn't it? Anyway, as I was saying, my client has a matter of pressing concern and has hired me to find her." I didn't see any need to discuss Shana's untimely demise as well. I took out one of my business cards and gave it to him. Then I showed him the picture of Pat Humphrey that Rose Taylor had given me. "Are you sure you haven't seen her recently?"

He studied the picture for a minute and handed it back. His nails were manicured. "I'm sorry, but I can't say that I have."

"Can I speak to the person that runs the place while you're gone?"

The reverend sighed. "I wish you could. Unfortunately, Brother Sisley left for Bolivia last night."

"What a pity. And when will Brother Sisley be back?"

"In two or three months. I can give you his address in La Paz if you want."

I told him I did want it just to see what he'd do. The reverend disappeared into his office and came back empty-handed a few minutes later.

"That's funny." He scratched his neck. "I was positive I had the address. I must have mislaid it. If I find it, I'll definitely send it to you." And he made a show of rereading my card. "I see you've come all the way from Syracuse." He tsk-tsked. "Such a long drive for a fruitless errand. Perhaps you'd like to share a meal with us before you leave. It's the least I can do."

"Thanks, but I'll pick up something on the way home."

The reverend waved his hand around. "I'm sorry I couldn't

be more help. I wish you success in your venture. Please feel free to walk around. And I hope you'll return another time and avail yourself of our facilities."

"You can count on it," I replied.

"Good." Looking at him as he put his hands in the sleeves of his robe and strolled away, the word smarmy came to mind.

By the time I left, the couple that had been walking on the shore was sitting on the jetty, dangling their feet in the water. I sat outside for about half an hour on the off chance that Humphrey would show up. When she didn't, I got into my car and drove away. I didn't believe what Sinclair had told me. Not for an instant. But I was too conspicuous sitting there like that. I'd come back later.

I didn't believe Sinclair hadn't seen Pat Humphrey. I didn't believe that she hadn't been here, but there was no point in calling him a liar—at least not yet. A couple of miles later, while I was mulling over my options, I spotted a minimart by the side of the road, pulled over, put in twelve bucks' worth of gas, and went inside.

"Do you know this woman?" I asked the clerk behind the counter.

He tore his attention away from the television and focused on the picture I was holding out to him. His eyes lit up. "What's she done?"

"Nothing. I need to talk to her."

"Oh." His shoulders slumped. He frowned. "I thought it would be something interesting. Like she killed someone and chopped 'em up."

"Maybe next week. So you have seen her."

He scratched one of the pimples on his face. "What will you give me if I tell you?"

I did my best tough-guy impersonation. "I'll let you live."

The kid snickered. "Seriously."

It was nice to know I couldn't even intimidate a seventeen-year-old boy. "Here." I dug in my pocket and took out a wadded-up ten-dollar bill and threw it on the counter. "This is all the cash I have."

"What do you live on? Food stamps?"

"If you feel that way . . ." And I reached over to take it back.

"That's all right." The kid smoothed the bill out and put it in his pocket. "She was here about three hours ago. She bought some gas and a couple of chocolate bars."

"She didn't happen to say where she was going?"

"Nope. Just gave me her money."

"Do you know where she's staying?"

"Yeah. With that loony up the road."

"The Reverend Ascending Moon?"

"Ascending Moon my ass. My ass. Get it?" The kid cackled and slapped the counter. "I don't know. Sometimes I just crack myself up."

I took a piece of bubblegum out of the box on the counter, unwrapped it, and popped it in my mouth.

"Hey, what about the gas?" the kid yelled as I walked out the store.

"Deduct it from the ten I gave you."

"You owe me twelve."

"Oops." And I got in my car and went back to the center.

A group of five men and women were doing tai chi under the evening shade of a maple tree, while another woman was looking at the river through a pair of binoculars.

The lobby of the lodge was empty when I walked inside, although I heard voices. I followed the sounds into the dining room. Ten people were sitting at two round tables in the small wood-paneled room. I stood at the entrance for a few seconds and watched them pick at the mass of brown-colored food on their plates. Then I went inside and showed them all Humphrey's picture. No one in the group had seen her.

"We just got here a little while ago," one of the men explained.

Before I could ask him anything else, Sinclair appeared at my elbow. "You've come back, I see."

I wondered if the smile he was wearing would fool his guests. "I already told you I need to talk to Pat Humphrey."

Sinclair's smile grew till it threatened to split his face. "You can see she's not here."

I allowed him to take me by the arm and steer me back into the lobby. "The kid that works at the minimart said she was."

Sinclair started laughing and ended up snorting instead. "You're taking his word against mine?"

"Yes, I am. Maybe I should start knocking on the cabin doors."

"You can't do that," Sinclair protested. "I won't have you disturbing my guests any more than you already have."

"Call the cops."

Sinclair wrung his hands. "This is a place of peace."

"I need to speak to Pat Humphrey."

"And I'm telling you she's not here."

"And I'm telling you I don't believe you."

"Please." Sinclair came around the counter and touched my shoulder. "Let's go into my office and talk this out."

As he spoke to me, his eyes flickered out toward the lake and back and then toward the lake and back again. It was a slight movement—it couldn't have taken more than twenty seconds—but it was enough. I turned my head and followed his glance. At first, all I saw was one of the motorboats that had been tied up putt-putting away from the dock. Two figures were sitting in it. They both had hats on. They were both dressed in khakis and short-sleeved white shirts. One was thinner than the other. I couldn't see their faces because the setting sun was reflecting off the water in a way that obscured my vision, but from the look on Sinclair's face, I had a pretty good idea who one of those figures was.

I cursed under my breath and ran out of the lodge.

"Wait. Come back." Sinclair's voice floated behind me as I

sped down the lawn toward the woman standing on the shore, gazing at the sunset through her binoculars.

"I need those for a second," I told her as I wrenched them out of her hands.

"What are you doing?" she cried.

"I'll give them right back," I promised as I focused in on the two figures in the boat.

I felt something hard prod me in the ribs and heard Sinclair's voice say, "Do it now."

Chapter Seventeen

I whirled around. Sinclair was holding a bolt-action rifle. The woman grabbed the binoculars back from me and scurried away, pausing every now and then to look over her shoulder. Probably to make sure I wasn't coming after her. In a short while, she disappeared into the lodge.

"I don't know who sent you, and I don't care," he said. "What I do know is that you're upsetting people, and I can't have that."

I gestured toward the weapon. "That's not very peaceful of you."

"Sometimes peace needs to be protected." Sinclair took a couple of steps back, but he was still aiming his rifle right at my midsection. "I want you to get in your car and drive out of here. And I don't want you coming back."

The boat I'd been watching was moving on the water now at a good clip. It dodged another motorboat, then headed into the open waterway. I wondered where the hell Humphrey was going.

"First tell me where Pat Humphrey is heading and I will."

"I don't think you're in a position to insist on anything," Sinclair said, emphasizing his point by jabbing me in the ribs with the barrel of his rifle again.

That was his mistake.

First Geoff had pointed his Glock at me, and now here

was Sinclair with his rifle doing the same thing. On another day I might have been scared, on another day I might have left. But not today. Today I was pissed. Sometimes there are definite advantages to being in a really bad mood.

"Don't you know you're not supposed to poke people with that," I snapped. "That's for shooting deer."

Then, before Sinclair knew what was happening, I'd grabbed the barrel of the rifle and wrenched it out of his hands. Sinclair's jaw went slack with surprise as I aimed the weapon at him.

"How do you like it?"

He put his hands in the air palms out and began backing away. "Please don't shoot me," he pleaded.

"Don't worry. Not that I wouldn't like to, but you're not worth serving jail time for," I told him. Then I turned and started for the lake.

"What are you doing?" he cried as I flung the rifle as far away from the shore as I could manage.

"My own weapon-management program." I watched it sink below the waves. "This way no one gets hurt." In the mood I was in, I was afraid I might plug him if I had the chance.

When I turned back, Sinclair looked as if he were going to cry. He rubbed his hands across his chest. "Do you know how much that cost?"

"I thought Wal-Mart sold those things pretty cheap."

He flushed. "You had no right to do that. None. I have to be able to defend my property."

"Against what? Marauding squirrels?"

Sinclair drew himself up. "I will protect my clients' right to privacy to the death."

"Oh, please. Now where did Pat Humphrey go?"

He took a deep breath and shrugged. "I didn't even know she was in that boat. You were the one looking through the glasses, not me."

Talking with him was pointless. I started back up the grass, with Sinclair tagging along besides me. His skullcap kept slipping off his head, and he kept pushing it back on. Finally, he gave up, took it off, and put it in his pocket.

"Try bobby pins," I told him. "It works for the Orthodox Jews." When I got about twenty feet away from the lodge, I stopped and studied the area.

"You have to go," Sinclair yammered in my ear. "If you don't go, I will be forced to call the police."

I ignored him and concentrated on trying to figure out where Pat Humphrey had been staying. There were only two possibilities. The lodge or the cabins. But the lodge had only one entrance, which ruled that out, because Pat Humphrey would have had to have gone by me when she left and she hadn't. I checked the outside of the building just to make sure I hadn't overlooked an exit, then went inside.

"What are you doing?" Sinclair squeaked as I walked behind the counter and pulled the sign-in book toward me.

"What does it look like I'm doing?" I said as I quickly ran my finger down the pages.

Apparently the Center for Enlightened Self-Awareness hadn't caught on with the holiday crowd yet. Not many people had registered over the past month, and Pat Humphrey wasn't one of the people that had—or if she had, she hadn't done it under her own name. There was only one other thing I could think of to do: look in the cabins. Which meant I needed the passkey, because Sinclair was not about to help me. I scanned the area around the counter. It wasn't there. It wasn't by the mailboxes, either.

"Come out from there." Sinclair slapped the counter. "Come out this instant. You're not allowed. That's for employees only."

"Pretend I am." The damned thing had to be here somewhere. And then I spotted it hanging on a hook over where the telephone was.

"Leave that key alone," Sinclair cried as he reached over the counter and tried to grab it.

But I was faster. I got it first. Sinclair straightened up and dabbed at the beads of perspiration covering his forehead with the sleeve of his robe while I clenched the key in my hand.

I came out from behind the desk. "Tell me which cabin Pat Humphrey is staying in and I won't go into the others."

"But she isn't here," Sinclair wailed.

"Okay. Wrong tense. Was here. Fine," I told Sinclair when he didn't answer. "If that's the way you want it." I walked out the door and strode across the lawn. Sinclair, holding his robes up to mid-calf, dogged my steps.

"And even if she was, what difference could it possibly make," a panting Sinclair demanded.

I skirted a tree stump. "I don't know. Maybe it's not going to make any, but as long as I'm here, I'd like to see for myself."

"You mean you're going to go through all of these cabins?" Sinclair said as I knocked on the first one.

"That's the general idea."

I waited for a response. When there wasn't any, I knocked again. A moment after that, I opened the door and went inside. The first thing I noticed was the musty smell, the same smell as the cabins in which I'd stayed in the Catskills when I was a kid.

"You should open a window and air this place out," I said as I looked around.

The room was large. The furnishings consisted of matching made-up twin beds, two nightstands, an oval-shaped rag rug, two white dressers, and an old chair in the corner. The place looked untenanted, but I checked the closet and the dresser drawers to make sure. They were empty. I walked into the bathroom and peered into the medicine chest. Those shelves were empty, too.

"See," Sinclair cried triumphantly as I closed the door to cabin one and went on to cabin two. "What did I tell you? You're just wasting your time."

"Let me be the judge of that."

But that was vacant as well. So was cabin number three.

"How long are you going to do this for?" Sinclair demanded of me while I trudged toward the fourth cabin.

"Until I find what I'm looking for."

"The woman in here is sick," Sinclair said when I reached it. "She's resting, and I won't have her disturbed."

"I think I'll let her tell me that."

He stepped in front of me and spread his arms out, attempting to bar my way. "She's under a doctor's care."

"Really?" I went around him.

"Yes, really." Sinclair's voice rose.

"If she's that ill, why isn't she in a hospital?"

He grabbed my arm. "Her emotional state is extremely fragile. Are you prepared to take responsibility for precipitating a crisis?"

I shook him off. "Absolutely. I've done worse." By now I was about five inches away from the door.

"At least let me go in and prepare her."

"I don't think so."

He went for my arm again. This time he knocked the passkey to the ground. I ignored it.

"Wait," he said as I rapped on the door.

"Who is it?" a woman asked.

A moment later, Amy stepped outside.

Chapter Eighteen

A my froze when she saw me. She was wearing a white robe and a pendant similar to the one Sinclair had on. Her dark hair looked as if it needed to be brushed, and her eye makeup was half rubbed off.

"Well, well, well," I said. "What a pleasant surprise seeing you here."

"I tried to keep her away," Sinclair told her.

Amy moved her hand away from the doorknob and managed a slight smile. "It's all right. No harm done."

"I take it you're a member of this particular establishment?"

Amy flushed. "What if I am?"

"Nothing. I was just thinking about how pleased your mother will be."

"My spiritual life is none of my mother's business."

"In this case, given the circumstances, I think I'm going to have to disagree."

Amy shrugged. "Then tell her. I don't care. In fact, I want you to. I insist on it." She began raking her fingers through her hair. "You know, I feel sorry for her."

"And why's that?"

"Because she has no connection with anything other than her own base needs. None of my family does."

"Maybe that's a good thing."

Sinclair broke in. "Sister Uma. I was telling Robin you were sick. That you needed your rest."

"Sister Uma?" I raised an eyebrow.

Amy drew herself up and grasped her medallion in her right hand. "It's Hindi," she informed me. "It's my chosen name. It means Blessed. It comes from Genesis in the Bible." And she closed her eyes and recited, " '*I will bless her, and she shall be a mother of nations: kings of peoples shall come from her.*' "

Looking at Amy, I decided if she were God's idea of blessed, I'd take another road.

"I'd still come here even if the center didn't exist." Amy indicated the area. "I love it here. I always have. The colors. The smells. The sounds of the water and the wind. The cows in the fields. I used to dream about them when I was a little girl." Amy straightened her shoulders. "Coming here for me is like going to *sessin*. The Reverend Ascending Moon helps me focus," she said. "He helps me center myself."

"You mean you're off-kilter?"

Amy glowered at me. "You can make fun if you want, but it just shows how closed off to new thoughts and feelings you are. They threaten you."

"Have you thought that the reason I'm speaking to you this way is because I'm tired of being lied to."

Amy took a deep breath. "There is truth in everything."

"Really? How profound. Do you know that the Reverend Ascending Moon, as you call him, is Paul Sinclair, a two-bit petty crook from Buffalo."

Amy ran a hand up and down the chain of her pendant. "I know all about the reverend's past history. It's irrelevant. People change. People evolve. You have to allow for that possibility."

"Fine. Tell me where Pat Humphrey evolved to and I'll leave."

"I don't know," she whispered.

"Can't you see how upset Sister is?" Sinclair demanded of me.

I ignored him. "You do know what happened at the estate?"

"I know," Amy whispered.

"I'd think you'd want to be there lending your mother moral support."

Amy picked a strand of dark thread off her robe. "She doesn't need me."

"Are you sure?"

She looked down at the floor.

"But she needs Pat Humphrey, right? Is that why you're not going to tell me where she is?"

Amy remained silent.

"Did you also know that your brother might be in trouble? That he might be charged? That Pat Humphrey might have information relevant to Shana Driscoll's death?"

"I want to lie down," Amy said.

"When we're done."

"Can't you leave me alone," she wailed. "We didn't talk. I swear I didn't even know she was here." She dissolved in a puddle of tears, but I was unmoved. I had the feeling she was one of those women that started crying the moment she didn't like how things were going.

I pushed by her and went inside the cabin. The odor of sandalwood hung in the air.

"Hey," Amy cried as I walked inside. "You can't come in here. What are you doing?"

"Checking things out." I scrutinized the room. There were two beds. Both were unmade.

"I'm sick," Amy said sullenly. "I need rest."

"So Sinclair told me."

It suddenly occurred to me that he wasn't there anymore. I wondered if he really had gone to call the police. Hopefully, I'd be out of here before they arrived.

Amy shook her head. She watched me as I walked over to the nearest bed, picked up a bright red shirt that was on it, and held it up to the light, then dropped it back down. It was too big to be Pat Humphrey's. I glanced at the clothes lying on the other bed. Small-sized linen pants. A silk T-shirt. A silk bathrobe.

"Who's your roommate?" I asked Amy.

"Those are my clothes."

I held the pants up. "No they're not."

She flushed again and began fiddling with her pendant. I dropped the pants back on the bed and walked over to the closet and looked inside. Three white robes, just like the one Amy was wearing, were hanging on the steel rod, along with a selection of slacks and blouses. My glance traveled downward to a suitcase lying on the floor.

"That's mine," Amy said, moving toward me.

I bent down and read the tag before she could take it away. "You always travel with Pat Humphrey's suitcase?"

"She lent it to me a while ago."

I just stared at Amy. She bit her lip and stared back at me. By now she was breathing hard, but I couldn't tell if it was from anger or exertion.

"Has it ever occurred to you," she said, "that Pat Humphrey doesn't want my mother to find her."

I remained silent.

"Don't tell her," Amy begged. "Please."

"Why not?"

"Pat has her reasons."

"You were the one in the boat with her, weren't you?" I intuited.

Amy blanched.

"Where did she go?"

"I wasn't with her."

"You're lying."

"That's enough."

I turned around. Sinclair was standing by the door. He had a nasty smile on his face and two unsmiling, powerful-looking men flanking him. Somehow they didn't look like members of his congregation. I think I would have preferred seeing the police.

"These two gentlemen will escort you off the premises," Sinclair announced.

"Gentlemen? Now there's a misnomer if I ever heard one."

"Be quiet."

"Where'd you get them from?" I asked.

Sinclair folded his hands together in an attitude of prayer. "I think there have been enough questions asked here for one night."

"And if I don't agree?"

"I said that's enough," he yelled.

Amy cringed at the loud noise. He went over and stroked her arm.

"I'm sorry, my dear," he said. "I didn't mean to scare you."

"That's touching."

He pointed at me. "Get her outside. Now."

One of the men took one arm, the other took the other, and they marched me out of the room. Sinclair joined them a moment later.

"It must be tough having to keep that sensitive front up all the time," I said.

Sinclair came up till he was about two inches in front of me. "Just be glad I don't beat up women," he hissed. "Unlike the person who did that." He pointed to my jaw. "Though if I see you again, I'll make an exception to that rule. Do you understand what I'm telling you?"

"Absolutely. You couldn't be clearer."

"Good." He turned to the two men. "Make sure she leaves the area."

"So you guys trying to find inner peace, too?" I asked both of them as they escorted me to the parking lot. "Or are you here for the fishing?"

They could have been deaf for all the response I got. They walked me to my vehicle and stood there, arms crossed, while I got in.

I waved to them as I hit the accelerator. " 'Bye, assholes."

The bigger one growled and started toward me. But it was too late. I was already in motion.

"Next time, guys." And I gave the car more gas.

It was probably the letdown, but all of a sudden I realized I was ravenous. My stomach was rumbling. I drove into the first rest stop I came to after I got off Wolfe Island, bought two Big Macs, a Coke, and a large order of fries, and called the Taylor estate. Moss Ryan got on the line. He sounded tired and edgy.

"It's late to be calling here," he said to me.

I licked the ketchup off my fingers. "Don't you ever go home, or have you taken up permanent residence?"

"Of course not," Ryan snapped. "I'm just staying here till things calm down. Rose can't handle all of this by herself."

"Where's Geoff?"

"With Rose. She's very upset by everything that's happened."

"I can't understand why."

"Do you have anything to tell me or not?" Ryan said impatiently. "Because if you don't . . ."

"Actually I do." And I told him about my evening's adventures.

There was a brief pause on the other end of the line, and then he said, "I can't believe you lost her."

"Hey, you think someone else can do better, be my guest and go hire them."

"No. I want you to go back and see if she's still there."

"Now?"

"Tomorrow."

I guess I should have been politer to the two gentlemen in Sinclair's employ. Either that or come back armed. "And if she is?"

"Call me."

"And then what?"

"We'll take it from there."

"And if she's not?"

"Then you're to keep looking."

I finished off the last five French fries and unwrapped the second Big Mac. "Are you sure Rose will agree to this?"

"Absolutely positive."

"Maybe I should talk to her."

I could hear his sigh of exasperation. "You can call her tomorrow morning if you want. No earlier than ten, though."

"Why can't I speak to her tonight?"

"Because she's already taken her sleeping pill for the evening."

"I see."

"What's that supposed to mean?" Moss Ryan demanded.

"Nothing."

"I'm sorry," he said. "It's just been a zoo around here."

"I can imagine."

"And it's only going to get worse."

That I could believe.

Chapter Nineteen

A t seven o'clock the next morning, I got a call from Pat Humphrey. I'd been in a deep sleep, the kind you have to claw your way out of when the phone rang.

"I hear you've been looking for me," Pat Humphrey said. "What do you want?"

I sat bolt upright. The phone started to slip through my sweat-slicked fingers. I caught it just before it hit the bed.

"Who told you?" My voice was thick with sleep. I shook my head to clear it and tried to focus.

"Amy. Tell me what's going on."

"Rose was worried about you."

"She shouldn't have been."

"Well, she was." A sparrow lit on my windowsill. We stared at each other for a few seconds before it flew off. "It looked as if you'd disappeared."

"I was helping my neighbor with an emergency."

"But the hose and the door," I protested.

"Her ten-year-old was supposed to take care of that. He forgot."

I wondered what the emergency was as a narrow band of sunlight moved across the floor and onto the fluttering shade in the window across from my bed, but she didn't tell, and I didn't ask. "She wants to see you."

"She will. I just need some time to myself. I understand you found my pendant."

I moved my legs over the side of the bed and reached for a cigarette. "You stay fully informed."

"I try to."

"Louis has it."

"Louis is a thief."

"Why don't you call the police?"

"I might, although I think he's in enough trouble at the moment, don't you?"

I found my lighter. The flame flared up when I clicked it, and I moved back. I tried again. This time I succeeded. "You know that message you left on my machine the other day, the thing about blood and the dark? Well, don't do that anymore."

"Why not?"

"Because I don't like it."

"You should be grateful."

"Stick to your paying clientele."

"You know, Murphy has things he'd like to say to you."

"Can the crap and stick to your animals. If I want to hear from my dead husband, I'll consult a friggin' Ouija board." And I slammed the phone down without trying to find out where Pat Humphrey was staying. Which was not good, since that's what I was being paid to do. The woman was making me crazy.

I tried redialing, but this time star 69 didn't work.

I finished my cigarette while Zsa Zsa watched me disapprovingly.

"Yes, I know I shouldn't be smoking this early," I told her. I put it out, hopped in the shower, threw on some clothes, and raced over to Pat Humphrey's house.

I wanted to make sure she hadn't been calling me from there. But if she had, I was too late. She'd already come and gone. The breakfast dishes on the table in the backyard had been cleared off. The doors were locked. Her mailbox was empty, and there was no paper on her stoop. I spoke to the neighbors. One of them had seen her leave. She'd just waved at him as she'd driven by, but he had no idea where she was going.

I rang up the Taylor house on my way to the store. Moss Ryan got on the phone, and I told him about my early-morning phone call.

"Find her," he told me. "Find her now."

I pressed the OFF button. It was a little after nine in the morning, and I felt as if I'd been up for hours. The day was already hot. Flowers drooped and people watered scraggly lawns as I listened to the announcer on the radio predicting it was going to go into the nineties. I felt as if someone had hooked me up to a vacuum cleaner and sucked all the energy out of me. I stopped at a minimart on my way to work and got a large Coke to go, but it didn't help much.

I was still wondering why Pat Humphrey had called when George came through the door of Noah's Ark carrying a take-out bag and two coffees. As I watched him approach, I realized that one of the things I loved about him was that he fed me.

George plunked the bag down on the counter. "I thought this would make a change from your chocolate-doughnut diet," he announced as he took the coffees out of their cardboard holder and unloaded three types of bagels, cream cheese, juice, and the morning edition of the local paper.

"Thanks." I grabbed a bagel and cut it in half as George looked over the news.

"Hello." He whistled. "Here we go." He took out the Metro section and folded it, indicating a two-column story, tucked below the fold, headlined: *"Fatality in Cazenovia,"* and handed it to me.

I emptied three packets of sugar into my coffee and stirred. "It's not getting much play," I observed. Stories placed under the fold in newspapers are traditionally deemed less important than those above the fold.

"Maybe not, but it's still in." George took a bite of his bagel. "Even Rose Taylor couldn't keep it out."

"True." I spread some cream cheese on mine and wondered what people down in New York City would have to say about the bagel I was eating—banana orange. When I was growing up, bagels came plain or with onion, garlic, or poppy. Now they're at least double the size and come with everything from sun-dried tomatoes to chocolate chips. Sometimes, I decided as I settled down to read the story, choice is not a good thing.

According to the piece in the paper, *"Shana Driscoll, an employee of well-known philanthropist Mrs. Rose Taylor, was found floating in the pool on the Taylor estate by Mrs. Taylor's husband and a guest. When attempts at resuscitation failed, Mr. Moss Ryan, prominent lawyer and family friend, called 911. Police are investigating the possibility of foul play."*

"I'm a guest?" I said to George.

The police sure hadn't treated me like one when they'd arrived at the scene. From the way they'd carried on, I'd expected to be marched down to the Public Safety Building and booked. Fortunately, it hadn't come to that, although I'd had to go down there again to give another statement.

He took another bite of his bagel. "Evidently."

"Possibility?"

"That's what it says."

I spread more cream cheese on my bagel and added some jam. "So reading between the lines, what they're saying here is that the police think someone fed Shana Driscoll a large quantity of alcohol and then proceeded to hold her under."

George broke off a piece of his bagel and gave it to Zsa Zsa. "That would appear to be the case."

I thought back. "I didn't see marks around her throat; in fact, I didn't see any bruises on her at all, but there wouldn't have been if someone pushed her in and held her head underwater. It probably wouldn't have taken all that much strength to do, either."

"Not if she were drunk enough."

I visualized the two whiskey-filled glasses I'd seen sitting on the coffee table at the cottage and the half-empty bottle of Jamieson's on the arm of the chair out by the pool. The scene wasn't hard to read. She and her killer had started drinking in her cottage and then continued out at the pool. Then her killer had suggested they go for a quick swim—and bye-bye Shana.

"Whoever killed her was definitely someone she felt comfortable with. Otherwise she wouldn't have let them into her house," I reflected.

George removed the lid from his cup of coffee and tossed it into the trash. "I've always said that stranger danger is an overrated concept."

I picked a strand of lint off my linen skirt and decided I should have sent it out to have it ironed instead of taking it directly out of the dryer and putting it on. That way maybe I wouldn't look like an unmade bed. "How high do you figure her blood-alcohol level had to be?"

"High." George fed Zsa Zsa another piece of his breakfast.

I studied my dog, who, having gobbled down George's last handout, was prancing around his feet in the hopes of getting more. "She is getting really fat."

"Spheroid. Maybe you should consider feeding her—dare I say the word?—dog food."

"Dog food?" I laughed. "No, I don't think she'd appreciate that too much. Maybe I'll just feed her less." I lit a cigarette, took a puff, then reached for my coffee.

I told George about the reception I'd gotten at Sinclair's.

"It's amazing how many of these cult places have men with guns hanging around them," he observed as his glance strayed down to the picture tacked up on my cash register.

I explained about Raul and the picture.

"I didn't think people died from TB anymore."

"They do if it's not treated." And I made a mental note to go down and get a TB test.

George snorted. "And you're really going to try to find this woman?"

"If I can."

"Why?"

"I suppose because I would want someone to do the same thing for me." And I changed the subject. "You want to take a boat ride with Zsa Zsa and me?"

"Where?"

"Around Wolfe Island, of course."

I readjusted my baseball hat against the sun, rubbed some more suntan lotion on my arms and shoulders, and thought about how nice being on the water was. As I listened to Zsa Zsa bark at a water-skier whizzing by, I watched a seagull diving for something below the water's surface. The wake from a passing boat set ours rocking. I took two Sam Adams beers out of the Styrofoam cooler sitting next to my legs and passed one of them over to George.

"Thanks," he said, lowering the binoculars. He twisted off the cap and took a swig. "I should get one of these," he mused aloud, referring to the twelve-foot fiberglass runabout we'd rented from the marina down the way. "Maybe even get something a little larger. They're not that expensive. I could winter it over in my garage, then dock it on Ontario in the summer. I always wanted one."

I grunted and stretched my legs out. "Anything yet?"

"Just some people doing tai chi over by the trees."

"See Sinclair?"

"Nope. No Sinclair. No Amy. No Pat Humphrey. No anyone you're interested in seeing."

I was betting that Pat Humphrey had come back to the center, that she hadn't left the area after her phone call to me, but the only way to find that out was to wait and watch. If she had skipped out, I reflected gloomily, finding her was going to be a bitch. Unless, of course, I could get Amy to talk.

"Here." George handed me the binoculars. "Your turn."

Our vantage point of about thirty yards out on the river gave us an unobstructed view of the main lodge of the Center for Enlightened Self-Awareness, eight of the cabins, the lawn, about one-quarter of the parking lot, and all of the shore and the jetty. We'd been playing at spying for a little over an hour.

We'd kill the engine and bob around for twenty minutes or so, then start her up, ride around for another ten minutes, and come back again. This was in case anyone was watching from the shore. I didn't think anyone was. But George believed in being careful. At least that's what he said, although I thought that his being careful had more to do with taking the runabout for a spin than with anything else.

So far, the only things we'd seen were a middle-aged couple walking by the shore, a couple of dogs wading in the water, a man throwing a fishing line off the jetty, and the aforementioned group of tai chiers. Not that I minded. We had a cooler filled with beer and tomato-and-cheese sandwiches. There was a nice breeze blowing off the river, and the late-afternoon sun felt pleasantly warm on my shoulders and back. I even caught the scent of the sea in the air. I put my toes in the water, wiggled them, and watched the ripples lapping against my toes.

"You know," I said to George as I scanned the center with my binoculars, "I could do this all day." Actually, we were going to do this until it got dark—four and a half hours away.

"It certainly beats sitting in a car."

I rested the binoculars on the seat next to me and rubbed some more suntan lotion on my shoulders.

"You should invest in some of that high-tech surveillance equipment."

"I like being low-tech."

"I know you do." George paused for another swallow of his beer. "But the world's becoming a high-tech place."

"You think I'm not aware of that?"

"Even a Luddite like you has got to move with the times."

"I will." I leaned over and watched the ripples in the opaque water and studied the way the color shifted from lighter to darker green. Then I lifted my head up toward the sun and closed my eyes. "But not today."

* * *

George and I stayed on the water for the next three hours. It was getting cooler. I rubbed my arms and wished I'd brought a jacket along. The breeze had a definite chill to it now. Or maybe it was just my sunburn that was making the wind feel that way.

"What's Manuel up to these days?" George suddenly asked.

"Why?" George didn't approve of him, thought it was wrong of me to have given him the key to my house.

He shrugged. "Just making conversation."

"He's checking out Louis's girlfriend for me."

"What's she got to do with anything?"

"I don't know. She's just popped up in too many places recently."

"Just like my ex-wife," George muttered.

I waited for him to say more, but he didn't, and I didn't ask. His ex-wife was one of those out-of-bound topics of which we had far too many. The river had grown quieter in the last hour. Lacy patches of fog drifted up from the water, obscuring vision. Most of the boats had gone in for the evening. Soon we'd have to go in as well.

George yawned. The sun and the water, not to mention the beer, had made us both sleepy. "How about we give it twenty more minutes and then call it a night?"

"Fine." It would be too dark to see anything soon, anyway.

He pointed at the sky. "Look at those clouds."

I nodded. I'd been watching them for the last ten minutes. They were black and moving in from the west at a rapid clip. "The weather report didn't say anything about rain."

"It looks as if it's coming, anyway."

There was a clap of thunder far off in the distance. Zsa Zsa whined. She didn't like storms. If we were home, she'd be hiding in the closet.

"We'd better head for the marina," George said.

"Wait a minute." I held up my hand as I watched a figure make its way down to the shore. "I think that's Sinclair."

George cursed under his breath. "Are you sure?"

I held out the binoculars. "See for yourself."

"I believe you. What's he doing?"

"Nothing at the moment."

Sinclair had come down to the water's edge. He had his skullcap back on. His robe was moving in the breeze that had suddenly sprung up. He stared straight out. For a moment I shrank back, thinking he was looking at us, but then I realized he was looking at the yacht that was passing by. We bounced around in its wake.

George held out his hand. "It's starting to rain."

"I know." I could feel the drops on my nose and cheeks. "Come on, Pat," I murmured, willing her to appear. "Don't make me have to run all over God's creation looking for you."

"Why doesn't Sinclair go inside?" George demanded.

It started to pour.

Sheets of wind-driven rain swept across the water. I blinked the water out of my eyes. Then, suddenly, we had the answer to George's question. Pat Humphrey appeared as if I'd conjured her up.

"Now this is interesting," I said.

George grunted.

"You don't think so?"

"I think I'd like to get out of the rain."

My eyes were glued to Pat Humphrey as she walked down from the lodge. Her head was bare, but she was wearing a long dark raincoat. Underneath it I got glimpses of a white shirt and skirt that stood out like a beacon in the dim light. As if sensing her presence, Sinclair faced in her direction and held out his arms. They embraced, and then they kissed. His hands were all over her body.

"They're a good pair," George observed.

"They certainly have a commonality of interests."

Zsa Zsa rubbed the side of her muzzle against my leg. I reached down with my free hand and stroked her while I watched Sinclair and Humphrey. They kissed for a long time.

"Whatever happened to motel rooms?" George asked.

"Maybe they're economizing."

"At last," he said as Sinclair turned and started back up the path to the lodge. "It must be fun walking in those wet robes."

Pat Humphrey was still standing by the water's edge. She knelt, picked up a handful of stones, and began tossing them, one at a time into the river.

"What the hell is she waiting for?" George demanded.

"You got me."

By now the chop was getting really bad. I could feel my stomach turning queasy, so I was relieved when she turned and started up the way Sinclair had come. "Let's get out of here."

"Good," George said. "I could use a drink."

"Two," I said. I reached for my cigarettes, but they were soaked, too.

A few seconds later, we heard the crack of a rifle shot.

Chapter Twenty

It's funny how you experience things when you're not expecting them.

How sometimes you think they're something else.

For one split second I'd thought that the crack I was hearing was the sound of a branch falling from one of the trees along the river. Or maybe I'd hoped that's what it was, because I knew better even before George had yanked me down off my seat.

A dull pain ran up the middle of one of my thighs as my knees hit the floor. I rubbed the spot above my elbow where George had grabbed me and cursed under my breath. I could almost feel the bruises forming.

"You want to get shot?" he hissed, pointing to the hole near the hull of the boat.

The bullet had entered about three inches from where I was sitting.

Close enough.

I'd been shot before. I squeezed my eyes shut for a second and took a deep breath to steady myself and tried not to think of the shattered muscle and bone. Of pain. Of the time shut away in a hospital bed. Of the gratitude at just being outside in the fresh air.

I indicated the hole. "I wonder if the rental place is going to make us pay for this."

"Maybe if we ask the shooter nicely, he will."

"Maybe."

The water streaming off George's face outlined and highlighted its contours. His eyes stood out bright with anger. I raised my head above the side of the boat and surveyed the shore. The fog coming off the water, combined with the rain, reduced everything to varying shades of gray. Water and sky looked the same.

"I don't see anyone. Maybe they left."

George snorted. "I wish I'd brought my weapon." He had a nine millimeter that he kept in a lockbox in his bedroom.

"I wish I'd brought my cell phone."

"I wish we were on land."

I thought about the rifle I'd grabbed out of Sinclair's hands yesterday. I shouldn't have thrown it in the lake. I should have shot the bastard when I'd had the chance. Now it was too late. I tried to picture him or one of his goons standing behind a tree, the gun heavy in his hand, intent on the sound of our voices or the waves slapping on the boat's hull. He'd lift his weapon and pull the trigger, the revolver bucking in his hand, a smile of satisfaction on his face. Somehow, though, I couldn't put Sinclair's face on the shooter. It wouldn't stick.

I wiped the rain out of my eyes and pulled the brim of my hat farther down on my head, but it didn't keep the water off my face. The drops ran down my cheeks and soaked my shoulders. It felt as if I were submerged in a watery grave.

The wind picked up, sweeping a curtain of water across the river, blowing it into George's face. He hunched down, reached over, and pulled the starter. The motor coughed and died.

"Fuck." George tried again. This time nothing happened. He brought his foot back and kicked it.

"That's going to help."

The boat dipped alarmingly low to the water as George swiveled to face me. "You have another suggestion?"

But before I could make it there was another crack. We

threw ourselves onto the boat's floor. Little slivers of metal peppered my face like bee stings as the bullet ripped through the boat hull. How far could bullets go underwater, anyway? I tried to remember. Fifty feet? Half a mile? Less? More? Above me I could hear George's litany of curses rising and falling, intertwined with Zsa Zsa's whining.

After a minute, I raised my head. By now the runabout was rocking back and forth, and water was sloshing in over the sides. Zsa Zsa tiptoed around the edge of the boat, trying to avoid getting her paws wet in the puddles that were forming. I touched my cheek. My fingers came away wet, but I didn't know if they were wet with rain or blood.

George took my face in his hands and studied it. "You just got scratched. You'll be fine. But the shooter wouldn't be. I can promise you that. He's going to wish his momma had never pushed him out into the light of day." He sounded angrier than I'd ever heard him. Then he turned back to the engine.

I pulled the tendrils of hair that had plastered themselves across my cheek away and checked for the life jackets.

"See if there's a wrench in there, too," George said, his voice an echo on the wind.

I rifled through the compartment the life jackets were supposed to be in.

The first one was filled with rope, empty beer cans, and fast-food wrappers. The second one was stuffed with paint cans and brushes and rags that smelled of gasoline and turpentine.

"So far there's nothing here we can use."

"Well, keep looking. Maybe we'll get lucky. I don't know why I let you talk me into these things," George complained.

I raised my head. "These things, as you refer to them, was just going to be a nice day on the water. Which it was up until about fifteen minutes ago."

"Have you found anything yet?"

"Only this." I held up the ratty-looking life preserver I'd located in the third compartment. According to the notice pasted on the compartment door, the boat was supposed to have a minimum of six flotation devices.

"That's going to get us far," he observed, eyeing the duct tape on it.

"It's better than nothing."

"Barely. No wonder the rental was so cheap. When we get back to the marina, I am going to personally and cheerfully strangle the guy who rented us this piece of shit."

"At least it's floating."

"But not for long if this keeps up."

George was right. More water was coming in over the sides. Zsa Zsa whimpered and tried to sit on my lap. No sense, she probably thought, in everyone getting wet.

Another crack sounded.

We ducked down for the third time.

"I'm getting tired of this," George said. "Real tired."

After a couple of minutes, we poked our heads back up, and George went back to working on the engine.

It was dead.

I repositioned Zsa Zsa on my lap. "Maybe you should let me try."

"I'm almost there." George yanked on the string again. This time the engine spluttered. "See. She's coming." He pulled again. The engine coughed and died. He patted it. "Come on, baby," he coaxed. "You can do it, you know you can." George yanked the cord again. The motor roared to life. "That's it," George cried. "We're out of here."

But just as he opened the throttle up, a bolt of lightning flashed across the sky. For an instant everything went white. The smell of ozone filled my nostrils. The hair on my arms stood up.

"Jesus, that was close," I said.

Another bolt crackled above us, dazzling us with light.

George gestured upward. "It's time to go in. Unless, of course, the idea of becoming a French fry appeals to you."

"No. I've sworn off fried foods."

"I just hope that the shooter has gone home for the night."
And with that George turned the boat around and headed it
toward Sinclair's dock.

"So do I."

By now the runabout was bobbing up and down like the
proverbial cork in the ocean. The rain was coming down in
sheets. Zsa Zsa whimpered and wiggled under my legs as another crack of lightning exploded in the sky.

"Great," George said to me. "I don't get it. All summer it's
nice, there's no rain, and we have to be out on the water on
the one evening it storms."

We were a couple of inches from the dock when George
cut the throttle. I reached out to pull us in, but a wave
slapped us against the jetty. I pulled my hand back just as the
hull smashed into the wood. The thought that Sinclair would
not be pleased flashed through my mind as we rammed the
dock again. Somehow that made me feel better.

"I can't get up there to tie us down," I yelled as another
wave pulled us out toward the river.

By now we were about a foot away and traveling fast.
George tried to start the motor again, but it coughed and
spluttered and died. He pounded it with his fists. It didn't
help.

"We don't even have any oars," he said as he hunched
over the motor.

I watched the shoreline recede, come closer, and recede
again. Then suddenly there was a loud crunch.

"That doesn't sound good."

"No shit. We've hit something," George said at about the
same time I looked down to see what was knocking against
my legs.

It was the cooler floating around. Which was when I became aware that there was about six inches of water—though
it was difficult to gauge the exact amount in the dark—in the
boat.

"We have to get out of here," George yelled.

"We could bail."

"I don't think we can bail fast enough. How's your swimming these days?"

I wiped the rain out of my eyes. We weren't that far from shore. "Tolerable, and yours?"

"Good enough for this."

By now the water was over my shins, and the runabout was riding lower. "What about Zsa Zsa?"

"I'll take her. I bet she'll never go in another boat." And George grabbed the whimpering dog and plunged into the river.

I said a prayer and followed him. Considering the hot summer we'd been having, the water was colder than I expected. The shock of it took my breath away. I swallowed a mouthful of river, gagged, and began coughing.

George paddled toward me. Zsa Zsa was clutched to his chest. He grabbed the back of my T-shirt with his other hand. "Light, you're not going to drown on me, are you?"

I raised my head and struggled to get my breath back. "No." The buffeting waves made me feel as if I were in a churn. "I'll be fine."

"You sure?"

I treaded water while I got a bearing on the land. "Absolutely." It was easy to see how someone could panic and end up swimming the wrong way in the dark.

"Because I wouldn't want to be stuck with your damned dog."

"Won't happen," I assured him. "It's okay. You can let go of my shirt now. Really."

He did, reluctantly. "You go first and I'll follow."

I nodded and started doing the crawl toward the shore. As I swam, I tried to time it so I took a breath when I was on top of the wave, but every once in a while I'd miscalculate and swallow some more river and gag on it. I lost all sense of time. It seemed as if I were swimming forever. What had looked liked a short distance in the boat turned out to be a lot farther in the water.

I settled into a rhythm, switching from the crawl to the sidestroke and back again, stopping every once in a while to check and see that George and Zsa Zsa were still behind me. As each moment went by, my arms and legs seemed to grow heavier and heavier. By the time I crawled up on the shore and collapsed in the dirt, my legs were shaking from exertion. I felt as if I'd run a marathon.

Chapter Twenty-one

A moment later, George sprawled out beside me. Zsa Zsa jumped out of his arms, ran over and licked my face. I hugged her to me. She licked the corners of my mouth and my chin, then rubbed up against my shirt, trying to get some of the water off her coat. After that she snuggled up by my side. The three of us lay like that for I don't know how long, too spent to move or talk, the cold water having leached the warmth from our bodies. Even if someone had come up and tried to shoot us, I'm not sure I could have summoned up the energy to move.

Instead, I watched the lightning and listened to the thunder. The smell of wet dirt and vegetation and ozone lingered in the air, but the storm was moving off. The lightning was over the hill now, the time between the thunderclaps and the flashes longer. Over to the west I could see glimpses of the moon as the clouds scudded across it. The rain felt soft as it caressed my face. I listened to the wind whipping the branches of the trees back and forth. The friction of the leaves rubbing against each other sounded like sandpaper. And there was something else as well. Something higher.

I turned my head toward George. "I think I heard a moan."

"I didn't."

"There it is again." A picture of Pat Humphrey flashed

through my mind. In the excitement I'd forgotten about her. She'd been there at the edge of the shore, and then she disappeared. I pulled myself up. My legs felt as if they were made of rubber. My arms were still partially numb from the cold water. "I'm going to check it out."

"Don't be stupid. The shooter could still be out there."

"If he were, we'd be dead already."

"Come on, Light." George rested his hand on my calf.

"There. You mean you didn't hear that groan?"

George grunted and got up, but I was already on my way. Zsa Zsa circled my legs as I followed the sound. The smell of wet pine needles surrounded me. They scratched at my calves and ankles. I stepped over rocks. Pebbles embedded themselves in my feet. Somewhere along the way I realized I'd lost my shoes. I moved a branch that had been downed by the storm, and its sap stuck to my hands. I went around a large lilac bush that someone had planted as a specimen tree. Then I went around another one and stopped.

Pat Humphrey lay sprawled out on her stomach. The bullet had dropped her down where she'd stood. It had entered her back, rendering it a dark pulpy mixture of flesh and fabric. Here and there I caught a glimpse of something white and shiny, something that my mind shied away from identifying as her spine.

I swallowed down the bile rising in my throat and forced my eyes downward toward her skirt, which was plastered to her legs. Then my eyes rose again, unable to turn away from her. Her face, an oval slashed with the shadows her eyes and mouth created, was half-turned toward the right. Her lips were parted. Her eyes open. One arm was extended outward, as if she were pointing at something. She looked like a discarded rag doll, just as Raul had. She was still moaning, only the sounds were softer now, as if she were running down.

I went over and knelt down next to her. She looked at me and blinked. Her eyes were surprisingly calm, her face peaceful. Then she smiled. A trickle of blood ran down the side of her mouth. I wiped it away.

"It's funny. All that time at the gym and now I can't move anything."

"You'll be all right."

"No, I won't."

I started to get up. "I'll go call someone."

"Don't bother. Just stay with me."

I reached over and took her hand in mine. Her skin was cold and wet to the touch. I massaged it. "Is there anything I can do for you?"

She shook her head. "That stuff about Murphy," she whispered, her voice so low I could hardly hear it. "It was all a con. I'm sorry. Forgive me?"

"Of course. But how . . ."

". . . did I know?" She gave me a tiny smile. "The newspapers . . . I remember things . . . I always have . . . but the dark and the blood. That was real."

"Shh."

"I just didn't think it was about me." She started to cough. The cough turned into a gurgle. "That's the trouble with this kind of thing," she continued on when she could speak again. "I see things, but I never know what they're about."

"Who did this? Who shot you?"

"I . . ."

"Was it Sinclair?"

She said something, but I couldn't catch it.

"I'm sorry. Tell me again." And I put my ear to her mouth. She made a noise in her throat and died.

"What did she say?" George asked.

I jumped. I'd forgotten he was there. "I don't know. I couldn't hear."

"Did she say the shooter was Sinclair?"

"I just told you I don't know." I straightened out her skirt and reached over and shut her eyes and tucked her hair behind her ears.

"So it could have been."

I stood up. "I suppose."

"I want to talk to him."

"You're not on the force anymore. And even if you were . . ."

My voice trailed off. Looking down at Pat Humphrey, all I wanted to do was go home and have a drink. I could feel the comforting slide of the scotch down my throat, the expanding warmth in my limbs, hear the clink of the ice cubes as they went into the glass, and see the gold color.

"I know what I am. I just want to see Sinclair's face when we come through the door—that's all."

I should have argued. I knew that. I didn't like the look on George's face. But I didn't have the energy. So I just went along.

No one was at the lodge. There was a fire burning in the lodge fireplace, but the lobby itself was empty. I noticed we were tracking water and small clumps of mud across the polished floor.

"I wonder if they have a bar around here?" I mused aloud. The thought seemed very attractive.

George looked at me, opened his mouth to say something, and changed his mind.

"You got a problem with that?" I demanded.

"No. I think you might, though."

"Meaning?"

"Let's not do this now."

"Fine with me."

George massaged the back of his neck. "He's got to be here somewhere."

"What are you going to do when you find him?"

"Sinclair? Nothing. I already told you I'm just going to talk to him."

"You know . . ." I was starting to say when George made a shushing noise and put his finger to his lips.

I heard the voices, too. One was sobbing, and the other one was making soothing noises. The voice that was making soothing sounds was Sinclair's.

George looked at me, and I looked at him.

"Maybe we should call 911," I suggested again.

George clicked his tongue against the roof of his mouth.

"We're going to. Later." Then he looked at me. "Hey, if you don't want to do this, you don't have to go in with me. You can wait outside."

"I just don't want you to do anything stupid."

"I'm not going to do anything stupid. I just want to talk to the man. Nothing wrong with that, is there?"

"No," I said softly. "I guess not."

George grinned. It wasn't a nice sight. "It's the polite thing to do," he said as he headed to where the voices were coming from.

"I can't believe it," the woman was saying. "I just can't."

"It'll be all right," Sinclair replied. "Let me help you."

"No, it won't be. It won't be at all."

"You have to believe that it will."

"She said this would happen." The woman wailed. "She saw it. How could that be? I don't understand. I don't understand."

I couldn't hear what Sinclair said next, but it must have been something to the effect that the woman should calm down, because the next thing I heard her say was that she was all right. She'd be fine.

"You're obviously not," Sinclair replied.

By now we were almost in front of the office behind the front desk. The door was closed. George and I looked at each other. I knocked.

Sinclair opened the door half an inch. His eyes widened when he saw me. "I thought I told you not to come on this property anymore."

"She's really bad at listening," George said, flinging his weight against the door.

It flew open, and Sinclair went flying.

"Sorry to interrupt," I said as I stepped inside.

George followed.

Sinclair struggled to get up from the floor where he'd landed. Blood was running out of his nose. He touched it and winced. "Damn. I think it's broken," he announced in an unbelieving tone as he stood up. "You broke my nose."

Neither George nor I said anything. Our gazes were riveted on Amy.

Her eyes were swollen from crying.

Her skirt was hiked up to her thighs.

She had blood on her shirt and a gun in her hand.

"My, my," George said as Amy pointed the weapon at us. "What do we have here?"

Chapter Twenty-two

Amy's eyes darted from me to George to Sinclair and back to me again. With her free hand she tugged her skirt back into place.

"I can see religious life has its benefits," I said to Sinclair. "First Pat Humphrey and now her." I nodded in Amy's direction. "Not bad. Of course, the gun might be a little bit of a turnoff. Unless you're into that kind of thing. Are you?"

"What are you? Nuts?" Sinclair mumbled as he wiped blood away from his mouth with the back of his hand. "She came on to me. Not the other way around."

"It's not my fault," Amy said in a high, piping voice.

"Nothing ever is," Sinclair muttered to himself. "It's your family's."

"Of course it's not." I kept my voice low and soothing and my glance on the gun in Amy's hand.

"It's Hillary's. This whole thing happened because of her." Amy's breasts strained against the white shirt she was wearing as she gulped in air. The shirt was translucent from being wet, and her nipples were visible through the fabric. "I'm not taking the blame for my sister's mistakes. Not this time I won't."

"You're right. You shouldn't have to."

Amy used her free hand to wipe her eyes. "Don't you humor me." Her tone was fierce.

I put my hands up and inched closer. "I'm not trying to."

"Yes, you are. Everyone always does."

"What's not your fault?" George asked.

Amy spun around toward him. "Who is he?" she demanded as if she'd noticed George was in the room for the first time.

"He's a friend of mine."

"Why is he here?"

"I came along for the ride," George answered.

"Ride? What ride?"

"It's just an expression. Now, why don't you give me the gun?"

Amy glanced down at the automatic in her hand. She looked surprised to see she was holding it.

"Or," George continued, "if you don't want to do that, you can put it down on the desk."

"That's right," Sinclair cooed. "Give it to us."

Amy took a step back. "It's not mine."

George took a step forward, an unwilling partner in an awkward dance. "We know that."

"I found it."

"Of course you did." His voice was like syrup.

Amy raised the revolver. "Stay where you are."

"Why is the whole thing Hillary's fault?" I asked, trying to divert her.

"Because she called you," Amy replied without taking her eyes off of George. "If my sister hadn't called you, none of this would have happened."

"Are you saying I'm responsible?"

"I'm not saying that at all." A bead of water dripped from her hair onto her shoulder. "It's just that your visit set certain things in motion."

"What things?"

"I told her." Amy's voice rose. She lifted the gun a little higher. "I told her it was a bad idea."

I nodded encouragingly. "I remember you did."

"But she wouldn't listen. No one ever listens to me."

Then Amy smiled. "But you're listening to me now, aren't you?"

"Absolutely. Is there anything I, we, can do to help you?"

"Yes. Don't let him get near me."

"Who?"

"Him." She nodded in Sinclair's direction. "The reverend. If I give you the gun, will you promise to keep him away from me."

"Now, Amy . . ." Sinclair began. The "Amy" came out through clenched teeth.

"No . . ." she cried. "He tried to rape me . . ."

"Amy, you know that's not true."

"Yes, it is," Amy said, appealing to me.

Sinclair fixed his gaze on Amy. "I want you to take deep breaths. You know you tend to become agitated—"

Amy pointed. "He did." Then she turned to Sinclair. "You want everyone to think I'm crazy."

"Of course you're not crazy," he cooed. "You're just over-wrought, which is very understandable in the light of what happened. You'll be fine as soon as you start taking your medication again." Sinclair turned to George and me. "Evidently Amy's let her prescription lapse."

"Leave me alone," Amy screamed at him. "Just leave me alone." And she closed her eyes blotting out the scene.

Before George or I could stop him, Sinclair leaped across the floor to Amy and grabbed the hand that was holding the gun.

She screamed, "Stop," as Sinclair tried to pry her fingers open.

"Give it to me, goddamn it."

George dashed across the room and wrapped his arms around Sinclair's shoulders and attempted to pull him off.

"Let her go," he shouted. "You're making things worse."

"Get away from me," Sinclair screamed.

I ran to help George. I grabbed for Sinclair's arm and came up with a piece of his robe.

The gun went off. My ears rang. I smelled hot metal.

"Oh, my God," Amy said in a voice filled with wonder. A few seconds later, she crumpled to the floor. I knelt down besides her.

"You sonofabitch," George growled at Sinclair.

I watched Sinclair's face go from white to ashen. He looked as if he were going to be sick. "Someone had to do it," he cried as Amy clutched her side and writhed on the ground. "You saw." He appealed to me. "You saw I didn't have a choice. She was going to kill us all."

"Really." I saw George's fist bury itself in Sinclair's midsection. I watched as he doubled over. George lifted him up and hit him in the kidneys. Then he landed one on his cheek, right underneath his eye.

"Please," Sinclair cried, dropping to the floor. "Don't."

"That's it," I yelled as George lifted his foot to kick him. "No more."

George paused and glanced down at Sinclair. A dark puddle of urine had formed around his legs. He was sobbing, the sounds muffled through his hands.

George swallowed, dropped his hands to his sides, and walked out the door, self-contempt for what he'd just done inscribed on his face.

Later, on the way home, I tried to talk to George about what happened, but he didn't want to. His face was as tightly closed as a fist. I touched his arm, and he pulled it away. I gave up trying and turned on the radio.

"You blame me," I said when he finally dropped Zsa Zsa and me off at my house.

"Why would I do that?" His voice was carefully neutral.

"For putting you in that situation."

"Don't be stupid."

But I knew he did.

I went inside and poured myself a drink. By the third one, I was feeling good enough to consider the possibility of sleep. It occurred to me at some point as I was walking up the stairs that maybe George was right. Maybe I did have a drinking problem. But then I decided I didn't care.

The next day, I got a phone call from the director of the Hispanic Alliance. He had spoken to the clerics. It was decided. A collection would be taken up for Raul's burial. I donated two hundred dollars for the cause.

A day later, I found myself seated in Moss Ryan's office, waiting to hear why he'd called me in. The way the receptionist was dressed and the flower arrangement on her desk reconfirmed that Hinkle, Ryan, Packard & Maxwell was one of those law firms that specialize in the problems of the rich and the corporate. Ryan had made the call for this appointment himself, which I thought was fairly unusual. I didn't have to sit around long, either. The receptionist buzzed me through as soon as I'd announced myself after asking whether I wanted anything to drink.

I sat down in a modern brown leather chair; Moss Ryan remained seated across the desk from me. He had his jacket unbuttoned, his chair pulled out from behind the desk, and he was tapping a silver mechanical pencil against the palm of his hand. He was freshly shaved, and his blue suit was immaculate, as was his white shirt and blue tie. But he appeared tired and unhappy. It was easy to understand why he would.

I glanced around. His office came as something of a surprise. Given the reception area, I'd expected Moss Ryan's office to be done up in international style—all teak and leather and chrome. But that wasn't the case at all. The bookshelves were mahogany. The drapes were brocade. There was a set of highly polished armor standing in the corner. Broadswords, crossbows, and lances decorated the walls. A cloth pendant hung over the bookcases. It looked like a medieval banner. The background color was silver. Two rampant griffins sat on either side. There was a border of flowers on the bottom. Two lines of writing were inscribed in the middle. I sounded it out.

"*Amor stemman non cognosce/sed ad virtutem cede.* That's Latin, isn't it?"

He nodded. "It is indeed. Sounds nice, doesn't it? Too bad the church abandoned it." He absentmindedly traced the jagged edges of a large piece of quartz that was sitting on his desk with two of his fingers. "I used to enjoy listening to Mass as a child. It's not the same anymore."

I indicated his collection. "Where did you get all of this stuff?"

"Here and there."

The afternoon sun was coming in through the slats on the blinds, dancing around the room and making shadows on the walls. I leaned back in my chair and watched them while I waited to hear what Moss Ryan had to say. He seemed lost in thought for a moment or two; then he pulled himself together and spoke.

"You'll be happy to hear Amy is doing well." He tapped his pencil on the desk. "She should be out of the hospital in a day or two."

"That's good." Her wound wasn't as bad as it had first appeared. It turned out she'd shot herself in the shoulder, the bullet traveling upward and out, tearing tissue as it went but, fortunately for her, nicking the bone instead of shattering it. "Her mother must be relieved."

"Her mother doesn't know."

"You're kidding, right? What about the report I sent in? Didn't she read it?"

"I read it to her. Or rather I read the relevant parts to her."

I studied his face. He was serious.

"Which is why we're having this conversation." Moss Ryan took a deep breath. "Rose wants to speak to you."

I waited.

"As I said," Ryan went on, "she doesn't know about Amy, and I don't want you to tell her anything that happened. Yet."

"Where does she think Amy is?"

"She thinks she's vacationing in Mexico, and given the fragile nature of Rose's health, I prefer to keep it that way—at least for the time being."

I crossed my legs, then uncrossed them. "Somehow Rose

Taylor strikes me as a woman who wouldn't enjoy having things kept from her."

Ryan gave a short bark of a laugh. "Oh, we'll tell her. There's no danger of our not doing that. But Pat Humphrey's death has been an incredible shock to Rose's system. When we told her, Geoff and I were afraid the news would precipitate another stroke, especially coming, as it does, on top of her nurse's unfortunate demise."

"Unfortunate demise is a nice way to put it. What's new on that front?"

"You know as much as I do."

"So the detectives haven't said anything to you."

"Just that her parents are flying in to claim the body. A thing like that makes me glad I never had a child." Moss Ryan paused for an instant, then said, "To get back to the matter at hand, I'd like to give Rose a little time to adjust before we hit her with more bad news."

"What if Amy's indicted?"

"Hopefully it wouldn't come to that."

I thought about the blood and the gun. "I wouldn't be so sure about that if I were you."

Ryan dropped his pencil, leaned forward, rested his elbows on his desk, and steepled his fingers. "I've heard Amy's story, and it sounds extremely credible to me. She tells me she stumbled across Pat. And I mean that literally. She fell over her. Naturally, in the dark she didn't realize what had happened. She thought Pat had had some sort of seizure. Evidently she'd been complaining about headaches." He sighed. "Amy tried to rouse her, and that's when she must have gotten the blood on her shirt."

"Funny thing, but when I got to Pat Humphrey, she was talking. How do you account for that?"

"Perhaps she passed out from the bullet, then came to again. The doctors I've consulted have told me that that can happen."

"Even so, why didn't Amy call the police?"

"Because she was in shock."

I thought about how George and I had found her. "She certainly has a unique way of showing it."

Moss Ryan frowned. "Everyone is different. Don't forget, Amy thought Pat Humphrey was dead."

"And the gun?"

"She found it on her way to the lodge as she was going for help."

"And Amy just picked it up and brought it with her?"

"Stranger things have happened."

"But not by much."

Moss Ryan stiffened. "It's possible."

"Anything's possible. Is the D.A. preparing an indictment?"

"Not to my knowledge."

"And you believe Amy's story?"

"Absolutely." Moss Ryan straightened his tie. "The idea that Amy shot someone, let alone Pat Humphrey, whom she adored, who was aiding her in making contact with her favorite childhood pet, is ludicrous. Why would she? As I said, Pat was helping her. She was the only person that could. Added to everything else, Amy is terrified of guns. She always has been."

"Childhood pet?"

Ryan had the grace to look abashed. "I'm told the dog's name was Corky. It was some sort of mixed terrier. Amy watched a car run over it. Maybe because it happened soon after her father died, Amy never got over it. Pat was helping her achieve closure. Look," Ryan said, "I know it sounds stupid, but it was important to Amy. Very important."

"Maybe Corky told Amy it was her fault that she died, that she should have had her on a leash and she got angry and killed the messenger."

Moss Ryan rubbed his eyes. "I'll tell you the truth, I don't know what to think anymore." He picked up his pencil again, clicked it twice, put it down, and leaned back in his chair. "The only thing I do know is that Rose wants you to come out to her place at seven-thirty tonight so she can discuss hiring you to investigate Pat Humphrey's death."

"The police are doing that."

"Over the years, I've observed that the police tend toward the ready-made and the obvious when it comes to suspects."

"Like Amy."

Ryan shot his cuffs. "I've always conducted my life along the motto that forewarned is forearmed. Actually, if the investigating officers look further, I'm sure they'll find that Amy isn't even their best suspect."

"Meaning?"

"We can talk more about this later if it becomes necessary."

I rubbed my arms. They had goose pimples on them. The air conditioning in the office was beginning to get to me. "And Rose doesn't know about any of this."

"No. Not at the present time."

"How does she think Pat Humphrey died?"

"She knows she was shot, if that's what you're asking. I just didn't read her the last part of your report."

"Is getting me involved in this your idea?"

"Actually, it was Rose's. But if she hadn't suggested it, I would have."

"I'm not equipped for this type of thing."

"Just listen to what she has to say."

"Without telling her about her daughter? What if she asks?"

"Lie."

"I don't think I can do that."

"Please," Moss Ryan begged. "When you see her, you'll understand."

Chapter Twenty-three

It was a little after seven-thirty when I pulled into the Taylor estate. I was hot and thirsty and thinking I should have stopped at Burger King and picked up something to eat and drink on the way over as I watched a crow pecking at a dead squirrel in the driveway. He hopped away when I neared, then returned once I'd parked the car.

Remnants of the yellow crime-scene tape fluttered from the hedges and hung from the trees, a remembrance of the violence that had recently jarred the serenity of the place. I was surprised everything hadn't been tidied up already and consigned to the dustbin. Even if money can't buy happiness, it can buy order. It was probably my imagination, but the grass and the bushes looked a little scragglier than they had the last time I'd visited.

Geoff rushed forward to greet me as I got out of my car. He'd been leaning against the doorframe, biting a cuticle, when I'd pulled up. The last week had aged him, too. His face looked bloated, as if he'd been spending too much time with a bottle for company. He had dark circles under his eyes, and his hair, normally perfect, had several cowlicks sticking out around the back of his head.

As we walked to the front door, I noticed he had a grease splotch on the front of his polo shirt. "You spoke to Ryan, right?" he asked me. "He told you about not mentioning Amy?"

I nodded. "I said I'd try not to bring her into the conversation, but if her name came up or questions were asked, I told him I wasn't going to lie."

Geoff opened the door for me and escorted me inside. "It would kill Rose if she knew, just kill her."

"Well, we wouldn't want to do that."

"No, we wouldn't."

I noticed the flowers in the vase on the table to the left needed to be replaced. "So how are you dealing with Shana's death?"

"Managing." He paused for a second as a new thought occurred to him. "Ryan didn't say anything about Shana and me, did he?"

"Not that I recall."

Geoff was so close to me that his breath tickled my ear. "Are you sure?"

"Positive."

"Because if he does, you can tell him for me to say it to my face."

"I think you should tell him that yourself."

"Maybe I will." Geoff continued his walk down the hallway. The polished marble floor, the high ceilings, gave off a chill despite the warm summer night.

"I have a question for you."

"Yes?"

"How could you afford to give Shana Driscoll a pair of earrings from Tiffany's?"

He stopped. "That wasn't a question."

"No. I guess it wasn't."

"Why assume it was me?" he demanded. "She could have been seeing someone else."

"I suppose she could have, but I don't think they would have typed the card. I think they would have signed their name."

Geoff folded his arms across his chest. "I don't know any-thing about it."

"All right." I changed the subject. "How's Rose doing?"

"Rose? As well as can be expected, given the circum-stances. We had her doctor here this morning. He prescribed some tranquilizers. We gave them to her, but I'm not sure that they're doing much good."

I'd assumed Rose would be in her sitting room, but Geoff led me to the sunroom, the room in which I'd first seen Rose. She was sitting on the same sofa, wearing slacks and a long-sleeved linen blouse. A heavy gold chain hung around her neck. Her cat was sprawled out across her lap.

"This is my favorite place," she said to me when Geoff and I entered, answering my unasked question. She made a sweeping gesture with her right hand. "The plants give us so-lace, don't they?" she asked Sheba, who twitched her tail in response and slightly altered her position on her mistress's lap. "You can leave," she told Geoff. "I'll be fine."

He hesitated while Sheba regarded him disdainfully out of unblinking cobalt blue eyes.

"Really."

"But . . ."

Rose made a gesture of dismissal. "If I need anything, Robin will get it for me."

Finally, after hesitating for another few seconds, Geoff walked out the door.

Rose continued petting her cat as I sat down in the arm-chair next to the sofa. The events of the last few days had taken their toll, but given what Moss Ryan and Geoff had said, I'd expected Rose Taylor to look a lot worse than she did. It's true she looked frailer, almost translucent, as if a piece of her had been rubbed away, but she was fully made up, and even though her eyelids drooped slightly, her eyes re-garded me with a shrewd, measuring gaze.

"Geoff and Ryan." She shook her head. "They think I'm going to come apart. It hasn't occurred to them I wouldn't have gotten to where I am if I wasn't tough-minded. But women are stronger then men. Much stronger. Even though men don't like to admit that. The truth is, men go on being little boys, but the moment that baby comes out from between your legs, a woman has to grow up."

I remember my grandmother saying something along the same lines to me. I hadn't agreed with her then, and I wasn't sure I agreed with Mrs. Taylor now, but I nodded, anyway.

"Good." She smiled. "Which brings me to why I sent for you. I'm sure you're wondering."

"I assumed you wanted to talk to me about the report," I lied.

"That was fairly clear-cut. Not much to discuss in it." She buried her hand in Sheba's fur. "Except for the fact that while it's true you found Pat Humphrey for me, you unfortunately didn't find her soon enough."

I didn't say anything.

"If you had been faster, Pat Humphrey might be alive today."

"I'm not so sure. She had a reason for disappearing the way she did."

"And what was that?" Rose snapped.

"She was scared of you."

Rose laughed derisively. "And who told you that, Hillary?"

"Actually it was Amy."

"Even better. She has no idea what's going on, none at all. Of course, none of my children do. I can't figure out what I did wrong."

"She seemed pretty convinced."

Rose studied her perfectly manicured nails for a minute before looking back up at me. "Amy was also convinced that Louis raped her when she was fifteen. Did you know that? And in case you're wondering, no, he didn't; he was playing football at the time. Naturally I checked." Rose took a deep breath. "Unfortunately, to be blunt, my daughter is a liar. She makes up stories. She always has."

I thought about Amy's yelling that Sinclair was trying to rape her. I hadn't believed it then. I believed it even less now.

Rose continued. "I've been told it's the only way she feels she can get attention. I've tried to explain to her that there are other ways to go about that. I've offered to pay for a personal trainer so she can lose some weight. I've even offered to send her to a plastic surgeon, but she isn't interested." Rose waved her hand in the air. "It's sad, but one has to accept the truth and move on. Stop moving and you die."

A vision of a tiger shark endlessly circling around a coral reef came to mind.

Rose went back to petting her cat. "Now, what were we talking about? I've lost my train of thought."

"You were talking about your children."

"Before that."

"You were saying that Pat Humphrey would be alive today if I'd been faster finding her."

"It's true, isn't it?"

She looked at me expectantly. I was sure she had her arguments marshaled, but I didn't give her a chance to trot them out.

"So," I said instead, "if you were dissatisfied the first time, why do you want to hire me now?"

"Because I think you can do better. Anyway, you already know everyone. It would be more time consuming to bring someone else up to speed."

"Is that your idea of a compliment?"

"As anyone who knows me will tell you, I don't give compliments out easily." She tapped her fingers on the sofa. "I want you to get up and go over to the desk on the far left-hand corner and open the top middle drawer. Take out the large white envelope addressed to you."

I did as I was told.

"Now open it."

I peered in. The envelope was stuffed with hundred-dollar bills.

"There's ten thousand dollars in there," she told me.

I took a deep breath. Down in someplace like New York City or Silicon Valley ten thousand dollars was walk-around money, but in my world it was a lot. Judging from what she said next, Rose Taylor knew that.

"I want you to use it to find out who killed Pat Humphrey," she told me. "There's enough there to allow you to concentrate exclusively on this. Hire someone else to run your store for you. By the way, that money is in addition to any expenses you incur. To be reimbursed for those, just submit your receipts to Moss."

It pained me, but I closed the envelope flap. "That's very generous of you, but I can't trump the police on a homicide investigation."

"I realize that. But you can speak to people."

"The police will, too."

"Exactly my point."

"I don't understand."

"I know you don't." Rose Taylor bit her lip. She looked down at her hands, then back up at me. She took a deep breath and let it out. "This is just hard for me to talk about."

"If it upsets you . . ."

"No." She brushed my objections aside. "It's simple. You're my insurance policy."

Moss Ryan's statement about being forewarned is forearmed flashed through my mind.

"It might not happen, but I'm afraid that sooner or later the police are going to stumble on a certain fact, and when they do, I'd like to have a name to give them."

"And what fact is . . . ?"

"That Pat Humphrey was my daughter."

Chapter Twenty-four

I got up, went over to the sideboard situated on the opposite wall, picked up a tall glass etched with gold trim, and poured myself a healthy shot of Black Label.

"Pour one for me, too," Rose said. "A long one. And add some ice to it if you don't mind. Use the tongs," she instructed as I opened the ice-bucket lid. "That's what they're there for."

The ice cubes clinked as I filled the glass with them. I put in a couple of fingers of scotch and handed Rose her drink. "You forgot the napkin," she said. "Not the paper ones, the cloth ones over on your right."

If this was any indication of what Geoff had to put up with, I wondered if the cars and the clothes and the money were enough compensation as I went back and got Rose her napkin. It was hand embroidered Irish linen.

She took it out of my hand, then looked at the coffee table and back up at me. "I don't know what you do in your house, but in mine we put coasters under our glasses."

A *House Beautiful* was lying on the table. I pushed the magazine toward her. "In mine we use these."

Rose glared at me for a second, and I glared right back. After another second she laughed. "Most people automatically do what I tell them to."

"So I've observed."

"Which, I suppose, is why I want to hire you."

I waited for Rose to speak, but she just sat there lost in thought, holding her drink in one hand and petting her cat with the other, while I listened to the clock on the other side of the room ticking the minutes away.

"Are you sure about Pat Humphrey being your daughter?" I finally asked.

"As sure as I can be." Rose took a sip of her drink and set her glass down on the magazine. The cat flicked her tail in annoyance at being disturbed, but Rose took no notice. "Evidently, Patti got her birth certificate, or if we're going to be precise, a copy of the certificate—originals are never given out—from the agency that handled her adoption. I saw it. My name was there, typed in on the line that says mother."

"I didn't think agencies were supposed to do that. I thought that was illegal."

"They're not, and it is. Unless I give my consent. Which I didn't. Nor would I have. As far as I was concerned, that part of my life was closed. I certainly didn't want to open it again. But Patti can be, could be, terribly persuasive."

"Do you still have it?"

"The certificate? No." Rose gave a dry little laugh. "Patti took it back."

"That's convenient. What did she do with it?"

Rose brought her free hand up and let it fall back down in the equivalent of a shrug. "I suppose what most people do with documents like that. Put it where she thought it would be safe."

By now the police would have sealed off Humphrey's safe-deposit box, her bank account, and her house. If the birth certificate was in there, Rose was right. It wouldn't be long before the police were knocking at her door.

"And it looked authentic to you?"

"I'm not an expert, but yes, it certainly did, insofar as reproductions go."

"Did it have a seal?"

Rose picked up one of her cat's front paws and touched

the pads. The cat twitched its tail in annoyance and unsheathed its claws. Rose smiled and dropped the paw. "Of course it had a seal. That's one of the first things I checked."

"Do you remember the name of the adoption agency?"

"That's a stupid question. It was the Oxford Agency." She leaned forward a little. "Listen, do you have a cigarette on you?"

"Always. But they're unfiltered."

"Doesn't matter."

I sat down, took my pack of Camels out of my backpack, and passed the cigarettes and the lighter across the table to Rose.

"Thanks." I watched her light up.

I lit a cigarette of my own and inhaled, taking the smoke down into my lungs, then releasing it to the air.

"It's been a long time." Rose pointed to a small, valuable-looking, crackle-glazed oxblood ceramic pot on one of the tables. "Bring that over." She gave me a sly look. "Unless you use something else in your house."

"An ashtray."

Rose didn't respond to my comment. Instead, she watched me as I positioned the pot between us. She took another puff of her cigarette and flicked the ash into the pot as I sat down. "Sanford would have a fit if he saw me do this. Of course, he would have had a fit if he saw me smoking. He hated it. Said it was a filthy habit." Then she fell silent. I waited for her to continue. Finally, she did.

"Really, it's an old, boring story. High-school sweethearts. Madly in love. He wanted to marry me when I told him I was in the family way. Quaint phrase that." Her lips turned up. "But our parents wouldn't hear of it, and in those days you didn't run away and set up housekeeping in San Francisco—at least no one in my circle of friends did. His parents left town and took him with them. Later, I heard they sent him off to military school.

"My parents sent me away, too. I spent eight months in a little town in Pennsylvania. I remember writing letters to my best friend—her name was Edna; I wonder whatever happened to her—but the people running the place confiscated them. They wouldn't allow me to mail them. My mother told everyone I'd gone out there to help care for a sick aunt. I never even saw the baby. They gave me a general anesthetic, so I wasn't awake. Everyone said it was better that way. Less painful. They were probably right."

Rose took another puff of her Camel and contemplated the ash for a few seconds before continuing. "I'd almost talked myself into believing that the whole incident had never happened—it's amazing what you can forget if you work at it—when Patti showed up with my cat." Rose shook her head. "What's so genuinely odd is that Sheba really had run away and Patti did find her. Patti did have genuine ability, just like my grandmother had. I never had that ability. I was a good athlete. I was smart. But I could never see things. Grannie was famous among the neighbors for knowing things. They came in the afternoons so she could read the tea leaves for them. She never took any money. Ever. She said she had a gift and that she owed it to the world to share it."

Rose sighed, held up her drink, and studied the amber liquid for a few seconds before taking another sip. "Patti told me that at first she had no intention of contacting me. She wanted to look at where I lived—that's all. But then, when she found Sheba on a walk around my property, it seemed as if fate was calling to her. She told herself she just wanted to meet me, and then she'd walk away.

"But we became friends. There was something there. I knew it the moment she walked in the room. We had the same taste in clothes and in art. We thought the same way. And so, after wrestling with her conscience, she decided to tell me. I didn't believe her. Or rather, I didn't want to, but when she showed me her birth certificate with my name on it . . . well, you can see I had no choice but to believe her.

"And you can also see what the police will think when they find out," Rose went on. "They'll suspect one of my children in Patricia's death. And nothing I say will convince them otherwise."

"Do your children know?"

"No. At least I don't think so." Rose's voice was trembling, but whether from fear or rage, I couldn't tell. "That's the problem, you see. I'm not sure. I can't bear to think that I raised someone who could—" She stopped.

"Would you like me to get you some water?"

"No." She stubbed out her cigarette. "I should have known better than to take Patti in. Sanford always said, 'if you have three cats and you bring another one inside, you're going to have trouble.' But I couldn't say no. For God's sake, I should be entitled to do what I want at this stage in my life."

I didn't point out that she already had.

She straightened up. "I want you to find out who Patricia's enemies were."

I looked her straight in the eye. "Aside from your children?"

"There's no need . . ."

"I'm afraid there is."

Rose pressed her lips together and bowed her head. She could have been praying. When she lifted her head, her eyes were shuttered, all expression gone. "You're right. I need to know about them, too. I need to know what kind of people they are. I'm afraid I've avoided that for far too long."

"Who did know about Pat Humphrey being your daughter?"

"No one knew."

"No one?"

"That's right, no one," Rose repeated in the face of my disbelief. "I didn't tell anyone."

"Not your lawyer. Not your husband."

"I didn't see any reason for them to know. Why should they?" Rose rubbed the rim of her glass with her index finger. "In today's parlance, I don't like putting my business out on the street. Of course, I can't say the same for Patti. She may have told someone. Even though I warned her not to."

A picture of Pat Humphrey and Sinclair embracing on the shore flashed through my mind. I wondered if Humphrey had told Sinclair and started a chain reaction in which Sinclair told Amy and Amy told Louis and Louis told Hillary. Sort of like the game telephone we used to play when I was a kid. And then I wondered how Shana Driscoll fit into the scenario? Because despite what Moss Ryan said, she did. How were Shana and Pat Humphrey linked? And did Geoff come into the equation? Was that why he seemed so nervous? Or was it just the stress of the last days catching up with him?

I gulped down the rest of my scotch. As I did, I wondered how easy it would be to fake an adoption certificate. Not that difficult, I'd warrant, especially in today's world of copiers and scanners. Especially since Pat Humphrey had supposedly shown Rose a copy of the original to begin with. The question was: If the certificate was a forgery, where had Pat Humphrey gotten her information from? How had she known that Rose Taylor had borne an out-of-wedlock child so long ago? How had she been privy to all the details?

"So you'll see what you can do?" Rose said, interrupting my thoughts.

I told her I would.

The next day, I had to go downtown to do some banking. Since I was in the area, I decided I might as well visit Paul in his office and check out his new digs. He'd set up shop on the fifth floor of the State Tower Building. The large brick building, which towered over the Syracuse skyline, had been constructed sometime in the thirties and still had the mail chute, the art deco overhead lighting fixtures, and the glass doors of that era. I took the elevator up and walked almost to the end of a long, angled hallway.

The smell of wet paint and take-out Chinese food hit me as I opened the door to Paul's office. The small waiting room was sparsely furnished, with two straight-back chairs, a waste-paper basket, and a piece of bad art on the wall. I knocked and walked into the office proper. Moderately large, the desk had been set flush up against the far wall. Three chairs had been arranged near it, while a brown sofa and a coffee table sat across the room. The rest of the space was taken up with bookcases and file cabinets.

Paul glanced up at me from his computer screen. He'd buzzed his hair since I'd seen him last, which made his nose look even bigger than it already was and highlighted the gray.

He threw his pen down and swiveled around in his chair. "Don't have anything new for you, darlin'. Nothing except what I already gave you." He made to turn the screen around. "I can show you if you want."

"It's okay."

"I told you, you want to find out about this Humphrey, you're going to have to drive that pretty little butt of yours out to the town she was raised in and talk to the people there."

"Anything new on the Oxford Agency?"

"Long gone. It was taken over by something called Helping the Children. They're gone, too. Busted for extortion."

"Nice."

Paul grinned. "But I do have somethin' for ya from one of my friends downtown."

I rested my backpack on the floor. "Which would be?"

He smirked. "That would depend on what you have for me."

"Don't you have any sense of loyalty?"

"Sure I do. But if you and George were serious, you'd be living together already. Not doing this separate-lives thing."

"Have you ever thought that we may like it this way?"

Paul shrugged. "Hey, things go forward or they fall apart."

"Do you think we can skip Paul's Personal Rules for living?"

"If that's what you want. But you're missing some pearls

of wisdom." He winked, unwrapped a stick of gum, shoved it in his mouth, and began to chew. "The bullet that killed Humphrey was a .3006 caliber fired from a bolt-action rifle."

Just like the one I'd taken away from Sinclair and tossed in the river. Of course, every deer hunter in the Northeast used one.

"Sinclair has a nice little collection of those. Claims he does a lot of hunting. None of them have been fired. And the paraffin tests on him and the woman are negative. Not that they couldn't have hired someone."

"They gonna look for the rifle?"

Paul shrugged. "Haven't heard."

I thought about what Ryan had said about Amy's finding the gun near Humphrey. It looked as if she'd been telling the truth, that the gun she'd had in her hand when we'd walked through the door was Humphrey's. Humphrey must have been carrying it for protection. Not that it had done her much good.

"Nice for her."

"Isn't it." I perched on the edge of his desk. "I want you to run these people for me."

Paul reached for his pen. I gave him Geoff's, Hillary's, Amy's, and Louis's names. "See what you come up with."

"You got money for this?" he asked as he jotted them down.

I showed him the deposit slip for Rose Taylor's cash.

He whistled. "That's rather a departure from the usual low-life scum you deal with."

"Charming as always."

He winked again. "That's why the ladies love me. I'll give you a jingle when I have something. And listen, my offer about working with me, it still stands."

"I'll bear that in mind. And Paul . . ." He looked up. "You're working the thirties-gumshoe bit a little too hard."

On the way back to the store I stopped at George's house and knocked on his door. I wanted to see how he was doing after the other night. Not well, I decided when he came out-side. His eyes were bloodshot, and his clothes, a stained T-shirt and a dirty pair of shorts, looked as if he'd slept in them. He needed a shave, and I wasn't sure, but I thought I smelled the faint odor of alcohol coming off him.

"I'm working," he told me when he saw me. He had a withdrawn expression on his face.

"Can't I come in for a few minutes?"

George glanced at his watch. "I'm sorry. I haven't got the time. Is there anything else?"

"So now we're doing polite?"

"Robin, what is it?" And he tapped his fingers on his thighs while he waited for me to complete my sentence.

"I think we should talk about what happened with Sinclair."

"Let's not." George's expression hardened even more. "There nothing to discuss. I lost my temper, I punched him. End of story. Hopefully, he wouldn't file assault charges."

"George . . ."

He lifted a hand. "Stop."

"But . . ."

"No. I don't like who I am when I'm with people like Sinclair; I don't like what I become. That's why I quit the force. So I wouldn't have to deal with this kind of thing. I'm happy where I am now, studying history. I enjoy going to the library and teaching my classes. The other night . . . It just swept everything away, and I was back on the street again.

"I don't want that." Then he added, "Although, I'd rather be dealing with the crackheads on the corner than with the group you are currently mixed up with. At least with them you know where you stand." And with that he went inside and left me standing in the heat.

I had a lump in my throat all the way to the store.

Chapter Twenty-five

Later that evening, I went to hear Hillary sing in a North Side bar called Quotations. The full moon's reddish tinge and the clarity of the air gave the streets the feel of a Rousseau painting. A gust of wind had kicked up, and I was watching a sheet of newspaper dancing across the pavement when Paul called me on my cell phone.

"Darlin'," he said, his voice sounding slurred from too much drink. I heard the plaint of country western playing in the background. "I got the info you wanted."

"Where are you?"

He giggled and told me what he'd found out. But aside from the fact that Geoff had been a tennis pro before he met Rose and had two DWI arrests and that Hillary also had a DWI in her past, he hadn't been able to turn up too much of interest.

"You wanna join me? Keep old Paulie company? We could look together."

"I don't do country western." And I pressed the OFF switch. As long as I was on the phone, I tried George again, but either he wasn't in or he wasn't answering. "You'd better start talking to me," I told his machine as I turned onto North State Street. Then I turned off my cell and considered what I was about to do.

Hillary and I hadn't parted well the last time we'd spoken.

She'd accused me of betraying her to her mother. Even though I hadn't, I could see her point of view. I wondered what she'd say to me now, especially in light of what had happened recently, as I parked in front of Quotations.

Located in a working-class neighborhood, the club faced the backside of Saint Joe's, offering an extensive view of the hospital's concrete wall. It had been in existence for a little over six months. If the number of people sitting at the bar was any indication, getting through months number seven and eight was going to be somewhat iffy.

I'd been told that the owner was a twenty-four-year-old college dropout called Little Johnny Q. He'd picked up his nickname to distinguish him from the four other Johnnies in his Cazenovia elementary-school class. The only son of a former county district attorney, he'd flunked out of Cornell due to his penchant for alcohol and weed, at which point he'd gone down to the city, kicked around, and come back after deciding he wanted to be Syracuse's new impresario.

His father, who was not exactly poor, had come up with the backing, and the kid had bought an old neighborhood bar, gutted the place, and decked it out in classic Soho industrial style. Quotations had a long, gleaming steel bar, a raised dance floor, exposed wires and pipes, and wall studs that would rip your sweater if you got too close—as well as lighting so dark you'd have to light a match to read the menu. And that, of course, was the problem. Johnny Q had put a trendy club in a neighborhood where the restaurants had never stopped serving mashed potatoes, iceberg lettuce, and Spanish rice. People that lived here not only didn't get "it" but didn't want to, and from what I could see, the place wasn't drawing anyone from the other side of town. It was Thursday night, traditionally a night to hit the clubs, and this one was three-quarters empty.

I paid my entrance fee, got my hand stamped, and walked inside. Hillary was up on the small stage making like Billie Holiday to a handful of chattering people who weren't paying attention but should have. Because the lady was good. I was surprised at how good. Somehow I'd thought she'd be strictly amateur, one of those karaoke wanna-bes, but she had a real edge to her. She could have sung in any club in New York City and come out okay.

Despite the heat, Hillary was wearing a long-sleeved black cotton sweater over a white tank top and a tight black rayon skirt that was slit up to her thigh and made her look even thinner than she already was. Her black hair formed a lank curtain around her face, and her eye makeup was smudged under her eyes, giving her face a bruised quality. She was leaning against the piano, her eyelids half-closed, her hands clasped around the mike, swaying very gently from side to side, seemingly oblivious to the whirring of the ceiling fan above her.

She gave off the feeling that she was singing to herself and that I'd wandered into someplace private, someplace I wasn't supposed to be. Her voice was rich, with a vibrato that she could turn on and off. And then suddenly it was over. The piano player stopped playing. Hillary opened her eyes, replaced the microphone on the stand, and abruptly walked off the stage without glancing at the audience or giving them a chance to applaud. The piano player, who looked as if he worked as an actuary in an insurance agency in his button-down short-sleeve shirt, got up, gave an abrupt little bow, and followed Hillary down the two steps and into the back.

I shook off the seeds of sadness her song had planted in me, walked over to the bar, and ordered a Sierra Nevada Pale Ale from the bartender. A good-looking guy in an aging-hippie kind of way, he was broad-shouldered, stood a little over six feet, and sported a suntan and a long gray ponytail, but there was a vacancy around the eyes that didn't inspire confidence. When he put my glass down in front of me, I asked him when Hillary was going to be singing again.

He shrugged. "You got me. Sometimes she does two or three sets a night. Sometimes she just packs it up and goes home. It all depends on her mood. And the audience." He pursed his mouth as he took stock of the room. "Tonight I have the feeling she's going to go home early."

"She's good."

"If you like that kind of music." He stifled a yawn and glanced at his watch. "Myself, I prefer listening to something a little more upbeat." His eyes drifted off, following a girl in tight white pants, a tank top, and mules who'd just gotten up.

"I need to speak to her."

"Hillary?"

"Who else are we talking about?" I took a sip of the Pale Ale and made a face. "This is stale," I said, pushing the stein back toward him.

He took a sip. "Tastes all right to me."

"I wouldn't brag about that if I were you."

"So you want something else or what?" the bartender asked, dumping the beer down the drain without taking his eyes off the girl as she sashayed across the floor.

"What's your name?"

"Russell." He said this with his eyes still firmly fixed on the girl's ass.

"Okay, Russell. What I want is to speak to Hillary."

"You the person she's waiting for?"

I lied and told him I was.

He watched the girl take a left into a hallway and disappear from view before turning back to me. "That's funny," he replied, plastering a smirk on his face. "Hilly said she was waiting for a guy."

I slid a twenty across the bar. "Sex-change operations can do wonderful things these days."

He slipped the bill into his pocket as a man signaled to him from the other side of the bar. "She's in her dressing room. That's two doors down from the bathroom. Tell her Russell said he's still waiting. She'll know what I mean."

"Tell her yourself." And I left.

* * *

If the bar area was dark, the hallway was even darker. The only light came from wall sconces decked out in dark-red-and-purple shades. The first time through I miscounted the doors, because what I thought was the third door turned out to be the bathroom, while the door after that was an office. Outlined in a halo of bright light, I caught a glimpse of a young, well-dressed guy and a couple of Hispanics in cutoff jeans and stained sweatshirts arguing. They stopped when they saw me. We stared at each other for a few seconds. Then I apologized, shut the door, and retraced my steps. The second time I got it right.

The door to Hillary's dressing room was slightly ajar. I pushed it open and walked in. The place was stifling. Windowless, it smelled of sweat, talcum powder, nail-polish remover, and smoke. I noticed a fan sitting unused over in the corner. Looking around, I got a quick impression of a sofa with ripped cushions shoved against the far wall, a chair piled high with clothes, a grime-stained rug with its pattern long since worn away, and urine-colored paint on the walls. Hillary was sitting in front of her dressing table. Her head was bent down. She was holding a nail file and considering the nails on her left hand.

The door creaked when I closed it.

"What the hell took you so long?" Hillary asked without looking up.

"I've been asking myself the same question."

Hillary's head shot up. She dropped the nail file and quickly shoved something lying on her dressing table underneath a crumpled-up towel. "What are you doing here?" she demanded, swiveling around to face me.

"You invited me to hear you sing." I found myself staring at Hillary's shoulder blades. They protruded from her skin, as fragile as a wren's wing. "I really enjoyed you out there. Have you recorded anything?"

"A couple of CDs under a local label. They never went anywhere." She cocked her head. Her hair fell over one side of her face. She pushed it back behind her ear. "So that's why you're here? To tell me how much you liked hearing me sing?"

"Among other reasons."

She looked at me uncertainly, not sure of what was coming next, then slipped into her best Emily Post manner. "Well, thanks for coming. It was nice of you to tell me, and now that you have, I'd like you to go. I'm tired, and I need to rest before I go on again."

"This will just take a few minutes. It's about Pat Humphrey."

Hillary stuck her jaw out. "Whatever I had to say about her, I've already said to the police."

"Say it to me."

Hillary stared at me for a moment. "Who sent you? Ryan? My mother?" She searched my face. "It was my mother, wasn't it?"

"Yes, it was."

"Well, screw her. I don't have to talk to you."

"She's worried about you."

Hillary snorted. "That would be a first." She turned her back on me. I could see her reflection in the looking glass mounted on her dressing table. "You have to go."

"After we've talked."

Her hand moved toward the towel and back again. "No. Leave now." Her voice had grown higher. I noticed her hands were trembling. "This is my dressing room. Do I have to call Security?"

As I watched her, suddenly everything fell into place. Her extreme thinness. The way she was always wearing long-sleeved shirts and sweaters when everyone else was stripped down to tube tops and shorts. I cursed myself for not having seen it sooner, but then you usually only see what you're looking for.

"What are you doing?" Hillary demanded, turning toward me as I crossed the room. "I told you to leave."

"Show me what's under that towel." I pointed to the dressing table.

"You're crazy." Hillary's eyes widened.

"Maybe. Maybe not." I leaned over.

Hillary grabbed my wrist as I reached for the towel. "How dare you?"

I shrugged her off easily; her grip was as insubstantial as a bracelet of dandelion flowers, but she was on me again like a leech. "Get out of here," she shrieked as I disentangled myself and threw her back in her chair.

She jumped up and grabbed the nail file she'd been using as I raised the edge of the towel. A set of works—a syringe, a length of rubber tubing, the whole schmear—was sitting on a little lacquered tray.

"Can't get away from the Chinese motif, can you?" I told her as a starburst of pain went off.

I looked down. I saw blood on my arm. Then I saw the red-stained nail file Hillary was holding. I wrenched it out of her hand, grasped both of her shoulders, and shook her.

"Are you crazy?"

"You have no right," Hillary was screaming when the door banged open and someone said, "What the hell is going on here? I can hear you down the hall."

Hillary and I both turned at the same time. The guy I'd seen in the office was standing in the doorway. He appeared larger than he had when he was sitting down. A tribal tattoo ringed his neck.

"Nothing, Johnny," Hillary whined, taking her seat and surreptitiously lowering the edge of the towel. "Nothing is going on."

He glared at both of us. "There better not be. I don't need that kind of shit in here. I've warned you before." Then he looked me up and down. "Who the hell are you?"

"An old friend."

His brow furrowed. "So if you're an old friend, how come you're fighting?"

Hillary threw me a pleading look.

"We were just arguing over a pocketbook." I gave him my best smile. "It's one of those women things."

It was an embarrassingly bad story, but Johnny must have decided I wasn't worth bothering with because he grunted and turned his attention back to Hillary. "I don't want any more crap from you."

"You won't get any."

"I'm doing you a favor letting you be here at all."

"I know," Hillary whispered, and she hung her head.

Johnny looked from one to the other of us and back again. He jerked his chin at me. "I hear any more and you're out and she"—he pointed to Hillary—"never sings here again. Got it? Got it?" he repeated when I didn't answer immediately.

"Like crystal," I said.

"So, how long have you been shooting up?" I asked Hillary when he left the room.

"I'm not."

"And I raise roses for a living." I took a tissue out of the box on the dresser and pressed it against the cut on my arm and watched the blood form a pretty design on the thin white paper. It took two more tissues before I stanched the bleeding.

"It's my friend's stuff. Really," she protested as I threw the bloodstained Kleenex into the trash can.

I reached over and yanked her cardigan down over her shoulders. There were track marks on the insides of both her right and left arms. She flushed and pulled her sweater back up.

"I repeat. How long have you been shooting up?"

She threw me a sullen glance. "What do you care?"

"I don't, really. I'm not going to lecture you on the evils of drugs. Some of my best friends used to . . . indulge."

"Big fuckin' deal. If you're going to go into one of these look-how-cool-I-am raps, forget it."

"Don't worry. I'm not going to bore you." I kicked the chair against the wall over, threw the clothing on it on the sofa, and sat down next to her. "These days, I thought most people smoked it. I guess you're just an old-fashioned kind of girl."

"I guess I am."

"Either that or you're suicidal."

"I'm not HIV positive, if that's what you mean," Hillary said.

"But you will be if you keep this up."

She shrugged. "I'm careful. I don't share needles."

"All it takes is one time."

"Maybe the pleasure is worth the risk. Have you ever thought of that?"

"What I'm thinking is that you're just some stone junkie, a Billie Holiday wanna-be romanticizing yourself as someone too sensitive to live in this world."

Hillary's eyes blazed. "Fuck you," she spat.

I leaned over. "No. Fuck you. You know why I didn't tell your boss?"

"I don't care."

"I didn't tell him because I want you to answer my questions. And if you don't, then I'll march right down to his office and tell him you're a user, and then, if he doesn't do it, I'll pick up the phone and tell the police."

Hillary gestured toward her dressing table. "First-time offender? I'll get off with probation."

"You're right, you will, but the arrest will be reported in the papers, and you'll lose your teaching job. Schools don't like to let addicts teach—especially elementary-school kids."

Hillary tried to meet my eyes but couldn't. "I'm not an addict."

"Fine. User. Dabbler. Experimenter. Smackhead. Hype. Pick whatever word you want. Let's not do stupid on top of everything else."

Hillary's chin came up. Her gray eyes became lighter. She studied her nails. "It would almost be worth it to see the expression on my mother's face when the neighbors start calling."

I took out a cigarette and lit it. "You guys put the D in dysfunctional."

"And I suppose your family is perfect."

"As perfect as apple pie," I lied. "Do you want to answer my questions or not?"

Hillary squared her shoulders. "Answer them. What other choice do I have?"

"None." I looked around for an ashtray and finally settled on an empty soda can. "Now, tell me again why you hired me to investigate Pat Humphrey?"

Hillary spun her ring, a gold band with a black opal in it, around her finger. "I already told you, I hired you because I was afraid Pat Humphrey was ripping my mother off. And it wasn't just me. Louis and Amy agreed."

"But you were the driving force."

"I was the one that suggested it. Yes."

"Because you didn't want to see all your money go to waste."

Hillary glared at me. "There's nothing wrong with me looking after my assets. Our assets," she corrected herself. "Those of my sister and brother."

"Absolutely." I took another puff of my cigarette and flicked the ash into the soda can as a trickle of sweat worked its way down between my breasts. A cool shower would be wonderful, but that was still a ways away. "Especially when a person has expensive habits to maintain. Incidentally, what's the going rate for a hit of heroin these days?"

Hillary clamped her lips together.

"Okay. Here's my next question. How would you feel about splitting your mother's money four ways instead of three?"

Hillary smoothed down the front of her sweater. "I don't understand what you're talking about."

"I think you do. Your mother gave a substantial chunk of change to Pat Humphrey. I'm just wondering what you'd feel like if you found out she was legally entitled to more."

"I still don't get it."

"According to your mother, Pat Humphrey was your half sister."

"I never heard anything so ridiculous," Hillary scoffed, but her tone of voice and facial expression made it clear that contrary to what Rose had told me, I wasn't telling Hillary anything she didn't already know.

"Your mother says she had a baby and gave it up for adoption."

"So?" Hillary leaned forward slightly. "That doesn't mean that Pat Humphrey is that child."

"Evidently she showed her the birth certificate."

Hillary snorted. "Which is about as credible as my mother's cat telling Pat Humphrey where she lived."

"You're saying you believe it was forged?"

"What do you think? Look, my mother is old. My mother is lonely. My mother had a stroke. She's scared of dying alone. She'll believe anything if she thinks you care about her."

"Which you don't."

"We're not a Hallmark-card kind of family." Hillary started moving her ring up and down her finger again. "I used to. She was the one who didn't care about me. She didn't care about any of us. We're all disappointments to her."

"How do you know?"

"She's told us. An infinite number of times. She wanted Louis to go to law school. He barely made it through high school, let alone graduating college. And then he goes and joins the postal service. And me! She wanted me to be the wife of . . . I don't know . . . someone famous . . . someone rich. She wanted a daughter she could brag on at the country club, not a teacher, not someone who sings"—Hillary swept her hand around her—"in a place like this. And as for Amy . . ."

"What about her?"

Hillary wiped the corner of her eye with the back of her hand, smudging her makeup even more. "Well, you know what she looks like. You've seen my mother. Imagine what she's had to say about that."

I didn't have to imagine. I could hear Rose's voice in my head telling me. "And then along comes Pat Humphrey . . ." I let my voice trail away.

"So neat. So cool looking." Hillary's voice shook with indignation. "She played my mother. I don't know how she did it, but she knew what my mother wanted to hear, and she gave it to her." Hillary took a deep breath.

"So then you didn't shoot her?"

Hillary glared at me. "I don't like guns."

"That doesn't mean you can't use them."

"Anyone can use one, for God's sake. It's not terribly difficult."

"It sounds as if you know how."

"My father and mother used to go hunting in Africa before he got sick. Of course I know about guns. Everyone in my family does. We have them all over the place."

"Including Geoff," I murmured, thinking of how he'd greeted me.

"You'll have to ask him about that."

"I will. So where were you when Pat Humphrey was shot?"

"I've already been through this with the police. I was at my house." Hillary smiled unpleasantly. "The neighbors saw me. Not that that means anything. I understand these days you can pay a couple of thousand to have someone kill someone else."

"Did you?"

"No. But if I find out who the shooter is, I'll give them a reward."

A phone rang, and Hillary burrowed into her bag to get it. "Where are you?" she said, turning away from me. "Well, come as soon as you can."

I got up, accidentally dislodging a magazine and sending it onto the floor.

"No," Hillary replied to the person on the other end of the line. "I just knocked something over. There's no one here." Then she turned off the phone.

"Your friend get held up?"

"You have to go."

"Do I?"

She plucked at her sleeve with long, skinny fingers. "Please."

I studied her. Hillary had crossed her arms over her chest and was kneading her shoulders with her hands. A phrase my grandmother used to use popped into my head. She used to say of someone that they looked as if they were held together with safety pins. The phrase seemed to fit Hillary.

"Don't worry," I said. "I'm leaving."

"Are you going to tell my mother about me?"

"That's what you want, isn't it?"

Hillary swallowed and turned her head away. When I left, she was sitting with her back to the door, her face buried in her hands.

I walked out of the bar, got into my car, and waited to see who was going to put in an appearance. It didn't take long.

Thirty minutes to be exact.

Chapter Twenty-six

I sat in my car, licking the last three squares of the old, melted chocolate bar I'd scrounged out of the glove compartment off its foil wrapper, watched the moon, and contemplated Hillary's relationship with her mother. Talk about fucked-up. Hillary was willing to jump over the cliff as long as her mother was watching. But then, who was I to say anything? Mine wasn't all that much better.

What had the last fight we'd had been about, anyway? That fight in the hospital room crammed with orchids and roses. And me, dumb schmuck, standing there with my get-better bunch of carnations clutched in my hand. I crumpled the foil wrapper up into a tight little ball, tossed it out of the car window, and wiped my fingers off on the front page of yesterday's newspaper.

Had we fought about my hair being so messy or the dress I was wearing or why I was walking around on shoes with run-down heels? That's what we usually argued about. Only, of course, it never was about that at all. It was about everything else. The man I was seeing and later married. The fact that I wasn't living my life the way she wanted me to. I'd stormed out of the room, and that had been that. A week of not calling had turned into a month and then six and then a year. My mother had come up for Murphy's funeral. And gone home the next day. Both of us stiffly polite. Both of us wanting to say things and not being able to.

I watched an old, rusted-out Honda Civic chug by. I should call. I knew I should. I should call before it was too late. I'd told myself that before, but this time I actually took my cell phone out of my backpack, and before I had time to think, punched in the old, familiar number, but the moment I heard my mother's voice on the line, I pressed the disconnect button and called Manuel on his cell instead. I guess I was scared. At least that's what the therapist I used to go to would have said.

"Speak to me," Manuel said.

"I am, moron. You got anything for me on Debbie Wright yet?"

"I do. I do."

"Well," I said after a moment had gone by.

"I think this might be worth more than a hundred bucks . . ."

"Manuel, I am not in a good mood," I told him as I fished around in my backpack for my cigarettes. I took one out, then put it back. I'd been smoking way too much lately.

"Okay. Okay. She's moved out of her family's house and is livin' over on Catherine Street. She works at one of those toy stores in the mall part-time and deals dope on the side. Nothing big. Some pills, a little E, pot, dabbles in smack once in a while. Strictly amateur night."

"This is not a big surprise."

"What?" he squawked. "You know how long it took me to get this info?"

"Knowing you as I do, you probably knew it already."

"Come on, Robin. Don't be cheap."

"Don't tell me you've been out to the casino again."

Manuel was suddenly silent.

"You've got to stay away from there."

"I know. I know. You know what else Debbie told me?"

"What?" I asked as I eyed the street.

"She said that Bethany's dad is shipping her off next week and that he's got her under house arrest."

"Manuel, what did you expect? Hold on a second. Debbie's boyfriend is here."

"The weirdo?"

"That's so politically incorrect."

"What the hell is that supposed to mean?"

"Never mind."

Louis was walking up the other side of North State Street. His height and weight made him impossible to miss. He would have stood out in the middle of a crowd in Times Square on New Year's Eve. Not that that was a problem, since at the moment there was no one else on the street.

"Man, I don't get it. Debbie, she wouldn't give me anything, but she's hooked up with this guy who wears dresses."

"Maybe she gets off on making him up."

As I watched Louis enter the club, I began to feel sorry for Rose Taylor despite myself. She'd asked me to tell her what I found out about her children. The way things were looking, she was going to get way more than she bargained for. I asked Manuel to go to my house and walk Zsa Zsa and hung up.

The wind had died down. Everything was still. A man wheeling a shopping cart filled with dirty clothes walked down the middle of the street talking to himself as I studied the marquee. I realized that someone had made a mistake and put an apostrophe between the n and the s. I wondered if I should say something as I locked up and went back inside.

It took a minute for my eyes to readjust to the dim lighting. I glanced around the room and spotted Louis sitting at the bar. Which surprised me. I'd expected him to go directly to his sister's dressing room. Or maybe he already had. Maybe he'd made his delivery and come straight back out. In any case, he was sitting opposite the door, watching something outside my range of vision, off to the left. When I walked in, Russell had just finished putting a beer down in front of him. I went over and said hello.

"My, this is a coincidence," I chirped, slipping onto the bar stool next to Louis's.

He turned around to face me.

"I almost didn't recognize you dressed like this."

He looked down at his polo shirt and khaki shorts, then back up at me. "Is that supposed to be some kind of joke?"

"No. How was the party?"

"I never got to go."

"I hope you're not blaming me for that."

Louis grunted.

"You'll be happy to hear my jaw is fine."

He took a sip of his beer. I couldn't take my eyes off his hands. They were so large, they nearly hid the glass. No wonder my jaw still ached. I was lucky it wasn't wired shut.

"I wasn't worried."

"That's not what Debbie said."

He grimaced. "Debbie doesn't know shit. I told you I used to box pro. You shoulda listened. What are you doing here, anyway?"

"I came to hear your sister sing."

"That makes two of us."

"Oh. I was thinking you might have come for another reason."

Louis's eyes narrowed. "Such as?"

"You might have brought her something she needs."

He tapped the counter with his fingertips. "And what, pray tell, would that be?"

"I don't know. Throat spray. Lozenges."

Louis gazed at me for a few seconds, assessing me, his face expressionless, before turning back to his drink. "She takes care of those things herself." He took another sip of beer. As I watched him, I could hear one of the guys at a table near us telling his friends what a dead place Syracuse was. "Hillary is good," Louis added.

"So I've been told," I agreed.

"Too good for here," Louis observed. He picked up his napkin and began shredding it. Then he took the shreds and placed them in the ashtray next to him.

"So how come she is?"

He shrugged. "I'm not sure. I think she owes the owner a favor."

I thought back to the scene I'd witnessed between Hillary and Johnny Q. Somehow that wasn't the impression I'd come away with.

"It's amazing this place is still open." His eyes took in the surroundings. "It reminds me of a factory."

I didn't tell him that was the whole idea.

"Why anyone would want to come here is beyond me."

"It doesn't look as if many people have."

He gave me a half-smile. "I keep telling Hillary she should get out of here and go down to New York City."

"Why doesn't she?"

Louis shook his head. "She went down when she was younger. Something happened—I don't know what—and she never went back."

"Is anyone else in your family musical?"

"My mother is. She has a very good voice. Amy and I can't carry a tune." He took another sip of his beer and lifted his glass. "Hey, let me buy you one of these."

"Thanks, but I think I'll pass."

"I insist. To make up for your jaw." He called to Russell, who'd been talking to someone down at the other end of the bar. "Bring her whatever she wants," he said to him when he came over.

"Can't stay away," Russell said to me.

"It's your compelling personality."

"Oh, I thought it was the beer."

Louis shot me a puzzled look.

"I was here a little earlier," I explained. "I liked your sister's singing so much I decided to stay around for the next set." I turned to Russell. "Do you have Black Label?"

Russell shook his head. "We have Johnny Walker Red." He put both hands on the bar and leaned toward me. "You look familiar," he said, scrutinizing my face. "Why is that?"

"Because you saw me earlier this evening?"

"No. I thought that when you came in the first time. Are you someone I should know?"

"Doubtful. I have a generic face."

Russell snapped his fingers. "They did a story on you a while ago in the paper. You found someone's dog for them or something. You're some kind of pet detective or something weird like that . . ."

"She investigates things, for God's sake," Louis said.

"Did Louis lose his Chihuahua?" Russell asked.

I smiled unpleasantly. "No. I'm investigating you." What can I say? The man irritated me.

He raised an eyebrow. "Really?"

"And this place."

"I thought you had to have a license to do that kind of thing."

"I work under Paul Santini's," I lied.

"Find out anything yet?"

"No. But I'm sure I will."

Russell grinned. "You want a private Q & A, all you got to do is ask me."

"I'll bear that in mind."

He wiped his hands on the towel he'd slung over his shoulder. "So, did you say you wanted a Sex on the Beach?"

"No. I said I wanted a shot of Red Label with a glass of ice and water on the side."

"If you insist." And he winked at me. "But you'd like my suggestion better."

Russell poured my drink and moved down to the other end of the bar.

"What a schmuck," Louis muttered, nodding in Russell's direction. "He has to come on to anything that walks."

"So how's Debbie?" I poured the scotch over the ice, then added a little water.

"Debbie's fine." Louis pointed to the ceiling. I followed his finger. "They had a tin ceiling here, and Johnny just ripped it out and threw it away. You know how much it was worth?"

"As much as Pat Humphrey's necklace?"

Louis studied the room for a few seconds before answering. "I know I have a problem."

"Several."

"I'm seeing a therapist."

"And that gives you carte blanche?"

"I didn't say that. But Pat understood."

"That's not the impression I got."

"She did." Louis frowned. "I apologized. I was going to return it." Louis took another sip of his beer. "I haven't been to Wolfe Island in years. Not since they redid the docks. Amy and I used to catch frogs there." He took a handful of peanuts out of the bowl near him, then shook his head as if to clear it. "It's a shame what happened to Pat. I liked her."

"Who?"

"Pat Humphrey."

"Your sister didn't," I told him while I watched Johnny Q come out from the back and walk over to the bar. He lifted up a hand and beckoned to Russell, who drifted over.

"You mean Hillary, I take it?" Louis said.

I nodded.

"She's a very jealous person."

"But you're not?"

"Not of her."

"What would you say if I told you Pat Humphrey was your half sister?" I asked him, watching his face carefully to see what his reaction was.

"I'd say wow." He'd opened his eyes wide in a caricature of girlish astonishment, the gesture making his face look grotesque.

It was obvious Louis wasn't surprised by the news, either, even though he was trying hard to act as if he were. And if he knew, Amy probably did, too. The question was: When had the three of them found out? Before Pat Humphrey was shot or after? And how had they found out? Rose had sworn she hadn't told anyone. And I more or less believed her. At least if she had a reason to lie, I didn't know what it was. Which meant that Pat Humphrey was the one who had talked.

"I'd say you were crazy." Louis paused for a few seconds to study my face. "You're not kidding, are you?"

"No." I told him what I'd told Hillary as the lights in the bar dimmed even more and she and her pianist came back onstage.

Hillary looked calmer. Her brow wasn't furrowed up. Her hands weren't shaking. Obviously, she'd gotten what she needed. The question was: Had she gotten it from Louis or from someone else?

I took another sip of my drink and settled down to listen to her sing. Louis excused himself and walked toward the back, where the bathrooms were located. I noticed he stopped to chat for a minute with Russell and Johnny Q before continuing on his way. The pianist had just sat down at the piano when Johnny Q came over and sat down next to me.

"You know Louis?"

"We've met."

Johnny Q played with the zipper of his shirt, revealing a tuft of chest hair. He shook his head and gestured toward the club. "So whaddya think?"

"I like it."

"I'm getting tired of it myself. I think things should always be changing, you know?" He twisted the band of silver he was wearing on the upper portion of his thumb. "You got to reformat. Otherwise it gets boring. Speaking of boring, you must really like Hillary to stick around for her second set."

"Don't you?"

"No. She's old." He pronounced the word as if it were a disease that he was going to do his damnedest not to catch. "That stuff she sings should stay in the forties where it belongs."

"Then why is she here?"

He clicked the metal ball in his tongue against his teeth. "Because she's paying me."

"Paying you?" I asked as I wondered why he'd gotten his tongue pierced and how much it hurt.

He grinned. "Yeah. This is like a showcase."

"That's fairly low rent. Kind of like one step up from a scam."

He didn't even look affronted. "You think? I'm just doing what everyone else is—trying to stay afloat and make a buck. And anyway, it's hard to say no to family."

"I didn't know you're related."

"Very distantly." Johnny Q rubbed his tattoo. It was impossible to hide. A black band of abstract shapes, it came halfway up his neck like a choker. I wondered what he'd do if he ever went corporate. "So you and Hillary kissed and made up?"

"We've come to an understanding."

"Good. Because I wouldn't want to have to throw her out."

"And lose that money."

"Hey," Johnny Q protested. "Do you have any idea how much it costs to keep a place like this going? The liquor, the help, the electricity, garbage pickup . . ."

I interrupted. "How much is she paying you?"

"Enough. Enough to make it worthwhile." He looked down at my glass. "What's in there?"

"Johnny Walker Red."

"Don't drink that crap." He raised his hand and beckoned to Russell. "Bring her some from my private stock." Then he turned toward me. "Russell says you're an investigator. He says you're investigating the club." And he moved closer, grazing my leg with his. I glared at him, and he moved his leg away—fractionally.

"Is that why you're here?"

"No. I've always wanted to meet a lady detective."

"Then you should go back to your office. I just said that because your bartender was pissing me off."

"Well, Russ does have that ability." He put his elbow on

the bar, leaned his head on his hand, and studied me. "Would you tell me if you were?"

"Investigating you?"

"Yes."

"That depends."

"On what?"

"What tactic I think would be most effective."

"It must be a dangerous job. Especially for someone like you." And he favored me with a nasty smile.

"You mean, because I'm a woman?"

"Exactly."

"I've found that weapons equalize things."

"Not always." He straightened up. "Not when you can't see things coming."

Russell set a glassful of an amber liquid in front of me, then moved away.

"Meaning?" I said.

"Nothing. I was just making an observation. Here. Try this," Johnny Q said, pointing to the glass. "It's the real deal. Single malt. Aged twenty-five years."

He watched my face as I took a sip. The taste exploded on my tongue and moved to the back of my throat. "Good, isn't it?"

"Very."

He clicked the metal ball in his tongue against his teeth again. "That's what they're selling down in the city. Can't keep the stuff in stock down there, but I can't push it up here. No market. If I go through a bottle every two weeks, I'd be doing well. The people that would buy it don't have the money, and the ones with the money have taste up their asses."

I took another sip and rolled the scotch around in my mouth before I swallowed it. "Why did you pierce your tongue?"

Johnny leered. "Ask some of my girlfriends. They'll tell you."

"I think I'll pass."

He grinned. "Oh, well. No harm meant. You are an investigator, though. Russell was right about that."

"Yes. But I'm not here in that capacity."

"Then what capacity are you here in?"

"I already told you. Hillary and I had some business we had to settle."

"And what kind of business is that?"

"The none-of-your-business kind."

"You don't look like the type of people she usually does business with."

I shrugged. "I can't answer that, since I don't know what those people look like."

"They're definitely on the scummier side of the equation, the kind that deal dope out of the front seat of their cars."

I turned slightly and watched as the pianist seated himself at the bench and began to play. No one in the room paid any attention. Hillary walked up to the microphone and adjusted it. It let out a loud screech. For a moment people were startled into silence, then they went back to chattering.

Johnny Q tapped his fingers on the bar. "I'll be glad when she's gone," he muttered in my ear.

"Despite the money she's paying you?"

"Yes. I don't need the kind of trouble she brings with her."

I watched Johnny take another sip of his drink. "Besides that, she's a downer. People want to go out and have a good time, not listen to the crap she's singing."

"Then why do you let her up there?"

"I already told you," he replied.

"I just thought there might be more to it."

He clicked the ball in his tongue against his teeth. "Like what?"

I shrugged my shoulders. "If I knew, I wouldn't be asking."

I went back to studying Hillary. She was ignoring everyone. She closed her eyes, flung her head back, and opened her mouth. The notes from "Can't Help Lovin' That Man of Mine" floated out into the air.

As my gaze roamed around the room, I caught sight of Debbie Wright.

She was standing in the hallway, beckoning to me.

When she realized I'd seen her, she shrank back against the wall.

I told Johnny I was going to the bathroom and went to see what she wanted.

Chapter Twenty-seven

As I neared her, Debbie grabbed me and pulled me farther down into the hallway, away from everyone's line of sight. "I shouldn't be doing this," she said, looking over her shoulder.

"Doing what?"

"Telling you this, but that drink Johnny gave you. Don't have any more of it. It's doctored." She kept shifting her head to study the main room, then turned back to look at me.

"With what?" I asked, even though I thought I already knew.

"Roofies."

What else? This generation's Mickey Finn. A new wrinkle on chloral hydrate. Christened the date-rape drug by the media. The scourge of college campuses. The reason there are signs in university bars telling people to take their drinks with them. Short for Rohypnol. Featured in *Time* magazine. Colorless, odorless, tasteless. Dissolves easily. Originally used in surgery. Ingested, it makes you compliant but blocks all memory of what has happened.

I studied Debbie's face. She'd changed her hair color to purple. In the dim light it made her look like one of the living dead, but I suppose that was the general idea. "How do you know?"

"Because I heard Johnny talking to Louis. Louis didn't want to have anything to do with it."

"But he didn't stop it, either. Legally, that means he's liable as well."

Debbie bit her lip.

A couple of thoughts surfaced while I watched Debbie fiddle with her necklace. Like why was Johnny doing this? I was almost certain he'd believed me when I'd told him I was joking about investigating his bar. And even if I weren't, why call attention to yourself? Why not just give me my drinks and hustle me out? And then there was Debbie, virtually implicating her boyfriend in this little scenario.

"I don't get your reason for telling me this."

Debbie twisted a piece of her hair around her finger and turned her toes in till she was standing pigeon-toed, making her look like a baby vampire. "Because Manuel likes you," she said. "And I want to do something that puts me in good with him."

"Really?" I ticked off the points I was making on my fingers. "Number one, I didn't think he was your type, and number two, aren't you already seeing someone?"

She canned the little-girl act. "Okay. If you really want to know, Bethany's dad, he's talking about having me arrested. I just thought that maybe you could put in a good word for me. I'm doing that quid bro"—she waved her hand—"that latin thing."

"You mean quid pro quo? Why don't you ask Hillary for a recommendation?"

Debbie tittered.

"After all, she's one of your satisfied customers, isn't she?"

Debbie ducked her head and began chewing on one of her cuticles. "That's not what I meant."

"I know."

The more I thought about it, the less I trusted her. "You're putting me on about the drink, aren't you? Is there anything in it?"

"I was just trying to help you, but if you feel that way . . ."

Her voice drifted off. She went to leave, but I latched onto her wrist. "Let me go," she demanded, trying to pull away.

"Tell me."

"It could have happened," she whined as she tried to peel my fingers off.

"But it hasn't. Has it? Has it?" I insisted.

Debbie didn't say anything.

"That's what I thought. What are you? A pathological liar?"

Her eyes blazed. "Don't pull that number on me. At least I'm not lying to myself." This time she managed to yank her arm away from me. "Which is more than I can say for you."

"Save your rap for someone who cares."

"Fine. But you think you're doing good by finding Bethany. Being the good guy and all the rest of that pathetic stuff. Well, you aren't. You should have left her alone. She was better off with her friends than that family of hers."

"That is not true." I was about to say something else when a door opened. The light spilled out, and one of the men that I'd seen in the office earlier with Johnny stepped into the hallway.

"*Que pasa?*" he demanded.

"Nothing," I replied as Debbie took off down the hall. "Nothing at all." As I looked at him, I realized I'd seen him before, and then, after a few seconds, I remembered where. "You're one of Sinclair's goons aren't you?"

"Sinclair. Who is this Sinclair?"

"You escorted me to my car."

He made a shooing motion with his hands. "You better go back. This area is for employees only. It's not safe to be here."

"What are you doing here?"

The man moved forward. "Did you hear what I just said?"

"Yeah, I heard." Suddenly, his English was okay. But instead of doing what he'd requested, I went through the nearest door, mostly because it was so obvious he wanted me out of there.

Eight Hispanics turned away from the television program they were watching when I came in.

"I told you not to go in there," Sinclair's man said as he dragged me back into the hallway.

Someone got up and closed the door, but I'd seen enough. The cramped room with the dirt-streaked walls. The coffee table littered with soda bottles and Styrofoam coffee cups. The television playing a Spanish station. The fear on the men's faces when they saw me.

"Sinclair said you were trouble," the man growled.

Suddenly he was holding a knife to the base of my throat. A big one. Not that it would have mattered if it had been smaller. The results would be the same. In this case, size doesn't make a difference. I wondered where the hell he'd been hiding the knife, although that didn't matter, either. I had an overwhelming urge to swallow. I suppressed it.

"He said you'd be back." He stuck his face close to mine. I could see the cyst on the side of his cheek.

And that's when it struck me. "Sinclair told you I was an INS agent, didn't he?"

"I'm not going to let you harm my friends."

"You're the one with the knife."

Now everything made sense. Sinclair's attitude, the paucity of guests at his place, the way I'd gotten escorted off his property. Sinclair was running undocumented workers through the Center for Enlightened Self-Awareness, an easy enough thing to do considering the center's location between Kingston, Ontario, and the United States. Smuggling has always been big around that neck of the woods, right from Depression days, when they'd smuggled liquor in from Canada. Today the traffic leans toward dope, cigarettes, and illegal immigrants, although most of the traffic comes through farther north.

"Think about it. Do I look like INS to you?" I asked him. "Would I come in here like this if I were? Would I be that dumb? I don't think so."

The guy hesitated. The point of the knife receded slightly.

"Come on. What's your name?"

"Estevez . . ."

"Okay, Estevez, put the knife down before you hurt me and get yourself into serious trouble. My identification is in my backpack. I'm not here for you or your friends. I'm here to ask questions about a woman named Pat Humphrey. Go on, look," I urged.

I held my breath and waited while he made up my mind.

"Bueno," he finally said.

Thank God. He had gone through most of my stuff when he turned to me. "Who is this?" he asked.

I realized he was holding the picture of Dorita and her children in his hand. "I don't know." As I explained, Estevez sucked the air in through the gap in his front teeth.

"Can I keep this?" he asked when I was done.

"Sure." I reached over and scribbled my phone number on the bottom of it. "Call me if you find anything out."

He nodded. Then, before I could say anything else, Johnny Q was walking toward us. His cologne preceded him by a good ten feet or so. "What's going on here?" he demanded.

"Nothing. Your friend and I were just having a little chat."

Johnny Q nodded at Estevez. "Go on. Get out of here. Tell Russ we need some more glasses."

Estevez nodded and left.

"He's a little on the slow side," Johnny Q said to me. "But he mops a mean floor."

"I bet he does. Probably for free."

"Would you care to elaborate?"

I picked up my backpack and fished around for my cigarettes. I felt an urgent need for one at the moment. "You're Sinclair's partner, aren't you?"

Johnny raised his eyebrows. "Sinclair? Who is Sinclair?"

"The Reverend Ascending Moon."

"I'm supposed to know this name?"

"You should," I said to Johnny after I'd lit a Camel and taken a puff.

"You're not making any sense."

"You and he are running undocumented workers through Wolfe Island. Sinclair brings them in from Canada, and you let them stay here, before they go off to do whatever. Like work in the restaurants downtown. Pick apples. Garden. Go down to Long Island."

Johnny chuckled. "You have a good imagination. You should be writing fiction."

I pointed to the door I'd opened. "Who are those guys in there?"

"They're friends of Estevez—not that it's any business of yours. I'm just doing them a favor by letting them hang out here a little while. They drink a little beer. Play a couple of hands of cards. Watch the fights. You have a problem with that?"

"You're a nice guy."

"Yes, I am. Since when is being nice illegal?"

"I'd be willing to bet that most of the guys in that room don't have a green card."

Johnny shrugged. "I wouldn't know. I never asked. It would be rude. What am I supposed to do? Check and see if everyone who comes in here has one? Where are we? In Russia?"

I took another puff of my cigarette and stubbed it out. My throat felt raw, and it was only making it worse. "I don't believe you."

"Like I give a shit."

"You should. I'm sure if the authorities went over your books they'd find some interesting things."

"Like the fact that I'm losing money?"

"That's why you don't care if this place turns a profit or not. It's just a cover."

"Think whatever you want."

I moved closer to him. "Well, this is what I'm thinking. I'm thinking that somehow or other Pat Humphrey found out about this operation and was going to report it. Which is why one of you guys shot her."

"Hey, hey, hey." Johnny adjusted his belt. He looked flustered for the first time. "Just slow it down. I didn't kill anyone. I'm a vegetarian, for God's sake."

"A vegetarian? There you go." I put my hands out palms upward. "A first-rate defense."

"I don't kill things. I don't believe in it."

"Does your father know you're a vegetarian?"

"Leave my father out of this."

"I'm not sure that's going to be possible."

"It had better be. I'm serious about that."

"Or you'll what?"

"Trust me, you don't want to push this." Johnny ran his hand through his hair. "I'm telling you for the last time, these guys are friends of Estevez. I'm doing them a favor letting them hang out here."

"Favor? That's an interesting turn of phrase." I flicked my cigarette on the floor and ground it out. "So now you're a humanitarian? An upstanding member of the community? The last of the good guys?"

"You're goddamned right I am. The people in that room are legal."

"How do you know? You just told me you weren't sure."

"Fuck you." Johnny shook a finger at me. "But even if they weren't—so what. You know what their lives are like back home? Why do you think they come here? At least here they can earn a living. They can send money to their families back home."

"Washing dishes and taking out trash."

"It's better than nothing."

"Not always." I thought about the way Raul had looked when I'd found him on the road. His skin so hot and dry. His lips cracked. His cough. "Sometimes people don't pay them for their work. Sometimes they don't have enough to feed themselves or to see a doctor if they get sick."

"Hey. I'm sorry if that's the case, but that has nothing to do with me."

"How much of a percentage are you taking off?"

"Me? I already told you I'm not getting anything."

"I don't believe you. I don't think the INS will, either," I added.

"Go ahead. Call them if you want. But before you make a fool out of yourself, go talk to Sinclair. Talk to the woman he got the house from. She knows."

"Rose Taylor?"

"No. Her daughter. Amy."

"How does she fit in?"

"Find out for yourself."

"I think you're lying."

Johnny shrugged. "I don't care. Believe what you want. And by the way, don't come in here again. You're not welcome."

"I can live with that," I told him. As I watched Johnny stride back to his office, it occurred to me that he was going to call Sinclair and that I didn't want him to do that before I got to speak to the reverend first.

Johnny was so involved in his own thoughts that I don't think he heard me following him. I don't think he heard me come in the door. He didn't hear me when he picked up the phone on his desk and began punching in the numbers.

"What the hell?" he said as the phone went dead on him.

Which is when he turned and saw me with the cord that I'd yanked out of the phone jack in my hand.

I smiled sweetly. "I understand the phone company is having a problem these days with their maintenance, which is why so many people are going cellular. Or is it digital? I always get those two confused."

Johnny started toward me. "You are going to be very, very sorry you did that."

"Maybe. Maybe not." And I brought up my other hand, the one that was holding the canister of mace I always carry with me. It wouldn't injure Johnny, but it would make him very, very unhappy for a short amount of time.

"Fuck you." But now he was moving away from, not toward, me.

If he'd been the tough guy he wanted to be, he would have charged me and taken his chances, but he wasn't. He was a pampered middle-class brat, used to his comfort, afraid of pain. I told him to get into the closet.

"They said you were crazy," he told me as he backed up toward it.

"And they were right."

"What are you going to do?"

"Give myself a little time. Now open the door and step inside."

"No." He planted his feet on the floor and folded his arms across his chest. "I'm not taking another step."

"If you don't think I'll spray you with this, you're seriously mistaken."

Johnny Q hesitated.

"Your eyes are going to burn. Your skin is going to feel as if it's on fire. You're going to wish someone would take a gun and shoot you."

"I don't believe you."

"That you'll feel that way or that I'll do it to you?"

"That you'll do it to me."

"Because I'm a woman? Don't bet on it, buster. Actually I have to be nastier than your average guy. Otherwise no one will take me seriously."

Johnny didn't say anything. I could see he was trying to decide if I would or I wouldn't.

"Fine," I said. "If that's the way you want it." I started to depress my finger.

"I'm going," he said, and went inside the closet.

I moved a couple of steps closer, but not close enough so that he could grab me. "Now shut the door."

"You're a dead woman," he said as he did.

I reached over and clicked the lock. "Maybe, but not today." Then I took his desk chair and jammed it underneath the lock.

"Light . . ." he growled as I removed his phone from his desk and stuffed it in my backpack.

"Relax," I told him. "Maybe you should take this opportunity as a gift to think about your direction in life."

I ignored the stream of obscenities that were coming out of the closet, found a piece of paper and a marker, and printed out *"Gone for the Evening."* I studied my writing for a moment, decided it looked good, then taped the sign to Johnny's office door and walked back inside.

"I'm leaving now," I told him. "Sleep tight. Don't let the bedbugs bite." And I locked the door and left.

On my way out, I stopped at the bar to talk to Russell. As I did, I noticed that Louis and Debbie had left already.

"I have a message from your boss. He said to tell you he had to leave. He wants you to close up."

Russell wiped his hands on the towel he'd slung across his shoulder. "What happened?"

I shrugged. "I'm not sure. He didn't say. Some kind of emergency."

"Typical," Russell muttered, and he started wiping down the bar.

As I left Quotations, I started having second thoughts about the wisdom of what I'd just done. But it was too late. It was a fait accompli.

Chapter Twenty-eight

As the *Wolfe Islander III* clanked away from the pier, I stared down at the water, so different now from the other night. Now the waves were lapping peacefully against the boat's hull instead of trying to rip the boards from the boat frame. I breathed in the air, the hint of pine, the smell of fish and diesel oil, and studied the stars overhead. At two o'clock in the morning the last ferry out of Kingston was almost empty, the only people on it sleepy-eyed and tipsy from their night in the bars.

Their tiredness must have been contagious, because suddenly I felt exhausted, too. The adrenaline I'd felt after leaving Quotations, that had buoyed me up on my ride over here, had vanished, leaving me doubting my judgment. Maybe I shouldn't have done this. Maybe Johnny Q would bust out of the closet and call Sinclair before I could get to him. Maybe I should have dialed the INS right away and let them handle it. But I wanted to have a look at Sinclair's records before they moved in and shut the place down.

If the records were still there. I figured it for a fifty-fifty possibility.

Because the truth of the matter was that even if the INS wasn't there, the homicide guys had probably already sealed off the place and carted them away. I wouldn't know until I arrived. It wasn't as if I could dial them up and tell them to

wait for me. I was a nobody. I had no official status whatso-
ever. No one had to talk to me. Nor would they except to ask
me what the hell I was doing back here and drag me down
and take another statement from me. Something I preferred
to skip.

This trip might turn out to be a gigantic waste of time. But
I didn't care. Even now, with my bones aching with fatigue, I
didn't think I'd be able to sleep. The idea of motion, of movement, seemed both a necessity and a solace. I had the feeling
that if I stopped, if I remained still, I might fall apart. It was
better to keep going. After all, things in motion remained in
motion. It was an immutable physical law. Stop and you
risked going over the edge of the whirlpool. And anyway, if I
was doing something, I wasn't drinking.

I spent the rest of the twenty-five minutes it took to make
the crossing from Kingston to Wolfe Island staring over the
railing at the black water below and seeing Murphy and myself in the wooden motorboat he'd dredged up from somewhere, cackling maniacally, drunk off our asses, sailing down
the East River. How we'd managed not to kill ourselves or
anyone else, I didn't know. I was thinking about how it had
taken us four tries to dock the boat at the City Island slip
when I realized that the ferry had stopped. We were here.

Once I drove my car off the ramp, there was no one on the
road, and I made good time. I'd been thinking that there'd be
a squad car around keeping an eye on things, but except for
a screech owl on a branch of one of the pine trees, the parking lot of the Center for Enlightened Self-Awareness was
empty. The guests had left. They'd certainly gotten a lot more
than they'd bargained for. They'd come here for a little peace
and gotten a lesson in the duality of the universe.

It looked as if Sinclair had gone, too. I wasn't surprised.
Given Sinclair's history, it was the logical thing for him to do.
It's what I would have done in his place. Why stick around
when there's trouble? It's better to just disappear. He was
probably on his way to points south by now, planning his

next scam. It looked as if George could stop worrying about getting stuck with an assault charge. Although I didn't think that would make George feel better. George. Man oh man. Just thinking about him made my stomach churn.

It wasn't my fault he'd lost it with Sinclair and beat him up. It wasn't my fault that it had brought back all of his bad memories. That it had ruptured the view of himself as an academic that he was so carefully constructing. Not talking to me wasn't going to help. I was really, really tired of his withdrawing every time anything went wrong. I was tired of waiting for him to decide that it was okay to talk to me. I chewed on the inside of my cheek. Well, screw him. If he didn't phone me soon, it was going to be a long time before he heard from me again. I could see our relationship ending, as Eliot wrote, "not with a bang, but a whimper."

I took a deep breath and told myself to think about Sinclair. He was simple. His motives were clear. I focused on how much money he'd taken with him as I drove over the lawn, up to the lodge, and got out. A sign on the door read: *Closed Until Further Notice*. Down a ways I could see the flickering of the yellow crime-scene tape, a reminder of where I'd found Pat Humphrey.

Twigs from the branches brought down by the storm crunched beneath my feet as I walked down there. A warm breeze was coming off the river, bringing with it the smell of fish. The pop, pop, pop of fireworks going off floated by in the wind. I studied the tape's boundaries, looking for what, I wasn't sure.

There was nothing to see, nothing that was going to help me with Humphrey's death. I crouched down and sifted the dirt through my fingers. A beetle crawled onto my hand. I let it get to my palm before I brushed it off, wiped my hands on my pants, and stood up.

On impulse, I went over to a rock where a small clump of wild asters was growing, plucked a sprig, and laid it on the place where Pat Humphrey had died. It seemed the least I could do. I said a short, silent prayer, went back to the lodge, and got a flashlight out of my car. The cops had padlocked the door and sealed it, not that that was going to stop me.

I picked up a big rock, walked around to the side away from the lake, and smashed one of the windows. When I finished knocking the remaining pieces of glass out of the sash, I hoisted myself up and climbed inside.

I went directly into Sinclair's office. I'd pretty much expected the police to have impounded his records, but they hadn't. Everything seemed the way I'd left it when I'd last been here, right down to the splotches of blood from where Amy had shot herself. I drew the curtains, covered the lamp with a cloth to dim the light further, and got down to work.

I spent the next two hours going over Sinclair's records. His records for the center were in good shape. His accountant would have been proud. He'd kept all his tax, water, and phone bills. Nothing unusual in any of them, although I noted that Sinclair had made frequent calls to Pat Humphrey's and Rose Taylor's numbers. By now I was positive Rose Taylor was the person who had set up the foundation that was responsible for giving Sinclair this house. The question was, what relevance did that fact have? Rich people often donated property to religious and educational institutions so they wouldn't have to pay taxes on it. That Rose Taylor had didn't mean that she knew what Sinclair was doing here. On the other hand, all her help was Hispanic. Coincidence? Maybe. Maybe not.

I moved on to another file, which listed the center's members and the amount of money each one had donated. Most had given between three and five thousand dollars, some had given as much as ten thousand, while a couple of unlucky souls had donated twenty grand each to the building of a temple. Sinclair even had a brochure printed detailing the structure. It was supposed to have stained-glass windows and everything. All told, I figured Sinclair had between one and two hundred thousand grand in the bank from contributions alone. Not bad for an ex-con who'd gotten religion. And if he had just left it at that and invested it in the stock market, things would have been fine, but he hadn't. He'd branched off into another sideline.

Maybe someone had suggested it to him. Or maybe he was in Canada and someone had approached him and asked him for a lift over to the island. Offered to pay him. And he'd agreed. And the man or woman Sinclair had transported had told his friends and they'd gotten in touch with Sinclair. And then he'd started providing other services.

The money was so easy, it had probably seemed irresistible. It was strictly a no-muss, no-fuss operation. He had a couple of boats already. Just bring the undocumented workers over from Canada on them, put them up in a few of the cabins, and then transport them to wherever they were going and get paid for doing it. Due to the beefed-up presence of border patrols on the Mexican-U.S. border over the last few years, it was now cheaper and easier for someone to fly to Canada and come into the United States that way than to pay a smuggler to get him across the border down South. Go figure.

Of course, so far I hadn't found records or evidence detailing any traffic of that sort. Either Sinclair had been smart enough not to record his profits—or do something like claim a tax deduction on wear and tear on his boat, as someone that had recently been arrested for cigarette smuggling had done—or he'd taken his records with him. A more likely possibility. Or there were no records and I had an extremely overactive imagination. I pulled out a couple of cartons by the desk into the middle of the floor and dumped them out. There was nothing in them but old newspapers and magazines. I thumbed through half of them in case there was something of interest, but from the looks of it, Sinclair had been saving them for the recycle bin.

After I searched his desk, which yielded nothing except a collection of bad pornography and a number of pens and pencils, I went through the clothes in his closet, at which point I finally found something of interest. A theater stub for a movie that Sinclair had attended the night Shana Driscoll had been killed was in one of his pants pockets. According to the time marked on it, Sinclair had been happily watching cars exploding and large men beating each other up when Shana was being drowned. That was good to know, not that it helped me much. I put the stub back where I'd found it, replaced the boxes with the newspapers, and tidied up and closed Sinclair's file drawers before I turned out the lights and left.

It was now a little past three in the morning. I decided to have one more look at the cabin Pat Humphrey and Amy had been staying in. I wasn't expecting to find much there, either, but I couldn't get off the island until 5:45 A.M., when the first ferry of the day went back to Kingston, so this seemed as good a way as any to kill a few hours.

Even with my brights on, it was difficult staying on the path, and I bumped and humped my way down it, my tires crunching over rocks. As I got out of the car, I saw bats flitting around under the trees. They were eating the mosquitoes the rain had brought out. They weren't doing a good enough job, though, because the mosquitoes started biting me as soon as I stepped outside. I kept slapping at them as I walked to the cabin, wishing I'd brought bug spray with me.

The door was open. No one had bothered to secure it. I stepped in and flicked on the light. Someone had tidied up the place. The beds were made, the clothes that had been lying on them were gone, but the room was still impregnated with Humphrey's perfume. I looked around some more. Except for a couple of aspirin, the nightstand was empty. I got down and glanced under the bed frames. There was nothing there except for some dust bunnies and a lone white sock. The dresser drawers were empty, too, but in the closet, all the way in the back, buried behind a couple of ripped screen windows, I found a box filled with stuff.

I lifted it up, carried it over to the bed, and tipped the contents out. The mattress groaned as I sat down on it. There were pictures of Pat Humphrey when she was growing up. A six-year-old Pat Humphrey—dressed up for Halloween as a fairy princess holding a wand in one hand and a goody bag in the other—with her mother and father. An older Pat Humphrey embracing the family dog, a golden retriever, who was wearing a T-shirt and hat. Pat Humphrey and family at a country fair. Pat Humphrey and her date at the senior prom. Pat Humphrey's high-school graduation picture, posed with her family in front of her high school, G. B. Delworth. The name was printed right on the front of the school in big black letters.

I slipped the picture into my backpack and continued looking. There were pictures of Pat Humphrey in her twenties in a bathing suit at a beach and pictures of her on a tennis court holding a racket and ball and smiling. I picked up some recent pictures of her in a waitress uniform, standing in a dining room in front of a large stone fireplace with a fire going in it, holding a trayful of drinks aloft.

I found a notebook from a class she'd taken in English poetry and a small stuffed dog, the kind they give out as prizes at county fairs. I found a couple of small trophies that she'd received for winning tennis tournaments when she'd been in high school and one for winning a swimming competition and another one for gymnastics.

I picked up Pat Humphrey's photos and shuffled them around, dealing them out like a pack of cards, but they didn't provide any answers. Neither did staring at them. I got up and stretched the kinks out of my back, then returned everything to the carton. I knew I should put the carton back in the closet where I'd found it, but I decided to take it with me instead. Just in case.

I stood in the center of the room and let my mind go blank. Johnny Q had told me to talk to Sinclair and Amy. Sinclair was gone. Amy wasn't. She was at home, having just been released from the hospital. But she had been here. Yet there was no sign of her presence. It looked as if someone had come and collected her possessions and left Pat Humphrey's. Why?

My gaze drifted around the room. If there was anything else here, I couldn't see it. I closed the door on my way out and went on to my last stop. As long as I had time, I figured I might as well check out the cabin Sinclair's other guests—the ones that weren't signing the register—had been staying in. I was calculating that the cabin was set somewhere back in the woods, away from the main drag.

The trees got thicker and the path smaller and rougher as I drove down the trail that was doing stand-in duty for a road. Finally, I was driving over stones and branches, and I had to stop before I ripped the bottom of my car out. I halted, took my flashlight out, and began walking. A fog was rolling in, making it harder to see, and the dew on the long grass soaked my legs and sandals. The hoarse croaking of a bullfrog broke the silence from time to time. I found myself tripping over twigs and stones as I walked farther into the pine grove. I was just about to turn back when I spotted what I was sure was the cabin I was looking for ahead.

I was positive I was right as I got closer. In contrast to the other cabins, this one looked neglected. The screen door was ripped, and a shutter was hanging down from one of the windows. A trash can outside overflowed with refuse. When I pushed on the door, it opened with a creak. There was a hole where the lock should have been. When I walked inside, the smell of unwashed bedding overwhelmed me. I tried the light switch, but it didn't work.

I shone my light around the room. It was filled with beds, twelve of them, each arranged as close to each other as possible. A few of them had stained mattresses; others had bottom sheets over them. The floor was strewn with fast-food wrappers. A table in the middle had paper plates with pizza crusts on them, piled grease-stained pizza boxes, and half-empty bottles of beer. I picked up the pizza box. Someone had scribbled a bunch of addresses and phone numbers on it.

It was too early in the morning to call them now. Instead, I copied them into my notebook, closed the door, went back to my car, and drove down to the ferry. Once I got to the parking lot, I called the local investigation unit of the INS on my cell and left an anonymous tip. Somehow it seemed simpler that way. Experience has taught me that the less I have to do with the federal government, the happier I am.

I checked my watch. I had an hour and a half to go before the ferry came in. By the time I got to the pier, a few streaks of light were visible on the horizon. I was the only car in the lot. I closed my eyes and tried to sleep, but the damned birds were chirping so loudly I couldn't.

I raised my windows to shut out the noise, but then it was too hot.

Finally I gave up, opened the windows back up, and lit a cigarette, the last one I had in the pack. I took out the sheet of phone numbers and addresses I'd copied down off the pizza box and looked at them carefully.

Which was when I realized that I knew some of the addresses on the list.

Chapter Twenty-nine

Manuel was sound asleep on my living-room sofa when I got home. He was curled up on his side with Zsa Zsa snuggled up against him. When she saw me, she jumped off and came running over, stopped a couple of inches away, made sure I was watching, squatted, and peed on the floor to tell me exactly what she thought about my leaving her alone.

"Bitch," I said. But in a nice way. She was right.

She came over and allowed me to pet her, after which she pranced back over to Manuel, wagged her rump, and jumped up next to him. I knew she'd forgive me—that's one of the good things about dogs—but not before she made me suffer for a little while.

"Be that way," I told her, and headed into the kitchen for a roll of paper towels.

I checked my answering machine. There was a message from Rose Taylor's lawyer asking me to call and a message from Tim telling me he was opening the store, and that was it. Nothing from George. If that's the way he wanted it, I told myself, fine. Screw him. I opened the fridge door and downed some of the orange juice Manuel had bought and devoured a half-eaten doughnut that was sitting on the kitchen counter. But that just made me hungrier. I felt slightly guilty about finishing the box of Frankenberry Manuel had also purchased but not guilty enough to not eat it. Then I wiped up Zsa Zsa's mess, went upstairs, turned on the fan, and collapsed on my bed. I fell asleep instantly.

I woke up at two o'clock in the afternoon feeling groggy and out of sorts. Zsa Zsa was splayed out next to me with her head on my pillow. I knew better than to tell her to get off. I stumbled out of bed, took a long shower, got dressed, and headed downstairs while she looked on. Manuel had left a note for me in the kitchen.

"Thanks for eating all my food," he'd written. *"You owe me $7.53. We need milk, eggs, and more cereal. Catch you later."*

It dawned on me as I read the note that Manuel was planning on staying for a while. Again. George wouldn't like it, but that didn't matter. Manuel made me laugh. Which, at the moment, was a hell of a lot more than I could say for George. I balled up the note and threw it in the trash.

I tried returning Moss Ryan's call, but he wasn't in. I left a message, then fed the cat, who'd just come meandering in, whistled for Zsa Zsa, and headed out the door. It was late, and I had several people I wanted to speak to. I figured I'd start with the Petersons, Bethany's parents, since I already knew them. Their address had been one of the ones listed on the pizza box. I stopped at the minimart, gassed up the car, grabbed a large coffee and a couple of doughnuts, and headed off to Caz.

As I came around a bend in the road, I caught glimpses of Cazenovia Lake between the trees. It was filled with Saturday sailors manning their boats. A wedding reception was in progress at one of the inns. Cars were parked all along the town's main street. But once I got near to where the Petersons lived, everything was quiet except for the hum of the occasional lawn mover. I hadn't called to tell them I was coming, and Millie Peterson seemed flustered to see me when she answered the door. She was wearing an old stretched-out T-shirt and stained Bermuda shorts. Her face was shiny with sweat.

Her blond hair stuck out in clumps. Specks of dirt clung to her cheeks. I apologized for dropping by without calling first.

"Arthur isn't here right now," she told me, wiping a strand of hair off her forehead with the back of her wrist. "He went out for a run."

I wanted to ask if she needed his permission to talk to me. Instead, I asked if I could come in, anyway.

Millie Peterson hesitated. "I was gardening."

"I can keep you company while you work, if you'd prefer."

"No. That's all right." And she motioned for me to come in. "He should be back soon."

Somehow I couldn't imagine Arthur Peterson running. He was too short and heavy. His wife must have thought so, too, because she said, "I don't know why he decided to take this up."

The house's air conditioning felt chilly on my bare arms and legs. "So how's Bethany?" I asked as Zsa Zsa and I followed Millie Peterson through the hallway and into the living room. I noticed her gait was stiffer. She was moving more slowly since I'd seen her last.

"She's fine," Millie said. "Just fine." And she curved her lips up in an apologetic smile. "Is this about the check? I'm positive Arthur said he sent it."

"He did. Can I speak to Bethany?"

She turned to face me. I noticed she'd developed a tic under her left eye. "Is that why you're here?"

"One of the reasons."

Millie bit her lip. "Arthur said . . ."

"What did I say?" Arthur asked as he walked into the living room.

Millie and I both jumped. Neither one of us had heard him come in.

Arthur Peterson was wearing running shorts and a tank top. His face and hair were slick with sweat, as were the chest hairs curling out of his top. His complexion was beet red. His chest was heaving up and down. He looked as if he were about to have a coronary.

"My, this is a pleasant surprise," he told me, although the expression on his face said otherwise.

"About Bethany . . ." his wife offered.

Arthur glanced at his wife. "Those shorts have seen better days. You should throw them out," he commented. I watched her flinch as he turned to me. "Bethany is fine. Didn't you get the check I sent you?"

I nodded. "So she's still here? I thought she'd be gone by now."

"She leaves for Florida next week. She's grounded until then. No guests. No phone. No TV. No radio."

"Can I see her?" What Debbie had said to me about Bethany must have bothered me more than I was willing to admit, because for some reason I needed to reassure myself that Bethany was okay.

Arthur Peterson raised his tank top and wiped the sweat off his beard with the bottom of it. "You came all the way out here to check up on her; that's very admirable. I hadn't expected such diligence."

"Is there a problem?"

"Not at all." He nodded to his wife. "Millie, why don't you bring Bethany out. You know, my daughter may not be happy to see you," he added as his wife scurried off to do his bidding. "Sometimes," he continued, his eyes following her, "it's hard for people to do the unpopular thing."

"Like your wife?" I hazarded.

Arthur Peterson sighed. "My wife is a lovely person, one of the sweetest I've ever known, but she thinks with her heart, not her head. She wants to take our daughter in her arms and make everything all right, but sometimes that approach doesn't work. Believe me, I wish it did."

"And you think your way is better?"

Peterson took a small white towel that was hanging on the back of one of the chairs and wiped his face with it. "I've been a family therapist for twenty years now. In my practice,

I've found that setting limits works. It may be painful. For everyone. But someone has to take charge. Obviously, you can't have a fifteen-year-old girl running around the streets."

"Obviously."

I looked up as his wife brought Bethany into the room. She was smaller than I remembered, and paler. More tentative in her movements. Her face was scrubbed; her blond hair had been redyed to a brown color and was pulled back in a ponytail. She wasn't wearing her gold jewelry. But the expression on her face was still the same—sullen.

"Say hello, Bethany," her father instructed.

"Hello," Bethany parroted.

"So?" I said. "How's it going?"

"Considering I'm a prisoner in my own house, just great."

"Now, Bethany . . ." her mother admonished.

"What? I'm not?" She faced me. "Satisfied?"

I didn't say anything.

"Here to collect your blood money?"

"I already have it."

She jutted her chin forward. "Then what?"

"I just wanted to see you."

"That's why you came?"

"One of the reasons."

"Bullshit," Bethany sneered. She picked up a fashion magazine and started to thumb through it. "I'm nothing but a check to you."

"So why are you here?" her father asked before I could answer her.

I turned back toward him. "A couple of reasons." I showed him the picture of Dorita that Raul had handed me. "Does she look familiar?"

Peterson shook his head.

"Are you sure?"

"Of course I'm sure. Is this it? Are you done?"

"Not quite." And I pulled out the list of addresses I'd copied down and handed it to Arthur Peterson. He looked at it and handed it back to me.

"Are these supposed to mean something?"

"One of these addresses is yours."

"I can see that."

"They were taken off a pizza box that I found in a cabin on Wolfe Island, a cabin that was a clearinghouse for undocumented workers. I was just wondering why they had your address?"

Peterson raked his beard with his fingertips. "May I ask what this is in relation to?"

"A case I'm working on involving the recent death of a woman called Pat Humphrey."

"Never heard of her."

"She was a pet psychic."

Peterson rolled his eyes. "Lord, grant me the strength to withstand this New Age gibberish."

"So you have no idea why you're on this list?"

He shrugged. "I don't have a clue. Maybe they were copying down phone numbers at random."

"You're such a friggin' hypocrite," Bethany cried. "You make me want to puke." And she threw down the magazine she'd been reading, turned, and stormed off to her room.

"See what I mean," her father said to me as we heard a door slam. "She's impossible."

"Why should she say something like that?"

He shrugged again and pulled on his beard. "Why does she say or do anything? I wish I had an explanation other than the fact that she's fifteen."

Out of the corner of my eye I watched Millie Peterson. She was studying the sofa. Her fingers were nervously plucking at the waistband of her shorts, as if she were playing a harp.

"Millie, do you know why she said that?" I asked.

"Me?" She gave an incredulous laugh. "I don't know why she says anything these days. I wish I did." But her eyes weren't meeting mine.

"I told you that trailer park should be cleaned up," Arthur pontificated to his wife. "I've said it from the first. But no one wants to listen. No one wants to do the hard thing anymore.

Everything is spin control. That was probably a list of people whose houses they were planning to rob. I'll bet anything on it."

"I doubt that," I told him.

He glared at me. "And what, may I inquire, makes you such an expert on this topic?"

I gazed out the living-room window at the landscaping. "How much land do you own?" I suddenly asked.

Peterson furrowed his brow at the question as he tried to figure out where I was going with it. "An acre," he answered. "An acre and a half. Why?"

"That's a lot to keep after."

"I hire a gardening service."

"Speaking of that," Millie said. "If you'll excuse me, I have to get back outside. The weeds are calling."

I put my hand out and stopped her as she went by. "One quick question."

"But I don't know anything," she wailed. "Arthur does all the hiring."

"But you're here."

"Could you get to your point?" Arthur Peterson said, interrupting.

I ignored him. "Millie," I said. "The man I picked up on the road that day. You knew him, didn't you? He'd worked for you. That's why you called your husband to the door, isn't it?"

"Don't be ridiculous." She bit her lip and studied the brown-and-orange patterned rug on the floor as if there were going to be an exam and she would be asked questions on it.

"My wife doesn't know what you're talking about, and neither do I," Arthur Peterson blustered.

I turned to face him. "I think you both do. I think you hire these people along with half the inhabitants in this area. That's why you're on the list."

"You have no basis for making that statement. None at all." He pounded his right hand into his left for emphasis. "If I had known you were going to come in here and insult me in my own house, I certainly would never have hired you. Now get out before I call the police."

"Gladly. But there's something I think you should know."

"I doubt that."

"That man in my car. He died from TB."

"Remember, I was there," Peterson replied. "I heard what the EMT guy told you. It has nothing to do with us."

"If you say so."

"Out," said Peterson, pointing to the door. "Now."

As I walked toward my car, I could hear Arthur Peterson yelling at his wife. His voice seeped out through the cracks in the door, disrupting the serenity of the late-Saturday summer afternoon.

Chapter Thirty

Zsa Zsa and I stopped at a couple more of the addresses on my list before heading over to the Taylor estate. The responses I encountered were pretty much the same as the ones I'd gotten at the Peterson house. Puzzlement. Outrage. Lots of rejoinders like: "I don't know what you're talking about" and "Who do you think you are?" I wasn't surprised. After all, who was going to admit they knew they were hiring undocumented workers to clean their kitchens and mow their lawns? These were the kind of people that wouldn't talk to Saint Peter on the final Judgment Day without proper representation. Why the hell should they talk to me?

Geoff opened the door when I rang the bell to his house. He was wearing tennis whites and carrying a racket.

I stopped leaning against the doorframe and straightened up. "Where's the maid?" I asked.

"It's her day off. What do you want?"

He didn't look pleased to see me, but then, so far no one had.

If I had less of an ego, I might have taken it personally.

But despite Geoff's costume, from the way he was looking, I had to surmise two homicides were not what he'd been counting on when he'd signed on as Mr. Taylor. The polished, I'm-so-cool look had been replaced by sprouting facial hair and bloodshot eyes with puffy lids. Evidently he hadn't been sleeping too well these days.

"I'd like to talk to your wife, if you don't mind."

"The boss lady?" He chuckled mirthlessly. "Even if I did mind, what difference would it make?" He tore at one of his cuticles with one of his fingernails.

"None." I watched Zsa Zsa chase a squirrel a short way before coming back and flopping down next to me.

"Does this have something to do with Pat Humphrey?"

"It might."

"God." Geoff ran his free hand through his hair. I noticed his fingers had a slight tremor to them. "I rue the day that woman ever came into this house."

"I bet you do." I looked around.

The grass had been mowed, the bushes clipped. The water in the swimming pool was a limpid blue. The sprinklers were making hissing noises as arcs of water shot out from them. Everything looked the way it had the first time I'd set foot in the place, with the notable exception of the outdoor staff, who seemed to have disappeared. Or maybe I was just being unduly suspicious. Maybe they all had the day off. Then I wondered if Johnny had gotten out of the closet yet. I should probably call Russell and make sure.

"So how are things going?" I asked Geoff. "How is Rose doing?"

Geoff let out a strangled laugh. "My wife? Better than I am, if truth be known."

I gestured toward the house. "Are you going to let me in? I need to see her."

"She's not in there."

I waited and watched Zsa Zsa sniff around one of the laurel bushes. "Well, where is she?" I asked after a minute or so had gone by.

Geoff gazed off into the distance, seemingly tracking the lone cloud in the sky. "With Amy," he finally said.

"At the hospital?"

"No. Our little murderer has been released to the fond embrace of her family." He waved his tennis racket in the air. "Bad joke. Sorry. Forget I said that. She's staying in the cottage for the present."

"The place Shana was living in?"

Geoff nodded. "That's right. Pretty bizarre, isn't it? But you know what Rose said when I made a comment? She said, 'Life goes on.' "

"Maybe she didn't like Shana as much as you did."

Geoff gripped my arm and pulled himself toward me. I could smell the whiskey on his breath. "What's that supposed to mean?"

"Well, you did like her, didn't you?"

Geoff swallowed. He let go of me. His eyes drifted in the direction of the swimming pool. I wondered if he was seeing himself and Shana there. "She was a nice woman," he allowed. "Fun to be with. When you gave her things, she had this neat habit of cocking her head and looking as if your present was the best thing in the world. It didn't have to be anything big, either." He paused. "I still haven't been able to take a swim in the pool." He shook his head. "I ask you, is that stupid or what?"

"Not really." After finding Murphy's body in the garage, I hadn't been able to go into it for six months. I'd parked my car in the driveway.

"I wanted to keep her dog," Geoff said. "Maurice liked me. He really did. I thought it would be nice to have him around."

"So why didn't you? What happened?"

"Rose wouldn't hear of it. Claimed the dog would ruin the carpets." Geoff ran his fingers over the tennis-racket strings. "It seemed the least I could do."

"Where is Maurice?"

"I found a home for him with a friend of mine. He'll be fine." And Geoff lapsed into silence.

I lit a cigarette.

"Got an extra?" Geoff asked.

"I didn't know you smoked."

"I quit when I met Rose," Geoff said as I handed him my pack.

"You know," I said after he'd lit up, "given the way Amy is, I'm surprised that she consented to stay in the cottage. I would have thought she would have refused. Negative karma. Ghosts. That sort of thing."

"God, this is good," Geoff said, taking a deep puff of my Camel. "They have her so doped up she could be in the Taj Mahal and she wouldn't know the difference."

"But why not the house?"

Geoff made a wry expression. "Amy has someone watching her. Rose said she didn't want to be disturbed by all the comings and goings." He shifted his weight from his right to his left foot. "And now, if you don't mind, I've got to get onto the courts. I have a tournament coming up at the club, and I'm going to need all the practice I can get in."

Given Geoff's present condition, I'd say he was going to need a lot more than a couple of practice rounds on the back court to win, but I wished him luck and walked down to the cottage to find Rose.

The first thing I saw when I pushed the door to the cottage open was a man standing in the middle of the kitchen who could have been a stand-in for one of the World Federation Wrestling bad guys. He was about six feet four, probably weighed at least three hundred pounds, and had biceps the size of cantaloupes, a chest you could break things on, and a shaved head that looked as if it had been polished. The hoops he was wearing in his ears only added to the impression of menace. He put down the sandwich he was eating and turned to face me. The expression on his face was far from welcoming.

"Yes?" he growled.

"I'm Robin Light, and I'd like to speak to Mrs. Taylor."

He gave me a quick appraising glance and must have decided I wasn't going to be any trouble, because he said, "She's busy with her daughter. Come back later," before returning to his sandwich.

"I need to speak to her now."

"Didn't you hear what I said?" Annoyed, he slapped the sandwich down on the plate and started toward me. "I told you to come back later."

"Listen, bud, I'm trying to be nice here."

"Or you'll . . ." He sneered.

"Leave."

"It's all right, Tom."

We both turned. Rose Taylor had wheeled herself into the room. Her hair and face were immaculate. She was wearing an expensive white linen blouse and matching pants. A strand of pearls circled her neck.

Tom touched the edge of his hand to his forehead in a mock salute. "If you say so, Mrs. T," and went back into the kitchen.

"You're hiring bodyguards now?"

Rose looked up at me and frowned. "Tom is a nurse. He comes highly recommended."

From where? I wondered. The state psychiatric facility? Attica?

"Moss has been trying to get hold of you," she continued. "He wants to know what progress you're making."

"I called him back earlier today. He wasn't there."

"He's at the club." Rose absentmindedly brushed the pearls with the tips of her fingers. "You can reach him there. So where have you been?"

"Out at Wolfe Island. Among other places."

"Wolfe Island," she mused aloud. "It's been years since I've been there. Sanford and I used to have a nice time there when the children were little. His father built the place as a fishing lodge."

"That's what Louis said."

A smile flickered across Rose's face. "He used to love to catch frogs when he was little. He always wanted to bring them back with him. He used to cry when I made him let them go."

"The lodge you're talking about. Did you turn it over to a man called Sinclair?"

"Sinclair?" Rose looked puzzled.

"The Reverend Ascending Moon, the one who renamed your place the Center for Enlightened Self-Awareness."

"Oh, yes." She nodded. "Him. Of course. How could I have forgotten?"

"I was wondering the same thing myself."

"Do you know how many charitable donations I give each year?" she demanded. "Exactly," she said when I demurred. "Amy begged me to." Rose rested her hand on the pearls. "The reverend needed a place, and he seemed to be doing Amy some good. She seemed quieter, more at peace. I couldn't see any harm."

"And you get to write the property off."

"That, too," Rose agreed. "I won't deny it. I don't see anything wrong with helping someone as well as getting a little bit back for myself. Isn't that what enlightened self-interest is all about? I'm not religious, but when Sinclair told me about his beliefs, I thought they made a lot of sense."

"What are they?"

"You have to give back."

"Mostly to him, it seems."

"It's a good principal nevertheless."

"Did Amy also tell you Sinclair has a sideline?"

"I know he teaches yoga."

"Besides that."

"Tell me," Rose ordered. "I don't like guessing games."

"He smuggles undocumented workers into the country."

Rose's eyes narrowed. She compressed her mouth into a thin line. She looked angry, but I couldn't tell if she was angry because of what Sinclair was doing or because I'd found out about it.

"That's a serious accusation. Do you have any proof?"

"I'm sure the authorities will find some if they look."

"Can I infer from your comment that you've already notified them?"

I didn't say anything.

"How enterprising of you." Rose steepled her fingers together and rested her chin on them. "And what does Sinclair say to this?"

"He doesn't. He's gone, along with the men he brought over."

"So where's your evidence?"

"The guy who owns Quotations . . ."

"Fred's child . . ."

"If you say so. He's involved. I think he'll testify."

Rose tapped her nails on the wheelchair's railing. "You realize you're talking about a relatively minor offense here?"

"Possibly," I conceded.

"Definitely," Rose corrected. "In addition, I know Fred. He's extremely well connected. Believe me, he's not about to let his only son go to jail. Or allow himself or his friends to be caught in whatever you're conjuring up."

"I'm not conjuring up anything."

"Perhaps. Perhaps not. Now my question to you is, do you think this alleged sideline of Sinclair's is connected in some way to Pat Humphrey's death?"

"It might be."

"Might isn't good enough. I'm paying you a rather large sum of money to investigate a specific subject, not go tearing off after anything that takes your fancy."

"This found me. I didn't find it."

"How far have you gotten with Patti? What have you found out about my children?" Then, before I could reply, Rose raised her hand. "No. Stop. Don't tell me. I don't want to know. Tell Moss. I don't think I can take anymore."

We heard a low moan.

Rose sighed. "That's Amy."

Tom moved. It was like watching a boulder come to life. "Do you want me to take care of her, Mrs. T?" he asked.

"No." Rose shook her head. "Finish your lunch. I'll see what she wants. If I need you, I'll call."

I followed Rose into the bedroom. She looked as if she wanted to tell me not to come in, but she didn't.

Amy was lying in the bed Shana had recently occupied. One of her arms was in a sling, while the other lay down by her side. She was dressed in a white cotton nightgown. Her usually wild hair had been combed off her face and secured with a large barrette. She was watching television with the sound turned off. Her eyes were dull. Her face slack. A thin strand of saliva made its way out of the corner of her mouth and down her jaw.

"She's been like this since we took her home from the hospital," Rose explained as she wheeled herself toward her daughter. She reached over and patted Amy's hand. "Everything will be fine," she told her. "I promise."

Amy continued to watch television.

"What is she on?" I asked Rose.

"Something to quiet her nerves."

"It must be a pretty strong something. I'd say it's doing a little bit more than that."

"The doctor says he'll be able to lower her dosage after a while."

"She didn't seem bad enough to warrant this the last time I saw her."

"She got worse in the hospital. Much worse." Rose turned to look at me. "Moss says this is the best thing to do."

"Do you always follow what he says?"

"Not always, but he is my adviser. Which is why I'm not holding it against you that you didn't tell me about Amy's involvement in . . . you know . . . Patti's . . ."

"Death?"

"Yes."

The telephone rang. A moment later, Tom called Rose to the phone. I went over and sat down next to Amy. She didn't look at me. She kept her gaze focused on the television. I took her hand in mine and stroked it.

"How's it going?" I asked her.

She kept watching the screen.

"Sinclair's taken off."

She didn't raise her eyes.

"I think the police are going to arrest him."

"Good." Her eyes were still on the screen, and her voice was so low that it took me a minute to realize she was speaking.

"I thought you liked him."

"Not anymore."

"Why?"

"Because he lied to me."

"About what?"

Amy scrunched up her face. Tears rolled down her cheeks. "He told me he loved me. He told me we would be together. If it wasn't for me, he'd still be back in that crummy apartment."

I thought back to the scene I'd witnessed between Sinclair and Pat Humphrey on the beach. "When did you find out that he was seeing Pat Humphrey?"

"The morning she died." Amy looked at me for the first time. "I know this is a cliché, but I thought she was my friend. I thought she cared for me. But she didn't. She betrayed me. Just like everyone else. She's a liar. She lied about everything. Everything. She said she didn't, but she did."

Now Amy's tears were falling faster.

"How did you find out about her and Sinclair?"

"I saw them. I saw them together. I wanted to talk to him. I'd had an idea about how to attract more people to the temple, and she was coming out of the room."

A picture of Amy, her skirt pushed over her hips when we walked in on her and Sinclair after we'd found Pat Humphrey's body, flashed through my mind. "Yet you and he—"

I didn't get any more out before Amy started yelling, "He made me. It wasn't my fault. It wasn't my fault." She brought her hands up and began clawing at her cheeks. Lines of blood appeared.

I reached over, grabbed hold of her hands, and wrested them down to her side. "Stop it," I ordered. "Just stop it."

Tom materialized by my side, hypodermic in hand. Amy screamed as the needle went into her forearm. She went limp almost immediately.

"Get away from her," he growled as I let go of Amy.

"You see what I mean," Rose Taylor said from the doorway. She was clutching the pearls around her neck with her right hand. "You see what I'm telling you. My daughter is crazy."

The string broke, and the pearls cascaded onto the floor. Tom got down on the floor and began picking them up.

Chapter Thirty-one

The thwack of Geoff's racket hitting tennis balls punctured the stillness of the afternoon. I caught sight of him as Zsa Zsa and I rounded the bend in the path that led to the cottage. He was totally engrossed in what he was doing. I don't know a lot about tennis, but the serves he was dishing up looked pretty good to me.

As I glanced up toward the house, I caught a glimpse of the maid who'd let me in the first time I'd come around, the maid Geoff said wasn't here. She was carrying a laundry basket. I started toward her, but when she saw me, she turned and limped back inside. I went around and knocked on the back door, but she didn't answer, and after peeking in the kitchen windows, I finally gave it up for a bad job and walked away. Whether or not she had a green card wasn't my business. I didn't really care.

I've always thought that line about breaking a few eggs to make an omelette was a crock of shit, but now I'd gone and done just that. A woman like Rose's maid would be gone in the blink of an eye. I phoned the guy at the Hispanic Alliance and told him what had happened. He said he'd see what he could do, but I still felt lousy as I walked back.

As I started up my car, I decided that contrary to what her mother wished to believe, Amy wasn't crazy—unless crazy with guilt counted. Geoff's comment about welcoming "our little murderer" home was a distinct possibility. If Rose Taylor wanted to, she certainly had the power and the money to keep Amy a virtual prisoner in that cottage. Maybe that was the idea.

As I drove to the country club, I contemplated which would be worse, being a ward of the state or a ward of Rose Taylor. The parking lot was crowded with Saabs and Mercedes and SUVs, and I had to circle three times before I could find a space for my dented-up Taurus. I stopped briefly to admire an MGB. I wondered if Geoff had finally gotten his present from Rose as I took in the clubhouse terrace. Moss Ryan was sitting at a round table, under a striped umbrella, drinking a beer and playing cards with three other men. Everyone was laughing and looking as if they were having a good time.

When he saw me approaching him, he said something to them, put his cards down, pushed his chair away, and stood up. As he came toward me, I saw he was wearing his golfing clothes, a yellow Izod polo shirt, and bright lime green slacks, and I wondered again why it was that when men play golf, any sartorial intelligence they've acquired seems to vanish. Then I noted that Ryan looked slightly ill at ease in his togs, as if he couldn't adjust to being out of a suit.

"Let's go back inside the club, shall we?" he said as he steered me into what was the main lounge.

It was a cozy kind of place, with large, overstuffed sofas and club chairs, the kind of place where you'd sit in the winter and have a cup of hot mulled cider. But this was summer, and the large room was empty. Everyone was outside. Moss Ryan leaned against the wall of the fieldstone fireplace. "I was just speaking to Rose. She called me a few minutes before you showed up."

"And?"

"She's extremely upset."

I put my backpack down and massaged my shoulder. I really had to take some things out of it unless I wanted to have a permanent kink in my back. "I kinda figured that out. The pearls tipped me off."

"They're South Sea," Moss Ryan absentmindedly informed me. I felt as if I were suddenly taking a tour of a landmark house. "Hand-strung and knotted. Very expensive. Sanford gave them to her on their second anniversary. I helped him choose them."

"How nice." Murphy had given me a set of knives he'd picked up at a discount place for our second anniversary. I changed the subject. "I take it she's not very happy about my handling of Sinclair."

"Among other things."

"Like Amy?" Always go with the obvious. That's my motto.

Moss Ryan nodded. "She needs peace and quiet. What she doesn't need is someone barging in and upsetting her."

"I'm not the thing that's upsetting her." I waited for Moss Ryan to ask me what I meant. When he didn't, I said, "Tell me, you don't really think you can establish an insanity plea by keeping her doped up like that, do you?"

"I'm not establishing anything." He feigned stifling a yawn. "In fact, I have nothing to do with Amy's legal troubles. I handle civil matters, not criminal ones. My role is Rose's legal adviser. That's it.

"But," Moss continued, "you saw Amy. She's hysterical. She's self-destructive. She's begun to mutilate herself." He shuddered. "She needs to be protected from herself. I think there can be very little argument about that."

"If that's the case, she needs to be in a good psychiatric hospital."

"I don't think that Rose's strategies—not a felicitous word choice, I admit—need to concern you at the moment."

"Let me guess. She's firing me."

Moss Ryan waved hello to someone out in the lobby before replying. "Not firing. It's true she wants you off the case for now. But what she wants to do instead is keep you on retainer so you'll be there if any future problems arise. To that end, she wants you to keep the money she's given you as a gesture of goodwill."

What a nice, polite way to buy someone off, I decided. So this is how the rich did things. "I take it you want a report."

"Of course." He smoothed the front of his polo shirt down. "But there's no great hurry."

"Why the change?"

"I think, if truth be known, that Rose doesn't want to know what her children have been doing. She says she does, but she doesn't. Mind you," Moss Ryan continued, "I don't agree with Rose's decision. But it's not mine to make. And now, if you'll excuse me"—he made a sweeping gesture with his hand—"I have to get back to my friends. I'm winning, and I don't want my luck to change."

I picked up my backpack. "Just so you know, I'm putting the rest of the money in the envelope with the report."

"You must do as your conscience dictates."

"I intend to."

Moss Ryan shrugged and walked away.

As I watched him, I wondered why Rose was trying to pay me off. Who was she protecting?

Did she already know that one of her children was a heroin user and the other a transvestite? That her son, Louis, was involved with a drug dealer?

Or maybe I was wrong.

Maybe Moss Ryan was telling me the truth.

Maybe it was a matter of scale.

After all, ten thousand isn't a large sum of money to someone like Rose Taylor.

It was like my spending a dollar on the lottery. If it paid off, fine. And if it didn't, so what.

I was still mulling over my conversation with Moss Ryan as I went back outside. This must have been Rose Taylor family day, because I was halfway down the clubhouse steps when I spotted Geoff coming toward me, tennis racket tucked under his arm.

"I don't know why he bothers competing," I overheard

someone in back of me say. "Ever since he married Sanford's widow, he's lost his edge."

"He was good playing mixed doubles, though," his companion replied as the two men came abreast of me.

"He's gotten fat. And slow."

"So what do you think about the Orangemen making the playoffs this year?"

"You know, I'm not sure." Then the two men walked by me, and I couldn't hear any more of what they were saying.

As Geoff came closer, he raised his free hand in a salute. "Fancy meeting you here."

"I came to talk to Moss Ryan."

"I know. Rose wasn't too pleased with you."

"So I understand."

"She's given orders to the staff to have you shot on sight. Just kidding," Geoff added. "Just kidding."

"So what do you think about Amy?"

He shrugged. "I'm not paid to think. I'm paid to shut my mouth and do what I'm told."

"That must be difficult."

"It all depends on what you want out of life."

"And what do you want?"

"I used to think it was to be able to play tennis and live in a fancy house and drive a nice car. Now I'm not so sure." He glanced at his watch. "The tournament is going to start soon. I'm going to be late."

I watched him vanish into the afternoon heat. Then I went back to Noah's Ark, but I couldn't settle down. I kept seeing Amy's face. I kept wondering why Rose had called me off. Then I started thinking about George and what I should do about him, call him or not, break it off or not—which somehow was even worse—so I went back to thinking about Rose Taylor.

Later that evening, after I'd closed the store, I went over to the apartment where Amy lived. I figured, if the police hadn't been through her stuff, maybe there was something in there that could shed some light on what was going on. After all, just because Rose had told me to stand down didn't mean I had to. Especially since I still had her money in my bank account. She'd told me to keep the whole ten thousand. If you thought about it, I was actually doing her a favor by just billing her for the hours I was going to put in and returning the rest.

Amy lived in an apartment on James Street. The building was one of those mansions that had seen better days and was now divided into several apartments. I got the landlady to open the door by telling her I was Amy's sister and that I'd come to collect some of her belongings.

"I was wondering where she'd gotten off to," the landlady, a skinny redhead with a bad tattoo of Daffy Duck on her shoulder, said as she handed me the bundle of Amy's mail that she had sitting on a table in the foyer of her apartment. She had to raise her voice to be heard over the noise of the television set. "Usually, she checks in. Isn't she coming back?"

"Probably not," I replied, amazed, as always, by how readily most people will take somebody's word. "She's pretty sick."

"Poor dear." The landlady clicked her tongue against the roof of her mouth. "She's got eight months on her lease left to run. Who's going to pay me?"

"Get in touch with this person." I scribbled Moss Ryan's name and address on a piece of paper and gave it to her.

She glanced at it. "Because this puts a different complexion on things, as it were. I can't be letting you take her stuff if she isn't paid in full."

"She just wants me to get her a couple of CDs. I'll leave the rest." I handed the woman a twenty-dollar bill.

"I suppose that wouldn't hurt," she allowed, slipping both the money and the paper into the side pocket of her jean shorts. "Just so you don't take anything else."

Amy's apartment turned out to be on the second floor. "So no one has been here?" I asked as I followed the landlady up the stairs.

"No. Her husband hasn't been around for a while. Usually, he shows up once a month or so. I guess he travels for a living."

"Husband?" I couldn't keep my voice from rising in surprise.

The landlady stopped in front of Amy's apartment. "You're telling me you didn't know she was married?" she said, favoring me with a suspicious glance. "You can't be much of a sister if you don't."

"We've been estranged for the past couple of years," I explained.

"I'll say."

"We've just reconnected," I improvised. "I can't believe she didn't tell me she and Neff finally got married."

"Sinclair," the landlady corrected.

"That's right." I snapped my fingers and laughed. "How stupid of me. I always forget that guy's name. They've had one of those off-again, on-again relationships for years. He's one of the reasons my sister and I stopped talking."

"Yeah," the landlady said. "I've had a couple of those myself." A wistful look crossed her face. "They're hell on the digestive system."

"I'll say," I said, thinking of Murphy. I tipped her another twenty and took the key out of her hand. "If you don't mind, I'll just let myself in."

Amy's apartment looked like mine had after I graduated college. The sofa and chairs in the living room were shabby and mismatched; the coffee table was one of those large wooden spools the utility company stores its wire on. The bookcase that ran along the dining alcove wall was made of unstained wooden boards and bricks, while the scratched table and chairs looked as if they had been picked up in the Salvation Army. A curtain of red and pink plastic beads separated the kitchen from the dining room. I was thinking that I hadn't seen something like that since the seventies when I heard the front door open.

"Hillary?" Sinclair called out.

I walked back to the middle of the living room. "Guess again."

"What the hell are you doing here?" he demanded.

"I might say the same of you."

He peered around nervously, ready to flee out the door if need be. "Where's your friend?"

"George? At home."

Sinclair relaxed a little.

"You look a hell of a lot better than the last time I saw you." The marks from the beating George had given him had almost faded.

Sinclair pointed to his side. "Yeah, well, my ribs don't feel any better. I should have had him charged with assault."

"Go ahead." I waited for Sinclair to reply. When he didn't, I said, "I thought you'd be on your way to California by now."

"Don't worry. I will be soon enough." He glanced around the room. "Where's Hillary? The landlady said Amy's sister was here."

"She couldn't come. I'm playing surrogate. You should have told me you were a married man."

A look of surprise crossed Sinclair's face.

"The landlady told me," I informed him.

He straightened up. "Good. I'm glad you know. I don't like secrets."

I tried not to laugh. "So how long ago did this happy event take place?"

"About eight months. Give or take."

"This is just a wild guess, but would that be right around the time you got the use of the lodge?"

Sinclair didn't say anything.

"I'm assuming you and Amy didn't invite Rose to the nuptials."

"Amy didn't want to. She said it would make things too complicated."

"I bet it would have. So are you going to tell her?"

"I just have. I've just come back from seeing her."

"That must have been a nice surprise for her. Having such a distinguished son-in-law."

Sinclair shrugged. "When it comes down to it, she's a sensible person."

"I bet. When it comes down to it, you're two of the same kind. What are you doing here?"

"I've come to get my suit. I have an appointment at the Federal Building. Rose's lawyer has been kind enough to arrange for representation for me."

"How nice of him. But then I suppose it's in everyone's best interests. How much has Rose been paying her help, anyway? Or is all of it just going in your pocket."

Sinclair moved by me. "I resent that accusation. I think you'd better leave."

"I don't think it's going to be so easy for your wife when it comes to Pat Humphrey. Or for you, for that matter. A homicide rap is harder to work around."

Sinclair stopped. "She had nothing to do with that."

"It certainly sounds as if she has. She certainly acts as if that's the case."

"It isn't."

"Well, if you say so, then I guess everything is fine. But here's what I think. I think Amy was jealous of her. I think she was furious at her. Not only was she going to take her inheritance from her; she was screwing her husband. Give me a better motive than that."

"It's true," Sinclair admitted. "Pat and I had something going—it didn't mean anything. Pat was like a guy in that regard. Just because she went to bed with you didn't mean she wanted an emotional attachment. In fact, she was hung up on some other guy. But as for the inheritance angle, I don't know what the hell you're talking about."

"Yes, you do. Pat had Rose convinced she was Rose's long-lost daughter, the one she'd had when she was young and gave away. In fact, I wouldn't be surprised if you were in on the scam with her."

"Don't be ridiculous," Sinclair scoffed.

"I'm not. Rose told me."

"Well, maybe Rose's stroke killed off more brain cells than anyone is admitting. Trust me, I know. Pat and I talked. She never mentioned anything like that."

"Maybe she didn't tell you."

"Why the hell wouldn't she?"

"I can think of lots of reasons—like she was going to get all this money and she didn't want to share it with you."

"No. Pat wasn't like that."

"Like what?"

Sinclair chewed on the inside of his cheek while he thought about what to say. Finally, he came out with this: "Look, scam artists are like everyone else. You do what you're used to doing. You have something that works for you, you continue in that vein. You don't change in midstream. Embezzlers don't run cons. Pat Humphrey had her thing, her pet psychic thing. Not," Sinclair quickly added, "that Pat was without psychic ability. She did have it. She was the genuine article. Sometimes she had these flashes . . ." Sinclair's voice drifted off.

"I know," I said softly, thinking about what Pat had said.

"It always gave me the creeps," Sinclair said. "The way she'd just blurt this stuff out. But the thing is that sometimes it worked and sometimes it didn't. She couldn't always count on it. Her pet-psychic shtick was half-true, half-bullshit. Sometimes she really could understand animals. I always thought it was just because she was very observant.

"But in the end that really doesn't matter. What matters is that it was working for her. It was making her a good living. She was getting a large clientele list. Hell, vets were sending clients to her. There was no reason for her to do something like what you're saying. Something that would open her up to prosecution. She really did not want to go back to jail."

"Maybe she was greedy."

"No. She wasn't."

"Then why would Rose lie about something like that?"

"Why does Rose do anything? Because she wants to."

Chapter Thirty-two

As it turned out, I didn't have to take a day off to drive out to where Pat Humphrey's parents were living to find out whether or not she'd been adopted. According to the pet sitter, they were in Syracuse, staying with a cousin in Eastwood. She didn't tell me much else, though, because between the bad connection and the dogs that were barking in the background I had trouble hearing what she was saying. I called the cousin and she told me to come over.

Ann Fitzsimmons opened the door for me when I rang the bell. She was a large, blowsy woman, and the only resemblance I could see between her and Pat was in the shape of her mouth and the coloring of her skin.

"Everyone is in here," she said, motioning for me to follow her into the living room.

The room, the antithesis of Pat Humphrey's place, was crammed with cheap furniture, photos, and tacky souvenirs. Pat Humphrey's parents were huddled together on the sofa, holding hands. They had that dazed look that people get after an accident or a fire. Small and fragile, they seemed lost in the expanse of black leather that framed them. Even though the temperature outside was in the eighties, and it was probably higher in the house, they both were wearing cardigan sweaters.

The cousin introduced us, and we shook hands. "They're having trouble understanding," she confided to me, referring to them in the third person, in the way that some people speak about children even when they're in the room.

I nodded and carefully placed the box with their daughter's possessions on the coffee table in front of them. Pat's mother stared at it and wet her lips. Her eyes were vacant. As if her heart had traveled to somewhere else and wouldn't be returning.

"It's just not right a child dying before her parents," she declared, aiming her statement at the world in general.

Her husband patted her hand. I don't think she noticed.

"I never thought I'd be having to pick out Patti's tombstone." She shook her head at the wonder of it. "I was thinking about getting one of those nice little angels carved on it. Do you think she would have approved?"

"I'm sure she would," I replied, even though I thought from my brief acquaintanceship with Pat Humphrey that she wouldn't.

The mother went on as if she hadn't heard me. "Because, you know, our tastes. They weren't alike. She never liked the clothes I used to send her. Claimed they weren't stylish enough. I like prints. Things that are bright and cheery. But Patti just wanted beige and brown and black. Time enough for those when you're an old woman, I told her."

The mother stopped talking as she realized what she'd just said. Her lips trembled, then collapsed. She hid her face in her hands. "I'm fine," she said to her husband as he hugged her. "Really. Just give me a moment." A few seconds later, she raised her face. Her eyes were shiny with unshed tears.

"So," she said to me, her voice bright in a ghastly parody of social chatter, "I know you told my husband when you talked to him on the phone, and he told me who you are, but tell me again. I've forgotten. I seem to be doing that a lot lately." She unconsciously brushed the edge of her hand across her forehead. "Not being able to keep a thought in my head. Were you Patti's friend?"

"No," I said gently. "I'm a private detective. But I've met your daughter."

"She was nice, wasn't she?" the mother asked as she leaned over and dipped her hands into the carton that I'd brought.

"Very," I said, watching her lift things out and reverentially place them on the table.

"She had the gift, you know."

"Yes, I do."

She paused and searched my face. I got the feeling she was seeing me for the first time. "She told you things, didn't she?"

I nodded.

A hint of color bloomed on her cheeks. "She used to do that with me, too," she confided. "Especially when she was little. Just used to blurt things out. It used to drive me crazy, because you never knew when it was going to happen. Once, when we were at the grocery store—Patti must have been about three then—she went up to this woman and told her her dog was peeing in the house because his wee wee hurt. It turned out he had a bladder infection. I just about died."

She fingered her cardigan. "My mother had the gift, too. It skipped me. But I'm glad. I never really wanted it. I never saw what good it does having it if it doesn't tell you to get out of the way when a truck is coming."

"So then Pat wasn't adopted?"

"Adopted?" Her mother stared at me incredulously. "Whatever makes you say something like that?"

I made a noncommittal noise. "It was just something someone told me."

"Well, I don't know where they got that from. I really don't," she complained. "I tried to get pregnant for years. I had to stay in bed with Patti from my sixth to ninth month. Complete bed rest. I could only get up to pee. Ask Fred here." She indicated her husband. "He'll tell you." She picked up the stuffed dog that had been lying in the carton and buried her face in it. "But she was worth it. My little baby. This smells like her."

"Sorry."

"She didn't tell you she was adopted, did she?" her mother demanded, putting the dog on the coffee table as the thought crossed her mind.

"No," I reassured her as she took the photographs of her daughter out of the box, studied them one at a time, and laid them out on the coffee table.

"She was a really good athlete," the mother was saying. "We have a case in our den devoted to her trophies. I don't know where she got that from, either. No one else in our family is at all athletic." She picked up the photo of her daughter as a waitress. "She got a job in this place just so she could use the courts. Of course, she had to play after hours, when the members weren't on them."

I stared at the photo of Pat Humphrey in front of the fireplace, smiling as she held a tray. I'd seen that fireplace before.

In fact, Moss Ryan had been standing in front of it when I was speaking to him.

Pat Humphrey had worked at the club as a waitress, and she played tennis. I remembered the tennis racket I'd seen in her hall closet and the trophy for winning a singles—or was it a doubles?—tournament. I couldn't remember.

Geoff played tennis there, too.

"How long ago did she work at the club?" I asked.

"Let me see." Pat's mother thought for a little while, then gave me the answer I was expecting to hear. "Of course, she's always given readings on the side."

"Of course."

Here it was. Pat Humphrey's entrée into Rose Taylor's house.

I could see it all. She and Geoff meeting on the courts, the conversations, tentative at first, something along the lines of, wouldn't it be funny if—Everything just a joke until it turned serious. Who had come up with the idea? It must have seemed so simple. A little money for everyone. No harm done. Only now Pat Humphrey was dead. No wonder Geoff looked the way he did.

The next day, I tracked down the tennis pro at the country club. I wanted to make sure that I was right before I said anything to anyone.

I found him in the shop straightening out shelves. He was about forty-five and had the kind of ready smile people in his business have to have if they want to stay in it for any length of time.

"Oh, sure," he said when I showed him Pat Humphrey's picture. "Her. Had a very good backhand."

He slipped my card and the two hundred dollars I'd pushed across the counter into the pocket of his tennis whites. It was around one o'clock on a hot, sunny Monday afternoon, and the courts were deserted. Twenty years ago they would have been filled with women playing a round before the children came home from school, but now most of the women worked, too—even in this income bracket.

"She played every chance she could get." The pro took a shirt off the shelf and slipped it underneath the rest of the pile. "She used to sneak on the courts when she wasn't supposed to. Not that I was going to kick her off."

"And why was that?"

When he didn't answer, I said, "Was it because she was friends with one of the members?"

He got busy rearranging the next pile of shirts. "Listen, if you're looking for someone to swear out an affidavit in a divorce proceeding, you're speaking to the wrong person. If I talked about everything I see going on here, I'd be out of a job."

"This has nothing to do with a divorce. It has to do with a possible homicide."

The pro lifted his head. His expression indicated that as long as no one was killed on his court, he didn't care. "This is a very small community. I say something to you, and you say something to someone else, and pretty soon everyone knows where the story originated, and bang, I'm out of a job."

"I'm not asking you to say anything."

"Then what are you asking me to do?"

"To nod if I mention the right name."

"Which is?"

"Geoff."

"There are a lot of guys that go by that name here," he observed as he nodded, picked up a racket, and started inspecting it.

"Obviously."

"Look," he said, putting the racket down and picking up another one. "What people want to do among themselves is their own business. I'm just here to give lessons and make sure everything runs smoothly."

"I realize that. And believe me, I don't want to do anything that will create waves. Really." I gave him another hundred. "Did he pay you to let her on the courts?"

"That's a harsh way of expressing things." The tennis pro looked around, checking to make sure that no one had come into the shop before speaking, then beckoned me to come closer. "But I will say that when I help out some of the members here, they've been known to show their appreciation."

"I can understand that."

"Sometimes," he continued, "you have to bend the rules to make that happen. But I always figured, if no one gets hurt, what difference does it make. Besides, some guys got full-time jobs up at their houses, if you know what I mean. His wife—I used to deliver papers for her when I was a kid. She was tough. Tried to stiff me out of the bill a couple of times. So it wasn't as if he couldn't use a little relaxation now and then."

I thought back to Rose's nurse. "I think he had something going on already."

The tennis pro winked at me. "All the more power to him."

I peeled off another hundred and gave it to him. "So he and Pat Humphrey were hooked up?"

"Like this." And the tennis pro bent his two index fingers and hooked them together and pulled. "Just like this."

"Tell me," I said as another idea occurred to me. "I get the impression you've lived in this area all your life."

"Aside from a couple of years I spent in the navy, absolutely."

I peeled off another hundred. "I don't suppose you would happen to know if any of Rose Taylor's childhood friends are still around? One was an Edna something."

"Name doesn't ring a bell, but I know who to ask. Of course, I'll have to give him something for his services."

"Of course." And I put another hundred dollars of Rose Taylor's money on the counter.

I called Paul and told him what I'd found out as I was driving away.

"And you want me to do what with this?"

"Nothing. I just thought you'd like to know."

"And why should I care?"

"No particular reason, I suppose."

"Exactly. May I ask why you care?"

"I don't like unfinished business."

He snorted derisively. "Now there's an expensive luxury most of us can't afford. You want my advice, stop spending the money the Taylor woman gave you and use it to pay your back taxes. Come have dinner with me and I'll impart more words of wisdom."

"No, thanks."

"How's George these days?"

"George is fine."

"Who's the blond I saw him with?"

I hung up, went downtown, and spent the rest of the afternoon in the bar.

The full name of the woman Rose had mentioned was Edna Busch. I got to see her the next day. It was in the upper nineties again, and I left Zsa Zsa in the cool of the air-conditioned store. It was so hot that she hadn't even protested my going.

That the tennis pro had gotten Edna's last name and address for me so quickly didn't surprise me. It simply under-lined one of the advantages of living in a small, as opposed to a large, city. I'd called and explained that I wanted to speak to her about Rose Taylor.

"Oh, God," she said, atwitter with excitement. "I haven't seen her since high school." Then she added, "Is this about what happened out in Caz?"

"It could be," I replied cautiously.

"I was told you're a private detective."

"That's right."

"I'm so excited. *Murder She Wrote* is my favorite show."

"Well, I'm not sure this is like that."

"Believe me, it's the closest that I'll ever get."

I laughed, and we agreed that I should come out to where she lived at two the following afternoon.

The Pines was one of those assisted-living places that are popping up all over the country. Whenever I see an ad for one of them, with the healthy, smiling couple talking about all the fun they're having—as though they're back in summer camp—all I can think of is the word warehouse. But I guess most other people don't share my opinion, because they fill up as soon as they open.

"Do you carry a gun?" Edna asked me first thing when she greeted me in the main lobby, one that could have done a stand-in for the lobby of a three-star hotel.

She was wearing jeans, sneakers, and a maroon short-sleeved shirt. Her hair was cropped, and her eyes were danc-ing with excitement.

"Sorry. Are you disappointed?"

"A little," she admitted. "My nephew promised to show me how to shoot his pistol, but he keeps on forgetting," she added as she took me up to her apartment on the second floor.

"This is her," she told a woman coming down the hall and pointing to me. "I'll talk to you later." And she whisked me inside.

Her apartment was a small three-room affair that would

have benefited from a color on the walls other than white, but the rooms were well proportioned, and there was enough light for the violets growing on the windowsills to flourish.

"Nice place," I said to Edna as I followed her into the galley kitchen when she was making us tea.

"I like it." She got some biscuits out of a tin, arranged them on a plate, and turned on the light under the kettle. "I admit I was full of trepidation at first. Giving up my house and all that. But it's really quite liberating. Now I don't have to worry about taking care of things. But the best part, as far as I'm concerned, is the communal dining hall. I don't think people are meant to eat alone, do you?"

"No," I said, thinking back to all the meals I'd eaten in the last couple of weeks. Aside from the couple I'd had with Manuel, they'd all been catch-as-catch-can affairs on the run. "I don't."

"I'm so excited you want to talk to me. I've told everyone on the floor. They can hardly wait to hear about our meeting. You're making me a celebrity." The water boiled. Edna made tea, and I helped her carry the cups and the biscuits out into the living room.

"May I ask why you want to know about Rose?" she inquired as she sat on the sofa.

I explained about Pat Humphrey.

"That's simply ridiculous," Edna said. "Rose wouldn't even let a boy touch her in high school, much less anything else."

"She never had an affair?"

"Never."

"There was no boy she was madly in love with?" I asked, repeating Rose's story.

"Don't be silly. I mean, she used to go out with someone— he was the captain of the football team—I forget his name. I can find it if you need it." Edna gestured around her room. "I kept all the yearbooks."

"That's okay." I took another sip of my tea.

"But she never really cared for him."

"How can you be so sure?"

"She told me." Edna spooned sugar into her tea and stirred. "Listen, Rose and I lived across the street from one another almost all our lives when we were growing up, and if I can tell you anything, I can tell you this. She was never pregnant when she was in high school. I saw her every day. I would know. She was never passionate about anyone. If she had an affair, it was all in her head."

"Maybe it happened a year or two later."

"Nope," Edna declared. "I used to go out with one of her cousins. I would have heard if anything like that had happened. She was what we called a cold fish back then. The only thing she liked about sex was that it gave her control. If she couldn't have control, she wasn't happy."

"Then why would she say something like that?"

"Why does anyone make up stories? To get attention."

"You don't like her much, do you?"

Edna put down her spoon and took a biscuit. "No. I don't. Rose wasn't nice then, and I don't expect she's gotten any better now. Contrary to what the books say, people don't get nicer when they age. They just become more of what they are."

Chapter Thirty-three

I went directly from Edna's place out to Rose Taylor's estate. A few clouds had started massing in the sky to the west, but according to the weather reports, they were a tease. Promising rain but not delivering. On my way to Caz, I called George and told him I wanted to talk with him tonight, and we set a time. I could feel my stomach clenching as I hung up. I told myself I'd done the right thing. The adult thing. For a change.

We had problems. Our relationship wasn't going anywhere. According to Paul, it was already over. You were supposed to talk about things like that when you reached my age. But the problem was, where did I want us to go? I reached over and got my cigarettes out of my backpack and lit one.

The truth was, I decided as I slid a Willie Nelson tape into the tape deck, then swerved to avoid a squirrel that had darted out into the road, I didn't know. I admit I don't do introspection well. Never have. Even though I'm supposed to, being a woman and all. And then I decided, fuck it. Who the hell cared, anyway? I did. And that was the biggest problem of all.

When I drove through the pillars that demarcated the beginning of the Taylor estate, I was in for a little surprise.

Something new had been added to the decor. Or rather two new things: a barricade and a guard to go with it. With his tight body, the opaque expression on his face, the reflective sunglasses, and the buzz cut, the guard looked like a moon-lighting cop. When he spoke, he sounded like one, too.

He put the bottle of water he'd been drinking down on the ground, strode over, and stuck his head in my window. "Can I please have your name, ma'am?"

"How long has this been going on?" I indicated him and the barricade, a couple of D.P.W. sawhorses that a VW could have broken through.

"Please, ma'am."

"Fine." I fanned my face with the edge of my hand to get a little air circulating. "Robin Light to speak to Mrs. Taylor."

I watched Rose's house shimmer in the sun while the guard walked back to the chair he'd been sitting in, picked up his cell phone off its arm, punched in some numbers, and talked into the receiver. He kept saying, "Yes, ma'am," and, "No, ma'am." His face was expressionless when he hung up. Walking back over to me, he'd hooked his thumbs into his belt loops, giving his gait a roll.

"I'm sorry," he said. "But you can't go in. Mrs. Taylor doesn't want to speak to you at the present time."

A bee flew into my car, buzzed around the windshield, and left. I was hoping it would fly down the guard's shirt, but it didn't.

"What if I have something important to tell her?"

The guard remained silent.

I tried again. "What if the fate of the free world depends on my talking to her?"

He didn't crack a smile.

"How much are you getting paid to stand out in this heat? I can pay you more." Never let it be said I wasn't generous with other people's money.

The muscles on his lower jaw tightened. "I'm going to have to ask you to leave now."

"And if I don't?"

"Please, ma'am. I'm asking you to be sensible." A hint of pleading registered in his voice. I figured that the last thing he wanted to do right now was get into it with someone in this heat.

I agreed. It was too friggin' hot to argue. And I could be sensible. If necessary. In fact, I could be the poster child for that particular virtue.

"Fine." I put the car into reverse and made a U-turn. "But when the world ends, remember it's going to be your fault."

Somehow he didn't seem convinced.

I stopped about half a block away and parked my car along the opposite side of the road. The blacktop stuck to the soles of my shoes as I crossed. As I clambered over the stone wall that enclosed this part of Rose Taylor's property, I wondered why she had bothered with the barricade and the guard. It wasn't as if she were living in a secured facility complete with electric fencing and attack dogs. Anyone could get in if they wanted to. The wall was only waist-high. Maybe she figured the illusion was enough. Maybe she figured no one would look any further. But not this time.

Since I was closer to the cottage where Amy was being kept, I checked there first. It was cool in the grove. The piney smell of evergreens surrounded me as I moved through them. I touched the needles, and the sap stuck to my fingers, releasing its scent. Little flies buzzed around my head. I swatted at them, then absentmindedly wiped my hands off on my jeans. My skin felt taut and itchy from the sun and the needles. I wished I were inside as I focused my attention on the cottage. From my vantage point, I could see a man opening the fridge, taking out a carton, drinking from it, then replacing it and closing the door. He stood staring off into space for a few moments, then walked back into the living room, picked up the newspaper, and sat down on the sofa.

He was thinner than Tom, Amy's last nursemaid, and seemed to move a little easier. I shifted my gaze to the left and spied Amy. She was where I'd left her. In her bedroom. I could see the reflection of the TV screen through the window.

I wondered if she did anything besides sleep and watch the screen. After a few minutes, I continued on.

The sun attacked me when I left the shelter of the trees. It scorched the top of my head and shoulders, making me remember I'd forgotten my hat in the car. No one was by the pool or the tennis courts. The only things moving were the sprays of water from the sprinklers. Their hiss followed me as I went toward the house.

I entered through the back way. The door was unlocked. I pushed it open and stepped inside. The first thing I spotted was the maid bent over the table, rolling out pie crust. She looked up when she saw me coming through the door. The color drained from her face. She put her hand to her chest, leaving the white imprint of her hand on her black uniform.

"It's okay," I said. "Don't worry." She started to say something, but I put my finger to my lips, and she stopped. "Is your mistress in?"

She nodded, her eyes looking behind me, wondering who else was coming through the door.

"Anyone else?"

"Tomás."

Great. Tom. Amy's nurse. The one who looked as if he could pick me up, toss me across the room, and not even break a sweat.

"Where is he?"

Her eyes came back to my face. "In the shower."

"Anyone else here?"

The maid shook her head. Her eyes strayed back to the door.

"There's no one with me, if that's what you're thinking."

She looked down and spotted the flour on her uniform and brushed it off.

"Where is Mrs. Taylor?"

"In the sunroom." The maid put her hands on her hips. "You leave her alone."

"I just want to ask her something."

"When I got sick and need an operation, she pay for the

doctor," the maid continued. Her hand strayed toward the phone.

"Calling her would be a mistake," I warned. "Unless, that is, you want to get yourself in trouble. This is none of your business. It has nothing to do with you."

I watched the hand flutter with indecision, then move back to the table.

"Go back to making your pie crust," I advised. "Everything will be fine."

The maid wiped her hands on her apron and muttered something about *gringa estúpida* to herself. Then she snapped, "Next time, you clean your shoes before you come in here. You tracking pine needles all over the floor."

I looked down. She was right.

I found Rose Taylor in the place where I'd first met her. She was studying a delicate pale yellow orchid with a magnifying glass. When she saw me, she put down the glass and pushed her wheelchair away from the table.

"Nice little blossom," I said. "Is that one of the thirty-thousand-dollar ones?"

"How did you get in here?" she demanded.

"I don't know how much you're paying for your security, but you're not getting good value for your money."

Her eyes blazed. "I suggest you leave."

"I will after you tell me why you lied about Pat Humphrey."

"Don't be ridiculous."

"That's the same phrase Edna used when I asked her if you'd ever been pregnant."

"Edna Busch is senile."

"She doesn't seem that way to me."

"She is. Anyway, what gives you the right to come in here and question me?"

"When someone uses me, I like to find out why."

"I want you out of here. I want you out of here now." Rose reached for the phone. "I'm going to have you arrested for trespassing."

"By the way," I said as I headed for the door, "congratulations on the marriage of your daughter and Sinclair. I'm sure they'll make a lovely couple."

"Tom," Rose yelled. "Tom. I need you."

I was already out the front door when I heard him scream, "Stop."

Yeah. Right.

The thing about being as bulky as Tom is that it slows you down.

Unfortunately, I couldn't say the same thing about the guy that had been guarding the front of the house. I was more than halfway to the stone wall when I looked to my left. The guard was coming toward me. And he wasn't slow. He was closing the distance between us way too fast for my liking.

By now I could feel the heat searing my lungs. Sweat was dripping into my eyes. It felt as if someone were sticking a knife through my ribs. For a couple of brief seconds I considered giving up. After all, what was the worst that could happen? They'd take me down to the station house, and I'd get a ticket. Big deal.

But then I heard Tom yell to the guard, "Hold the bitch."

I turned and got a look at his face. His mouth was turned up in a tight little smile, relishing what he was sure was going to come next, and his eyes were flat, devoid of expression or emotion. That was all I needed to put on an extra burst of speed.

I was gasping as I got to the stone wall. I could hear stones falling behind me as I scrambled over them and ran for the car. I had the door open when the guard grabbed my shoulder. I spun around and kicked at him. I could feel a crunch as my foot connected with his knee cartilage. His grip loosened, and I slid in and slammed the door shut. I had my key in the ignition and was turning it when his arm snaked in through the window and grabbed my hair.

"Good try, but not good enough," he said, pulling my head toward him. "Hey"—he turned and yelled to Tom—"I got her."

"I'll be right there."

I could see the expression on Tom's face in my mind's eye as I frantically felt for my keys.

"I knew there was a reason I always liked girls with long hair," the guard said as he yanked harder.

My scalp felt as if it were on fire. I groped for my key chain. My fingers made contact. I grabbed it just as the guard opened the door and pulled me out.

"You owe me for making me run."

"You forgot to mention my kicking you. What do I owe you for that?" And I brought the little canister of mace I have attached to my keys up and sprayed him in the face.

His hands went to his eyes. He screamed and doubled over. I hopped back in my car and started it up. Tom reached me as I peeled off, peppering him with the gravel from the side of the road.

By the time George dropped by that evening, I'd taken a long shower, downed four Tylenol to ease the aching in my head and neck, had a short, dreamless nap, and shared some take-out Mexican with Manuel, after which I'd informed him that I wanted him to vacate the premises for the evening.

"But where am I going to sleep?" he complained as we walked Zsa Zsa around the block.

I breathed in the scent of my neighbor's honeysuckle. "On the sofa at one of your friends' houses, the way you usually do."

"But you might need me." There was real concern in Manuel's voice, and I felt a rush of gratitude.

"Leave your cell on. I'll call if I do."

We walked for another couple of feet, then Manuel asked, "So why you giving George the heave-ho?"

"I'm not. I think we need to talk about our relationship."

He made an impolite noise. "That's such a load of shit."

"Don't talk to me like that, and it's not."

"Hey, if you really believe what you just said, how come you're so smart and all and you lie to yourself like you do?"

"I don't."

"All I know is that when a girl says that to me, she's already made up her mind that things ain't working out, and it don't matter how much talkin' we do. It don't help." And he kicked at a soda can someone had left in the street, lofting it into the air.

I thought maybe he was right as I watched Zsa Zsa chase it down.

It was twelve-thirty. I was sitting on a lounge chair on the deck in my backyard, enjoying the cool night breeze, sipping a scotch and listening to Patsy Cline, when George walked in. He looked in better shape than he had when I'd knocked on his door how many days ago? I was beginning to lose track. He'd shaved. His shirt was clean, and his khakis were pressed.

"I thought you might not be coming," I told him.

"No. I just had a few things I had to think through. I always liked this deck," he murmured, looking around as he petted Zsa Zsa. "It's well designed. Murphy and I did a good job on it."

"Yes, you did." They'd worked on it every day for two weeks after work. I couldn't wait for them to finish so I could hear something besides electric drills and banging. I started to get up. "Can I get you a drink?" Suddenly I was talking to a guest instead of a lover.

He waved me back in my seat. "I think I'll pass. I've been doing a little too much of that recently."

I felt a knot forming in my stomach. "Aren't you going to at least sit down?"

"No. No, thanks." His voice was somber. "I'd like to just say what I need to, if you don't mind."

My throat started to close. "Go ahead."

He folded his hands across his chest. "I've been considering our relationship a lot over the past few days. And this is the thing. I don't think I can be with you anymore if you continue to do what you're doing. It brings me back to a world I don't want to be in, a world I'm trying to get away from. It makes me do things I regret. Like what I did to Sinclair. There was no reason for that. None. I know I've said this before, but this time brought it home to me here." And he pointed to his gut. "I wish it wasn't the case, but it is. And maybe we could find a way around it, but when you add in all the other stuff between us . . . I'm sorry. It's not working. I wish it was, but it isn't." He put my house key on the table, turned, and walked away.

I watched him go. Then I got up, went into the house, and got the bottle of scotch and brought it outside.

I heard his car taking off as I poured myself a long, stiff drink.

Screw him. This was for the best.

After all, it's what I said I wanted, wasn't it?

Chapter Thirty-four

I didn't sleep well. At some point in time, though, I must have dozed off, because I woke up the next morning hot and sweaty and with a sour taste in my mouth, an ache in the front of my forehead that wouldn't go away, and vague memories of dreams I didn't want to recall. I felt as if I'd drunk too much, which I had. Taking a shower didn't help. Neither did a cigarette or a shot of scotch. In fact, they just made me feel worse. And they didn't help me stop thinking about George and what he'd said or about Rose Taylor and her family. Somehow I'd allowed them to seep into my life. And I didn't want them there.

I was tired of trying to figure out who was telling the truth and who was lying. Because maybe George was right. Maybe I should be doing something else. Maybe on a cosmic level none of what I did mattered. The problem was it mattered to me. As I looked around for my car keys, I decided I was glad I was going into work. Taking care of the animals would give me something else to focus on. But that wasn't the way things worked out.

I'd just turned on the lights in the store when the phone rang. It was Moss Ryan telling me that if I set foot on Rose Taylor's property again, I'd be arrested.

"She's not kidding, either," he said.

I took a sip of my coffee and fed half of my doughnut to

Zsa Zsa. "So I gathered," I replied, thinking back to yesterday afternoon. My scalp still hadn't recovered.

"I just don't want there to be a misunderstanding on this matter."

"No. It's pretty clear." I took a cloth from under the counter and started dusting it.

"Good. Because I don't know what you did to Tom, but he'd really like to get his hands on you."

Wonderful.

"Tell me," I asked Moss Ryan. "Did Rose hire those guards to keep me out or to keep Amy in?"

"You've been warned," Moss Ryan said. "I felt I owed you that much." And he hung up.

I'd swallowed a couple more Tylenol to relieve the pounding in my head and was staring at the phone, telling myself not to call George, when it rang. Paul was on the line.

"Did you see the morning paper yet?" he asked.

"I haven't even had time to finish my coffee, let alone open the paper."

"Well, check it out. Second section. Second page. Toward the bottom." He paused for a few seconds before continuing, then casually added, "So, I understand you and George aren't an item anymore."

I could feel myself flinch. "Jeez, that was quick."

"I met him jogging along the canal this morning. Must be tough for you. How much time you guys spend together?"

"I don't know. Four, five, six years. Something like that." I didn't want to do the math. It was too depressing.

"Well, if you ever want to talk or anything . . ." He left the word "anything" dangling in the air.

"So you've said."

Man, George just couldn't wait to tell everyone, could he? I fought off the impulse to pick up the phone and tell George what I thought about him. Instead, I opened the paper and looked for the article Paul had told me about. It was small enough, just a couple of short paragraphs, and I might have missed it if I hadn't been looking for it.

The gist of it was that Sinclair had agreed to help the federal authorities in their investigation into the ongoing problem of the illegal transport of undocumented workers into this country from Canada in exchange for immunity from federal prosecution. It also made mention of his status as the Reverend Ascending Moon and the fact that his "church" had at least one hundred and fifty members and was located on Wolfe Island.

The article went on to say that the site had recently been the location of a homicide, although so far investigators had found no link between Sinclair and the victim or a link between the victim and any members of the church. Amy's name was notable in its absence. Authorities also declared that Sinclair was not under suspicion for the homicide at this time and that the investigation was continuing. A variety of leads were being pursued. Anyone with information was asked to call. A number was given, and anonymity was promised.

"So what do you think?" I asked Zsa Zsa.

She barked and started chasing one of the geckos that had escaped from its cage a couple of weeks ago across the floor.

I folded the paper back up and drained the last of my coffee. What had Sinclair said to me when I was up in the apartment about his having to get his suit because he had an appointment at the federal building that Moss Ryan had set up? Well, it looked as if the meeting had been a success.

And then I thought about Amy crying when I'd spoken to her. About how she'd told me she was glad Sinclair was leaving. She certainly hadn't seemed surprised when I'd told her. She'd known. I reached for my cigarettes and lit one. I wondered if she'd already confessed to her mother that she and Sinclair had gotten married. Maybe in light of her husband carrying on with Pat Humphrey she'd decided her marriage wasn't such a good idea. Maybe she'd asked her mother to undo it. And she had. She certainly wouldn't want Sinclair as a son-in-law. Too lower class. Among his other failings. The undocumented workers would be the perfect tool to pry him loose.

I could see Rose talking to Sinclair and offering him a deal. Leave my daughter and I'll make your problems disappear. Don't and you'll be tied up in court for a long time.

Naturally, Sinclair would say yes. What choice did he have?

Then Rose would call up her friend, Fred, the father of the kid that owned Quotations, and explain the situation to him. And Fred would get on the phone to his pals in the U.S. Federal District Court, and they'd chat over coffee, and one of them would call Moss Ryan and suggest that they meet, and Moss Ryan would say something like What about a round of golf at the club?

And they'd agree because it's nice to be able to transact business and do something pleasurable at the same time. And anyway, the truth of the matter was—what Sinclair had done wasn't a big deal. He was a small fish in a world of piranhas, a world where people made billions of dollars moving people from one country to another. He wasn't connected. He couldn't lead them to anyone. He'd be an irritant to the feds, a mote in their eye, but that was it. However, I figured he was a hell of a lot more than that to Rose Taylor. I couldn't see her letting that marriage remain. And so she'd bought him out.

I picked up the phone and called Paul back.

"Do me a favor and see if you can find out where Sinclair is staying these days. I have a few questions I want to ask him."

"You sound awful tense. Sure I can't interest you in a beer later tonight? It'll help relax you a little."

I hung up without answering. As a figure in an ongoing homicide investigation, Sinclair had to register his whereabouts with the police. It wouldn't be a big deal for Paul to locate him. Then I wrote a check out to Rose Taylor for five thousand dollars and slipped it in an envelope to give to the postman when he came with the morning's mail. Between my expenses and reimbursing myself for the money I'd given out, I figured that was a fair figure. Actually, I thought I deserved it all, but half was as much as my conscience was letting me keep.

I spent the rest of the morning cleaning out the reptile cages, catching up on my paperwork, and trying to tell a customer—at length—why he didn't want a monitor lizard for a pet.

Paul got back to me at about two-thirty in the afternoon. I could have saved myself the call. It seems that Sinclair was still staying in Amy's apartment. Although he'd only be there until later that afternoon. He was booked on a six o'clock flight to Taos. I called Manuel and asked him to cover the store for me. When he arrived, I went to see Sinclair.

It was like soup outside. Two steps and I was blinking drops of perspiration out of my eyes. The sky had turned dark. The trees glowed against the clouds as if they were backlit. Out toward the west a fork of lightning pierced the sky. A storm was blowing in. It was just a matter of when. By the time I got to Sinclair's place, my shirt was sticking to my back.

One thing was for certain. When I knocked on his door, he definitely wasn't happy to see me.

He cracked the door to his apartment open and stuck his head out. "I don't have to talk to you, and I'm not going to," he declared. He began to close it, but I yanked it open and stepped inside before he could.

"You're right, you don't." I looked around while he glared at me. Two open suitcases sat on the floor. Stacks of sweaters, underwear, and shirts were piled on the coffee table. "What? No robes?" I asked.

"Not this trip. And yes, the police know I'm leaving," he said, anticipating what he thought was going to be my next question. "I'm going to Taos for a while. I'm visiting one of my congregates there."

"I know."

He clasped his medallion in both hands. "If you know everything, then why are you here?"

"I was wondering if you'd answer a couple of questions for me. Just for my own information."

He opened his eyes wide in feigned amazement. "And why, pray tell, would I want to do that?"

I shrugged. "Because you have nothing to hide. Because you're a reasonable man who would rather conduct his business in a civilized fashion."

"Is that a threat?" He drew back, suddenly nervous.

"Not at all. I don't do things that way."

Unconsciously, Sinclair brushed the side of his face with the tips of his fingers. "Your friend does."

"My friend isn't here." And I took two one-hundred-dollar bills out of my wallet and held them out. "Here, have some more of Rose Taylor's cash."

He made a show of scratching his lower lip with his thumbnail. Then his hand shot out and grabbed the money with the speed of a chameleon snagging a fly. "I guess a person could always use a little extra," he observed, tucking the bills away in his pants pocket. "What do you want to know?"

"How much is Rose giving you to get lost?"

"I wouldn't put it that way."

"Then how would you put it?"

"Rose is giving me a contribution of two hundred and fifty thousand dollars so that I can bring my work to other parts of the country."

"That's not bad if you consider the amount you already have in the bank."

"It costs money to do God's work."

"It's funny how everything has gotten more expensive these days. I wonder how much Jesus would need if he were alive today?"

"Ask the fundamentalists." There was a crack of thunder. Sinclair moved to close the windows as it began to rain, the drops pelting the panes and wetting the sills and the floor.

"And you're not taking Amy with you."

He pushed down on the sash of the window on the right,

his face knotted up with the effort. "I wish I could." Sinclair's tone was anything but regretful. "Unfortunately, Amy has some issues she needs to deal with. I don't think she'll be able to travel for quite some time."

"Not from what I saw."

He went and closed the window next to the kitchen. It came down with a thud.

"They have her on some fairly strong medication."

"You've seen her?"

"No. The lawyer told me." He turned from the window, crossed his arms over his chest, and made an impatient noise. "Is that all?"

"Not quite. The evening Pat Humphrey was killed. When George and I came through the door, you and Amy—"

"It was her idea," Sinclair said quickly, a little more unsure of himself.

"But she already knew about you and Pat?"

Sinclair flushed and studied the stream of water running down the windowpane.

"So then why?"

He wet his lip with the tip of his tongue. "Who knows why women do anything?"

"I would have thought she'd have been furious."

He remained mute.

"What did she say?"

He swallowed. "Nothing."

"You're lying."

"Fine. She said she was scared. She said she wanted me to hold her. And then she wanted a little more. Satisfied?"

"Not really." I studied him. His eyes shifted this way and that, studying the beaded curtain in the kitchen entrance, then moving to the coffee table.

"What was she scared of?"

He went back to staring at the rain. It was coming down in torrents now, as if the sluice gates had been open.

"That she was going to be arrested for shooting Pat Humphrey?"

"Look, all I know is that I've always wanted to live in the Southwest, and now I'm going to." Sinclair tapped the face of his watch. "My taxi is going to be coming soon. I have to finish packing."

"Do you think Amy killed her mother's nurse, too?"

"I don't think anything." And he turned his back on me and began transferring his piles of clothes from the table to his suitcase. "The world is a mysterious place where strange things happen."

I watched him for a while, but he wasn't going to say anything, and I finally left. The landlady snagged me on my way out the door.

"I did what you said," she told me. "I called that lawyer you told me to, and he took care of everything. He said Amy really isn't coming back. What's she got, anyway? Cancer?"

"Something like that."

"What a shame. There seems to be a lot of that going around lately."

"There certainly does."

At six o'clock I got a call from Hillary. I'd just finished feeding the gerbils and was repairing a leaky air filter from one of the aquariums when she rang.

"You've got to help Amy," she said when I picked up. There was no preamble. Her voice was cracked and raspy in the way people's voices get when they've smoked too many cigarettes.

I continued cutting a length of duct tape as I snugged the phone between my chin and shoulder. "I'm sorry. I don't know what you mean."

"They're going to arrest her for those murders."

"How do you know?"

"Because I know my mother."

"Are you saying your mother is setting her up?"

"I'm saying my mother is into damage control."

"Why would she do something like that?"

"I don't know."

I snipped off about three inches' worth of duct tape and put the scissors down. "I think you do."

Hillary started crying. "She's always singled Amy out. Ever since she was a kid."

"That's really not a particularly persuasive answer."

I could hear Hillary's sobs seeping in through the phone line.

"If you know anything," I told her, "you'd better tell the police."

"I don't."

"I'm sorry. I don't think there's anything I can do."

"Please."

I carefully wound the tape around the ripped tubing, making sure to get everything squared away. "If what you're telling me is true, what your sister needs is a good defense lawyer, not someone like me." And I hung up.

The phone rang again. Instead of answering, I went into the back and grabbed one of the beers I'd stored next to the brine shrimp. By the time I walked back to the front, the ringing had stopped.

I'd told Hillary the truth. There was nothing I could do for Amy. Not now. Besides, I thought there was a good chance the D.A. was right. She might be responsible for Pat Humphrey's death. She had the motive, the means, and the opportunity. And as for the nurse . . . well, that one didn't add up. But maybe there were things I didn't know.

I got a saucer out from the counter and poured a little of my beer into it for Zsa Zsa. As I stood there and watched her lap it up, I decided Amy's guilt or innocence wasn't my problem anymore. It was the police's. Let them deal with it.

It turned out Hillary's prediction had been correct. Paul called me two days later to tell me the D.A.'s office was going to bring in an indictment against Amy in the death of Pat Humphrey sometime next week. Which they did. Bail was set at one hundred thousand dollars, and Amy was remanded to a psychiatric facility for evaluation. There was no doubt in my mind that a deal would be worked out between the lawyers. If Amy spent any time in jail, I'd be surprised. Probably some form of house arrest would be what she'd get.

During the next couple of weeks, I threw myself into the store and tried to forget about Amy, her family, and Pat Humphrey. For some reason, I felt as if my skin had been sandpapered. Everything bothered me. Somewhere during that period of time, I took Paul up on his offer and went to bed with him to try and forget about George. It seemed like a good idea, even though Calli told me it was a mistake. I figured I'd get back in the game. The sex was okay, not bad, not good, but it just made me miss George even more, and I went home and cried.

Paul was still calling, but I didn't want to see him. Actually, I wasn't in the mood to see anyone, preferring to spend my time in the company of Mr. Black Label. I'd taken to drinking way more than I should have. I probably would have kept going except for Manuel. I think I was starting to remind him of his father, though he'd never admit to that.

He'd come in at three in the morning and found me sitting in the living room in the dark, staring out the window, drinking scotch for the seventh, or maybe it was the eighth, night in a row.

"You gotta stop doing this shit," he said. The disgust in his voice was palpable.

I looked up at him and grunted.

" 'Cause if you don't, I can't live here no more." And he left the room.

Listening to his feet going up the stairs, it occurred to me that when a seventeen-year-old street kid says it's time to clean up your act, if you're smart, you realize that you've gone as far down the road as you can in that particular direction and that it's time to turn it around.

Unless, of course, you're interested in making detox or AA a stop on your itinerary.

Which I wasn't. The last thing I wanted to do was to have

to go to those meetings and listen to people yammer on about how they were getting in touch with their inner selves.

Just that thought was enough to make me get up and pour the rest of my bottle of scotch down the kitchen-sink drain. Then I went upstairs to apologize to Manuel. But he'd fallen asleep, and I didn't want to wake him. The next day, over breakfast, neither of us mentioned last night's conversation, but the following afternoon, he brought a big bouquet of flowers to the store.

"Here," he said. "These are for you."

I ducked my head and fed Zsa Zsa a treat so Manuel wouldn't see my eyes misting over. I find I'm doing a lot of that lately.

Chapter Thirty-five

Things seemed to be settling down. I was feeling a bit better. Manuel and I fell into a pleasant routine of eating dinner together, then taking Zsa Zsa out for a nightly stroll in the cool of the evening. I started doing a little gardening around the place, pruning back long neglected bushes and spreading mulch on the flower beds.

I'd almost gotten Pat Humphrey and the Taylor family out of my mind, and I was making a conscious effort to think less about George. I was using the time in the evenings when I would have been seeing him to begin a short story, the first writing I'd done in years. I'd forgotten how pleasurable writing could be. I'd done seven pages when the head of the Hispanic Alliance called me at the store and everything started all over again.

"I think I found your woman for you," he told me.

"Who?" I asked as I fed the store cat a new brand of tuna.

"Dorita."

"Right." I could feel myself flush with guilt as I listened to the slurping noises the cat was making. Somehow, in the press of events, I'd managed to forget all about Dorita.

"Someone who was in here yesterday saw her in Samilito's buying coffee. That's down on Seymour Street," he added. "I hope that helps. By the way, the funeral for that man that you found is arranged for next Monday, if you want to come. It's taken a while to get everything settled."

I told him I'd be there and hung up.

Tim promised to close up the store, and I took Zsa Zsa and drove over to Samilito's. The place wasn't listed in the phone book, but it didn't take me very long to locate it. After all, we're not talking long distances and loads of retail outlets in this particular neighborhood. The place was your typical convenience store, selling milk, bread, soda, cigarettes, and beer, with a few half-rotten-looking plantains on the side. At seven, people coming home from work were lined up in front of the cashier, waiting to buy lotto tickets and beer.

When my turn came, I purchased a pack of cigarettes and showed the cashier the picture of Dorita. He said he hadn't seen her, but a weary-looking woman standing in back of me with a baby on her hip and another grabbing the hem of her skirt told me she thought she lived a few houses down in the big red house located in the middle of the block.

I thanked her and left. The moment I pulled up in front of the place, I realized I'd been here before, that this was the house Bethany's boyfriend lived in. I was deciding what to make of that when he came out the front door of the building.

I stuck my head out my car window. "Hey, Andrews," I yelled. "Wait up."

He definitely didn't look pleased to see me. "Jeez," he groaned as I hopped out of the car with Zsa Zsa on my heels. "What do you want now?"

"To ask you something."

"Come on." He held up his hands and did a little shuffle with his feet. "I told you I didn't know Bethany was fifteen. I never would have started with her if I had. I'm sorry, okay?"

"This isn't about her." And I showed him the picture of Dorita. "I'm looking for this woman."

"What did she do? Rob someone?"

"She didn't do anything. I have something to tell her." And I went into my song and dance about the guy I'd found on the side of the road, the one I'd named Raul.

Andrews scrunched his face up. "Jesus. Do you mean Javier? God, and I thought he'd run off." He combed his hair with his fingers. "Was he real skinny? Did he have a tattoo on his hand of a comet?"

"That's him. You know him?"

Andrews nodded. "Oh, yeah. God." He sucked in his breath, then let it out. "Dorita is going to be really, really upset."

"Is she his wife?"

"No. His sister-in-law. Or something like that." Andrews touched the Saint Christopher medal he was wearing around his neck. "Some relative. Or a neighbor, maybe. I don't know." He waved his hand, indicating the house he'd come out of. "I can't keep track. They come and go all the time. Every time you look, there's someone new living there. And my Spanish isn't that good. I mean, I had three years in high school. But these people talk so fast. I can just get every third or fourth word."

Zsa Zsa and I followed him back into his house.

"This way," he said, pointing to a staircase on the right.

The landing was filled with bundled-up newspapers. The stairway itself was narrow, just wide enough for one person to go up at a time. The walls had holes in it that had been plastered over with duct tape—a new low in the home decoration department. There were two apartments on the second floor. Andrews knocked on the door of the one on the left. A moment later, a woman stuck her head out.

"Get Dorita for me," Andrews said.

"So now that you need me to do something for you, you're talking to me," the woman replied.

"Just get her, Selma. This is important."

She moved her lips into a pout. "First you apologize to me."

"I'm not kidding."

"Neither am I."

"Hey," Andrews said as she slammed the door shut.

"Who was that?" I asked as I raised my hand to knock.

"One of Dorita's friends. Let me," Andrews said, banging on the door again. Selma opened it and slipped out in the hall.

She was gorgeous, all dark eyes, long, curly black hair, and curves. When I saw her, I understood why Andrews was doing what he was.

"Yes? You want something?" She cocked her head and stood there looking up at Andrews, chest thrust out, hands on her hips.

"I'm sorry. Happy?"

"Absolutely." Selma's lips curved into a lazy catlike grin of satisfaction. "I'll get Dorita." And she turned and closed the door in our faces again.

"What was that all about?"

Andrews shrugged. "Stupid stuff." He ran his fingers through his hair again, then peeled a spot of paint off one of his fingers.

"Could you be a little more specific?"

He laughed self-consciously. "It's not like it's a big deal. She and Bethany got into this thing, and I stepped into the middle of it, so she got pissed at me. By now I should know better."

"She knows Bethany?"

"Kinda. Selma used to clean house for Bethany's parents a while back. Now she works in a shoe store in the mall. She likes it a lot better."

"So what were they fighting about?"

Andrews peeled another spot of paint off his hand and favored me with a rueful grin. "Who knows? The two of them were screaming at each other. I had to drag Bethany away. God, she's strong." He shook his head at the memory.

A moment later, the door opened, and the woman I'd been looking for stepped out. She looked thinner than she did in the photograph. Her face had acquired worry lines about her eyes and mouth. Her hair was shorter, and she'd bleached it blond, but it was the same person.

"Yes?" she said, looking at Andrews and ignoring me.

"She has something to tell you," he said, flattening himself against the wall as if he wanted to disassociate himself from the bad news I was about to bring.

"Dorita?" I asked. "Is that your name?"

She nodded her head slowly and took a step back as if she already knew what I was going to say and didn't want to hear it. I felt bad as I handed her the picture and told her how I'd gotten it. The photograph slid out of her hands and fluttered to the floor.

"*Dios mío,*" she cried, her lips trembling. Then she turned and ran into the apartment.

I picked up the photograph. Andrews looked at me and made a hunching motion with his shoulders. Then we followed her inside. As I stepped into the hallway I could hear Dorita talking to someone in Spanish.

She looked up from the phone as we walked into the kitchen and said something into the receiver. A moment later, she handed it to me.

"Here," she said.

A woman in a thick Spanish accent said, "You wait for me. I will be there." Then she hung up.

"Who was that?" I asked Dorita.

"My *tia.*" And she burst into tears and ran out of the room just as Selma came in.

"I like your little dog," she said, pointing to Zsa Zsa. "My cousin, who lives in Austin, has one. Would you like some coffee?" she asked.

Andrews shook his head. "I gotta get out of here," he said. "I really do." And he headed toward the door.

"Hey," Selma called after him. "You're not seeing your little friend anymore?"

Andrews stopped and gestured toward me. "Ask her about that."

"You come and visit me. I'll make you dinner." Selma

watched him leave. "He'll come," she confided to me after he'd gone. "He likes my boobs. All the men do." And she disappeared into the bathroom. A moment later, I heard the shower start to run.

I wondered what it would be like to have that much confidence in yourself as I took a pretzel out of the bag on the table and bit into it.

Dorita's aunt came through the door an hour and a half later. Whoever I expected to see, it wasn't Rose Taylor's maid. She limped into the kitchen on swollen ankles and sat down heavily on the chair across from me. She looked tired and hot. The dress she was wearing, a simple blue cotton shirtwaist, was stained with sweat marks around the armpits and the collar. Wisps of hair were plastered across her forehead. Her upper lip was beaded with moisture. She leaned across the table and took my hand in hers and pressed it till I could feel the roughness of her skin on mine.

"It's true what Dorita says about Javier?"

"I'm afraid it is."

"No one," she said, her eyes flashing, "deserves to die like that, like a dog on the road. Worse, even. No one. All alone. How am I going to tell my neighbor? If it wasn't for me, Javier wouldn't have come up." She took a deep breath. "But this is why I am going to tell you something, something that I have seen. Something very bad."

"If it's that bad, why don't you tell the police?" I asked.

"No." She shook her head from side to side. "I can't do that. *No policía.*"

"But . . ."

She pressed my hand harder. "You have to promise not to tell them this came from me."

"I'm not sure . . ."

"If you do and they come to talk to me, I will tell them you are lying. You understand?"

"All right."

"You swear?"

"Yes."

"Say it."

"I swear."

She studied my face for a minute, then leaned even closer to me and began to talk.

The next afternoon, on my way to Kingston, I pondered what Rose Taylor's maid had told me. It had cooled off during the night, and the breeze coming through the window of my car brought with it the smell of new grass and cows. Zsa Zsa kept her head out. As I watched her sniffing the air, I thought about Javier Andante and Dorita and all the people that washed in and out of this country in a big tide.

I thought about how once upon a time my grandmother had come to this country on a boat from Poland along with so many like her. Now her kind were being replaced by Mexicans and Dominicans and Vietnamese and Chinese and Russian immigrants, even in upstate New York. The complexion of the city was changing, and that was, on the whole, a good thing, even if a lot of people didn't think so, even if sometimes things didn't work out so well.

It took me three hours to locate the men who had been piloting the ferry the day Pat Humphrey had been killed. I tracked one down to his house and the second one to his daughter's place, where he was baby-sitting his grandson. The second one told me what I needed to know.

"That's him," he said after I showed him the photograph I'd managed to dredge up.

"Are you sure?"

"Positive." He uncoiled a garden hose, then went over to the side of the house and turned on the spigot.

His grandson clapped with glee as his grandfather began filling the little plastic wading pool set by the vegetable garden.

"How can you be so positive? You get so many people on and off the ferry."

"I might not have remembered the face. But I remembered

the car." He paused and lifted his grandson into the pool. The little kid squealed with delight. "You don't see many MGBs around anymore. Not these days. I can testify to that."

"You may have to."

Chapter Thirty-six

Moss Ryan looked up from his desk as I came through his office door the following afternoon, having been on the phone most of the morning.

"My secretary said this was urgent."

"It is."

"Well." He tapped his fingers impatiently on the surface of his desk. "What is it?"

"I didn't know you were a local boy."

"What the hell are you talking about?"

"This." I slid the yearbook I'd gotten from Edna Busch across the desk. "You and Rose were named senior-class couple of the year. You also won awards for Latin and history."

He pushed the yearbook away. "And I won a letter in football, too. You forgot to mention that. I hope this isn't what you had to see me about."

"Why didn't you get married?"

"That isn't any business of yours."

I pointed to the embroidered pendant hanging on the wall, the one with the two rampant griffins on either side and the flowers down below. "What does the inscription say?"

"It means, Love knows no pedigree/cedes only to virtue. Could you come to the point of your visit."

"Where are those lines from?"

Moss Ryan composed his mouth into a thin line. *"The Song of the Knight of the Rose."*

"I've never heard of it."

"I'm not surprised." He began tapping his fingers on the desk again. "It's a fairly obscure thirteenth-century work."

"Is it like the *Song of Roland?"*

"Something like that. Now, if you please." His voice rose. "School is out for the day. I have a meeting I have to prepare for."

"You know Edna said you wanted to be a priest when you were in the ninth grade."

A puzzled expression crossed Moss Ryan's face. "Who the hell is Edna?"

"Edna Busch. She lived across the street from Rose."

"And I'm supposed to know her?"

"Well, she remembers you." I pointed to the banner. "Just one more question, I promise. Where did you get that made?"

He searched my face. "May I ask why this sudden obsession?"

"I've always been curious."

He gave a satisfied grunt. "There are companies that specialize in heraldic banners."

"Does it cost a lot?"

"Not really, no."

"Silver signifies purity, doesn't it?" I asked, referring to the banner's main color.

"And gold means nobility, and red means boldness," Moss Ryan informed me through gritted teeth. "You've already asked three questions. If you have any more, I suggest you consult your librarian."

I contemplated the banner some more. "I never noticed that the flowers are roses and that green looks like moss. The moss and the rose. I can't believe I didn't see it before."

"I don't know what you're babbling about, and I don't care. Listen, you can leave now or I can call Security and have them throw you out. Either one is fine with me."

"Just one more thing." I perched on the corner of his desk and picked up the piece of quartz. "This is rose quartz, isn't it?"

"I am reaching for the phone."

"You know," I continued. "There's a witness that saw you kill Shana Driscoll."

Moss Ryan's face went white. His hand hovered over the receiver and retreated. "I don't know what you're talking about."

"And the pilot on the *Wolfe Islander III*. He saw you get on the boat a couple of hours before Pat Humphrey was shot. He also saw you driving off. You took the last ferry out after the storm. You should have driven something more anonymous. First rule if you're going to kill someone: Try not to be noticed."

Moss Ryan looked horrified and fascinated at the same time. It was the look of someone on the track who sees the train coming toward them and knows it's too late to get out of the way.

"And why would I want to do something like that?"

"I'm not sure." I put the quartz back down. "I'm guessing because Rose was upset because of the way Geoff was acting and you couldn't stand it. After all, you're her protector, aren't you? The one who has to make everything right? Or maybe you just hated Geoff. Here he was, married to the woman you adored, the one you loyally served all these years, and does he appreciate her? Absolutely not. He takes advantage of her. Treats her badly. Just like her children try and do. He's sleeping with two other women. One of the women is taking large sums of money from Rose. Maybe you did it to punish him."

"You have very funny ideas."

I stood up. "I don't think so."

Moss Ryan leaned back in his chair, picked up the pen, and began clicking the top of it as he thought. I could hear the sounds of phones ringing in the corridor outside the office. He threw the pen back down and leaned forward. "Okay. How much do you want?"

"Nothing."

"Then why are you here?"

"Call it curiosity."

"That's it? If you believe I've killed two people, you're taking a big chance coming into my office to satisfy it."

"You're not going to shoot me."

"Really." And he reached in his desk and pulled out a gun. "You're sure are you?"

"Yes."

"Why?"

"Because you won't be able to wiggle out of it."

He bit his lip and put the gun down.

"What's to prevent me from running away?"

"Nothing. But I don't think you will. Where would you go? You've spent your entire life here. You don't know anything else. Besides, my associate has called the D.A.'s office."

"A call won't be enough to make them come."

"My witness is prepared to testify," I lied.

"And who would that be, I wonder?"

I remained silent.

"I think I can guess." Moss Ryan adjusted the knot in his tie, then swiveled his chair and stared out the window. "She'll leave before she gets on the stand."

"We'll see. But it doesn't matter. The pilot can identify your car."

"Circumstantial."

"Here's something else to think about. You don't fess up, they'll question Rose. They're obligated to? Do you want to involve her?"

"No," Moss Ryan said softly. "I don't. Anything else?"

"Yes. One last thing. That Mexican you had working on the Taylor estate."

"Which one?"

"Javier Andante."

"The name isn't familiar."

"He coughed a lot. He was the son of your maid's neighbor."

"I vaguely remember."

"You should have brought him to a doctor."

"He wasn't my responsibility."

"You told the maid you would."

Moss Ryan turned back around to face me. "I got busy. I forgot."

"He died from TB. I found him lying on the side of the road."

"That's too bad, but everyone dies sooner or later."

"That's true. But he would have lived if he'd gotten some medical care, and you wouldn't be in the position you are now."

Moss Ryan didn't answer right away. He stood up and faced me. His hands were clasped behind his back in an ecclesiastical pose. "Somewhere," he said, "I read that all flesh is grass. All people die. All people kill. It's the natural law of the universe. Isn't it better to serve the thing you love totally than to lapse into indifference?"

"I can't answer that question. I'm not a priest."

As I left, I could hear him talking to his secretary, telling her to dial the number of the biggest criminal lawyer in town.

The story made the front page, though it took a couple of weeks for it to hit the papers. I don't know why it took that long, but then I could never figure out the vagaries of editorial decisions even when I was working for the paper. Basically, the story said something to the effect that Moss Ryan, overcome with guilt over the prospect of another person bearing the consequences of his actions, confessed to involvement in the deaths of both Shana Driscoll and Pat Humphrey. The first, his lawyer stated, arose through negligence, while the second was the result of Pat Humphrey's threat to go to the police after having been a witness to the first death.

"So," Manuel said as we shelved the new shipment of gerbil food that had just come in that morning, "he's lying."

"Well, I don't think you can accidentally hold someone's head under the water."

"Then why did he say that?"

"Because it would be difficult to prove otherwise."

"What do you think is going to happen to him?"

I handed Manuel a couple of boxes of gerbil treats. "Oh. He's going to go to jail. The question is for how long. I doubt whether there's going to be a jury trial. Sentencing will probably be at the judge's discretion."

"They can do that?"

"It happens all the time."

We worked in silence for a little while. These days I didn't feel much like talking.

"Hand me the box cutter," Manuel said after five or so minutes had passed.

I tossed it to him.

"I ran into Bethany the other day," he told me while he sliced through the packing tape of another carton.

"Really?" I dusted my hands off and sat back on my heels. "I thought she was in Florida."

"Not anymore." He opened the flaps and started taking out the rabbit food.

If I didn't know Manuel so well, I might have let it pass. Instead, I asked where she was.

Manuel tugged his pants up. "I think this order is wrong."

"Fuck the order. Where's she staying?"

He studied the floor.

"Where, Manuel."

He averted my eyes. "With my mother."

I gave him my best glare.

"Hey, she had nowhere else to go. She called me."

"What did she do, run away?"

"Something like that."

"That was fast." Then I thought about Arthur Peterson.

"Do the words statutory rape mean anything to you? Her father will not be pleased."

"Hey," Manuel squawked, "we're not doing anything. Anyway, I think her father has other things on his mind."

"Like what?"

"Bethany's mom threw him out."

I reached for my cigarettes. "How come?"

Manuel shrugged. "Maybe she finally got wise to what her old man was doing behind her back. Can I have one, too?"

"Sorry." I showed him the pack. "It's my last one. How do you know what he was doing?"

"Beth told Debbie, and Debbie told me."

"What did she say. Exactly."

Manuel shrugged. "He was getting it on with the cleaning lady."

I thought back to Dorita's friend, Selma, and the fight she and Bethany had had. What had Bethany's boyfriend said about it? It had been over something that had happened in Bethany's house. Something that involved Selma. I wondered if Bethany had walked in on her dad and Selma? That would certainly explain Bethany's conduct. The sullenness, the slipping grades, the running away.

"She still can't stay with your mother."

"My mother doesn't care. She's glad to have her."

"That's not the point."

"Beth's mother thinks it's okay, too." Manuel unpacked some more of the rabbit pellets. "It's just for a little while, anyway. Until everyone gets there shit together. At least Beth's back in school. I told her she's got to go."

"So now it's Beth?" I said.

Manuel flushed and went back to studying the floor.

"Maybe you should go back to school, too," I added, unable to resist.

Manuel straightened up and dug something out of his pants pocket and thrust it into my hand.

"I was hoping you could help me with this," he mumbled

as I unfolded the crumpled pieces of paper. "I mean, if you can't, that's okay."

It was an application to OCC, the local community college.

I smoothed the pages out. "I think I can find the time."

Chapter Thirty-seven

I saw Rose Taylor for the last time about three months after Moss Ryan's arrest. She'd left a call on my answering machine saying she wanted to see me, and I'd rung back to say I could come out early that evening, if that was all right with her. Hillary returned my call to say that it was. I was surprised to hear her and said so.

"Oh, Louis and I moved back a couple of months ago," she informed me. "Given the circumstances, it seemed like the best idea."

"Where's Amy?" I couldn't imagine her being there, too. Especially after what had happened.

"She's out in California taking some sort of film course. Now she wants to make documentaries. God, she never quits." And she hung up.

Even though it was a little after six-thirty, it was already dark out when I drove up to the Taylor estate. Leaves crunched under my feet as I walked to the front door. The air smelled of spice and cold. A page from a newspaper had wrapped itself around a fir tree. The floodlight bulbs over the door had burned out, leaving me to fumble around in the dark for the doorbell. Hillary answered when I rang.

"What happened to the maid?" I asked as she led the way to the greenhouse.

"Oh, she went back home to Chiapas, or wherever the hell

she was from," Hillary replied. She looked as if she'd gained a little bit of weight since I'd seen her last, and the black circles under her eyes had diminished slightly.

"How come?"

"She came into a fairly large inheritance."

"How convenient."

"Not for me," Hillary said, tugging at her hem. This skirt was short, too; only it was black wool.

"When did she leave?"

"A while back."

"Like three months?"

"I don't know. I don't keep track. So far I've had two other girls, and I've had to fire both of them. I'm interviewing someone else tomorrow." Hillary sighed. "This one is a Dominican. I hope she turns out better than the other two have, that's all I can say."

By now we were in front of the door to Rose's room.

"I'm going to leave you here," Hillary said. "Don't tire her out," she warned. "She's very fragile these days."

I was shocked by Rose's appearance. She was sitting in an armchair by the sofa with her cat, Sheba, sprawled out across her lap. Pillows had been stuffed along either side of her to keep her upright. The fancy clothes, the makeup, the jewels, were gone. Now she was wearing a plaid housecoat and slippers. Her hair was held off her face with a barrette. Suddenly she'd become an old lady.

"Geoff left, you know," she said. She didn't indicate that I should sit down, so I remained standing.

"No, I didn't."

"He went home. He said he was going back to school to become a teacher. He said that's what he'd always wanted to do—teach." Her voice had a tremor in it. She moved her lips carefully as she formed each word. The effort obviously cost her a great deal. "And, of course, Moss isn't here. It feels strange without him around." She looked up at me, her eyes filmy with a layer of tears. "Why did you do it? Why couldn't you just leave things alone?"

"I suppose because I think it's wrong for someone to be punished for something they haven't done."

Rose lifted her hand to her mouth and wiped off a bubble of spittle that had formed. The veins in the back of her hand stood out like ropes. "Amy would have been fine."

"I wonder if that's what the sacrificial goat usually says."

"I don't think you did it for Amy's sake. I think you did it because you were mad at me."

"That, too. You used me to set up a motive. Tell me, did you and Moss Ryan discuss it between you?"

"We never discussed anything. We didn't need to. We understood each other perfectly. He's always been there for me, and now I have no one. Now I'm going to die alone."

I spread my hands out. "What do you want me to say?"

"Nothing." Rose Taylor rested her hand on Sheba's back. "You know, Pat told me this was going to happen."

"That she was going to die."

"No. That I was going to end up with my cat for company."

"You're not alone. Hillary's here."

Rose snorted. "So is Louis, if it comes down to that. Believe me, if I didn't have money, they wouldn't be around."

"Maybe you should try and be a little more charitable."

"Why?" She dabbed at the side of her mouth again with a hesitant gesture. "No one's ever been charitable to me. Anyway, it's the truth."

I turned to go.

"I hope you're satisfied," she called after me. "I just wanted you to see what you've done."

I let myself out. Hillary met me as I was leaving.

"What did she say?" she asked.

"She thanked me."

"Yeah. Right." Hillary gave a mirthless chuckle. "My mother is known for her kindness." And she closed the door behind me.

I walked down to the cottage because I wanted to talk to Louis, but Louis wasn't there. His girlfriend, Debbie, was.

"He's working," she said. "He's still got the night shift."

The cottage looked different. Someone had painted the walls a dark green with white trim. There was a chintz-covered sofa and matching chair. An upside-down bear, supporting a round piece of glass with his feet, served as a coffee table.

"You like it?" Debbie asked.

I nodded.

"Me, too."

"You living here as well?" I asked.

"No. I just stay here sometimes to help Hillary out. Now that everyone is gone."

"So everyone's one big happy family again."

"Yeah." Debbie laughed. "Just like the Brady Bunch. You know, Louie says Amy is the dumb one for leaving, but I think she's the only smart one."

I agreed. The best thing I'd ever done for myself was leave my family.

I ran my hand over the chair arm. "How come Louis came back?"

"Because his *mommy* asked him to." She gave the word mommy a scornful twist.

"Then Lila's gone?"

"Oh, no." Debbie crooked her finger, and I followed her into the bedroom. She flung open the closet door. It was filled with spangled gowns and shoes. "I think Lila will always be around. He just sneaks off at night. Personally, I'm glad my parents didn't lay that kind of guilt trip on me. I've always been free to come and go as I please. I'm lucky, I guess. I've got good ones. If you don't, they can really louse you up."

"It's true," I said, thinking back to mine.

About four months after that I was at a bar with my girl-friend Calli, trying to chase away the Sunday-night blahs. We were listening to a blues band and drinking beer when George walked through the door.

"Shit," I said. There was no way he wasn't going to see me.

"You want to go," Calli whispered in my ear, "we can. Just say the word. It's okay by me."

"No. I'll be fine." But my heart was thumping, and I could feel my stomach knotting up.

The knot in my gut got even tighter when George spotted me and walked over.

"You're looking good," he said.

"You, too." And he did. He was wearing the blue shirt I'd always liked.

When he signaled to the bartender, his arm touched my shoulder. I took a deep breath and reached for my pack of cigarettes. I needed something to do with my hands to steady them.

"You must be happy with the way the Taylor thing played out."

"Reasonably. You know Manuel is going back to school," I said to fill in the silence that was opening like a chasm between us.

"That's nice. Is he still at your house?"

"For the time being."

George turned and faced me. "Paul told me you and he have something going."

"It wasn't a big deal," I replied as I tried to read George's face. But I couldn't. It was expressionless.

"That's what he said, too." George took a sip of his beer. "So are you seeing anyone else?"

"No. Are you?"

"Not at the moment."

George ran his finger around the neck of his bottle. "I've been thinking maybe we could catch a movie sometime."

"I'd like that."

"Good. I'll give you a call." And he moved away to talk to some other people.

I could feel my eyes filling with tears as I watched him leave.

"You okay?" Calli asked as I blinked them back.

"Fine."

"Really?"

"Really."

But I wasn't.

My hand was trembling as I took a cigarette out of my pack, put it in my mouth, and reached for my lighter. Then I pushed it away, took the cigarette out of my mouth, and laid it down on the bar. For some reason, I didn't feel like smoking.